MOTHER NATURE
is the
ULTIMATE APHRODISIAC

She shook her head and set the bottle down next to her equipment. "You can't go out there now. Conditions are only going to go downhill—" The laptop beeped as she tapped the keys. Frowning, she checked an image on a small-screened portable radar. "I don't understand this," she muttered. "This cell isn't part of a hurricane band... it makes no sense. It's moving over us from the wrong direction. It's almost as though it formed *on top* of us."

There's a reason for that.

"You'll be fine as long as you stay inside the house," he said, recognizing his own voice, rough with a mix of desire and fear, and *bébé, you have no idea what you're in for....*

She didn't look up. "Stay inside. It's too dangerous out there—we'll figure it all out later."

He knew he should leave, knew what the hot rush of blood throbbing between his legs meant, but he couldn't take another step any more than he could look away as she nibbled on her bottom lip. Reaching up, he touched his own subconsciously, wondering how she'd taste against his mouth.

He had to get out of here, because when lightning struck again, it was going to be too late for him to stop himself.

RIDING

the

STORM

SYDNEY CROFT

DELTA TRADE PAPERBACKS

RIDING THE STORM
A Delta Trade Paperback / September 2007

Published by
Bantam Dell
A Division of Random House, Inc.
New York, New York

All rights reserved
Copyright © 2007 by Larissa Ione & Stephanie Tyler
Cover art by Tom Hallman
Cover photo copyright © 2007 by Rubberball/Jupiter Images
Cover design by Craig DeCamps
Book design by Sarah Smith

Delta is a registered trademark of Random House, Inc.,
and the colophon is a trademark of Random House, Inc.

Library of Congress Cataloging in Publication Data
Croft, Sydney.
Riding the storm / Sydney Croft.
p. cm.
ISBN 978-0-385-34080-9 (trade pbk.)
1. Supernatural—Fiction. I. Title.
PS3603.R6356R53 2007
813'.6—dc22
2007008340

Printed in the United States of America
Published simultaneously in Canada

www.bantamdell.com

BVG 10 9 8 7 6 5 4 3 2

Writing a book is never a solitary process, and the following people helped tremendously to get this project off the ground:

Deepest thanks to both Roberta Brown, an all-around amazing agent and wonderful person, for her never-ending faith and support, and to our fantastic editor Shauna Summers, whose insight, guidance, and enthusiasm helped to keep us focused.

Special thanks to fellow authors Alison Kent for her constant encouragement and advice, and the ladies at Writeminded (Amy Knupp, Sharon Long/Maya Banks and Janette Kenny) for their amazing generosity and help during some rough times.

Last but never least, for Bryan, Brennan, Zoo and Lily, for letting us slip into our ACRO world for long periods of time at the expense of forgetting the real one exists—and for always believing.

RIDING
the
STORM

CHAPTER *One*

T-Remy, where you at? Sa va mal.

"So what else is new, Dad?" Remy muttered, squinting through the darkness and rain the windshield wipers couldn't keep up with as he struggled to stay on the muddy road and redial his cell phone at the same time.

For his old man to say things were bad meant one of two things: Either everything was business as usual and he was being dramatic, or the world was coming to an end. There was only black or white with his father, which is why Remy found himself comfortably in the gray most of the time.

And really, things were always going badly for Remy Senior, and calling T-Remy, as he was known affectionately around these parts, was like calling in his own personal cavalry. Navy style. Except that Remy had resigned his commission last month and had taken his final leave from his SEAL team seven days earlier, something he was not looking forward to telling his father.

Following in the old man's footsteps, Remy Senior had told him proudly eight years earlier, then signed the papers allowing his son to enlist on his seventeenth birthday, right after he graduated high school.

The Navy had been T-Remy's way out of the bayou, and joining the SEAL teams had been one of the hardest things he'd ever done. Leaving them had been as well, but he'd always known, on every level, that he wasn't meant to be a team player.

So really, there was no excuse on God's green bayou not to visit and check on his father. Family was family, and all that crap, even though this was the last thing he wanted to do.

Still no answer. Not even a damned machine on the other end of either the house or cell line a full three days and seven hours since Remy senior's last call. He threw the phone down and pushed his truck forward on the muddy road leading to his old man's house. Hurricane season had hit the bayou hard this year, and he couldn't be sure if that's why his father had called.

Last night, Remy had been drawing again in his sleep—the same picture he'd been drawing since he was six years old, the same picture he'd been drawing every single night for the past six months, the fist against a background of clouds, clutching a handful of lightning bolts in a firm grasp—and he knew the hurricane that stirred from nowhere late last night was going to follow him inland from the coast. He'd always been a lure for storms. A human weather vane. Rumor held he'd been born during a hurricane, born and then left on the church's doorstep while the night winds howled around him.

There was no denying that there was something about him and weather. He could predict it, ride it out, always knew when Mother Nature was going to piss on his parade. His former teammates called him Storm, as more of a joke than anything and mainly when he wasn't around to hear it, because Remy never did take well to jokes.

Lately, Mother Nature had been working her magic overtime on him, necessitating the early retirement, and today was no exception. Especially when the bridge started falling away behind his truck. He tried not to look back in fascination as the heavy logs that had been there for as long as he could remember broke like matchsticks under the wailing wind.

Yeah, this couldn't be good. He didn't feel like taking a swim in the murky water below. Or losing his truck. Never mind his aching ribs, freshly injured from an attempted mugging when he'd left his apartment in Norfolk for the bayou.

He urged the accelerator slow and steady, not wanting to encourage the bridge to fall directly underneath him. Five more endless feet and he'd be crossed over into no-man's-land and he could worry about getting back out later.

Part of him wanted to stop the truck right then and there, stand in the middle of nature's fury and let her try to kick his ass. But his feeling of responsibility nagged at him harder.

No time for play, T-Remy.

But that didn't mean Mother Nature couldn't play with him in the worst possible way, and his cock hardened in painful reminder. He'd tried to ignore the urges that started last night while he slept, the ones that would normally drive him from his bed, hot, restless and prowling for anything to scratch his itch.

That wasn't going to happen tonight, and he forced himself to tamp it down, turn it off and, within fifteen minutes, his truck turned up the dirt path and pulled in front of the house he'd grown up in.

The place was still a shithole.

Three years away and a storm that split the heavens wide open over the bayou hadn't softened the memories, and he was glad he'd made the drive at night. Broad daylight wasn't going to be any kinder and he hadn't been expecting much anyway.

His truck moved easily over the pitted driveway and

stopped just short of the ancient garage that had long since lost its door. He strapped his knife onto his left biceps with a black band of Velcro, because the local gators tended to get riled up during a storm, especially when they were displaced from their bayou home. More than a few times during his youth he'd been surprised by one or two lost ones that were just as pissed to see him as he was them. He'd learned how to alligator wrestle the hard way, a necessary survival skill around here.

He got out, grabbed his bag and went toward the back door before he lost nerve and turned tail. And the more he thought about it, the angrier he got, until it balled in his gut and hung there as he reached the door.

He'd lost the keys to the house, and tried to lose his way back too, years earlier. Of course, his father never locked the door. Hell, he couldn't pay a thief to come through this place.

The first thing he noticed when he flipped on the light was that it worked. Admittedly, he'd flipped it on out of habit, but he'd figured it was a sure bet the electric, and other bills, hadn't been paid in months. The only thing he knew for sure was that his father had called him from the house and now there was no sign of the guy to be found.

The next thing he noticed was that the kitchen was clean. Scrubbed clean. No dishes anywhere but in the cabinets, and there was even a cheerful yellow dish towel hanging on the stove handle.

The third thing he noticed was the sound of water running. His thoughts immediately went along the lines of a broken pipe or a leak in the roof. He dropped the bag and moved toward the bathroom.

A simultaneous burst of lightning and crack of thunder made the power flicker and then putter out as he reached the bathroom doorway. The storm illuminated the small bathroom briefly, just long enough for him to get a very good look at the beautiful naked woman in the shower.

Beautiful and naked, but not friendly. Screaming like a swamp cat caught in a coon trap, she hurled a bottle of shampoo at him. He ducked a split second before it could hit him, and it bounced off the wall behind his head.

Welcome home, Remy. This was going to be worse than he thought.

HALEY MARIE HOLMES LOVED SURPRISES. She did not, however, love strange men surprising her in the shower. In the dark. That she'd been expecting the strange man at some point didn't matter. He could have knocked.

"Get out of my bathroom!" she shouted as she pulled the cheap plastic shower curtain around her. The *clear* cheap plastic shower curtain.

"*Your* bathroom? This is my goddamned house, so I think you're a little mixed up, lady."

The voice was a low, controlled drawl, the sentiment behind the words anything but, and the man she hoped was Little Remy stood outlined in the light from the storm, dripping wet in the middle of the small bathroom, wearing a T-shirt, cargo pants and flip-flops, like he was coming in from a day at the beach instead of the outer bands of a hurricane. Except she'd never seen any man wear a lethal-looking knife to the beach.

She shivered, raised her gaze to the strong masculine features of his face, then upward to his hair. She'd always been a sucker for dark hair, and he wore his short but longer than the ate-up military guys she'd known, and he'd slicked it back from his face, his fingers leaving wild grooves.

This was definitely Remy, that uniformed SEAL in the photo from the dossier she'd been given by her agency. The knowledge should have put her at ease. Instead, his alert stance, the way he seemed primed for battle despite the casual clothes he wore, set her even more on edge.

"Can you give me a minute here?" she snapped, then forced herself to not look away from his eyes, which narrowed into slits as he stared.

"I don't give intruders anything. And where the hell is my father?"

She shut off the water, glad she'd already finished rinsing, and took a deep, calming breath of steamy air. "I'm not an intruder, and if you'll get out of here I'll explain everything."

Everything but the truth. He wouldn't learn why she was really there. Or how, after her contact at the National Weather Service had forwarded Remy Senior's letter to her, she'd bribed him into calling Remy to beg him to come home, something that turned her stomach because she knew firsthand how much power parents had to hurt their children.

The old man had all the bad qualities of a used car salesman and only half the charm, and she hoped his son was different. Personality-wise, though, T-Remy's charm wasn't quite coming through the shower curtain.

In the bright glimmer of nearly continuous lightning, he studied her, the rigid lines of his brows framing an expression as hard as the man himself seemed to be. "I don't mind the view from where I'm standing. So why don't you start explaining now—because I'm not all that patient."

God, she hated military men. She'd hated them even when *she* had been in the military. No way would she roll over in submission like some trembling green recruit just because a big, tough ex-SEAL suffering from an excess of testosterone barked an order at her.

"I'll explain when I'm dressed," she said in a defiant tone that was probably lost to the storm.

She gathered the shower curtain more securely around

her—for all the good it did—and stretched toward the towel bar, but Remy was faster. He snared the towel and dangled it just out of her reach. In the flickering shadows that played on his face, she could make out a smirk—a smirk that shouldn't be sexy, but for some reason was. The storm must be getting to her.

Or maybe the stories about Remy were true.

Discounting that last thought because it was ridiculous, she made a grab for the towel, but he yanked it away. "Tell me who you are."

She hesitated, not because her cover identity was a secret, exactly, but because his military-clipped order chafed at several sore spots. Which was why she and the Air Force had been a disastrous combination.

"My name is Haley. Haley Holmes. And," she said, wringing water out of her long hair, "I'm not saying another word until I'm dry."

She shoved the shower curtain aside because it was useless anyway, the sound of the rusted metal rings scraping the equally rusted rod barely audible over the sudden roar of wind through the trees. Water trickled down her face, dripping off her chin and onto her breasts, and Remy's eyes, glittering in the flashes of light, blatantly took it all in.

The appreciation in his gaze made her swallow. Made her hot and tingly and feeling the need to shower again, but with cold water.

She stepped out of the tub, and this time, when she reached for the towel, he held it out to her. Her fingers closed on the fabric; his fingers closed around her wrist. The man moved like a striking snake, and her heart stopped as though she'd been bitten.

She lifted her chin, met his intense gaze. He looked down at her from his considerable height of at least six-foot-three and drew her a step closer to him, so close she could feel heat rolling off his large body. Her dad had always told her how her impulsive nature and utter lack of fear would get her into trouble someday, even as he encouraged those qualities.

Now, as her stomach flip-flopped, she made a conscious effort not to tremble. Stepping out of a shower naked in front of a complete stranger wasn't the smartest thing she'd ever done. Then again, after several weeks of studying the man right down to the name of his childhood dog, she probably knew him better than she knew the people she'd worked with for months.

"You've got five minutes to dry off and get dressed, and then you'll talk," he said, his voice rougher than it had been a minute ago.

The lights flickered, matching the quick-pounding of her pulse. Then they came on fully, leaving her standing bare-assed naked mere inches away from one of the best-looking men she'd seen in her life, with only a corner of the towel and a thin, swirling veil of steam between them.

She tried to wrench free of his grip, but he held her for a moment longer, as though to prove he could, his gaze traveling slowly from her face, down to her breasts, to her belly, her pelvis. Her skin tightened and prickled, her nipples puckered and heat spread in a languid wave from her cheeks to the juncture of her thighs.

His half-lidded blue eyes smoldered, but a vein throbbed at his temple, just below his hairline, and she sensed more than saw the battle that raged within him, even if she didn't completely understand it. And she felt certain he had no idea his thumb was stroking the sensitive underside of her wrist any more than he knew his fingers were digging painfully into that same wrist.

Thunder sounded in the distance, and he flinched, snapped his gaze back up to hers. "Like I said, five minutes. And you can get dressed now." With that, he released her wrist, pivoted with military crispness and stalked out of the bathroom.

Cursing, she slammed the door shut.

What. An. Ass.

It didn't help that her fingers shook as she held the towel to her chest as though Remy were still in the room, watching her with those intense, intelligent eyes that flashed even without the lightning.

She waited until her heartbeat slowed, until the storm outside had ebbed—the outer bands of a hurricane moved out as suddenly as they came in—and then she dried off and, with the exception of her underwear, dressed in the clothing she'd worn into the bathroom before her shower. She hadn't expected Remy to show up tonight, after all.

She'd been here in his house for forty-eight hours now, and she'd figured she'd have at least twelve more to review the files her agency had given her one last time, the ones containing his military records and an impossibly detailed account of Remy's entire life—including obscure information obtained by the agency psychics.

Since accepting the assignment five weeks ago, she'd unearthed personal statistics, like how he ate anything with shrimp, had an allergy to chocolate and that he shared her May third birthday, though he was three years younger. The most fascinating details, though, the weather details, came from the recordings she'd covertly obtained while talking to Remy's father.

In any case, she'd expected more time to prepare tonight, and then, tomorrow, to have met the man who supposedly drew weather phenomena like trailer parks drew tornadoes. Which was a myth, but a popular joke in her profession.

She'd rented the place for a month, had a cover story worked out, and if all went as planned, T-Remy Begnaud would never know he was the subject of a scientific study sanctioned by the government but funded almost entirely through private sources.

Unless the allegations against the man proved to be true, and then all bets were off. Her job would veer from research to recruitment, because the enemy could be knocking on his doorstep within days.

Except Itor Corp didn't knock. They forced their way inside, took what they wanted and destroyed what remained.

Of course, she fully expected her investigation to quickly reveal that the stories were nothing more than fantastical rumors, or that Mr. Begnaud—junior *or* senior—was a charlatan. Either way, she'd have enjoyed the opportunity to observe a late-season hurricane before moving on to her next assignment as a parameteorologist, something far more interesting—the possible existence of a weather machine.

She'd balked when orders to investigate the seemingly nutty ramblings of a television weatherman had come down the pipe, but really, the military had been trying to control the weather for decades. Cloud seeding, Project Cirrus...so if the thing existed and could cause violent weather, ACRO needed to get their hands on it before the enemy did.

First, though, she had to make it through the coming days with a man who, people claimed, could summon lightning at will. Who had emerged unscathed from the center of an F5 tornado. Who had supposedly screwed a woman insane during a storm that had made him insatiable.

Naturally, none of those claims could be substantiated, but as she reached for the doorknob and the power went out again, she swore she'd get to the bottom of the tales. If anyone knew about extraordinary weather phenomena, it was Haley. And after taking one look at her subject, she was more than willing to go wherever she needed to go to get the information she required.

Even if that meant testing out Remy's power in bed.

CHAPTER
Two

Remy's ribs began to ache in tandem with his head, and his balls, as another storm cell moved in and the evening hurtled rapidly downhill. He'd always appreciated the unexpected— didn't like it, but appreciated it the way he did a bag of gris-gris or the spell-casting voodoo queens he'd grown up around; yet this was beyond what he'd been prepared to handle.

Of course, he *could* handle Haley all right, palm the curve of her hips and push her thighs apart with one of his while the wind shook the world around them, breathe in the scent of soap and woman while he found her core with his fingers, his tongue.

She wasn't afraid of you. His cock twitched, and he looked toward the bathroom. She didn't look like she'd break easily.

Get a fucking grip. He wheeled around and pressed his forehead against the window that faced the backyard, closed his eyes and let the cool feel of the glass calm him a bit.

He should never have touched her. Just seeing her had been enough to push him close to the edge, but once his hand closed around her wrist and the quick tick of her pulse slammed into his palm, he knew it was going to be next to impossible to spend any length of time near her without having her. One of them was going to have to go.

One more second in the small confines of that bathroom and he would've taken her right there against the tile wall. He could barely control himself with a woman during normal storm conditions, and the way this one was intensifying, Haley Holmes had better run for her damned life.

As the storm's fervor rose, so did his, and it bound to him like a fever he couldn't shake. He wouldn't be able to until he got laid or jerked off a few times to ease the pressure, and even then, it wouldn't erase the longing, the need, until the storm died down and released him from her grip.

Unfortunately, his arousal would increase the duration of the storm, feeding off the other until both just burned out in a frenzy of hot, destructive need.

His fingers gripped the windowsill as his balls tightened— every nerve was on edge and screaming for some kind of sweet relief he hadn't completely found since all this began with the giant testosterone surge when he'd turned fourteen.

When he found himself near a woman during a time like this he'd force himself to hold back, afraid of hurting her, which wasn't satisfying to either party. The one time he did let loose, way back when, before he'd learned to get out of those situations fast when a storm was approaching and restraint was limited, things hadn't turned out well. He'd regained control before he hurt her, but shit, she'd been terrified. And she'd told all her friends.

His sexual tie to the storms didn't get easier as he got older, but with effort and planning and praying, he was able to keep himself in check. Still, it effectively killed any hope for a love life. He was so tired of scaring people, tired of being a freak and tired of being alone, even though that was the easiest way for him to live.

At twenty-five, he was pretty sure things couldn't get much worse, but over the past six months his needs had been increasing to such a degree that he could barely contain himself during a storm period. And he knew that the current need he was experiencing had never been this bad or lasted this long. Something different had happened in just the past forty-eight hours to shift the already skewed balance of power.

He ripped the knife off his arm, stuffed it into his bag and turned, seconds before Haley emerged from the bathroom, and watched her saunter into the living room wearing shorts and a T-shirt, her long brown hair, still damp, pulled back into a low ponytail. When the lights blew again after he left Haley in the bathroom, he'd only bothered to light one of the hurricane oil lamps by the kitchen, even though she'd scattered at least ten of them throughout the house. The less he saw of her, the better, even though the image of her wet, naked curves was burned into his brain.

The wind howled with a force that shook the walls as he watched Haley's long-legged strides. She didn't seem to notice the sudden surge, and he didn't bother telling her that three of his paychecks had gone to reinforcing the structure to withstand the brunt of most hurricane-force winds that threatened Louisiana and her precious bayous.

Mother Nature could be a real bitch when she was trying to make a point.

"So, you're Little Remy," she said over her shoulder, as she entered the kitchen.

"T-Remy," he said, teeth on edge.

She shrugged. "Same difference." She yanked open the door to the ancient fridge and bent at the waist, giving him a view of her ass hanging out of Daisy Dukes that should be illegal. She plucked out a Miller Lite, which was not his father's first choice of beer, and turned back to him.

She'd been here long enough to buy groceries.

"Actually, it's not the same difference," he said. "But since you didn't grow up around here, you wouldn't know any better."

"So how do I know you are who you say you are? I mean, I don't see any pictures."

"I'm half owner of this shithole—*tonnere m'écrasé si j'sus pas après dire la vérité*," he muttered.

"Translation, please."

Shit, he'd lapsed back into Cajun French without thinking. Never a good sign. "It means, may lightning strike me dead if I'm lying," he said with a smile, because she had no idea. She did, however, give him a strange look, probably wondering what kind of idiot dared Mother Nature during a storm. If she only knew. "And I'm starting to lose my patience with you."

"And I wasn't expecting you," she shot back.

"But my father did mention me to you. You know my name."

"He said he had a son in the Navy, but didn't say you'd be coming home tonight," she said, and as much as he wanted to believe that was the truth, he couldn't.

Remy Senior had always struggled to keep his son's freak weather ways out of the public eye, but that didn't mean he wouldn't try to make money off of it any way he could. Especially as the old man got older, drank more heavily and continued losing his hard-earned money, and T-Remy's too, on the ridiculous inventions Remy Senior thought would make him a millionaire.

Someone had loved his father once. Her death had taken away a piece of Remy Senior's heart that no one else had been able to fill. And Remy himself got that, understood what it was like to always feel that something was missing.

He gazed at Haley, with her smooth skin and tight, toned body as his own began to ache. "My father called me," he said. "He sounded upset. In trouble. Asked me to come home."

"Well, as you can see, he's not here."

"And what—you're his newest girlfriend or something?"

Her slightly upturned nose wrinkled in disgust she didn't bother to hide. "Hardly. I'm renting the house from him for the next month, and the last time I saw him, he was perfectly fine."

Fuck. Inviting some strange woman here was something his father would do, but why the hell would anyone come to Bayou Blonde if they didn't have to? "Are you on vacation?"

She snorted. "A vacation would mean Hawaii, not some godforsaken swamp. I'm here for work."

"What kind of work?"

He glanced around the room and saw the piles of paperwork and books on the floor next to the weathered desk in the corner, which was laden with electronic equipment, hard plastic cases and a laptop computer, which must be on some kind of serious battery backup. He swore, wondering how the hell he'd missed all that until now.

"I'm a meteorologist. I'm studying the ecological aftereffects of hurricanes."

"Why here?"

"Because this area has been relatively untouched by human hands since it was devastated by Hurricane Tessa twenty-five years ago." She twisted the cap off her beer and tossed it into the garbage can at the base of the counter. "Tessa was an anomaly, not only as a rare May storm, but in her behavior and unique pattern of destruction. By studying how an area recovers organically from an irregularity, we can learn how nature inherently protects itself from storms."

Yeah, Tessa was an anomaly all right, and so was he. What kind of mother abandons her kid outside during the worst hurricane the bayous had ever seen? He could never understand how he'd survived for three hours outside in the storm, the only cover being a thin blanket and the awning above the church steps, but his father always insisted that was how it happened.

He wasn't sure if that was bullshit, but he knew Haley's pseudo-environmental study definitely was. Because this area had never really recovered, and most would say, neither had he.

His skin tingled, and half a second later there was another lightning strike, too damned close for comfort. He checked Haley for a reaction, but she only pursed her lips around the beer bottle, circling the opening. He watched the way her throat moved as she took a few long sips, and realized he'd taken two steps toward her.

Her mouth would feel so good around him, cool lips, warm tongue inviting him to slide farther down her throat. . . .

Back it up, Remy. And he slowly did move away from her even though every fiber throbbed for Haley Holmes and that hot place nestled between those finely muscled, tanned thighs. If she'd just touch him, put a hand between his legs and stroke him through the fabric of his cargos, he'd be okay. He'd put his hands behind his back and let her take him, maybe instruct her to handcuff him so he couldn't hurt her, and then everything would be all right.

Except you hate being tied down. . . .

"Are you okay?" she asked, and he hated the concern in her voice, hated the fact that he'd let the low rumble of a groan slip from the back of his throat as the house swayed and the wind slammed the already battered exterior, like it wanted in.

He knew neither the wind nor he would stop until they got what they wanted, and he grabbed his bag in one last-ditch effort to save what he could. "Since you've already paid rent for the place, I'll be the one to vacate."

She shook her head and set the bottle down next to her equipment. "You can't go out there now. Conditions are going downhill—" The laptop beeped, and she tapped the keys.

Frowning, she checked an image on a small-screened portable radar. "I don't understand this," she muttered. "This cell isn't part of a hurricane band . . . it makes no sense. It's moving over us from the wrong direction. It's almost as though it formed *on top* of us."

There's a reason for that.

"I'll be fine, and so will you, as long as you stay inside the house," he said, his voice rough with a mix of desire and fear and *Bebe, you have no idea what you're in for.* . . .

She didn't look up. "Stay inside. It's too dangerous out there—we'll figure it all out later."

He knew he should leave, knew what the hot rush of blood throbbing between his legs meant, but he couldn't take another step any more than he could look away as she nibbled on her bottom lip. Reaching up, he touched his own lip subconsciously, wondering how she'd taste against his mouth.

A printer on the scarred old dining room table spat out a page, which she tore loose and scanned in the greenish glow from her equipment.

"Hurricane Center update." Dropping the page to the floor, she turned back to the radar image. "This is way more fascinating. Amazing . . ."

She was talking more to herself now than to him, lost in the weather. She glanced at her watch and then shook her wrist and frowned down at it, and he looked at the ancient clock that had sat on the mantel for as long as he could remember. The arms had frozen at nine-forty P.M.—the exact time he'd walked into the damned house.

A ragged breath shuddered through his chest. His pull was getting stronger and threatening the entire bayou, and Haley would figure some of it out soon. Sweat broke out on his forehead as nerves and muscles stretched. He had to get out of there, because when lightning struck again, it was going to be too late for him to stop himself.

Another flash, too close, and by the time the boom hit seconds later, his body had been taken over by its ruling member.

And while Haley was bent over, staring at the screen, her concentration on the impending storm outside rather than him, his brain fogged. Led by the heat of her body, he dropped his bag and found himself pressed to her, his thighs to her buttocks, his arousal straining to get out and into her.

She gasped when he wrapped his hands around her waist and pulled her upright into him. He gathered her shirt in his fist and pushed it up, needing to palm her full breasts as much as he needed air. Somewhere in the back of his brain, he heard thunder, and then the sound of electrical equipment popping.

Next, his hands were moving faster than his brain, to unbutton her shorts and shimmy them down. A violent tug and then they cleared her hips, and he barely heard her say, *"Remy,"* before the windows rattled as the storm surged forward against the house.

"Remy, please..."

With a grunt that came out like a howl, he jerked away from her, left her standing there with her shorts halfway down and, with no explanation, headed outside into the storm that was getting worse instead of better, a fact that no amount of Haley's research and equipment could ever explain, to get it all over with. Force Mother Nature to push him to his break point and, finally, let himself break.

It had to hurt less than this did.

HALEY SAGGED AGAINST THE DESK, heart pounding, knees trembling inside the shorts that were tangled around them. What had just happened? One minute she'd been trying to figure out where the storm cell raging above them had come from, and the next she was at the mercy of Remy's strong hands.

Not that she'd minded. Not when she felt the hard bulge of his arousal pushing against her, his hands under her shirt, massaging her breasts, pinching her nipples. His voice, gruff and low, had murmured phrases into her ear—some she understood, though they didn't make sense. *Touch the lightning?* Others she didn't understand, though she knew they had been uttered in smooth, sexy French.

Then his warm breath had fanned the back of her neck as he'd whispered, "Need you now," and shoved down her shorts. She hadn't had time to think, to protest or beg for the penetration that might follow, because he'd roared like a wounded bear and run out into the storm.

The storm. Oh, God, he was in danger. Quickly, she pulled up the shorts, not bothering to button them, and darted to the front door. When she turned the knob, the door blew open and slammed painfully into her hip, nearly knocking her off her feet. Rain stung her cheeks as she stepped outside. She squinted into the darkness, battling the wind with every step. Her bare feet sank into the muddy ground, and she tried to keep her thoughts on finding Remy, not on what might be squishing under her heels.

"Remy!" she screamed, but the wind swallowed her shout.

And then, outlined by a bolt of lightning that made the hairs on the back of her neck stand up, she saw him. There, a few feet away, one arm and his forehead braced against a swaying tree. Somehow, he'd lost his shirt, and in the backdrop of brilliant flashes and dappled shadows, the deep valleys and rounded peaks of his incredible muscles drew her gaze, even as thunder cracked, made her eardrums rattle.

Remy didn't so much as flinch.

"Remy!"

She staggered forward. What was he doing? Was he injured? The raindrops felt like tiny needles as she struggled for every step, desperate to reach him, wondering how she'd get him medical attention. Her van, parked in the back, would be useless if the roads had flooded.

"*Remy!*"

He didn't move. *No, please, no.* Her toe snagged a fallen branch, and she stumbled, careened off two trees with bruising force before she lost her footing and slipped downhill several feet. Ignoring the cutting whip of vegetation against her bare legs, she used vines and roots as handholds as she clambered back up the incline.

At the top, she found herself a few feet from Remy. As the lightning flashed and thunder threatened to rupture her eardrums, she noted his expression, one etched in misery. Pain.

She dragged her gaze down, to where his right arm worked furiously—and then she sucked in a breath of rain-saturated air with such force she nearly choked. His expression, dear Lord, his expression—not one of pain. One of pleasure.

His long fingers pumped up and down around the jutting length of his cock. Rain dripped into her eyes, and she blinked. Maybe the water was playing tricks on her vision. But no. Remy was braced against the tree, which sheltered him only slightly from the raging wind and rain, seemingly unconcerned that standing beneath a tree was the worst place in the world—short of a golf course or lake—to be during a thunderstorm.

She knew it was stupid to remain out there. She knew what she risked. She knew she shouldn't be watching.

But neither could she look away.

Each violent stroke of his fist caused her pulse to strum deep in her belly. Every time his palm cupped the head of his penis, heat worked its way lower in her body. And when he threw his head back and shouted at the storm, she felt her vaginal muscles clench and weep.

She'd known since the moment she saw him that she'd be willing to spread her legs for him. Sexual inhibitions had never been an issue for her, and even if she didn't need to bed him for scientific reasons, she'd do it for her own. She liked sex, and he looked like he knew his way around a woman's body.

It would be so easy to walk up and take him in her hand, her mouth. But doing so wasn't an option. Something was happening here, something intimate between Remy and Mother Nature, and she couldn't intrude. She could only watch from the darkness, a voyeur captivated by a powerful image of sensual, savage carnality.

The world spun as her own body reacted, hungry for something it hadn't tasted in a long, long time. Desire whirled through her as ruthlessly as the wind whirled around her, and unbidden, her hand slipped inside her unbuttoned shorts. Her fingertips slid down her flat belly, over the tattoo that seemed to have grown as sensitive as the day she'd gotten it. By the time she realized what she was doing, it was too late.

Her fingers found her slick folds, and fierce, biting pleasure radiated upward to where rain pelted her breasts like a lover's kisses. Her hips rocked against her hand, and she nearly cried out as she squeezed the pearl of nerves between her thumb and forefinger, the pressure agonizing yet soothing. And still, it wasn't enough, not when the fingers she wanted touching her were Remy's.

Lightning and thunder exploded simultaneously. A tree went down behind the house. Whether or not Remy had seen it, she didn't know. His only reaction was to bare his teeth and pump his hand even faster. Faster, and the storm raged harder. Each pull from root to crown ended with light streaking across the sky. Each thrust of his hips came with a shift in the wind direction.

Rain pounded her, ran in rivulets down her arm and along

her finger that stroked her pussy, the cool water easing the steamy heat there between her legs. Her fevered skin welcomed the rain even as it burned for the touch of the man in front of her.

"Remy," she gasped, and his head swiveled, his intense, glowing gaze capturing hers.

His sensual lips parted, and he said something, something she couldn't hear. Then his eyes closed and he turned back, braced his forehead against his forearm where it supported him against the tree.

Creamy moisture coated her fingers as she pushed two into her sex, where right now she only wanted the part of Remy that jutted magnificently from between his legs. Her internal muscles would pull him deep, ripple around his thick shaft as he stretched her sensitive tissue and drove her to orgasm.

Her legs grew shaky, her breath choppy. A twisting, wrenching sensation tugged at her, from her breasts that strained against the wet, cold fabric of her T-shirt to her pulsing, aching clit, which screamed for attention. Just one light caress would send her over the edge. A flick of her thumb, or better, a flick of Remy's tongue. But she waited, watching him, her feet inching her closer.

Remy's long fingers squeezed his hard flesh, stroked, and then his hips jerked forward and she heard his roar of release over the sudden tempest that broke over their heads like the heavens had opened up.

She smelled the acrid stench of ozone, felt her skin sizzle with electricity, and somewhere in the back of her mind she knew she'd never been so close to death—not even during her tornado-chasing days—but it didn't matter. Nothing mattered but finding relief.

She circled a fingertip around her clit, pressed against it in exactly the right place, and then her shout joined Remy's, and somehow, over the rioting storm, she heard their voices mingle.

When she could think clearly again—and she had no idea how long it had been—she found that the rain had stopped. The sky still flashed, but the lightning was distant, the thunderclaps muted. She blinked away water, and was surprised to find Remy a mere arm's length away.

He hadn't been the one who'd moved.

His chest heaved as he sucked oxygen into his lungs. He'd collapsed against the tree, his arms trembling. One hand still moved in slow, languorous strokes along his now semi-hard penis. A drop of liquid clung to the tip, but in the dark, she couldn't tell if it was water or cum. She wanted to fall to her knees, take him in her mouth and find out for herself.

As though she'd spoken her thoughts aloud, he fixed his sharp gaze on her, and her breath caught in her throat at the look in his eyes. He appeared exhausted, relieved and pissed off all at once. He shifted his gaze down, and her nipples tightened when he focused on them.

In one smooth motion, he tucked himself back inside his loose cargo pants and reached for her, his fingers stopping just short of touching one beaded nipple that pushed against the wet fabric as though it craved his attention.

Swearing, he pulled back. "Button up," he growled, and she realized her hand was still down her pants.

Like a teen who'd been caught in the bathroom with a nudie mag, she jerked her fingers from the damp bed of curls where they'd been nestled. Heat scorched her cheeks, and she was at once glad for the darkness and retreating lightning storm. She was no prude, had often stroked herself to orgasm during intercourse, but never had she masturbated in front of a complete stranger. Her humiliation completely outweighed her irritation at how Remy had just barked out an order at her—one she'd obeyed.

"Remy," she croaked, her voice sounding unused and harsh, "what . . . what just happened?"

His eyes narrowed, and he said nothing, but a muscle in his jaw ticked and his fists clenched at his sides. He looked so tired, so full of regret that it tore at her heart—something she'd thought withered and died a long time ago.

She took a tiny, cautious step forward, feeling oddly like what she approached was a timid fawn and not a full-grown, battle-scarred SEAL. His head came up, and his nostrils flared, and he watched her warily as she reached toward him. He flinched when she let her hand come to rest on his forearm. If she thought her skin had burned during the storm, it couldn't compare to the way white-hot electricity seemed to sear his.

"Don't," he said roughly. But he didn't move away.

Emboldened, she stepped closer, until her breasts touched his biceps, sending an erotic sizzle coursing through her. "We need to talk."

He glanced down at his crotch, where it was obvious that he had grown hard again, and suddenly, a bolt of lightning came out of nowhere. "Shit." He tore from her grasp and headed for the cabin. He didn't turn as he said loudly, "Get inside. A storm's coming."

three

"What the fuck were you doing out there?" Remy demanded. His anger had mounted with every step he took toward the house. Haley had barely crossed the threshold and shut the door before he'd turned on her.

She was breathing hard, her shirt soaked through and plastered to her breasts. Her nipples poked at the fabric, and he let his eyes trail to her shorts, still unbuttoned, remembering the way she'd looked when she'd touched herself. Wild, dripping with water, her tongue caught between her lips as she watched him with heavy-lidded eyes, her hand down her shorts, where he wanted to be.

"I was..." she started, then pushed wet hair off her flushed cheeks and stared at him. "I was worried about you."

"You shouldn't." Every one of his senses remained on heightened alert, and God, he could smell her, wanted to taste her, run his tongue between her legs and make her cry out his name the way she had out by the tree. And she would let him—he was sure of that.

Every one of his senses wanted her to worry about him, and that's what worried him the most. Where the hell was *that* coming from?

"I shouldn't?" She made an angry gesture at the window, flinging droplets of water onto the warped hardwood floor. "This weather is crazy. You could have been killed."

"I'm going to take my truck and drive away from here, and everything will get better," he said. "Trust me on that."

Didn't matter if the whole damned bayou had washed out—he'd sleep in his truck or in a tent or right out in the open in the middle of the rain; he'd done worse on missions. Besides, he'd slept outside more times than he cared to remember when he was a kid, when his father got piss-drunk or when he hosted his weekly poker games and his asshole friends would treat him like shit.

He and the weather had forged an uneasy truce for most of his life, at least until he ran across Hurricane Haley and her magic touch. Now all bets were off and both the weather and Haley were threatening to kick his ass.

His eyes drew to where her shorts gaped open at the fly, and the hair on the back of his neck rose. He wondered why he hadn't seen the symbol earlier, when she'd been in the shower. She followed his gaze, and then idly traced the tattoo on her right hip with her middle finger.

"I got it when I was in the Air Force," she said, because he couldn't stop staring. The roar in his ears got louder. "It was a stupid, drunken dare. I thought about having it removed once, but..." She shrugged.

"When?"

"When was I going to have it removed?" At his nod, she circled it once more. "About six months ago, I guess."

About the time Mother Nature had started messing with him even harder than usual.

A step forward, no touching, and he stared at the symbol and then at her. This was so *not* good. "Haley, you've got to tell me why you're really here."

"I told you, I'm here to study weather phenomena in the area."

"Bullshit." He balled his fists at his sides to keep them from reaching out.

"You don't think I'm a meteorologist?" She crossed her arms over her chest, and they pushed her breasts up and out. He swallowed dryly. "I'll have you know I got my initial training in the military, and then I got my degree in meteorology and worked for the National Weather—"

"Not that," he gritted out, dragging his gaze away from her breasts. "The reason you're here. It's bullshit."

She whirled away from him. "I don't have to prove anything to you."

Her hips swayed as she stalked toward her equipment, muddy feet squishing on the floor, and just as he knew the wind was about to pick up, he knew he shouldn't touch her. But he did it anyway. Grasped her elbow and swung her around.

"That," he said, looking down at her tattoo. "I've seen it before." He kept to himself the fact that he'd seen it in his dreams. That he'd been drawing it since he was six years old.

"Well, *there's* some solid evidence that I'm lying," she huffed, but he'd stopped listening, found himself on his knees in front of her to get a closer look at the tat.

He didn't mean to touch it—hell, his hands were still fisted at his sides—but his tongue snaked out to trace the cloud and the fist holding the lightning bolts, letting it linger on the smooth, sweet expanse of wet skin.

Going to have to ask her what the tattoo symbolized. Later. When he was done fucking her.

No point in denying that was going to happen.

She moaned when he licked an errant drop of rainwater from her belly, and her response encouraged him, let him trace circles that got wider and wider until he had to peel down the fly of her shorts for better access. And when he looked up at her, he wasn't surprised to find her watching him, her mouth already swollen as if in anticipation of his kisses.

He wasn't going to kiss her. They were well beyond that intimacy.

When the tingle started at the base of his spine and worked upward faster than it ever had, he closed his eyes, because he didn't want to see the darkness that was seconds away from descending.

When he heard the sound, like a train ready to smash through the center of the house, her computer went wild behind her, the printer furiously spitting out the graphs and charts neither of them needed to look at to know they were in for some major weather.

What she didn't know was that it was all his fault. Mother Nature wouldn't hurt her as long as she was with him, but the same couldn't be said for *him*. He shouldn't be here.

"Haley." Her name passed his lips as a plea, to which she responded by grabbing his shoulders, holding him against her.

She wouldn't let him break away from her touch—he could have easily, that they both knew, but her hands on his body mesmerized him, held him prisoner in ways that weren't physical. The pressure was beginning to build again; his earlier orgasm had done little to help him, and suddenly, it didn't matter why she was here. Nothing mattered except the anticipation of skin on skin and the need to feel her flesh contracting around him.

He rubbed his face against the wet denim of her shorts until his cheek felt raw, and then he tugged at the waistband, first with his teeth and then his hands. The shorts came all the way down, and he pushed her thighs apart roughly. She whimpered, kicked the fabric away from her feet.

His cock was rock hard by the time his tongue darted through her damp curls and into the hot flesh between her legs, leaving her no doubt that he was claiming her, with his mouth, the rasp of his tongue, the light stroke of his teeth against her clit that left her begging incoherently.

He freed himself from his own pants, his face still buried in between her thighs, refusing to break away from tasting sweetness and sin and everything in between.

The floorboards vibrated under his knees as he used one hand to work his cock while he licked her swollen sex, then probed, hard and fast. He was caught in a frenzy of need and want, and his free hand dug into her hip, and *God, she was so wet for him*. He was vaguely aware of her hands clutching his hair, pushing his face closer against her, and of her calling out, *Don't stop, please don't stop....*

Glass shattered somewhere in the house—windows blowing out—and she yelled above the sound as she came against his mouth. He swirled his tongue through her folds, easing her down from her high even as his hand worked himself toward his own pleasure, upward toward the pinnacle. Maybe if he could get there, he'd release enough steam that he could take her like a normal person, with no risks, no terror. He couldn't stand to make her afraid of him.

He loosened his grip on her hip, and she sank down to her knees, facing him. Desire had darkened her half-lidded brown eyes to a smoky umber, and her cheeks glowed with warmth. A sultry smile tipped the corner of her mouth, and he'd never seen anything so beautiful, so tempting. Damn, but he was in trouble.

She placed her warm hand over his that gripped his cock, and she looked into his eyes as she guided his fingers where she wanted them to go. Then, like a petulant child, she slapped his hand away and replaced it with hers.

His balls constricted almost painfully as her hand dropped to cup them, her fingernails scratching lightly at the sensitive spot behind them.

"Do you like that?" she murmured, and he could only groan, and then she peeled off her shirt and was on all fours in front of him, her curvy ass open to the air, her breath scorching the head of his penis.

His entire body trembled in anticipation as her lips hovered near the tip, nibbling, kissing, flicking her tongue against the weeping slit. Shocks of pleasure shot from his groin to his toes, and his skin rippled as if he could almost feel the light from the thunderbolts on his flesh.

"Don't tease, Haley," he said gruffly. "I can't...it's too dangerous...."

He couldn't finish the sentence because she took him deep into her mouth, and the only thing he could do was spear his fingers through her hair that had come loose from her ponytail, and thrust upward. She hummed or moaned or groaned—he couldn't tell which, but the vibrations rippled from the head of his cock to his balls, and the sensation almost sent him over the edge.

A crash. In his head. In the cabin. Shit. Another window had blown in the kitchen, and the storm continued to try to pound her way inside.

Dammit. He couldn't do this to her. He wouldn't. No matter how his body had tensed to the point of breaking, he wouldn't be responsible for breaking *her*.

Grasping her head with shaking hands, he lifted her away. "Go to the bathroom and stay there. It's the strongest part of the house." He'd stay here and take care of his raging need, send the storm packing.

He pulled them both to their feet, and as her hair whipped wildly about her face, she stared him down. "No. We're finishing this."

Anger and need collided in one massive ball of rage in the pit of his belly. "The goddamned hurricane is here! Go. Now!"

Instead of obeying, she reached for him again, closed her fingers tight around his cock. A strange buzzing noise bounced off the inside of his skull, and his mind whirred so fast, he couldn't think straight. He shoved her away, propelled her toward the bathroom and stalked to the broken window, his flip-flops crunching glass.

Standing in the wind, he closed his eyes, took three deep, long breaths. *Get it together, man. Get it together.* He needed to get out of here. Draw the storm away. Take care of his needs far from here, where the wind howled her fury at Haley like a jealous mistress.

"Remy!"

He whirled, teeth bared, darkness closing in on his thoughts and the cabin. She was walking toward him, her shadowed body wet, dripping, the dark triangle at the juncture of her thighs a beacon that made his cock jerk toward her.

"Not. One. More. Step," he heard himself say, though that voice wasn't his, not the way it sounded torn from the depths of hell. "You have no idea what I'm capable of."

"I need to know," she said, reaching for him. "Show me."

He shook his head, a last desperate attempt to hold on to control, but the moment her fingers touched his skin, the battle was lost. His tenuous hold on sanity snapped, and with a roar that drowned out the storm, he spun her around, bent her roughly over the back of the stained orange sofa.

The whirring in his head spun faster. The howling wind outside picked up speed. He grasped his cock, engorged to the point of agony, and thrust inside Haley's waiting sex. She cried out, and dear God, he hoped it wasn't in pain because he couldn't stop.

Gripping her hips with trembling fingers, he pounded into her, each thrust pushing her and the couch forward. Her pulsing walls sucked him deep, squeezed him so hard that his concentration centered only on the place where their bodies joined.

Son of a bitch, she felt good. Hot and silky and tight.

He looked down at his shaft, glistening with her juices, as he drove into her. Riveted by the sight of their mating, he trailed his thumb across her firm bottom and then spread her wide with his fingers. Lightning spanked her pale ass cheeks as he skimmed a finger along her crevice, circling her opening, making her squirm and moan.

"Remy..." She arched her back, taking his thrusts even deeper, testing his control. Normally he'd orgasm quickly and end the storm and the danger that came with it, but this was different, Haley was different, and he ground his teeth until he thought one would crack. He needed to do this right. He needed to taste her, needed every part of their bodies to meld.

With a growl, he bent over her, positioned his mouth against the gentle slope of her shoulder. He couldn't help but bite into the soft skin and hear her whimpers of pleasure when he didn't let go.

Every muscle screamed as he drove into her. Thunder shook the house, sent shock waves up his legs and into his balls, which slapped against her soaked lips.

"Harder," Haley cried hoarsely, and he couldn't believe she wanted more, not when every other woman he'd been with had begged him to ease up long before he'd made it to this point.

She reached between her legs, used two fingers to stroke his sac, and he knew he wanted more too, wanted to see her eyes when she came.

He grunted as he pulled out of her, and he didn't need to spin her around this time. She turned, thrust a leg between his to hook his calf and pull him down to the floor with her. They dropped heavily, and he barely had time to twist his body to take the brunt of the impact.

Somehow, he kicked off his flip-flops and stripped out of his pants, and then she was all over him, legs spread and wrapped around him. Strong legs that hugged him firmly around the waist and wouldn't let go.

He'd stopped thinking the second she'd touched him a moment ago. Now, sunk deep inside Haley's body, her center slick from orgasm but still tight enough to cause her to gasp, thoughts were starting to come through, thoughts about how she wasn't the least bit afraid.

And she was holding him, her arms wrapped around his shoulders, her eyes focused on his and dark with pleasure.

He'd been murmuring things to her, words, phrases in Cajun French, and somehow she was answering him, telling him she loved it.

"You like this," he murmured. "Like my cock buried deep inside you."

"Mmm, yes."

"Fucking you so hard you don't have any control," he said, pushing his palms against the floor for support; his knees scraped the old wood, and he didn't care because he was so deep in the rut.

She was still clutching him like he was more than just a screw, stroking his back, kissing his neck while she kept pace with the rocking he couldn't stop, matching him thrust for thrust.

He must have been talking, because she was telling him to come, telling him not to worry about hurting her, telling him it was okay to let go.

She had no idea what she was saying, but she'd said it, and that was all he needed. He rammed into her, dug his short nails into the soft skin of her shoulders. A red-hot spear of pleasure burst in his pelvis. A clap of thunder shook the house.

He shuddered as he came. Spilled inside her because the storm hadn't provided him enough time to think about protection and he didn't care—loved the way her tight heat milked him up and down, the way it felt to fill her up completely with his seed, which spilled out from between them and lubricated him for the next round.

He was still hard, steel encased in softness. And he was so far from done. Slowing, he caught his breath for just a second before he was thrusting into her again.

* * *

HALEY CRUSHED REMY BETWEEN HER THIGHS, lifted her hips to take him deep, arched so her nipples rubbed against his damp chest. Never had she been with a man who could match her hungers in bed—not that she and Remy had made it to a bed. But now, this was the best kind of research she'd ever done.

He spoke sexy things into her ear as he alternately nipped her lobe and then soothed it with his tongue. His voice was softer, gentler than it had been before his orgasm, and crazily enough, so was the storm.

Maybe there really was something to Remy Begnaud and the weather thing. Part of her, the curious, dedicated scientist, wanted to scrutinize every move he'd made since she'd met him, analyze how his behavior had paralleled weather events. But the extremely aroused female part of her didn't care about any of that, as long as Remy kept doing what he was doing. If the weather made him the strongest, most intense lover of her life, then let the heavens roar.

"Tell me what you want, *chere catin*," he murmured into her ear. "Tell me while I can still think."

"That," she said as he inserted a hand between their bodies to circle her clit lightly with one callused finger, his hot touch releasing an eruption of fiery ripples at her center. "Just. That."

Silver bursts of lightning made shadows dance on the walls, the floor, the skin of his shoulders, but the thunder was muted, allowing her to hear his whispered words—which she didn't recognize as English, but that spoke volumes nevertheless.

She closed her eyes, let herself feel and not think, because if she let her mind go, it would go places it shouldn't venture. It would wonder how Remy would react when he found out she was here to study him for possible recruitment into a super-secret agency. Or how he'd feel about being betrayed by his father. Or if he made other women come as hard as she had.

But really, none of those thoughts mattered, because she

didn't care. This was a job. Remy was a job. And he was doing a damn fine job at what he was doing.

She arched up, taking all of him, forcing his hand to touch her where she needed him to, forcing his cock to rake the place inside that made her wild. When he slowed the tempo of his thrusts, she dug her nails into the knotted muscles in his back. His response, a harsh breath that hissed between his clenched teeth, made her smile against his skin, especially when he drove into her harder than before. Her back scraped on the rough wooden floor, but she didn't care; the pain only made her more aware of the pleasant sensations between her legs.

Her body gripped his length so tightly that she could feel every ridge, every bump, every texture along his shaft, and she cried out at the sweet tension that began to coil in her core. The slide of his cock massaged her G-spot with each slippery stroke, dredging moans from the depths of her chest, urging her hips to roll frantically against his. Somewhere in the background, her mind registered the sound of the wind blowing open the front door, and then the crash of something heavy inside the house.

"I'm sorry," Remy said hoarsely, and plunged deep inside her.

"Don't be," she returned, her voice barely more than a moan. "This is...mmm, yes, oh, right there..."

The remaining windows rattled, and the roof creaked and popped like it was going to peel away like a can lid. Remy increased his pace, grabbed her head in both hands and forced her to look into his eyes. His eyes that had gone feral and luminous in the continuous flashes from the storm.

"Ground me."

It wasn't his voice. It couldn't be. Not unless he was the storm personified, because he sounded like the thunder. Only more powerful.

Goose bumps pebbled her skin. He'd asked her to ground

him . . . ground him in the here and now? How odd that he'd used an electrical term.

But she did what she could. She locked her gaze on his, watched the lightning reflect in his eyes, watched it emanate from somewhere deeper as well, from somewhere inside him.

"That's it, Remy," she breathed. "Let go. I've got you."

The fierce hunger in his eyes intensified, and he slammed hard, fast strokes into her. Her skin tingled and heat seared her flesh. Tendons strained in Remy's neck, his jaw clenched, and then he came, this time in silence, his hot semen burning her from the inside out like a current from a live wire.

The relentless pressure that had been building shattered, and shards of pleasure ripped through her body. The bone-deep orgasm tore her apart, left her panting, shaking, feeling at once wrung out and energized.

She couldn't recall the last time a man had worked her into more than one orgasm in a night, but she knew for sure that no man had ever done it so well.

As a meteorology geek with a passion for severe weather, she'd always harbored a secret fantasy, one that took her into the heart of a tempest with a man who was strong enough to stand up to Mother Nature.

It had been a safe fantasy, because no one was that crazy.

Wrong. Remy was that crazy. Even if the thing with the weather was a hoax or was all in his imagination, it didn't matter. Because he'd gotten off on the storms, and oh, man, so had she.

REMY BEGNAUD SR. LOOKED OUT Widow Johnson's window at the pouring rain and backdrop of lightning. Thunder shook the house. Snarling gusts of wind bent trees until their branches scratched like fingernails across the old tin roof.

T had come home.

Shit on a stick. He rubbed his jaw, rough after not shaving for two days. His mind had been elsewhere, on his newest inventions, on Widow Johnson's talent in bed, on the fact that he might have made a whopper of a mistake by telling that pretty little meteorologist about T-Remy's association with Mother Nature.

He'd done it for T's own good, and he dared anyone to think otherwise. Sure, Haley had given him a shitload of money for the info, but that had been gravy. The important thing had been to make sure T got help for his weather problems and a steady job outside the Navy so he wouldn't ruin his life the way Remy had. That Haley girl had promised T would get both if what Remy told her was true.

He closed his eyes and listened to the rain pelt the glass. It had seemed like such a good idea, letting her come to Bayou Blonde to study his son. A good idea until he helped the sweet young thing unload her equipment. All of a sudden, his blood had run cold and nothing seemed so good anymore. The way she'd talked, like T was a specimen in a petri dish and not a person, had filled him with dread and a sense of foreboding.

If T found out what he'd done, he wouldn't give a fig why. Remy could lose his son. Sort of ironic, he supposed, given that he'd gotten his son out of loss in the first place.

Raw pain welled up in his throat as though his twenty-five-year wound had been reopened. His lovely Fay Lynne, so supportive and trusting when he'd made the decision to leave the Navy after his first term was up, when she was six months pregnant and he didn't have a job to support them. If he'd only stayed in the military, had tried a little harder to be a team player and not balk at every command . . .

Shit, he could play the If Only game all night and nothing would change. Fay Lynne and his unborn son would still be dead, victims of a car accident he might have prevented if he'd had the money to fix the vehicle when he first noticed the brake vibrations. His life had ended with theirs that day, had spiraled out of control until three months later when he heard about a baby boy born on his own son's due date. Born during Hurricane Tessa and abandoned on the steps of the old Baptist church that sat across from the intersection where the accident had happened.

Remy wasn't one to believe in curses or voodoo or even superstitions, but he believed in fate. When the baby's mother turned up dead in the river and no one wanted him because everyone else believed in curses, voodoo and superstitions, Remy had found it easy enough to adopt the kid. Especially once the father, a married New Orleans blueblood, made it simple by greasing some palms to keep the whole thing quiet.

"Remy? You still worrying 'bout your boy?"

Nodding, he turned to face Widow Johnson, standing there in nothing but her skivvies, holding a candle for light. "He's home."

"He called? I didn't hear your cell ring."

"It didn't." Thunder rolled through the house, through his chest. "I just know."

"Then come back to bed."

Reluctantly, he followed her through the dark halls. He didn't deserve to sleep comfortably. Not when T was probably already under the microscope, being tested and poked and prodded after walking into a trap his own father had helped set.

Remy'd seen the meteorologist's communications equipment, and if that woman worked for the National Weather Service like she claimed, he'd eat one of them swamp rats that lived right outside the widow's back door. No, Miss Haley Holmes was backed by money and power, and once she figured out that his son could snap his fingers and level a town with a tornado, T was in trouble.

Gut clenching so hard that he stumbled, he did something he hadn't done since Fay died. He prayed. Prayed his desperation hadn't cost him the only person he had left in his life. Prayed his son would forgive him. Prayed his son wasn't right this very moment in trouble and hating life.

CHAPTER
Four

Haley was still there. Okay, maybe it was because she was partially trapped beneath the weight of his body, but she didn't look scared or upset when Remy stared at her face for traces of either emotion. She looked . . . satiated.

Son of a bitch, what the hell was he supposed to do with that?

She gently stroked a hand down his bare back, and he pulled away faster than if she'd slapped him across the face.

"Remy, wait," she said, but he grabbed an old blanket off the couch and handed it to her, the same one he'd used all those years that the couch had doubled as his bed and the only corner of the world he could call his. When she'd wrapped herself in it, he picked her up and walked her over to the couch.

"Stay put until I clear some of this glass," he barked, because he didn't know what else to say to her. Thankfully, she complied and sank back into the cushions. He yanked on his cargo pants, didn't bother buttoning them or looking for the shirt he vaguely remembered losing outside. Instead, he lit two of the closest hurricane lamps, since the electricity was still blown, and then grabbed a broom from the kitchen floor.

The storm wasn't over. He could feel it in the way his skin still tingled, stretched, like it was too tight for his body.

He could go again easily, right now, and the thought of swaying against Haley, into her, made the faint buzz in his head grow louder. He forced himself not to look back at her. Instead, he swept the glass and other debris into a neat pile by the back door and wondered what in the hell to do next.

Sex with her had been good—so damned good. Almost a real release, which he'd needed on more than one level, because it had been a while for him. Four months away in the desert with his team and his decision not to re-up had taken his focus mercifully away from sex and weather, even as he'd been forced to reevaluate exactly what the fuck he was going to do with the rest of his life when all he could ever think about was sex and weather.

He had friends who'd gotten into the lucrative business of mercenary work. The hours were long, but the pay rocked and the adrenaline rush couldn't be beat. Plus, it was something he could do alone.

But he wasn't alone now.

"Did I hurt you?" Haley was asking him. She was standing again, and the blanket had opened, baring her body to him. Even when he stared, she didn't pull it closed around her.

"Did *you* hurt *me*?" he asked in amazement, hating the way his voice shook. He shoved the broom aside and rubbed the back of his neck where he still felt the prickling on his skin.

"Your ribs. The bruises. I tried to be careful around them...." She'd moved toward him, reached a hand out to touch his chest, and for a second he was spellbound at the way her breasts swayed, still heavy and flushed from sex. Then he noticed the angry, crimson bite mark on her shoulder.

"Don't. Don't touch and don't worry about me," he said. She

didn't reach out to him again, but she didn't move away either, and for the first time in his life he didn't feel cornered having someone stand that close. Her presence was almost soothing, and he blamed his orgasm for the false sense of security.

That damned tattoo was throwing him too. And, as if she'd read his mind, her fingers played along the ink.

"You've got to tell me what that was all about," she said softly.

He wanted to ask her the same thing, wanted to put his mouth to her hip again and trace the familiar lines with his tongue, wanted to be buried inside of her to the hilt. Instead, he shrugged like none of this was a big deal and the pent-up energy still begging to be released from his body wasn't dangerous for both of them. "Hurricanes get me hot."

"Um, yeah, I'll say." She paused. "Those bruises didn't just happen tonight, did they?"

He glanced down at the dark blemishes that had formed almost immediately after the attempted mugging last night. Two men had cornered him by his car, while a third and fourth grabbed him from behind. They'd nearly taken him down hard, something that shouldn't have happened, given that he'd been trained to take out double that crew with no weapons other than his bare hands. At one point during the fight, his wrists had seemed bound together, although when he'd looked down at them, they'd been completely free.

"No, not from tonight."

"From work?"

"No," he said abruptly, and he willed her to use the blanket to cover her body. The lights in the house flickered on briefly and then buzzed off again. "Not from work. Are you sure I didn't hurt you?"

"You didn't hurt me, Remy," she said. "I'm tougher than I look." She smiled, and damn her, he almost let his guard down and smiled back. When he didn't, she sighed. "I think we both need to get cleaned up. I'll scrounge up some food and make a snack. We can eat while we talk about this."

For a split second, he wondered what it would be like, to talk to someone who might actually understand this roller coaster his body and Mother Nature took him on. Maybe she could explain it to him logically.

And maybe being inside her had screwed with his head, because he knew damn good and well his relationship with the weather had nothing to do with logic.

"There's nothing to talk about," he said. "Besides, I need to find my father." His gut tightened at the thought of Remy Senior, reminded him where he was and why he'd come home again.

"You can't go out there now to look for him—it's not safe."

He laughed. "*Bebe*, I know these swamps like my own fin-gerprints. There's nothing around here that scares me."

Except you.

"Your father obviously knows his way around here too," she pointed out. "I'm sure he's taken refuge somewhere, if he's even still in the area."

She had a point—if there was one thing the old man knew how to do well, it was take care of himself. He could go out at first light and do a sweep of the area. He could take some time now to clean up the rest of the mess, check the generator . . . or he could sleep.

He fought the urge to yawn, realized it had been weeks since he'd slept well. And storms like this one always wrung him out. The familiar, bone-weary ache had begun to settle in and he knew it was useless to fight it. He needed rest, and for the first time in years, he knew he could actually close his eyes and sleep.

She was still standing close, looking at him almost protectively. Which was ridiculous. He took a few steps away from her.

"I'm, ah, going to catch some sleep. I'll clean up the rest of this later," he said.

She cocked her head and watched him until he felt like a fascinating new microorganism on a microscope slide. "Are you always tired afterward? After sex?"

Not sex. Storms. But even though he didn't say the words out loud, wind stirred the air. The door had blown open, and he closed it, righted a lamp that had been knocked over.

"You might want to get some rest too," he said, ignoring her questions.

She was still staring at him, and then he realized he was staring right back, but not at her face. She blushed and tugged at the corners of the blanket, bringing them together to hide her lush curves. Disappointment ran through him, even as he yawned again.

"Okay, you rest," she said. "I'm not tired, so I'll start the generator and see what I can do about the rest of this place." She waved her hand at the mess. Normally, he would argue, tell her not to touch anything, but not this time. "Why don't you take my bed? It'll be quieter in the bedroom."

"I'll sleep out here," he said.

"But that old thing's so lumpy," she started, and he must have let his guard down, let his expression betray the lingering bitterness of his childhood, because she bit her lip and looked down. "I'm sorry."

"It's fine. I'm used to it." He left her alone for a minute to use the bathroom and clean up a little, and when he came out, she was already dressed and hovering over her equipment. Grateful that she'd found something else to study besides him, he sank into cushions that made the bare ground look comfortable, and settled in. His eyes closed and his breathing eased into a steady rhythm instantly, but his joints remained stiff, his muscles taut.

"Haley?" he murmured, turning to his side. "The storm's not over."

* * *

"HALEY, THE STORM'S NOT OVER," she muttered as she scanned the most current NOAA satellite pictures.

The storm was, indeed, over. It had skirted them and turned northeast as it fell apart. Aside from the stray cells drifting in from the Gulf, they should be free of significant weather until a front moved in, and the next low-pressure system looked to be at least two days away.

What puzzled her was the fact that nationally produced radar and satellite images indicated a category one hurricane with outer bands that had fizzled before they reached Bayou Blonde. According to the charts, this part of Louisiana had been in the clear all along.

It didn't make sense. She'd seen an intense echo pop out of nowhere on her portable radar before she'd run outside, yet that same echo didn't show up on National Weather Service products.

This shouldn't be happening. But Haley had learned a long time ago that as advanced as meteorological equipment was, Mother Nature could always throw a curveball. Unpredictable weather happened. Yet this...this was just plain weird. And as strange as the storm's behavior had been, Remy's had been stranger.

As the storm had grown in intensity, so had his agitation.

She didn't want to believe Remy was in any way connected to weather incidents, but to be honest, the events of the past few hours had riddled her with doubt. The weather had seemed to intensify every time Remy's mood did the same. Geez, she'd thought the house would blow down with every orgasm. So why the lack of data during the approximate times the weather had gone downhill? Why had the storm she'd experienced disappeared and left no evidence?

We've never been able to substantiate reports that Petty Officer Begnaud has ever directly affected the weather, because meteorological proof other than localized damage has never been found.

Now she understood what her boss at the Agency for

Covert Rare Operatives—ACRO—had tried to tell her. If Remy affected storms, he did it... invisibly.

Which was utterly absurd. She'd seen a lot at ACRO, enough to turn her conceptions of what was possible and what wasn't upside down, so while she couldn't rule out a form of telekinesis that controlled the weather, she couldn't wrap her brain around phantom storms that didn't appear in satellite photos.

Not so ridiculous, however, was the theory that weather affected Remy's behavior.

Atmospheric pressure, sunshine, humidity... those elements and more had forever influenced human, animal and plant life in ways not completely understood by the science community. Some could be rationalized, some couldn't. As a parameteorologist, it was her job to explain the unexplained. Or at least prove the unexplained does, indeed, exist. Mysterious phenomena like ball lightning, a controversial subject that sat solidly between two camps—believers and disbelievers—was a personal favorite. Remy, however, might just top ball lightning as her new fave.

The powers that be at ACRO would be disappointed if Remy couldn't control the weather, but they'd find a use for him even if some lesser connection existed. What they planned to do with him wasn't her concern; her career was, and her future depended upon her ability to learn the truth.

Learn the truth in any way possible, something ACRO's chief of operations, Devlin O'Malley, had made clear.

"Mr. O'Malley, I have a few questions," she said.

His fingers traced circles on the oak desk that separated them. He wore the same black BDUs every operative with an exceptional talent wore when they walked the halls of the main ACRO compound, and though he was the big boss, his white ID badge identified him as no one more important than an operative assigned to the Medium department in the Paranormal Division.

Haley fingered her own tag, bearing the light blue of the Science Division. As a "civilian" with no special abilities, she wore what she wanted, which usually meant pantsuits, but today she'd opted for a skirt, which left her feeling strangely vulnerable in front of this blind man whom she'd spoken with only twice, very briefly, before now.

"It's Devlin. Mr. O'Malley was my father," he said finally.

She nodded. His name suited him. Strong, mysterious, sexy. As dark as his short brown hair that was always spiky, like he couldn't keep his fingers out of it.

"Devlin, I've got some problems with the assignment I was given."

"Such as?"

"I don't want it," she said bluntly. "I don't have the kind of training your other operatives do. And I'm not a first contact person. I'm a scientist."

A scientist who was being asked to take a crash course in first contact procedures, which meant boning up on self-defense maneuvers, learning covert operation techniques and studying the psychological art of seduction. She'd gone through months of initial operative training when she first joined the agency, but it hadn't been the extensive military-type instruction the field operatives with special abilities received. Now, suddenly, ACRO wanted to remedy some of that.

"Not all first contact personnel have special abilities. More importantly, you're the only person at ACRO with the knowledge and background necessary to determine Remy Begnaud's talents. You're the only one we need," Devlin said, his own military background more than clear in his don't-interrupt-me tone as he stood, then paced, outlining his plan for her. "You have plenty of weapons, Haley. Brains, beauty. The whole package. Don't be afraid to use it the way you were taught."

His sightless blue eyes bore into hers as though he could see into her soul if he tried hard enough.

"You don't believe it yet, but sex is all about power and control. It's always been an underrated tool, and one that's fully at your disposal as an ACRO agent."

"Underrated, my ass," she whispered as she glanced over at Remy's sleeping form, at the way the fly of his pants had peeled back to reveal his sex that lay heavy and thick against his belly. Her body flushed with warmth, something the ice water she'd been gulping by the gallon to counter the sticky heat couldn't ease.

The reddened bite mark on her shoulder ached, but it was a good pain, the same good pain that made her sex tender from Remy's powerful thrusts. Oh, yes, she'd have fun uncovering the truth. And if the truth revealed no link between Remy and Mother Nature, he'd go on his way none the wiser, but she'd have indulged in the best sex of her life.

Her blood pooled and simmered in all her erogenous zones, as though her hormones were rebelling at the idea that she'd never experience his hands on her body again. Then he moaned in his sleep, and she forgot everything but the way he looked in slumber, strangely alert, but almost innocent, much like he must have looked as a boy.

She tried to picture a young Remy sleeping on the couch, probably for as long as he'd lived here, since the house had only one bedroom.

Why had Remy Senior even taken on the responsibility of a kid? He couldn't have known what Remy might be capable of, even as a baby—or had he?

Had any woman ever been around to help raise Remy? To bake him cookies and praise his macaroni art and pick up after him? She glanced at his muddy shirt, which she'd found outside the door when she'd been tossing out debris, and made a mental note to wash it once the power came back on and the washer wouldn't suck up the juice from the generator.

And then she wondered when she'd turned into such a domestic goddess, because any desire she might have had to take care of a man had been squashed years ago by her mom's unnatural devotion to her father. A devotion returned just as fervently, and one she'd resented and had never fully understood.

Her laptop dinged, and she shoved aside the thoughts she had no business thinking to scan an e-mail from ACRO. Both Dev and the Science Division director wanted a status report. After sliding a glance at Remy to make sure he was still sleeping, she brought them both up to speed, said she'd contact Dev if she determined that they needed to send in the Convincers.

She'd never had to deal with ACRO's last resort crew, the team called in to deliver "difficult" potential recruits to the New York compound. Haley's recruitment had come via a first contact person doing much the same job Haley was doing now with Remy. She just hoped the Convincers wouldn't be required. Out of necessity, their methods weren't nearly as gentle as Haley's.

As the e-mail winged through cyberspace, she considered her next move. The ACRO reports she'd been given detailed complaints by Remy's superiors and military team members that his mere presence seemed to cause electrical equipment to fail. Remy's father had claimed the same thing. Her own equipment had temporarily malfunctioned, but then, power surges provided the most likely explanation.

Tapping her chin, she watched Remy for a moment. If Remy affected equipment, how? And when? Was his effect on equipment related to whatever relationship he had with the weather? Remy wouldn't answer her questions, but she knew someone who might.

She just hoped Annika was in a good mood, because if Haley thought Remy was touchy, Annika made him look like a kitten.

CHAPTER
Five

ACRO Special Operative Annika Svenson was in a great mood. She might be alone in a haunted house whose electrical energy topped the limits of her modified multimeter's ranges, but she liked being by herself, and besides, she had her iPod and her own personal electric-shock security system that no one—ghost or human—was getting through.

So no, she wasn't afraid, but she was, however, cold. Even though it was only late September, Syracuse, New York, hadn't gotten the memo that it was fall and not winter.

Although, come to think of it, she didn't remember being *that* cold outside.

Whatever. She'd been on-site for two days, would spend the next few nights here, recording what she could and then reporting her findings back to Dev. An easy enough assignment, though she'd much rather be on the Louisiana job. Bringing in a man who could supposedly control the weather would be much cooler than sitting in some dusty old mansion recording electrical fields.

But Dev had grown up in this house, and it was special to

him. And he, in turn, was special to her, so he could ask her to walk through fire and she'd do it without question. No questions, but probably a lot of cussing.

Her cell rang, and she thought about ignoring both it and whoever was dumb enough to call her after midnight, but when Haley's Op code popped onto the screen, she gave in. Haley was the one person at ACRO besides Dev she could stand.

"Make it quick, Hays. I have to get back to my extreme boredom."

The connection sucked, and the fact that Haley was speaking in a low, hushed voice didn't help. Annika could barely hear the other woman ask if Annika was capable of shorting out electrical equipment.

"If I intentionally send a pulse into something, yes. But I don't kill projectors during movies, if that's what you mean."

"Could a person short out electronics without knowing it? Just by being in the room?"

The lights in the overhead chandelier dimmed. Nonchalantly, Annika stepped out from beneath the gaudy thing. If something wanted her attention, it would have to do more than conjure up cheesy parlor tricks.

"The existence of electromagnetic fields around every known object in the world is a fact. In humans, the energy varies in both strength and manageability. Some people can't wear watches because they short out the batteries. Others draw the dead with their energy. So I wouldn't rule out someone having enough energy to short out equipment when they do nothing more than walk by."

"But?"

Annika grinned. Haley might be uptight, but she wasn't stupid. "The thing is, they couldn't maintain that level of power without burning themselves out or someone noticing. If your weather guy shorts shit out, he probably can't control it."

"You can."

"I'm special." She ran a current of electricity across the surface of her skin just because she could. "If he's got some sort of electrical thing going on, it might be related to his weather ability. Have you established the existence of that talent?"

"Not yet. I'm trying to determine if the equipment failures are even related to him."

"If he affects equipment, it probably happens during periods of extreme emotion—piss him off or get him horny or something. Those are triggers for most uncontrollable powers."

Most powers, but not Annika's. She'd been in control of hers since the age of twenty months, when, at the height of a temper tantrum, she'd shocked a babysitter right into a Swedish hospital's burn unit. Since then, she'd identified the one switch that made her power unruly, and she avoided tripping it unless she was alone.

Annika's ears popped. "Shit. Haley, I gotta go."

She hung up. An unnatural stillness fell over the house, and then an electrical ribbon she could sense more than see snaked across the great room where she stood. God, she hated this supernatural bullshit. ACRO employed more than enough mediums to handle this—heck, psychics outnumbered people with rare talents like hers ten to one. Why she got stuck with this crap was beyond her.

The ribbon floated up the grand staircase. She reached for the volume on her iPod, prepared to blast her brain with Green Day as she followed the energy, but the sound of footsteps froze her to the floor. Slipping into battle-mode, she crouched low, crept silently to the room entrance. She flooded her body with electricity. She feared no one, living or dead; she did, however, fear capture by the enemy, and she'd die before she was taken again.

Of course, anyone who had the balls and skill to take her

wouldn't be clomping across the marble tiles like a Clydesdale horse.

She loosened her Beretta in its ankle holster, but rarely, if ever, did she need a gun. She was a walking close-range weapon, preferring the personal touch. Which cracked her up when she thought about it like that.

If she needed to shoot, though, her target didn't stand a chance. With the exception of one man, a sniper with extraordinary eyesight, reflexes and ego, she was the best shot at ACRO. Not that she bragged. Much.

Her knife, secured at her other ankle, saw even less action. If she was close enough to her opponent to use the deadly blade, she was close enough to use hand-to-hand combat or her gift.

The door to the room banged open, and her heart lodged in her throat. She struck, reacting on instinct and training that started nineteen years ago when the CIA stole her from her mother at the age of two.

Shoot first, leave nothing to question later.

A massive bolt of electricity ripped down her arm to her fingertips, enough volts to blow the soles off the guy's boots.

But when she grasped his leather-clad biceps, the dude didn't so much as flinch or smoke from his ears. He whirled, seized her wrist, and before she could fall back on her combat training and slam the bastard to the ground, he stepped back and dropped a duffel bag to hold up his other hand in defense.

"Why are you trying to kill me, Annika? You know we're supposed to pretend to get along, for Dev's sake."

Shit.

"Creed." The ghost hunter towered over her, dressed in his usual head-to-toe black leather, save for the black T-shirt, the tattoo that covered the right side of his face and disappeared beneath his collar nearly glowing against his tanned skin. The leather-clad Neanderthal peered down at her with amusement, which made her want to knock the smirk off his angular face.

Either that, or kiss him. He had the greatest mouth, full lips that were always slightly tipped up like he knew a secret and wasn't telling, and a pierced tongue that looked like it could create some of those secrets.

Apparently, a lot of women had similar thoughts, because his reputation as a player famous for one-night stands had been water-cooler talk for years. Not that she wasted time gossiping, but some rumors took on lives of their own.

"Dev's not around, *kukhuvud*, so I don't have to pretend shit."

"Kukhuvud?"

"Dickhead." Yeah, she must have been pissed as hell to curse in Swedish, something only Creed could do to her. The CIA had encouraged her to remain fluent in her birth language, which was why she hated to speak it. She needed no reminders of her life before ACRO.

He cocked an eyebrow, making the piercing there, a silver barbell stud, crawl up. It torqued her to admit it, but his tattoos and piercings fascinated her, made her wonder if the parts she couldn't see were similarly decorated. She'd always been a little envious of his capacity to express his individuality, since she was unable to do the same. Not in that way. No undercover operative in their right mind would adorn their body with identifiable marks. No, the ability to blend in made a good agent. An agent who stood out was a dead agent.

But that wasn't the only reason she disliked Creed. She also hated how his weird psychic energy that chased everyone else away had the opposite effect on her, drew her and buzzed through her like a vibrator with fresh batteries.

Not that fresh batteries did any good in her vibrators, since she shorted them out with the first orgasm.

Cursing to herself because her life was pitifully short on

orgasms and way too long on fried circuits, she released the energy she held before she shorted herself out. She could always shock people at will, but only rarely did she wield the power like a shield so that anyone or anything coming into contact would suffer a nasty surprise. Holding the shield too long drained her emotionally, physically and mentally, leaving her little more than a quivering blob for hours.

There was just one small problem. Her energy hadn't worked on Creed. And the strange pulsing sensation still raced through her body from the point where he held her arm, letting her know that, for the first time in her life, maybe she should be a little bit afraid.

CREED MCCABE HAD NEVER let anyone make him feel like a freak. He had a high tolerance for people and their suspicions and need to stereotype, had to really, because the way he looked had always drawn more than a few outright stares. Most of those gazes were appreciative, especially when he'd turned sixteen or so and many of the women—and men—he came into contact with thought the tattoo that swirled around his right eye and cheek and disappeared down his neck was cool.

Cool. Fuck, yeah.

They had no way of knowing he'd been born with those markings. He'd been home-schooled because his parents hadn't wanted him to have to deal with the teachers and school boards who would've accused him of being a punk. Especially because he'd decided to rebel by getting multiple piercings— tongue, eyebrow, ears and nipples—because he needed some way to rebel. But the girls he'd been with always had a good time discovering that the tat didn't end at his neck—and that it made the entire right side of his body extra-sensitive.

The tattoo—and the accompanying ghost he liked to call Kat—had been so much a part of him that being without either would've been like being without air. Or at least he hadn't thought about parting with either until the past few years had taken their toll on him.

He'd been born into ACRO—his parents were some of the earliest recruits when Stargate disbanded and Dev's parents began the agency with a few psychics and not much else. Creed's parents were ghost hunters—and best friends with Mr. and Mrs. O'Malley. He'd been rescued from an abandoned cave in Tennessee thought to be haunted by the famous Bell Witch, and adopted by the McCabes, who'd been trying unsuccessfully to have children of their own for years. They didn't care about his markings or the fact that he was followed by a spirit who claimed to be a direct descendant of the Bell Witch, and they'd encouraged the fact that he was able to speak to the dead through that spirit—a ghost translator, of sorts.

He'd grown up in the unreal world of Special Abilities, had watched Dev take over the reins and bring in even stranger types than Creed himself.

Types like Annika, who'd become something of Dev's special pet. If you believed the rumors, which Creed tended not to do.

"Can you let go of me now?" Annika asked, the blue of her eyes slightly less icy than normal.

He released her wrist and she rubbed her forearm where his fingers had splayed. "Did I scare you?"

"Yes, Creed. I'm shaking with terror," she muttered. "Dev didn't mention you were coming."

"Last-minute decision, based on your latest report," he said. He'd turned away from her, which was pretty hard to do because she was freaking gorgeous—blond and curvy and hotter than hot—but he sensed the change in climate from the second he'd walked into this place and couldn't ignore that. "When was the last activity you recorded?"

"A minute before you walked in the door," she said. He

turned to stare at her and she rolled her eyes as he grabbed the multimeter from her. "The last recording was an hour ago, centered in the upstairs hallway, right at the landing."

He took the stairs two at a time to see if he could catch the tail end of the energy, but it was long gone.

"How's your shadow doing?" Annika asked from behind him. "Maybe she could make herself useful and figure out all this."

He put his palm flat against the north wall and closed his eyes. "She's a ghost, not a shadow. Why don't you ask her yourself—she hates to be talked about like she isn't here." He felt the familiar itch at the back of his neck and knew the spirit was around him, and that she wasn't happy. Just like Annika.

His spirit was the jealous type—she didn't mind him sleeping with women, as long as they didn't mean anything. Anytime he'd tried to date, Kat would cause too much damned trouble for it to be worth it. At twenty-nine, he'd begun to want more than a one-night stand, and every time he saw Annika, he was reminded of just how much that want had grown.

He concentrated on trying to draw the energy from the house instead of worrying about the two warring women he was going to have to deal with for the duration of this assignment. "This is a portal."

"So we should set up the equipment here, then?"

He shook his head. "Not unless you want to be drawn in," he said, and noted she was hugging her arms to her chest. "Have you been cold all day?"

"Yes, since I walked in here. Can't you feel it?"

"I'm not affected that way. Are you sure you're not sick?"

"I'm not sick," she said.

"You're all flushed." He attempted to put a palm against her forehead, but she threw out an arm to block him. "Look, this is important. I need to know how this house is affecting you. If it's too dangerous for you to be here."

"I'm not leaving."

"Just sit down, Annika. I've got to put my hands on you."

"You're not touching me."

"I've got to make sure the presence that was here hasn't gotten into you," he said. "The only way for me to do that is to put my hands on your bare skin."

"You already touched me," she protested, and he wondered why the hell she was making such a big deal out of this. "Couldn't you get a read off of me then?"

"I didn't get any kind of read, which isn't normal. Just sit down with your back to me and pull your shirt up."

She stared up at him and muttered under her breath about Dev owing her. And then she sat down sideways on the staircase and slowly lifted her shirt to expose a smooth expanse of skin.

He admired her finely muscled back as he rubbed his palms together to warm them. He knelt close to her, closed his eyes and placed his palms on either side of her spine.

He felt a jolt that went straight through his body to his groin and forced himself to hold his hands steady as Annika drew in deep, erratic breaths. Shit. Not a good sign.

He shifted his hands farther apart so they skimmed her sides close to her breasts. He shoved his fingers impatiently under the fabric of her bra so he could feel skin on skin. She'd cocked her head to one side, and he moved his face close to hers so his cheek was nearly touching hers, his entire body attempting to draw out whatever had entered her.

His palms were nearly vibrating under the energy she threw off, and it took him a few minutes to realize he wasn't reaching the energy field of a rogue spirit. No, the feeling was purely Annika.

It pulsed through him like a sharp buzz, made his toes curl the way a good shot of Jägermeister would. Or an orgasm.

She turned her face toward his, her body angled back

against him, like she wanted to be closer to him, and for a moment she just watched him, her lips slightly parted. He could've sworn she was getting ready to kiss him. He would've reciprocated, too, if the window above them hadn't blown out.

"Shit." He scrambled up to stand in front of her, to cover her. But she was standing too, looking all around for the source.

"What's going on?" she asked.

"We pissed it off. We make a good team," he said, and Annika didn't look too happy about that possibility.

"Come here," he said, and didn't give her a chance to say no before he was holding her close, facing him. She tried to pull away from him, but he didn't let her, partially for her own safety and partially because he just wanted to touch her, to run his palms over every single square inch of skin, which would set his body to vibrating better than his old Harley ever did.

Without warning he shoved his hands under her shirt again.

"This is such bullshit, Creed," she said, even as the house began to hum again.

"It's called ghost hunting, honey. Trust me." But she didn't trust him, didn't truly trust anyone but Dev.

Creed liked pissing off Annika, mainly because it was easy to do, and he liked the flush it brought to her cheeks. Rumors held that she was frigid as hell and hot for Dev. Neither of which made complete sense, especially the way her body was reacting to his.

But none of that was his concern now. He was on the job. Paging the ghostbuster. Sort of.

His spirit was more like the bounty hunter who brought the goods to him. Through Kat, the ghosts would tell their story. Not like Oz, who could see through to the ghosts themselves. Of course, Oz was always contacted by the worst of the worst.

Oz would never answer Creed as to whether he could actually see the spirit who'd been with Creed since birth.

Oz had been gone from ACRO for a while now—three years by Creed's count. Supposedly, no one, including Dev, had heard from him again.

He wondered if Dev opened up about that to her, or to anyone. Oz would've been the natural choice to come here and feel for any leftover energy.

"I don't think there'll be much," Dev had told him last night. "But I'm looking to see if any spirit talks to you specifically about adoption. Or kidnapping."

Creed hadn't questioned further, had a feeling that Annika was sent ahead to scout out energy but wasn't sure what else she'd actually been let into.

For him, so far, there was nothing but a feeling of intensity in this house. In itself, that was normal for a haunting. Usually, the energy translated into a feeling of intense loss or sorrow, mixed with other emotions. But here, there was no confusion and pain. All those normal feelings were suppressed. Gone. Replaced with nothing more than a void.

Which was not normal at all.

"Tell me what you feel," he said, his hands firm against her upper back.

"I'm cold," she whispered.

"You don't feel cold to me at all," he whispered back. "I need you to touch me—put your hands under my shirt and touch me."

She complied, yanking his shirt out of his pants and putting her freezing cold hands on his back. Her body molded to his, seeking his warmth. He bent his head into her neck, closed his eyes so he could concentrate on the house ghost, who was now seeking its own warmth from Annika.

THIS WAS GOING TO END in disaster. Annika knew it. No good had ever come of her touching a man so intimately.

"Why is this thing pissed?" she asked, trying not to notice

how hard, how cut he was beneath her fingers. She definitely didn't need to note the raw sensuality emanating from him like some sort of masculine power grid.

"It wants possession of someone. It's attracted to your energy. And mine. But together, we're too strong for it."

"I swear to God, Creed, if you're making up this shit as an excuse to put your paws on me..."

Amusement flickered in the black depths of his eyes as he looked down at her. "You think I'm that desperate?"

"The raging hard-on jabbing at me says yes."

He thrust against her, his back arching, and her first instinct was to deck him. Even as she curled her hands into fists, she noticed how his entire body had gone rigid, his breath hissing through clenched teeth. No, this wasn't sexual.

"It's trying to separate us. Hold on to me—fuck...Dev's parents. Murdered."

Okay, she officially hated this paranormal shit. Dead people should not have this much power. "Tell the fucker that everyone knows Dev's parents were murdered. I'm not impressed."

"He says...here. In the house." Creed strained like he was trying to breathe, and she had no idea what to do except hold him like he'd told her to, and Christ, now she was starting to get scared. Not of the ghost, but for Creed. She just hoped his tagalong spirit, Kate, or Kat, or whatever she was called, was helping him.

"So...much...blood," he rasped.

"In the house?"

"Where we're standing."

A chill that had nothing to do with the temperature ran through her. She hadn't known exactly where Dev's parents had been killed, but now she couldn't help but imagine them bleeding out in the spot where her feet were. Poor Dev.

Annika hadn't known her birth father; her mother had never named him. And really, she'd never known her mother either. But she did know that her mother had bled to death, her throat slit, so she had an idea how Dev must feel about his parents' murders.

A presence broke in on her thoughts, a shadowy specter that writhed in the air all around her, until icy tendrils snaked around her shoulders. Instantly, she flooded her body with energy, too late realizing that the volts would pump into Creed as well as the apparition. Energy sizzled across her skin, crackled in her bones, stretched her muscles, and the cold fingers released her. Thankfully, Creed relaxed, completely unaffected by the massive output of electricity, just as before, when she'd tried to shock him out of his boots.

No one had ever been immune to her power, but she didn't have time to think through it because Creed dropped his head to her shoulder as though exhausted, muttering a few choice curse words.

"Did this thing kill Dev's parents?"

"No ghost could have done it," he said tightly, like he knew more than he was saying, and was trying to protect her. If he only knew the things she'd seen and done, he wouldn't worry about sheltering her ever again. Hell, he probably wouldn't even look at her. "Not like that."

"Itor," she breathed. "Bastards. Why is the spirit telling you all this?"

"It's trying to befriend me."

"Why?"

"It wants something from me," he said, and holy crap, his breath was coming out as white puffs of air, but she didn't detect a drop in temperature. This thing must not want him talking. "Spirits hang around for a lot of different reasons. Some have unfinished business. Sometimes, a spirit can get confused, although that usually happens to little kids or adults who die a quick, unexpected death and don't realize that they've passed on."

"So which one is this?"

Creed shivered, and she rubbed her palms up and down his back because, strangely, she was the warm one now. And was it her imagination, or was one side of his body colder than the other?

"This one's a guilty conscience," he said, and all around them, the house seemed to shudder in one large, collective sigh. "The spirit doesn't want to move on because it knows it'll be judged harshly for what it's done."

"And what, exactly, is that?"

"It won't tell me."

She became aware of his hands smoothing over her flesh, across her back, around her waist, and when the tips of his fingers probed under the waistband of her very low-slung jeans, her heart caught, mid-beat, but that didn't stop the pulse of desire that shot straight to her core.

This was so not happening. "Can we let go of each other now?"

"No. It's not safe." His hands kept roaming, each circuit dropping a fraction of an inch lower.

"My. Ass," she ground out, wriggling to escape, but he closed his arms tighter around her and buried his face in her neck.

"Shh," he whispered against her suddenly sensitive skin. "Kat is settling it down, leading it away. It wants to use one of us, so as long as we're together, we're okay. Too strong for it."

"Use us?"

He nuzzled her. "To get out. To talk. To get to who it really wants. Maybe something worse. Not sure."

So maybe he wasn't full of shit, but she seriously doubted

that being together required his hands on her butt. Or his erection at her belly.

But wow, he was big. All over. She'd noticed his size before; he was hard to miss. But being like this, against him, surrounded by him, she almost felt lost.

Then again, that could be because no one had ever held her, no one but Dev and the mother she didn't even remember, and she had no idea how to handle this kind of close contact.

Especially close contact that fired off sparks in every nerve ending and made her want to rub herself even more intimately against him.

Creed opened his mouth as if to say something—oh, please, something like, *The spirit is gone so you can let go of me now.* Instead he took a deep, shuddering breath and dragged his teeth over the tight cord in her neck.

"That had better be some sort of ghost-hunting technique, McCabe," she ground out, sounding a lot tougher than she felt, because right now her hips were undulating of their own accord, responding to the utter eroticism of his touch.

"I'm showing the spirit that it can't have either one of us."

Uh-huh, she was going to throw down the bullshit flag on that one, and she would have, except that he'd thrust his leg between hers and now she was rocking on his muscular thigh, nearly panting at the delicious pressure there against her center.

This was shockingly arousing. Every tiny movement sent vibrations of pleasure surging through her body. She could get off like this. Creed knew it, and he'd palmed her ass to hold her firmly against him, used his strength to keep them both upright.

Fuck. This was not going to happen. It was too dangerous.

Besides, she really hated Creed. Had ever since he'd turned her in for some stupid crap on a mission two years ago.

So it wasn't fair that he could get her so hot by doing nothing more than feeling her up *to fool the spirit*.

Yeah, right.

Slowly, deliberately, he ran his tongue, firm and wet, along her jawline to her ear. The ball piercing flicked over her earlobe, sending a current of desire sizzling down from her ear to her clit. She groaned, wondering how that magic ball would feel elsewhere.

"Is it gone yet?" Her voice was husky, too far gone with lust to pretend otherwise.

He slid his thigh back and forth between her legs twice, taking her to the edge, before answering. "Yes."

"Bastard." Her body screamed for release, but she pulled away, stood there glaring at him. "For how long?"

He shrugged. "Long enough to know you weren't acting."

God, she wanted to light him up. Why couldn't she?

Maybe the strange pulses his own body sent out made him immune to her electricity. Or maybe the spirit that had been attached to him, reportedly since birth, protected him.

Whatever it was, Annika was annoyed.

And strangely excited, because what if... Nah. Despite what had just happened, Creed didn't want her any more than she wanted him. He was just like everyone else at ACRO, jealous of her relationship with Dev. Sure, no one came right out and said it, but they all thought she and Dev were knocking boots, which wasn't true, but encouraging the rumor kept everyone at a distance.

"Are we done? I need a shower. I have to get the ick of creep night off my skin." Maybe she could wash away the feel of Creed too.

"We're done."

She marched down the hall toward her bedroom, and Creed followed, until she spun around and slammed her hand into his chest. "What the hell are you doing?"

"I don't want to leave you alone. The spirit likes your energy."

"So are you going to watch me shower, or what?"

"Do you want me to? Because I don't have a problem with that."

"You're such a jerk."

But she didn't say no, because if he wanted to watch, she could put on one hell of a show. Of course, Creed McCabe, the man who'd turned her in for breaking rules, would never spy on a naked woman in a shower. Too bad, too, because she was horny, in serious need of relief, and she intended to get it.

CHAPTER
Six

Haley stood next to Remy, her glass of ice water in one palm and her handheld barometer in the other. When nothing happened, she lowered the device until it rested against his arm in the lightest of touches. Still nothing.

Piss him off or get him horny.

Remy stirred, and the blanket that had been tangled between his knees slid into a puddle on the floor, the fly of his cargos gaping even wider. The sun-bronzed skin of his upper torso blended gradually into creamy perfection at the base of the zipper. No tan lines marred his sleek beauty, as though he spent at least some of his time outside in the nude, perhaps skinny-dipping.

Images sifted through her mind, of Remy slipping naked into clear ocean waters, of cutting across the surface with smooth, powerful strokes. She saw herself joining him despite the fact that she hated the water, sliding her body against his and using the wet friction to stir them into an erotic frenzy of limbs and skin and tongues.

Oh, man. Haley held the cool, sweating glass to her

forehead and willed her pulse to slow down. She wasn't given to daydreaming, preferring to expend her creative abilities on deciphering weather mysteries, and this sudden shift in behavior was not welcome. Besides, the flesh-and-blood man lay before her, eminently real and touchable.

No need to fantasize.

She set the water and barometer on the coffee table and kneeled on the floor. Gingerly, she skimmed a finger over his chest, recalling how his upper body, broad and powerful, had looked outside in the light from the storm. How rain had rolled in long streams through the deep-cut valleys between his back and shoulder muscles.

She let her fingertip follow her gaze down the line of crisp brown hair to where it grew thick between his legs, cushioning his sex. Stealing a glance at his face, still peaceful in sleep, she pushed the flaps of his fly open wider. A hot rush of anticipation shot through her at the sight of his shaft, swollen and flushed, but not yet hard.

Wetting her lips, she traced the veins along the underside, remembering how she'd licked him there, how he'd tasted smoky, like hickory, and clean like the rain that pelted him when he'd masturbated in the storm. Her ears still rang with the echoes of the thunder that had grown louder and closer the faster his fist pumped up and down on his hard cock.

She glanced at the barometer and back. At rest, he didn't seem to affect electrical equipment, but what if he became aroused? Became hot and sweaty and straining inside his skin?

Remy shifted, the couch creaking as he rolled from his side to his back. Gently, she took him in her fist and stroked, setting a rhythm that matched her rapid breathing.

He was long, thick, and as blood began to flood the veins in a tide of heat, her own sex spasmed as though remembering the incredible orgasms he'd given her. A rush of moisture dampened the panties she'd put on after a quick shower earlier. Damn, but she'd never wanted a man like this. Never had she felt so aroused, so electrified, as if currents arced between each nerve ending.

Electricity. Crap. She'd forgotten the experiment. The barometer indicated a slight bump in pressure, something normal and anticipated, since the trend was on the rise.

When she turned back to Remy, she swore his chest rose and fell a little faster than it had been. He grew more rigid with each passing moment, his shaft developing a more pronounced curve, the color deepening to a dusky crimson.

"Red at night, sailor's delight," she whispered, feeling silly and giddy, and blaming it on the fact that it was at least one in the morning.

What she couldn't blame on the late hour was her arousal, the way her breasts tightened and she grew impossibly wet. She wanted him inside her with a fierceness that felt as foreign as it did natural. All that hard muscle and restrained power bringing her pleasure again... She had to clench her thighs together to ease the ache before she started squirming.

A drop of milky fluid formed at the tip of Remy's cock, and she swiped her thumb through the slick wetness. His sharp breath startled her, but his eyes were still closed, his luscious lips slightly parted with each exhale.

Slowly, she spread the droplet around the head, leaving a thin, shiny layer of silken lubrication for her finger to slide through. When she returned her gaze to the barometer again, disappointment sank deep.

No malfunction.

Then the pressure took a dive. The screen went dark, and a hand engulfed her wrist.

"What the fuck do you think you're doing?"

Her mouth went so dry she could practically taste her guilt, but she managed a smile. "Your blanket fell off. I came over to put it back on, and I couldn't help myself." She gave his erection a squeeze for emphasis.

"Learn," he growled, and pushed her hand to her side.

Angling herself closer so he couldn't sit up without forcing her away, she closed her fist around him again. "I'm a slow learner."

"I doubt that," he said, as she flicked her thumb along the nerve-rich rim at the underside of the head, and he hissed through clenched teeth.

Excitement drilled through her, excitement and adrenaline at how the barometer had snapped off when Remy woke up, all grumpy and growly like a bear awakened early from hibernation. It might have been nothing. Then again, she might be on the road to an incredible meteorological discovery.

"Dammit, Haley," he breathed, but this time, he made no move to stop her.

The barometer crackled back to life, and curiously, the pressure remained where it had dropped.

Haley returned her attention to Remy, but avoided looking directly into his eyes. It was enough that she felt his smoldering gaze.

She circled the cap with the flat of one hand as she worked the other inside his pants to cup his balls, which were tight, drawn close to his body. When she stroked the seam between them, Remy bent his knee, allowing for better access.

The scent of his arousal, dark and musky, rose up in the muggy air, enhancing her own, and she nearly groaned. She shifted her weight to her knees so her sex settled on one heel. The pressure was good, too good, and the temptation to rock back and forth until she climaxed had her clenching her teeth.

A faint peal of thunder tested the limits of her hearing, but then Remy went taut, and she knew she hadn't imagined the sound.

Ignoring the need screaming inside her, she leaned forward and opened her mouth over the broad tip of his cock. Her lips didn't touch him as she blew a long, slow puff of hot air.

"Do you want me to stop?" she asked, already sure of the answer but wanting him to feel like he had control, a favorite Seducer technique.

"Remember his psychological profile," her Seducer trainer had said, *referring to the twenty-page document she'd been required to memorize. "Give him control to draw him in. Take it away to expose emotion and heighten pleasure."*

And her trainer should know, as one of two dozen specialized ACRO psychics who received psychic impressions only during sex, when, they claimed, no human could maintain the walls surrounding their minds.

Knuckles cracked as his fists clenched at his sides. He opened them, closed them and then opened them once more. "No," he said tightly. "No. You feel too good."

Though she'd expected the answer, she felt glad for her own reasons. She'd been alone for far too long, stuck inside the weather lab with only a handful of colleagues and no time for a relationship. Touching Remy, and being touched, satisfied a need she'd neglected for years.

Hungry for him, she brushed her lips over the hot stretch of skin the flared head to the base of his shaft, where she pressed the flat of her tongue firmly against the pulse above his balls. He arched up and his fingers caressed her scalp, encouraging but not demanding.

She dragged her tongue back up, and his tortured groan drifted down to her, deep and rumbling. It rumbled louder when she dipped her tongue into the weeping slit.

Hot and tangy, his male juices coated her tongue, drove her lust higher, and she wished he'd touch her between her legs, where all she wore beneath her button-down nightshirt were soaked panties. The thought of his fingers working her to climax made her shiver with want.

"You taste good," she said in a rush of breath. "Like a sultry summer rain."

As if in response, another drop welled up, and she took it greedily, applying suction until he rocked into her. Indecision tore at her: Oh, she wanted to go all the way, right now, with no regard to experiments or the weather or ACRO, but her career depended on what she learned from this. Remy's career did as well.

She glanced at the barometer. A thrill skittered through her at the slight decline. Still, one measly millibar fluctuation was hardly proof that he affected the weather, inadvertently or not. She needed more. Something the Seducers said about emotion and loss of control being a trigger gave her an idea.

"Remy?" She let her mouth hum around his shaft as she spoke.

"Mmmm."

"Do you like this? When I suck you?"

He tilted his hips, driving deeper, and he dropped one hand to her hip, where he massaged, his thumb rasping against her overly sensitized tattoo until she nearly cried out. "Fuck, yeah."

Oh, so did she. She wanted to spread her legs and touch herself, or better yet, let Remy touch her. His palm rubbed circles on her thigh, and his fingers, creeping behind, slid into the crevice between her leg and her sex.

"Stop," she breathed. "No touching."

"Haley—"

She sucked hard, drew his cock so deep it brushed the back of her throat. The sound of his panting breaths echoed off the wood-paneled walls.

"I want control, Remy." She scattered kisses along the crease on the underside of his shaft. "You had it earlier. Give it to me now."

And God help her, if he didn't give it to her right this second, she'd let him have whatever he wanted, however he wanted it.

His silence made her heart thump crazily, and she dared a look at his face. Oh, man, she shouldn't have risked it. Her breath hitched, locked down in her throat. The way he watched her, his stormy gaze so dominant and fiercely male, almost had her rolling over in submission. She'd always liked her men a little refined, more than a little minted lamb and pinot noir, but suddenly, she wondered why, because Remy was barbecue and beer, and not the least bit civilized.

Dev had said Remy could be dangerous if he possessed even a tenth of the power ACRO suspected, but she was beginning to see a very different reason for that danger. He was a menace to women everywhere. Funny how the psychics hadn't mentioned *that* important little detail.

Slowly he shook his head. "I can't give you what you want."

His words said one thing, the strain in his voice said another. She still had a shot.

Circling his cock with two fingers, she used her own saliva as lubricant to stroke him with brisk, wet flicks against the shiny rim. "Just for a minute. I want to take you with my mouth. And I want you to submit, let me suck you deep. Suck you off."

His fingers twitched where they rested just millimeters from her center. He cursed, but he removed his hands. The loss of his touch made her want to cry.

Remember the job, Haley.

She glanced at the barometer: 29.83. Another tiny drop. Not enough.

"Put your arms above your head. Clasp them together. If they come apart, I stop."

He obeyed, but more curses spilled from his mouth, and his muscles tensed, rolled angrily beneath his skin, which now glistened with sweat. Power filled her in a flood of energy, an aphrodisiac she'd not anticipated.

Three millibars: 29.80. *Yes.* She hoped her equipment on the table was recording outside conditions for comparison, because this drop was considerable.

Thunder rolled in the distance, but closer than before.

"Shit," he said raggedly. "I'm drawing it." She doubted he knew he spoke aloud, but the struggle to regulate his breathing and emotions was obvious in the tortured expression on his face, the way his eyes were screwed shut, his lips pursed and pale.

When a man comes, his walls crumble.

Beneath her fingers, Remy trembled, and she sensed his need to bring the encounter back to something he could dominate. Quickly, she swirled her tongue around the head of his cock, but nerves had made her mouth go dry. Her hand shook as she reached for her glass and sipped. One of the cubes tapped her teeth. Opening her mouth, she sucked it in.

Remy watched her, his eyes going wide when she closed her lips over him. The ice swirled around his shaft, and he hissed when she used her tongue to rub the ice up and down along the hard ridge.

"Jesus," he murmured. "No one has ever ... *damn.*"

His hand came down on her hip again, and she shook her head. His curse rang out, but she ignored him, used the heat of her mouth and the heat of his body to melt the ice cube on his cock. When it was gone, she hummed, sucked upward, and his breath grew labored, stopped and then rushed out with his primitive, violent roar.

His hips bucked, and he came in long, strong contractions that swelled against her tongue and teeth. The salty, heady taste drove her hunger for him even higher, and she eagerly sucked and pulled everything from him, loving how his body jerked and his cock pulsed at every upward stroke of her mouth.

As his flesh softened and his moans quieted, she licked him clean.

"God, Haley," he said, his voice raw and little more than a gasp. "That was..."

"Great?" she offered. "Amazing? The best ever?"

"Stupid."

"Not the answer I was looking for, really."

Shaking his head, still breathing hard, he levered into a sitting position, not bothering to zip up. "What were you thinking, playing with me while I was sleeping? And what did you plan to do with that?" He gestured to the barometer, and she silently swore, having forgotten to look at the readings when he climaxed.

Idiot. No wonder ACRO hadn't assigned her as an operative. Well, there was also the fact that she didn't possess any special abilities, like telekinesis or the power to electrocute with a touch.

"Nothing. I was just getting some post-storm readings."

He gave her a flat stare. "While giving me a hand job."

Busted. "No. I was—"

"Doing something you shouldn't have done. Don't you get it?"

This was it. The opening she needed. "Get what?"

He hesitated, distrust putting an icy sheen in his already cool blue eyes. Finally, he threw his head back against the back of the couch and pinched the bridge of his nose. "Shit. Nothing."

Sighing, she grabbed her water and tucked one leg beneath

her on the couch. She hadn't wanted to confess anything, but she sensed he required more from her in order to open up like she needed him to.

"Remy, there's something strange going on with the weather here, and I should know. I deal with bizarre meteorological phenomena for a living. I'm a parameteorologist."

His eyebrows slanted into a deep frown that matched the set of his mouth. "You're a what? Who employs people like you?"

Careful, Haley. Tell him the truth, but only to a point.

"Police detectives, insurance companies, sometimes, when loss occurs under strange weather conditions. Ditto for the NTSB. Physicians occasionally need expertise for odd injuries—usually electrical. Once a shipping company asked me to investigate a route where boat crews had reported blinding green flashes, up close during clear skies." She shrugged. "We're rare, but we exist."

Mostly, the handful of parameteorologists worldwide were employed by small private weather companies, as she had been, but she no longer worked in that capacity, and mundane investigations were no longer her responsibility. Her job with ACRO gave her more freedom, and more interesting assignments.

Like Remy. Sure, she hadn't wanted this job, but she also hadn't thought there was a chance in hell he had any real connection with the weather. Or that he'd be so hot.

"Well, now," he murmured in a deep, dark voice as he twisted around to face her and hold her with his equally dark gaze, "isn't it interesting that you're here."

She swallowed the sudden lump in her throat. "Remy, the weather in this area is legendary. People have reported storms that never showed up in official reports. Two tornadoes have flattened parts of this county, but satellite photos show clear skies. Hail has torn apart vehicles in the streets but left houses

unscathed. Hail in the shape of crucifixes fell near a brothel."
His eyes flickered with something—amusement? Regret? She
couldn't tell. But she had thrown him off track.

"This is prime property for a parameteorologist. And
now," she said, leaning so close to him that their noses nearly
touched, "I'm beginning to think it's no coincidence that you
grew up here."

God, she should be an actress. Maybe Devlin really had
known what he was doing when he gave her this assignment,
one she never should have had, because the agency had an
entire department designated to making first contact and
determining whether or not the subject would be an asset to
ACRO.

Unfortunately, as Dev had said, as ACRO's only parameteorologist, she alone was qualified to deal with Remy.

"Well? You got anything to say?"

A muscle in his jaw jumped, and his lips pressed into a thin,
grim line. "I don't know what you want, Haley. Just because
you got me off doesn't mean I have to engage in post-fuck
chat. So back off."

Haley sighed. Dev had been wrong. Very wrong. Because
parameteorologist or not, she was in no way qualified to deal
with Remy Begnaud.

CHAPTER
Seven

Sometimes, Devlin O'Malley was sure he could see light flicker through his sightless eyes. For just a second, usually when he first woke and his lids opened, more out of habit than choice, he was convinced the steady stream of pure white light he saw was real.

Once his body began to move, he realized it was part desperation, part gift and, finally, part warning. Step away from the light and all that bullshit. Which was why he hated mornings. And naps. They left him disoriented. Scattered.

In his haste to wake his own ass up from an impromptu one, he knocked several objects off his desk. From the sounds, he assumed his coffee mug and the glass ashtray were the most recent victims.

That was all right—the ashtray reminded him that he'd quit smoking, and he didn't like having to quit anything. Everyone needed a vice, but smoking had hindered his five-mile-a-day running habit, so it had to go. And ten years later, he still missed it.

"Devlin, are you all right in there?" Marlena West, his

personal assistant, asked through the slightly opened door of his office.

"Fine," he said. "I'm fine, Marlena." He stood, still a little unsteady, tilted his head from side to side to give his neck a stretch, the ache reminding him that working straight through the night wasn't the best idea.

"Creed just checked in. He met up with Annika, and they're making progress," she said.

"Good. Make sure he can always get through to me."

"And Haley's off-line since an hour ago, and she's not transmitting."

He raked his fingers through his hair and sighed as he heard Marlena walk away from the doorway. He needed a shower and shave—and then he'd change into the same unassuming black BDUs all the ACRO operatives wore on the compound.

The surrounding neighbors in the Catskill area of New York thought they were a private security firm, hired by wealthy companies all over the world. It explained the helo pads, the private jets and the men and women in BDUs seen around town, and for the most part they were accepted without question. The townspeople actually felt safer having the ACRO employees around, and Dev felt safer having moved the compound to a more out-of-the-way area than near Syracuse.

Winters here were tough; the amount of snow the area received made it difficult for him to deploy his agents, but it was even tougher getting in. And even though his Special Ability Operatives boasted that they could take on just about anyone, anywhere, anytime, Dev liked being able to provide them with a small measure of security.

He'd taken over as ACRO's chief somewhat reluctantly, but once inside he was fully committed to protecting his operatives. And recruiting new ones.

Recruitment was the biggest fight he had with the old guard

at ACRO. The veterans, mainly psychics who'd been here since the company's inception and who'd worked under his parents, didn't appreciate anyone with a military background telling them what to do. They were against actively pulling in new members, especially those with so-called uncontrollable abilities.

Dev came from a different place, preferred to call their newer agents *Special Ability Operatives*. They were facing a new enemy, a far more dangerous one than another country's government. Itor Corp used methods for collecting their operatives and treating them like specimens that turned Dev's stomach and made him more determined than ever to offer safe haven to Special Ability types in return for their helping to keep safe the world at large.

Speaking of safe, he hoped Haley was making headway on her current assignment. His investigators had discovered Remy's favorite flavor of ice cream, but not one of ACRO's psychics had been able to determine whether or not the former SEAL could actually control the weather. They were able to figure out that the weather controlled Remy, though, and Dev knew the man was going to need help no matter what. The sooner Haley got him back to the compound, the better. Itor had been running neck and neck with ACRO when it came to approaching potential agents and had recently stolen a few right out from under Dev's Convincers. He couldn't afford to lose another Special Ability, for ACRO's sake, and for Remy's.

Merging old and new had not been easy, would never be seamless, but things were running more smoothly now. All the operatives could agree on one thing—they'd never let the enemy win on their watch.

Dev had had his own demons to deal with during these years—as a teenager, he'd been haunted by a spirit who glided too finely along the line of good and evil. He'd long suspected that this same spirit, who'd mysteriously released him from its grasp when he'd entered the Air Force, had something to do with his C-130 crash and subsequent blindness.

His loss of sight, which was never medically explained, had gone on too long to be termed hysterical blindness. But the blindness had brought out his gift of second sight, and learning CRV—Controlled Remote Viewing—made popular by Stargate in the 1970s, brought that gift to a whole different level.

And now he suspected a mole, right here, among the operatives who'd sworn to love, honor and protect the world with ACRO's help. A betrayal that punched him in the gut every time he thought about it. The consequences of not finding the leak would be disastrous; the methods he would need to use to ensure success, doubly so. But now wasn't the time to think about that—not until he got a report from Creed and Annika.

He closed his eyes—again, habit—and began his normal routine of CRV. When he wasn't distracted, or exhausted, he could move through the compound easily, department by department, like he had some kind of security system in his brain.

He put his hands over his ears, something many operatives in the Paranormal Division did when things got too overwhelming—it was a useless attempt to block out the voices, but the pressure did take away some of the pain.

Sometimes, in all the combined chaos of the ACRO environment embedded into his brain, he thought he could hear his parents' voices too. But that was always a fake-out.

He didn't doubt that his parents' spirits surrounded him—the old guard wouldn't bullshit him about that, especially not Samantha Hawkins, one of ACRO's most well-respected psychologists and mediums. She'd been speaking to the dead, or them to her, since she was three years old.

She'd told him that his mom and dad were around him, most but not all the time, but they never said anything. Whether their silence was for better or for worse wasn't Sam's place to say.

He opened his eyes again on instinct, because Marlena stood in the doorway. He pictured her the way she felt under his touch—tall, slim, long hair reaching halfway down her back. His palms itched, fingers flexing along the soft brown leather arms of his chair before he motioned with a slight nod for her to come forward.

"You're tense," she whispered, running a cool hand along the back of his neck. He bent his head forward, let his face rest against her breasts to allow her hands greater access to his shoulders and back.

Since the accident ten long years ago, every other sense he had was more sensitive—almost too much. The line between pleasure and pain seemed to blur, especially when he was touched.

"The Lord giveth and the Lord taketh away," the old chaplain had told him. Stood over his hospital bed and tried that whole there's-a-reason-for-everything crap. Until Dev had proven to the guy that, while his eyesight was gone, there was nothing wrong with his fist.

The chaplain hadn't come back to see him for his entire stay in the hospital.

"Stop thinking, Dev," Marlena urged, and he sat back, lids closed, and let her unbutton his pants.

Stopping thinking was something he had to will himself to do. In fact, the ability to shut down the brain and just enjoy was becoming harder these days than ever. The old adage that the other senses strengthen when one was cut off was doubly true in his case. And lately his so-called powers had been increasing. Shifting. Doubling. He could determine the wind and weather forecasts from the pressure of the air on his skin and from the way the air smelled, could grasp the emotion in any room, coming off any person, from the second he came in close proximity. He could hear things that he shouldn't and his need to touch was constant, almost obsessive—to feel sensation beneath his fingertips was like the bridge between heaven and hell.

Marlena's mouth slid over his cock, demanding that he pay full attention to what she was doing, and he groaned. Sometimes Marlena got him maybe a little too much. She knew he could never love her. His heart was elsewhere, with someone who spoke to him in ways no one else had ever been able to.

His balls tightened, her fingers dug into his hips. His orgasms were as close as he was ever going to get to flying solo again. He accepted that, but would never come to peace with it. He'd give anything to replace his second sight with his original way of seeing the world. No matter how much he mourned his loss of vision, the pain never went away.

Stop thinking, Dev. Stop fucking thinking.

CHAPTER
Eight

Remy was pretty sure he knew what Haley wanted from him. And he was even surer that she wasn't going to get it. Maybe she could base her meteorological theories on a blow job, but he wasn't about to let himself become a sex toy for science.

Part of the problem was that he wasn't sure how he could answer her, even if he wanted to. His weather draw had been going on for so long, he was no longer sure where the weather ended and he began.

He stood, swore, raked his fingers through his hair. He needed out of this place, dammit. And a beer wouldn't hurt either.

"How long have you been here?" he asked her over his shoulder as he headed to the kitchen, even though he already knew the answer.

"I moved in the day before yesterday," she said.

Forty-eight hours ago—a day after his father had called, begging for help. Forty-eight hours ago, the urges started, stronger than they'd ever been, pulling him toward a woman who didn't appear to be scared of those urges.

None of this was coincidence. But he'd known that from the second he'd spotted Haley's tattoo.

He grabbed a beer and slammed the fridge door shut with enough force to rattle the cupboards. The bottle cap came off with a hiss, and then he flung it across the room in a smooth motion by flipping it between his thumb and forefinger, and took a long pull.

When he looked back at her, she was still sitting on the couch, wearing a loosely buttoned denim shirt. She'd showered and her hair was dry, free of twigs and leaves, loose and wild around her shoulders. He knew firsthand it was the softest thing he'd ever touched, and she hadn't bothered to style it or fix herself up the way most of the women he'd known had—like they were embarrassed to let him see who they really were.

Then again, he'd never spent real, quality time with any of the women he slept with, even the ones he'd been with during the calmer times.

Christ, the way she looked at him could take him down at the knees if he let it. She was watching him—studying him really—her eyes luminous and wide in the lamplight, and this time he could've sworn she wasn't doing it for science. But she was, and he would damn sure figure out her angle. If Haley wanted to play, he was going to give her her money's worth. Because he should get to have some fun during all this.

Hopefully, Mother Nature would cooperate, because he wasn't sure he could handle two strong women pulling at him at once. A team of tangos, yes, but none seemed to be available at the moment.

Over the years, he'd learned how to take better control, knew exactly what was needed to maintain his tenuous grip on his emotions—and subsequently, the weather. His rational mind could keep him in check, most of the time, but if he got injured or let his anger get the best of him, people needed to start running, because as much as Mother Nature could pull at him, he'd learned that he could push right back.

Now was time for that push.

"You know, they say that the bayou's a pretty magical place, *chere*," he said. "A lot of that weather stuff you're talking about could just be a built-in part of this area. Mysterious and unexplainable."

"I don't think so," she said.

"You don't believe in unexplained phenomena?"

"I think everything has an explanation, if you just look hard enough," she said.

He thought about pushing the shirt off her shoulders to expose her breasts again, and a low rumble of thunder sounded in the distance. She furrowed her brow, looked at the barometer, then back at him.

He shrugged, put on his best I'm-completely-innocent face and watched the color rise in her cheeks. This one was easy—his being horny didn't cause a storm to happen, but if there was one in the area when his cock demanded attention, he ended up drawing the energy in his direction. "I told you the storm's not over."

"And you know that how?"

"From living here for the first seventeen years of my life. From watching all kinds of strange, unimaginable things occur."

Like the time Melissa LaRue had taken his virginity—he'd been fourteen, she was sixteen, and that was pretty much the explanation for the hail that took out a few cars in front of Melissa's house. The hail in the shape of crucifixes had just been for practice. He'd also formed hail in the shape of devil's horns outside a church, just to be fair.

"And you never questioned them?" Haley persisted.

He'd never had to. He'd been born with this draw being as much a part of him as his fingers and toes were, and until recently, he'd managed to coexist with the sometimes strange electricity that lived inside of him. But lately, Mother Nature had been behaving like a petulant child, and he'd been repenting like hell, in hopes she'd ease up.

"I learned to enjoy what I couldn't explain," he said. It was more than a partial lie, especially the way these last six months had taken their toll on him—his life and his career—but she wouldn't know that. He took another swig of beer as hail began to strum the old roof. The left-hand side of the roof, to be precise. He watched with amusement as Haley leaped from the couch and hovered over her weather equipment on the table.

"This is impossible," she muttered as she scanned what looked like an on-demand radar image on her laptop, and he had to wonder just who she worked for to have such advanced satellite technology built into her computer.

"What's impossible?" he asked, though he knew.

"The hail," she snapped, probably annoyed that all her scientific crap couldn't explain a damned thing. "The closest storm cell is several miles away, according to this." She turned to a portable radar that didn't look all that portable, and how the hell had she gotten the thing in here? "My radar, however, indicates a sizable echo right on top of us, and if I run a loop—" she pushed a button, and the screen ran a series of images "—you can see that this echo formed almost instantly."

Yep, it pretty much had. Interesting. He'd never seen evidence of how his weather-weirdness worked.

"And outside, the pressure rose, the temperature dropped and the wind picked up, consistent with the hail that shouldn't be here." The desktop weather-station gadget blinked with all the updates.

Damn, she was hot when she was agitated, the way she kept sweeping her hair out of her face and biting her bottom lip.

She tapped a bunch of keys and looked up at the roof, where the hail still drummed.

He stopped it as suddenly as he'd started it, mainly because his stomach had started to growl. "Didn't you say you were going to make some food?"

"Food?" She leaned close to the radar, her gaze shifting between the machine and the weather station. "How can you think of food when—" She sucked in a harsh breath. "It's dissipating. Too fast. This isn't natural."

"I tried to tell you that things are mysterious and unexplainable around here." His stomach growled again, this time loud enough for her to hear it.

She turned to him. "I don't know what's going on, but I'm going to find out." Shaking her head, she sighed. "Tomorrow. When all the data is in, and I've gotten some rest. And food. I probably should clean up a little more, though."

For the first time, he actually surveyed the room, and it sobered him up again. He saw that four of the five windows in the living room and kitchen were blown out completely. Haley must've cleaned while he slept, and she'd tried to rehang the pathetic lace curtains that had been up for twenty-five years, if not longer. She'd straightened the pictures on the walls and piled the wet books and papers into a corner, and she'd added to the pile of debris he'd swept up earlier.

He'd never seen it this bad. But then, he'd never been coerced to remain inside when a storm raged. Even his team members had given up trying to keep him in once they realized things got better a few minutes after he stepped out into the storm. Besides, several of them had learned the hard way not to physically restrain him when his storm-fervor had him on edge.

But this...this had been really bad, and he drew a long, deep breath, took into his nostrils the burnt stench he always smelled after an episode, a combination of hickory and cinnamon, not unpleasant, not sickeningly sweet, just strong. Normally, he welcomed it, because it meant that things were over, but the way his skin still tingled, just below the surface, told him different.

Haley was still standing in the middle of the kitchen. She scrubbed her cheeks with her palms for a second and then nodded, like she'd made some kind of internal decision. She grabbed the broom and moved to sweep out the pile by the back door.

He leaned against the fridge and slowly shook his head. "Forget it. You can't sweep that outside."

"I can't leave it like this. The generator's nearly out of gas and I don't want one of us stumbling into the pile if we need to get to the door."

"We can use the front door instead."

"What's the big deal, Remy?"

"You just can't sweep it out the door. Not tonight," he said, realized he was going to sound like an even bigger freak, but hey, some things were so born and bred they could never be lost. "Look, it's an old Cajun superstition, okay? You're never supposed to sweep dirt out the door after dark."

"Why not?"

"It's bad luck," he said, watched her bite her lip and try, unsuccessfully, to hold back a smile.

She didn't make it—a small giggle burst from her before she covered her mouth. "I'm sorry," she said, but there was still laughter in her voice, something that made him feel... lighter. "It's just..." She motioned around them and he couldn't stop his own mouth from tugging up at the corners, until he let himself have a full-blown belly laugh right along with her.

"Yeah, well, you grow up around here, you're not going to escape without a few superstitions."

"Why do I have a feeling you've got more than a few?"

He smiled into his beer, thought about the time he tried to break a tornado when he was younger, by making a cross with two knives nine times in a row. "They exist for a reason, you know."

"Yes, to scare people into submission."

"I'd think, with your line of work, you'd have a little bit more of an open mind about things like this."

"I'm a strange combination of open mind and skeptic. I don't believe in frightening people—I believe in using science to prove fact. Once you know the facts, the reasons, well, it can be very freeing." She paused. "You don't buy it."

"Not a bit. You must have some superstitions, even if you don't really believe them."

"I don't walk under ladders, if that's what you mean. But that's because walking under a ladder is unsafe." She propped her hands on her hips, managing to look both serious and cute. "Now *I'm* starving—it's definitely time for food."

The kitchen had fared almost as bad as the living room. The cabinet doors had been wrenched from their hinges, and the silverware drawer had somehow slid out, spilling forks and spoons onto the floor. Only the dish towel Haley must have bought remained intact. It still hung on the stove, neatly folded and unscathed.

"I don't think we've got any dishes left," he said, without taking his eyes from the towel. And, as he watched, it slowly slid off the handle and onto the muddy floor below it.

He scooped up the towel and stared at it. "Shit," he muttered.

"What? Is there a dropping-dish towel superstition?"

"Means company's coming." And really, that one had always proven true for him. Maybe the old man was coming back ... or worse.

She looked past him, through the half-shattered kitchen

window. "*Bebe,* ain't no one comin' out in this one," she said in an exaggerated drawl.

"Ah, she thinks she can speak in Cajun tongues," he murmured.

"And soon I'll be learning to make gumbo and wrestling alligators." She took a step forward and winced. "Dammit, I thought I got all the glass up."

"You still should be wearing shoes, *bebe,*" he said, not giving a shit about his own bare feet. "Stay there." In three strides, he closed the distance between them and picked her up, carried her to the kitchen table and set her next to some of her equipment.

"That really wasn't necessary," she said.

"Just sit still." He cradled her foot against his thighs, saw blood oozing from the area surrounding the shard of glass lodged into the arch.

"It doesn't look too deep. Stop staring and just pull it out."

"Bossy thing, aren't you?"

She jerked her foot back and shoved him away. "I'll do it myself."

"Hey." He grabbed her foot again. "Relax. It was a joke."

"Sure it was. Because you're such a funny guy, Remy. A bundle of laughs."

He had no idea what had gotten her back up, but she was definitely riled. Curiosity tugged at him, but first things first. "I'm going to pull the glass out and see if you need stitches. I've got my medic kit with me, so I could—"

With a muffled curse, she yanked the glass out and hurled it to the floor. He grabbed the dish towel he'd draped over the back of one of the old, mismatched kitchen chairs and wrapped it around her foot to stop the bleeding.

"What the hell are you trying to prove, Haley?"

HALEY'S FOOT STUNG where she'd ripped the shard from her flesh. She tore her foot from Remy's hands.

"I'm not trying to prove anything to anyone," she said, even though it wasn't true at all. There was so much to prove—to the agency, to her old CO, to her parents. That her parents were dead didn't matter. "Can you give me a little space, please?"

"Yeah, just like you've given me. *Éspèsces de tête dure,*" he muttered with a shake of his head, but he didn't seem angry or upset.

"And what does that mean?"

"Means you're hardheaded." He ignored her request to back off and grabbed her foot again, used the towel to put pressure on the wound.

"I said, I can do it myself."

"I'm sure you can do a lot of things yourself, but that doesn't always mean you should."

"I'm like you, Remy. I don't count on too many people." She hadn't needed ACRO's dossier on Remy to know that either. His attitude screamed, *Loner.*

His gaze locked on hers, making her shift uncomfortably on the hard wooden surface under her, and she mentally berated herself for giving away more than she'd wanted to about her own life, not to mention how much she knew about his.

"That's no way to live. Trust me on that—I know better than just about anybody." His hand skimmed her calf in a light caress, and her breath caught in her throat. Her body, already primed from the sex play earlier, tingled. Acute awareness sharpened her senses as his fingers stroked behind her knee before continuing to her inner thigh.

Out of the calmness, lightning flashed through the windows, illuminating his eyes, the hard planes of his face. God, he was handsome, and she found herself wishing he weren't, because then when he dropped her foot and positioned himself so his body separated her thighs, she could have remained objective. Science-minded. She should have been wondering where the lightning had come from and how—and if—it was related to Remy's mood or sexual arousal.

But as it was, as his fingers moved upward until they skimmed the thin barrier of silk at the juncture of her thighs, objectivity took a backseat to pleasure.

"Like this," he murmured, exploring the hills and valleys of her sex through the fabric. "This, I know you can do by yourself. I watched you, remember? Out by the trees, when you put your hand down your pants, made yourself come."

Nodding, she leaned back on her arms and bit back a moan, fought the urge to push against his hand wantonly. She needed relief, but she didn't want to be this vulnerable, didn't want to believe she needed a man for anything she could do herself.

She especially didn't want him to know how his slightest touch affected her, but there was no hiding how turned on she was when he tunneled his finger under the fabric and pushed a finger into her warm, wet canal. A small whimper escaped her lips, and he added another finger and stroked slowly.

She felt his knuckles catch on the elastic leg opening, heard the soft rip of torn fabric as he split the crotch and plunged his fingers back inside her.

He circled her slippery bud with his thumb, and thunder rumbled close by. For a moment she wondered if they were in for another dangerous storm, but as the sound closed in, it became a low and soothing roll. His hand moved faster, in and out, spreading her moisture through her folds, bringing every nerve ending front and center.

Little shocks zinged upward from her clit with every stroke, and she quivered, ready to explode.

He took her close to the edge, so close she cried out with the first tremors of orgasm, and then pulled her back, almost as though on a mission. A mission to show her who was in charge.

He hadn't forgotten the incident on the couch.

Growling in frustration, she leaned forward and took his nipple in her mouth, giving it a sharp tug that made him groan.

"You play dirty, Haley," he breathed. "But this is my show."

She brought a hand down between her legs, parted her engorged folds to finish things. "I can take care of myself."

He pushed her hand aside with his empty one. "Not like I can."

As if to prove his point, he turned up the torment a notch, filling her with three fingers now, pumping faster, harder, until her breaths came in harsh gasps and her legs trembled.

"Do you want me to stop?"

Damn him. He'd turned what she'd done to him back on her, and she was too far gone to say yes.

"No," she moaned, and bucked when his fingers brushed the sensitive pillow of nerves deep inside.

Smiling, he leaned in, jerked her shirt open with his teeth. Cool air hit her breasts as the buttons lost the battle and hit the floor, and Remy moved in so close his hot breath wafted over her neck and his bare upper body brushed hers. Her nipples grew taut every time he touched them, and they were painfully so now. She rubbed against the hard wall of his chest, abandoned to ecstasy, not caring that she was rocking against him, seeking relief that only a screaming orgasm would bring.

"Then say it. Say it's my show."

No. But before she could stop herself, she obeyed, speaking the words between panting breaths. "Yes, Remy...your show."

"My house, my rules, and that's the way we play, all right?" he asked, and it wasn't fair, because at that moment she would've promised him anything if he'd just make her come.

Her calves curled around his ass and she locked her ankles against the base of his spine. She needed him there between her legs. Closer. She reached up to grab his shoulders, to pull him down on top of her, but he was faster. He kept one hand in her slick heat and the other grabbed one wrist tightly.

"My house, my rules," he repeated. "Give me your other wrist."

He opened his large hand, and silently cursing the reversal in roles, she did what she was told. He gripped both easily in his palm and then jerked her arms above her head so she was totally helpless. Vulnerable. Aroused like never before. He was getting his payback for the control she'd taken from him, and she hated it. Loved it. Wanted more.

He eased her thighs wider and stroked her with an easy rhythm that drove her mad, while his eyes looked on her calmly, with a mix of amusement and lust. When his thumb pushed up on her clit and then held it there with light but devastating pressure, he leaned over, whispered into her ear, "Say it, Haley."

"Your house, your rules...yes...yes...oh, God, yes!" Her orgasm exploded behind her eyes in a white-hot burst that put lightning to shame.

"See, something you can do on your own, but something that's much better when there's someone else involved."

Too spent to argue, she dropped her head onto his strong shoulder and inhaled the scent of musk and skin and all-man she would forever associate with Remy.

"You're so pretty, so beautiful, *chere,*" he murmured while he touched her hair, her cheek, almost as though he was in some kind of a trance.

With the exception of the strange comments Devlin had made, she'd never been called beautiful before, at least not after a guy had gotten what he wanted in bed. Capable, yes. "I'm not—"

"Yeah, you are. To me, you are, and right now, I'm the only one who counts."

Her head still felt fuzzy from orgasm, but his tone had punched through the haze, and she gave a small start. "You really mean that."

"You sound surprised."

"It's just that you don't know me very well." Not like she knew him.

"True. But we've already been through a lot, don't you think?"

Ignoring his question, because she didn't want it to lead to more she wasn't prepared to answer, she said, "I should let you get cleaned up, get comfortable."

"I'm pretty damned comfortable right now." His hand caressed the back of her neck. "And you're damned good at deflecting."

She lifted her head from his shoulder and stared. "What's your specialty with the teams?" she asked, even though she already knew. She also knew he had no specialty anymore, since he'd left the Navy.

He smirked. "Interrogation. So you don't really have a chance here."

He moved away from between her legs and sauntered to where his bag lay by the mantel. Crouching on his heels, he rifled through it while she fastened her shirt with the buttons that remained and admired the way his back muscles rippled, the way his skin glowed under the cloud-dappled moonlight streaming in through the window.

When he came back to her, he was holding a smaller black bag, the contents of which he unpacked on the table. Then he pulled up a chair and took her foot again. He opened a foil packet and removed an alcohol swab, which he used to clean her wound.

"Why the Chair Force?" he asked, said it more like a command than a question, but this time, she didn't bristle, even though he'd made fun of her military service. Even more puzzling was the way her heart stirred when Remy leaned in to blow air over where he'd just swiped the alcohol swab, cutting the sting.

Geez, she was easier than she'd thought. "I didn't have the money for college, and the Air Force had a great meteorology program."

She wondered if he detected the undercurrent of bitterness in her voice. Bitterness arising from the fact that her parents had suddenly found spare money for college only after she announced her intention of joining the military.

"What did your parents think of your career choice?"

"They were mortified."

"What would make your parents disapprove of the military so much?"

"My dad was a professional protester, and my mom was an environmental lawyer until she quit to protest with him full-time." She smiled at the mixed memories of growing up with ultraliberal hippie parents who'd planted pot next to the organic vegetables in the garden of their Oregon home. "They hated anything that represented government control, violence, war, you name it."

"Ah."

"Yeah. I grew up with no discipline whatsoever. I ate what I wanted, did what I wanted. Didn't even wear clothes or choose my name until I was four."

"You picked your own name?"

"They didn't believe in shaping a child's life with confining clothing or a name not of her choosing."

"Damned telling that given your parents' views, you did something so defiant as joining the service."

"I was rebellious," she explained, and some would say nothing had changed. "Funny how when you have no discipline whatsoever, you find ways to make your parents give it to you. I think I wanted to be told what to do for once." She shook her head. "I decided real fast it wasn't a good fit."

"See, talking about yourself wasn't so hard, now, was it?"

"Not for you," she muttered, and thought back to some of her first days at ACRO, when they'd kept her busy in interviews and counseling and testing. The question-and-answer sessions had been so intense, she hadn't been sure from one hour to the next if she was coming or going. At least, not until the ACRO people had shown her what her equipment budget, salary and assignments would be.

He pressed on. "So why weather?"

No doubt he knew exactly how to get her talking with subjects she enjoyed, and though she recognized the manipulation, she played along. Which was, of course, what he'd have expected.

"It's powerful. Too often unpredictable, no matter how hard we try. There's so much we don't know." She practically squirmed with excitement as she thought about all the discoveries yet to be made. Perhaps by her.

"When I was a kid, I watched ball lightning chase my neighbor through her house, and then catch it on fire. No one believed me. All through my career, my theories have been met with skepticism and outright laughter from other meteorologists. So I've always wanted to prove, without a doubt, that it exists."

And maybe, just a little, she wanted to justify her career path to her parents.

He nodded, didn't look at her like she was crazy, but he had to be thinking it. "I guess that sounds strange to you."

"Not really."

Bracing herself on her palms, she tilted her head back to get a good look at him. "Why did you join the Navy?"

"To get away from this shithole. To get away from my old man. To do something meaningful with my life."

His voice tore at her. She knew all too well what it was like to want to get away from something—the place where you grew up, your parents....

For the first time in years, she wanted to comfort someone, and wow, what an inconvenient time for her nurturing instincts to kick in. Before she could stop herself, she reached out to touch his shoulder. He pulled back. Like her, he wanted no one's pity. And, like her, he'd wanted more from life than what he'd grown up around.

"I don't think you need a stitch. A butterfly bandage should work, but you're going to have to stay off your foot for a while."

"Says the man with the bruised ribs."

"Do as I say, not as I do."

She arched an eyebrow. "Do I seem like a person who does anything someone tells me to do?"

Shaking his head, he smiled. "Not in the least." He smoothed a bandage over her cut. "I'll bet you gave your parents hell."

A twinge of regret pinched her gut, and she bit her lip. She didn't want to go there again. ACRO wasn't paying her enough to spill everything to a target. Then again, they hadn't paid her to have sex with him either.

Well, she supposed they had. Devlin wanted results, obtained by any means necessary. And Haley, feeling obligated to the people who had given her a dream job, had finally relented.

But never again.

Every shared detail, every touch, every smile took her off course, off the assignment and into hazardous personal territory she shouldn't be wandering around in.

"Haley?" Remy pulled her against him, and she realized she'd started crying. Her tears rolled down his chest, leaving clean tracks over skin that had been sprayed with mud during the storm and during the sex they'd had on the floor. "Shh, *chere*. What's wrong?"

She couldn't answer him because she wasn't sure. She wasn't one to cry. Remy must have stirred up more than just answers with his interrogation, something even ACRO's shrinks hadn't been able to do.

"I think...I think I'm just exhausted." That much was true. Last time she'd checked an isobar chart, the time stamp had said one A.M., and that had to have been an hour ago.

He stroked her back lightly, lulling her sobs and—damn him—drawing her closer. "It's been a long night," he said softly. "Feels like longer."

It did. Seemed as though she'd known him for years rather than hours, and that should feel stranger than it did. Of course, the whole night could be written off as one big *Twilight Zone* episode.

Right down to the strange chanting in her head.

THERE WERE TIMES that Creed was able to rely completely on his own sixth sense to guide him through a situation with a pissed-off ghost and times he needed the help of his spirit to sense anything at all.

This was neither of those times, and his own common sense told him to stay away from direct contact with the portal— and to stay with Annika.

For a few minutes, he stood outside her bedroom door, and then, once he heard the shower running, he stepped inside.

She'd left the door to the bathroom open, just enough for him to get a clear view of her in the shower.

She'd been sixteen when he'd met her—he'd been twenty-four—and she'd been too much of a kid for him to give her more than a passing glance.

Overnight, she'd grown into one hot mama, practically knocking him on his ass, especially the way she strode around

ACRO like she owned the place. Over the past years, she'd turned more than a few heads, but supposedly she hadn't taken any of the operatives up on their offers.

He hadn't offered her anything. Yet. And now he was all mouth hanging open, watching the warm water sluice over her body through the clear glass shower door.

She was perfect, with an hourglass figure normally hidden underneath the black BDUs she wore on a daily basis at ACRO—her shoulders were broad for her frame, her waist narrowed to nothing and that ass...

Heart-shaped. Made for his hands.

He started to sweat.

He'd already left his jacket by the door and now he pulled his T-shirt off as well, his spine against the cold plaster wall, and still he was getting hotter.

Soap ran off her back in creamy rivulets. She shook her head under the spray and his cock jumped, nearly led him into the water with her.

She wouldn't push him out—no, he was pretty sure she'd help him strip out of his pants and let him take her, her ass pressed against the glass or the tile or wherever else he balanced her.

The tattoos along his right side throbbed uncontrollably with a primitive, pulsing beat.

She'd be tight and hot when he entered her, her legs gripping his waist, his mouth on hers.

Or maybe he'd kneel down on the hard tile instead and spread her thighs, lick her sex until she came all over his face.

He swallowed hard and thought about leaving the room.

No, this is about her safety. The spirit had wormed its way in and discovered her deep connection to Dev. Add to that her electromagnetic charge, and she was like a lightning rod for this spirit to move through.

She turned slightly, enough for him to get a view of high, firm breasts, just big enough, with pink nipples that were already taut. She arched under the water, ran her hands up to play with her nipples, and he groaned under his breath.

His own fingers tugged the silver ring that ran through his left nipple as he attempted to bring sensation to that side of his body—to alleviate some of the pressure, to balance himself.

When one of her hands slipped between her legs, past the perfectly manicured blond triangle to the pink cleft under it, his groan turned to a low whimper. He unzipped his fly because there was no way he was getting through this without coming.

She was thumbing her clit, circling the nub slowly, interspersing that action by putting one of her fingers inside herself. Her mouth was opened, contorted with pleasure, and he heard a low, keening moan over the sound of the water.

His cock was leaking as he pulled it, back and forth, his fingers playing along the slit the way he imagined hers would.

His name was on her lips—he could see the way they pursed when they formed the *C*, the way her hand moved faster and faster, in rhythm with his. His balls tightened, his skin was so sensitive that the cold air from the house hurt.

And then she screamed—honest to goodness screamed as she came, as if the release was so uncontrollable she had no other way to express it.

Something sizzled through him, complete and utter pleasure as he started to come into the T-shirt he held.

The house appeared to shake with the force of their orgasms, enough for Creed to move out of view and Annika to open the shower door and call out, "Who's there?"

He stayed outside the bedroom door, listening to her dress, waiting for his legs to stop trembling... and thinking.

Well, now, this was an interesting turn of events, from both

Annika and the ghost. He'd been pretty sure he caught a certain vibe from the spirit when he and Annika were pressed face-to-face, downstairs in the hallway, but now he knew *exactly* what this ghost wanted.

He knew exactly what he wanted too.

CHAPTER
Nine

At first, Remy thought the chanting was only a figment of his imagination, a leftover mirage from spending time in this house again.

When it grew loud enough that Haley looked over his shoulder toward the front of the house, he knew it was no damned illusion.

Shit. "Haley, just stay here. Don't go near the front door," he said, pulling away from her. But that wasn't going to do any good, because she'd already ignored him, jumped off the table and pushed past him. And she still wasn't wearing any shoes.

"What's going on out there?" she asked.

"It's because of me," he said quietly, still unable to bring himself to turn and face the chanting. Or her.

His breath hitched for a second and that familiar feeling of dread pitched straight through to his gut. *You could leave now. Go out the back door and walk the hell out of Bayou Blonde.*

When he was younger, this kind of scene would always happen near Halloween, when witches and magic ran rampant.

And his old man would suddenly take charge, tell him, *Go into the bedroom and turn up the radio and don't come out until I tell you.* And then, after half an hour or so, Remy Senior would come in, to find him huddled against the headboard, trying his best not to show fear, not to give a shit at all, and never succeeding.

People get stupid about what they don't understand, T, Remy Senior would say. And he'd make dinner and they'd eat together and Remy Senior would stay home that night, barely drink, and that would be enough to make Remy happy.

But he wasn't that kid anymore. Or a coward.

"I said, don't go near that door," he barked, his voice firm with the inherent tone of command he'd grown accustomed to.

He turned in time to see Haley's spine stiffen at his words. But she'd stopped walking, at least. He moved quickly, brushed past her and flung open the front door, closing it behind him just as fast.

A quick head count showed fifteen people on the postage stamp of a front lawn, a mix of men and women with candles and lanterns, standing among the debris and destruction, and all because of him. How special. The welcome-home party that kept on giving.

His head began to pound, and he opened his mouth to speak, to tell them all to back the hell up, but nothing came out.

"Told you he was back," said one of the women he recognized as a self-appointed neighborhood voodoo priestess. She was really nothing more than a scam artist who sold tap water and called it miracle juice. And then she started chanting again in Cajun French, some curse-removal bullshit. Like any of them cared about helping him.

He'd never believed in curses, and he wasn't starting now.

"*Arète sa!* I'll give you two minutes to shut your mouths

and back away from this property. And then I'm going to start shooting," he said hoarsely.

The chanting died down to a soft whisper, drowned almost completely by the sound of branches cracking under feet as a handful backed away, even though he didn't have a gun in his hands. He recognized a few of the neighbors, even more people he'd once gone to school with, born and bred on the Bayou Teche and refusing to leave. He watched them until a single strong voice in the crowd cursed Remy, galvanizing the mob again, and then their faces grew hazy as his head began to spin. His skin tingled, the wind picked up and the chanting grew louder.

"Remy." Haley stood next to him, touching his arm even as the rain began to fall—large, heavy drops that splattered and hissed when they hit the grass. Steam rose and the images in front of him blurred and all their words ran together.

"Ah, T-Remy's got himself a woman."

"*Bonne chance, cherie.* With a man like that, you're going to need it."

"He's goin' to kill you, chile. He's done it before. . . ."

"You all need to leave," she called out to them, her voice calm and strong, and fuck, she was just as good at giving commands as he was. Maybe better, even, because everyone suddenly shut up, and for a second the humming in his brain stopped.

"Mebbe you need to get him outta here instead, lady," one of the men from the back of the crowd called. And that's when he noticed they all wore the familiar bags of gris-gris around their necks to ward off the evil spirits they were convinced held court in his body.

At this point, maybe they weren't wrong. And he didn't care anymore; he closed his eyes and prepared to let them chant the devil right out of him. But Haley shoved him hard, and he opened his eyes and stared at her. She stared back, her jaw clenched tight, her lips pressed into a thin, angry line.

"Don't you let them do this to you." She held the shotgun that had hung on the post inside the front door for as long as he remembered, slung comfortably across her arm. And he didn't see the same fear or hatred in her eyes that the crowd had in theirs. He saw understanding, but that had to be a trick of light.

This was all one big goddamned trick. "Go inside, Haley."

Something hit him in the chest—a bag of bones and herbs, most likely, followed by sticks and anything else the mob could get their hands on, all meant to drive him back inside so they could finish their spell-casting.

"I'm not leaving you out here alone," she said, using her weight to try to force him back toward shelter, but he stood firm, his bare feet planted on the wet deck. When a stone bounced off his shoulder, she snarled, spun around. "What the hell are you people doing?"

"We're throwing spells, sugar. You ever hear about the curse T-Remy's got on him?" One of the women in the crowd sauntered toward the porch, her hips swaying in cutoff jeans, and he recognized her as Suzette, a girl who'd been raised by her three brothers in a rusty old trailer. She had a few more pounds on her than he remembered, and her features looked harder, like she'd been through hell in recent years. But there was no denying that she was still a good-looking woman.

"If I need to know something about Remy," Haley said in a voice cool enough to send the local cottonmouths into hibernation, "I'll ask him myself."

She crowded possessively against him, put one foot in front of and between his so his thigh pressed into her ass, and he realized she was standing out here in nothing but a two-buttoned shirt and shredded underwear that, if there were more light, would be providing the men with a damned good show.

"Then ask him if he still likes these," Suzette said, cupping her breasts through the fabric of the tight tube top that barely covered them.

Damn, if this were happening at any other time, he might actually enjoy what promised to be a catfight worthy of any man's wet dreams.

"Maybe you think you're woman enough to take him on," Suzette continued, "but I don't think so."

"What, did you try and not succeed, *chere*?" Haley asked. She slowly leveled the shotgun at Suzette's chest, and cocked her head. "Because there's nothing about Remy that I can't—or don't want to—handle."

"He let me handle him a few times. *Gete toi*, sug." Laughter rang out as Suzette smirked at Haley, blew Remy a kiss and winked before she backed into the safety of the crowd.

"Go inside, Haley," he repeated. "This had nothing to do with you."

"It does if they're trying to hurt you."

"Doesn't matter."

"It matters to me." And then she fired the shotgun into the air, twice. "Those were your only warnings. Next time, I'm aiming for kneecaps. It'll be hard to run from the gators that way, don't y'all think?"

"She's bluffin'," someone called.

And then an old woman he didn't recognize stepped forward, dressed in a knee-length frock and granny shoes and looking for all the world like a kindly grandmother. "I knew yo mama, boy. You da reason she dead."

His gut clenched, his mouth opened—but nothing came out. The woman's face changed, scrunched up like she'd tasted something sour and nasty as she screeched out some sort of voodoo curse. The crowd shouted various chants, which became a muted roar, and a shower of rocks and wood and even a couple of candles pelted him. He roughly shoved Haley behind the shelter of his body, and then the smell of gasoline sent a stab of alarm up his spine. The whoosh of a fire cut through the night. In the crowd, someone had lit something.

He took a step forward, intent upon tearing some asshole apart before they burned down the house, but a glowing orange light screamed toward him. He ducked and struck out, deflecting the burning stick with his fist before it hit Haley. It spun to the muddy ground and the flame hissed out, but the gray smoke curled upward like it still wanted a piece of him. Fury seared him like the fire never could, the wind tore through the trees—and fuck, someone was damned lucky, because he'd have had to kill the son of a bitch who'd thrown it if Haley had been hurt.

"Get the hell out of here," she shouted, angling the gun a hair to the right of the crowd. She fired, took out the birdhouse hanging in an old sycamore at least fifty yards away. "Now." The boom of the shotgun once again filled the air, and mud exploded in front of the crowd, splattering the people closest.

"Remind me not to piss you off," he muttered as he watched the crowd back off. They didn't run, but the south did have a slow-moving rhythm to it, and in his estimation, these people were moving faster than they ever had.

"You mean, more than you already have?"

He knew she meant it as more of a joke, but it didn't sit well with him, not with the adrenaline pumping through his body the way it was.

"Give me the gun," he said, and she handed it to him without any further argument. The weather outside had calmed significantly since the crowd vacated the premises, but there was no way it was going to stay that way for long.

REMY'S HAND SHOOK when he shut the door. Haley wouldn't notice the slight tremble, but he hated himself for it. Remembered the times he would leave someone's house or front yard and he'd turn to see them sprinkling salt behind him. After all, that was what you did when you wanted to keep a visitor from returning to your home.

T-Remy's bad luck, bad news, bad everything....

Sometimes it worked for him, the whole bad boy image. Worked well enough that he could sneak over to the nearest town once the old man passed out. He'd steal the truck and cross the bridge into no-man's-land and the line of local bars strung along on the way to the bigger towns. They contained a rougher element than Remy had ever seen, although a few bouts with his father and the kids at school had more than prepared him to hold his own.

He'd been fifteen the first time he'd gone in, with no ID, no plan and a hell of a lot of balls. He'd walked right up to the bar and ordered a beer, then promptly got into a fight with two locals who recognized him as the freak of nature. Literally.

It didn't stop the women, most of whom were convinced they'd be the one to handle him. *Conquer Remy and his insatiable urges. Let him try to screw you until you lose your mind.*

He'd taken a lot of them up on their offers. Too many. And he'd gotten nothing in return except partial, temporary relief.

Thunder boomed outside and lightning tore at the sky, reminding him of who he was. Of what his future held. He closed his eyes and saw the tattoo—Haley's tattoo—flash on his brain.

"Why the fuck did you come outside?" he demanded suddenly, and grabbed Haley by the shoulders.

"Because they were going to hurt you! And you were just standing there, ready to let them." She didn't try to pull away. If anything, she pushed her chest toward him, chin jutted, like she was ready to go toe-to-toe with him.

The temperature plummeted as his emotions stirred again,

and the wind whipped the already battered house. He needed to keep it together, but somehow, it wasn't working. Not tonight, and no matter how hard he tried.

"You're dealing with something you know nothing about," he warned, but she refused to be deterred.

"I know those people are afraid of you. I know they wanted to hurt you. And I know that's not the first time something like this has happened." Her voice softened. "Tell me why they're afraid, T-Remy."

"Don't call me that," he said, as the familiar hum began to vibrate inside his skull. And Haley was reaching up to stroke his hair, his cheek. His cock began to harden, ache with need, and Haley looked at him as if she knew. Her body melded against his easily, the longing increased and he felt like he was breathing through water.

"Dammit, Haley, why didn't you just let me leave when I wanted to?"

"Because you need me," she said.

"I don't need anyone. Get that through your head."

"I can help you."

"No one can help me." He pushed away from her and covered his ears in an attempt to stop the pressure from building, but it was too late. The ringing in his ears was almost unbearable, like a train attempting to drive straight through his head.

His groin throbbed, rock hard, and Haley's touch to his arm made it worse.

"Tell me what's happening," she was saying, but her voice sounded far away. He reached out for her, because as painful as it was to touch her, things were going to be much worse if he couldn't be with her. And soon.

"I can't tell you. I can show you," he said after a minute, when he knew he couldn't wait any longer.

He grabbed her around the waist and pulled her so close that she went up on her toes, and then he started moving. She was forced to wrap herself around him, legs secured at his waist as he walked them both through the house and out the already broken back door, which tore off its hinges when he kicked it open.

The wind howled wildly, kicking up everything in a swirl at Remy's feet. And then the rain started, the large drops landing with small thuds into the already soaked earth in a large ring around them. He closed his eyes, held Haley tight against him and wondered if what he wanted to show her was going to work when he was already this far out of control.

He opened his eyes when he heard but didn't feel the raindrops. It took Haley a minute longer to realize that they weren't getting wet at all, and she stared from the sky to him and back up again, and he mustered every ounce of willpower to keep from pushing her into the soft earth and taking her while the rain spilled all around them.

"You're really doing this, aren't you?" she asked, touching his cheek like he'd just given her some kind of great gift. "How are you doing it?"

"It's complicated," he whispered.

"It's magical," she whispered back, and just like that, the mood broke. Because it wasn't magic to him. It was painful and freakish and everything he didn't want anymore.

He dropped her, waited until she was steady on her feet before walking away.

"Why are you doing this to me?" he yelled at the sky, fists in the air. Mother Nature answered in kind with flashes of intense lightning that were too close for comfort for most people. Not for him, and not for Haley either, because she was reaching for him.

He pulled away from her grasp, continued to rant at the sky, the way he'd wanted to earlier when Mother Nature had taken the bridge—and his only hope of getting out of there soon.

"What the hell do you want from me?" he yelled, the thunder rolling in his brain and in the sky, booming as loud as he'd ever heard it, until he didn't know if he was holding the sky hostage or if it was the other way around. Until he didn't care.

He sank to his knees. "I don't know how to handle this. I don't know what you want from me. *Quoi tu veux,*" he murmured, over and over, until the whirring noise slowed and his fingers curled deep into the mud.

"Remy, come inside."

"Leave me."

"No, I won't do that." Haley's hands were strong on his shoulders, pulling him up from the ground.

"Just tell her to leave me alone," he mumbled.

"Tell who, Remy?" she asked, and he started, as though seeing her for the first time. Her eyes were a deep brown, the color of soft earth, her cheeks flushed, her hair wild around her shoulders, and his blood surged hot. Nearly uncontrollable.

It was no use—he was never going to be free of this fever.

"Haley, you need to go. Get inside. Please." His voice sounded raspy, nearly unrecognizable as he begged her.

"I'm not leaving you alone out here. Come inside with me," she said, her tone more like a command than a request, and any semblance of control he'd had snapped.

He reached for her, pressed his body against hers as if readying her for that frenzy building inside of him. He'd had her before, and she'd liked it. He wasn't going to ask her to leave again.

"Coming sounds like a good idea, Haley," he murmured in her ear. "Are you going to come for me, with me, again and again, until you can't stand it anymore, until you can't see straight?"

"Is that what you want?" she asked.

"Not want. Need." He gripped her hips and urged her down to her knees. "Need to fuck you, right here. Need to be inside you now."

His scalp pulled tight, his skin itched and tingled like so many electric shocks that had built up along the pressure points of his body. Lightning illuminated the sky, partnering with the thunder right on its heels at an impossibly fast rate.

He ripped the shredded remains of her underwear off her hips in order to get to her before he eased her onto her back. He'd barely yanked down his own pants before he plunged into her, took her there, in the mud, with their legs tangled, bodies slick with rain and sweat, lifting her hips off the ground with each firm stroke.

He remained on his knees, with his arms fully extended for leverage so he could drive himself inside her deeper still, and Haley's hands were slipping off the slick skin of his shoulders as she attempted to climb him. When she finally succeeded, she wrapped her arms around his neck, pulling his chest to hers so they were locked together, moving as a single unit, his weight bearing all of hers.

She licked his throat, then suckled the sensitive skin at the base of his collarbone, and he groaned, fought to get a firm hold in the mud beneath his palms. He ended up on his elbows instead, and her hands began to roam his back, drifting lower. When she began to finger his ass, he jerked in surprise and found her smiling up at him.

"Jesus, Haley," he groaned, and still she continued to work him in a way he'd never allowed anyone to before, the pad of her thumb pressing the puckered hole, the balance of power slowly shifting with each of her caresses. When she penetrated, he came with an unexpected ferocity, his toes curling, yelling something even he couldn't understand. And then his body weight settled onto hers as though he'd never rise again.

But Haley, not through with him, surprised and roused him when she rolled them in one fast move. His back hit the warm mud with a loud, thumping squish, even as she kept a hold on his shoulders. He was still inside her, somehow still impossibly hard. He thrust his hips up, driving himself as far as he could, until he was the one who couldn't see straight. She was practically holding him down as she started a long, slow slide up and down his cock.

He struggled to sit up, to flip her, but it was no use when he was this deep in the pleasure she gave him. He wanted this, had to have this over and over, and it didn't matter what position he was in when he was getting his fill.

She arched back, her thighs pressing his as her slick heat contracted around him, and he let his next orgasm roll through him. Another one came fast on its heels and he was coming with such force that he wondered if he'd ever gain any kind of control over himself again.

A sudden surge of energy blasted through him, and he sat up, Haley still on top of him. He squeezed his eyes shut tight and put his forehead against hers.

"Make it stop, Haley. Please, make it stop," he whispered against her mouth, and then he kissed her, a hot, demanding kiss that jolted him to the soul. He heard popping sounds fill the air as if bolts of electricity were being released from his body, out into the universe, and he ripped his mouth away from hers as a hard rain whipped around them.

"*C'est pas le peine,*" he mumbled as Haley moved off of him, stood and dragged him determinedly to his feet and toward the house. "It's no use."

CHAPTER
Ten

Haley's brain had short-circuited. That was the only explanation for why, after seeing proof that Remy could do what his father said, she wasn't giddy with excitement.

The first contact instructors who'd prepared her for this mission had warned that people with special abilities often despised their powers, rarely understood them and most likely didn't have full control over them. Remy seemed to fit all three categories, and instead of being ecstatic about her discovery, all she wanted to do was help him find peace with who he was and what he could do.

Limbs heavy after so many orgasms she'd lost count, she led Remy into the house, which was dark, the generator having finally run out of gas. She'd expected him to give her more trouble, but he was strangely pliable. She knew that would change soon, that he would regain his hard-won control and shut her out again. For both their sakes, she couldn't allow him to slip back into a closed-off mode.

"In here, Remy." She urged him toward the bathroom, pausing briefly to snare a hurricane lamp from the end table.

She set it on the closed toilet lid and lit the wick quickly, the lamplight illuminating Remy's face and the emotions that crossed it. Confusion. Pain. Sadness. All of it fleeting, and all of it enough to make her heart break just a little.

Rain tapped softly on the roof as she grabbed a washcloth and ran it under the water in the sink. When she brought the cloth up to his face, he didn't even blink. She wiped the streaks of mud from his forehead, his cheeks, the tip of his nose, while he stared straight ahead, his posture all military bearing.

"Remy? Are you okay?"

"*J'aurais pas du de venire me fourer ici,*" he said, more to himself than to her.

"What does that mean?"

His jaw tightened as she ran the cloth over his hands, doing the best she could to get the worst of the mud off of them. "I shouldn't have come here. This place does me no good." He took a deep, shuddering breath. "God, I'm tired."

"Is it always like this?"

He dazedly looked down at the muddy tracks they'd left on the floor, but she didn't know if he actually saw them. "She's never fucked with me this hard. I don't get it. You're the meteorologist. Parameteorologist. Whatever. Don't you have some sort of inside track?"

"I wish I did."

A gust of wind shrieked through the trees, as if Mother Nature had heard Remy trying to get rid of her. "Fuck."

He took his hands from hers, held his fists at his sides, and his expression grew dark. Even in the dim light from the lamp flame, she recognized that look, the one full of heat and lust and a raging battle for control.

"What can I do, Remy? Tell me how to help you."

He didn't say a word, merely wrapped an arm around her waist and drew her into his hard body. Cold mud on his pants squished against her bare legs. His erection burned into the tender flesh of her belly and the even more tender tattoo, which had started to tingle again.

She reached down, touched him gently. "Is this part of your tie to the weather?" she asked, and he flinched. "It's okay, Remy. You can tell me. It is, isn't it?"

The ACRO investigators who'd probed Remy's past and present, who'd examined his movements all over the world, had included in their reports statements from women who claimed that when the weather turned bad, Remy's lust turned insatiable. Haley's own doubts had been dispelled not long after meeting him. Still, his desire could have been explained as some strange storm-fetish, which she shouldn't think was so odd, given that severe weather always gave her a sexual thrill, of sorts.

"Yes," he said through clenched teeth. "Storms. They affect me." He covered her hand with his, held it there against his crotch.

Hunger flashed in his eyes, so intense she squirmed as they stood there in the growing puddle of muck that dripped down their legs.

"We should clean up while the water is still hot," she said, lamely, because she had no desire to get clean. She wanted to get dirty in ways that didn't involve mud.

One corner of his mouth twitched in a half smile and he reached around her and turned on the shower faucet.

"No. It's dangerous to shower during a storm." And she'd investigated enough bathtub electrocutions to know.

"You were showering when I got here."

"That's because it wasn't storming. It wasn't until you got here..."

"Yeah," he muttered, and she wished she hadn't brought it up. "But we're safe. She won't hurt me."

Though Haley had her doubts, she allowed him to remove her shirt, not minding that his method of removal involved tearing it off so that the remaining two buttons scattered. If she spent much more time with him, she'd need a new wardrobe.

Her entire body throbbed already, and the ache drilled deeper as she watched his long, sexy fingers work the only button on his cargos he hadn't undone outside. The fly parted wide, and the full, thick length of his erection sprang free.

God, he was beautiful. And big. Her mouth watered with the memory of how he tasted, and her inner muscles clenched at the mere thought of how he filled her, despite the fact that they'd just had wild, hot sex.

A fog of lust and shower steam blurred her vision, until she could hardly see. He seemed to know, and he took his sweet time pushing his pants down. The hard globes of his ass shifted and flexed enticingly when he pivoted to kick the cargos into a corner, and it took every last ounce of willpower to keep from grabbing him. From reaching between his legs from behind and caressing his balls, maybe going to her knees and sucking them into her mouth as she reached around and stroked him in her fist.

Taking her wrist, he pulled her into the shower with him. The hard spray stung until he blocked it with his body, and she squirted a thick stream of coconut mango-scented soap onto her mesh body puff.

Mud sloughed off them, swirling down the drain as she gently scrubbed his chest, her looping, leisurely strokes at odds with the way her insides rattled and her hormones fired through her blood. Outside, thunder rolled, and with a groan, he tilted his head back into the stream of water. His throat worked on a hard swallow, and he threw out a hand to brace himself against the shower wall.

She washed her way up, to his arms and shoulders. His muscles rippled and bunched beneath her puff, and long, soapy trails wound through the valleys between. When she worked her way down, the wind outside picked up.

"Storms make you—"

"Want to fuck."

His head snapped forward, and he pierced her with a hard gaze. She shivered at the fierceness in his eyes, the crude statement. Her entire body went hot, so hot her damned tattoo felt like a fresh brand, with searing, tingling fingers connected to her sex.

"They make me want to fuck until I pass out. Is that what you wanted to know?"

"Yes," she whispered, unsure if he'd heard her over the shriek of the wind.

Her hand shook as she rasped the puff over his thighs. She let her arm brush his erection, each glancing touch causing his chest to expand sharply. Lightning bathed the bathroom in silver light.

"When you're aroused...like when there are no storms..."

"I draw any nearby weather." He hissed when she soaped up her palm and closed it around his penis, unable to hold off touching him intimately for another second. "Sometimes it forms out of nowhere."

There was so much more she wanted to ask, but he kissed her so thoroughly and for so long that the water started to grow cold even as her body grew hotter. How could it not, with the way he thrust into her soapy hands as though he didn't even realize what he was doing, the way he looked at her like he wanted to devour her.

Oh, she remembered how he'd devoured her hours earlier, how his tongue had swiped through her slit and then stabbed deep. Lick, plunge, repeat. Sweet Lord, she'd dance to that beat all night long.

"What..." She swallowed dryly and stepped back from the cool drops that sprinkled her skin. "What if there's a storm and you don't get sex?"

He shut off the water and shook his head like a big, powerful beast, sending water droplets splattering like rain on the shower curtain. "I have to. She makes me." He squeezed half the bottle of soap into his hand and stalked her, which seemed impossible, since they were standing inside a bathtub. "I can get myself off," he said, rubbing his palms together until creamy soap dripped down his arms, "but it's better to have a woman."

She couldn't breathe as he smeared her breasts and worked his way down to her belly and hips.

"Do you mind, Haley? Do you mind if I have you? Over and over?" He dipped his head, lapped at her shoulder. Shivers of pleasure rippled over her skin.

She didn't mind, and she had a feeling she'd never mind. But she was beginning to see why other women might. His files indicated that he never kept a girlfriend for long. His intense sexual needs, as well as the violent weather phenomena that followed him, probably scared the crap out of his partners.

Fortunately for him, Haley didn't scare easily, and never because of weather.

"Over and over," she swore.

Lifting his head, he speared her with a gaze full of a haunting hunger that broke her heart into a million pieces. "You can't be real."

There was no time to answer. He braced her face in his soapy palms, holding her as he lowered his mouth to hers. She'd never enjoyed kissing, but Remy kissed like he made love—with raw, primal skill that evoked a primitive feminine response she refused to analyze.

His tongue speared deep, stroked hers in a slow, drugging rhythm. When he sucked on her tongue, pulled on it with alternating firm and delicate pressure, she clutched at his waist and wondered if she'd ever let him go.

The kiss grew hotter, wetter, and so did her sex, until she couldn't stand the emptiness. She wrapped one slippery leg around his thighs, groaning at the pressure against her mound. Just a little gentle rubbing would get her there; her body was so willing and ready that he could probably talk her into an orgasm at this point.

Remy caught her bottom lip between his teeth and flicked his tongue over it, and oh, how she wished he'd do it again, only lower. Tilting her hips, she eased her throbbing ache against his hard thigh muscle. His erection tickled her belly, and though water and soap dripped down her abs, she could still feel the silky, hot pre-cum streaming from the tip.

Thunder boomed somewhere, but it was muted, distant. "Why isn't the storm bad anymore?" she asked, though she could barely understand herself, the way her voice sounded ragged and hoarse.

"Don't know," he said against her mouth. "Don't care." He brought his hands down, one sliding to her ass, the other dropping between them to cup her sex. "God, you're wet."

"It's mostly you," she moaned, as his middle finger slid back and forth in her cleft, making her twitch with every feather-light stroke across her supersensitive nub.

"Me," he murmured, his voice vibrating through her like some sort of secret trigger, because suddenly she was coming, and he was saying, "Only me, *bebe*, only me."

Her climax screamed through her, and he entered her while her pussy was still clenching with powerful spasms. The soap created a slippery, sexy friction as he took her against the cold tile.

"Harder, Remy." She wrapped herself tight around him and threw her head back.

He moved faster, thrust deeper, and he must have soaped up her back, because she slid up and down the wall like she rode on greased rails. It felt like being caressed in 3-D, from the back, the front, the inside, and God, she wasn't going to last much longer. The triple sensations were making her fly apart, making her straddle the precipice of a release that threatened to make all the others tonight seem mild.

His mouth came down on hers once more, sealing them together. And then, out of nowhere, lightning lit the bathroom, kept it lit as thunder damn near took the house off its foundation. Remy roared into her mouth, rammed into her, and blinding bursts of light speared her eyes as she came once more, her orgasm heightened by his.

Her release went on and on, a full-body orgasm she felt at the cellular level. She was a lightning rod, and Remy was the lightning, burning her to ash.

Sweat and soap and exhaustion bound them together, and she wondered if he could feel the feverish sizzle of her tattoo like a brand on his skin. He dropped his forehead against hers, his eyes closed, his breathing raspy. Outside, the rain stopped as suddenly as it had started.

Whether or not he was responsible wasn't clear. But one thing was certain: He had a connection with the weather. Which elements, and how, exactly, had yet to be determined. But ACRO had found itself a new operative, an X-Man, of sorts, providing Remy accepted their offer. And he would. No one turned down the elite secret agency that offered misfits something no one else could: a sense of belonging.

Not to mention the most interesting assignments imaginable.

She let herself relax in her assignment's strong arms, let herself be lulled by the sound of his heartbeat. She had to enjoy it now, because tomorrow, after she contacted ACRO with her news, relaxing with Remy would be a thing of the past.

CHAPTER
Eleven

Dev had let Marlena drive him back to his house; on the north side of the compound, it was still protected enough from intruders, by two gates, a security system better than any president's and, of course, bodyguards.

He hated the fact that he needed bodyguards. These days, more than ever, he wanted to be alone when he came home. Even though the men and women who had his back were competent, utter professionals he trusted with his life, just for one day he'd like to come home to a completely empty house.

Of course, if he turned off his second sight and tamped down his senses, he could pretend, but that never worked out as well as it sounded.

"Do you think Haley will be able to control the potential operative?" Marlena asked before Dev got out of the car.

"I don't think anyone can ever actually control another person," he said. "Not for long anyway."

Control. It had always been about control for Dev himself, a hard-won, nearly daily battle for much of his life, culminating in his loss of sight and the accident that took him out of the driver's seat and grounded him for life.

He walked through the familiar rooms on his way up the stairs, even though he knew he wasn't going to be able to sleep, letting his body rather than his powers guide him.

Maybe he should've let Marlena come inside with him—she could've helped him burn off some of this extra energy. But she'd also worry.

The leak at ACRO was eating him alive.

He could trust Ender, one of his most valued operatives, the man who'd saved his life in the fiery crash that took Dev's eyesight nearly ten years earlier. But if he told Ender now, the man's already rampant overprotectiveness would kick into higher gear.

No, he'd have to figure out on his own who the mole was. The two main psychics who worked directly with him were ready to admit defeat, but Dev knew what he had to do.

Sending Annika and Creed ahead to his childhood home was all part of the plan, one that could easily backfire in his face.

The extra powers that house seemed to provide were nearly too much for him; they had already broken him once before, three years earlier. It was the main reason why Oz, the best medium ACRO had ever seen, left after he'd helped Dev regain control.

He'd wanted Dev to promise that he'd never summon that spirit again, but of course Dev could never promise that. Not when his agency was at stake.

"I know how to control it now," he'd told Oz. "I know how to stop it from taking over."

"You're kidding yourself, Devlin. No one commands the spirit world. And if you're thinking like that, you're already too far gone."

Oz had slammed out of the office and out of ACRO and

hadn't been seen or heard from since. Dev's only consolation was that Oz was too good to get taken by Itor.

So yes, Dev knew something about trying to control powers that were nearly uncontrollable. He knew Haley had her work cut out for her... and he knew he'd be back in the office within a few hours, after he tossed and turned and pretended to sleep.

He wondered if he'd ever be able to stop pretending.

ANNIKA COULDN'T ESCAPE HIM. Creed was like the Terminator, all black leather, chains and ruthless persistence. When she'd wanted to nap after her shower, he'd insisted she keep the door separating their rooms open, and then he'd stretched out, shirtless, on his bed, a satisfied smile on his face that made her wonder what the hell he was up to.

And just now, she'd barely gotten to the kitchen and seated before he was pounding down the stairs. At least the creepy spirit that had shaken the house while she was in the shower had gone quiet.

"Did you get some sleep?" He clomped across the floor and took a bottle of water from the fridge.

Thank God Dev had hired a caretaker to keep the place clean, landscaped and stocked with drinks and nonperishable food. The caretaker had also put clean sheets on all the beds in the seven-bedroom mansion. Overkill, but the guy probably didn't have a lot else to do.

"A little." Very little, because with Creed in the next room, all she could do was think about him. Naked. Thankfully, he'd at least put on a new shirt. Black like the old one, but this one bore a Jack Daniel's logo. "You snore."

"That can be fixed." An impish gleam lit his eyes. "I only snore when I'm alone."

"I'll bet you snore a lot."

He laughed, a deep, masculine sound that shivered through

her and tickled all the places that needed to be tickled. Oh, this was bad. Sure, she'd gotten herself off earlier in the shower, but the release had done nothing to ease the strange cravings she was having for his body.

Every time she laid eyes on him, the knowledge that she couldn't shock him made him oh-so-tempting. To be able to have sex and not worry about her orgasm putting the guy into the hospital . . . heaven.

But why the hell did the one guy she could possibly fuck have to be the one guy she really, really couldn't stand? The one person at ACRO who seemed to go out of his way to annoy her? When everyone else scrambled away at her approach, Creed stepped into her path and made her either walk around him or shove him out of the way.

"You don't snore." Bracing one palm on the dining room table, he angled his big body close, invading her personal space in a way others feared to do. He licked his lips, so full and kissable, and his eyes darkened dangerously. "But you do make a lot of noise in the shower. You're a screamer."

Her breath exploded from her lungs. Had he taken her up on her sarcastic offer, after all?

She'd always been able to hang with the guys, talk like them, drink like them, kick ass like them. She'd never had an issue with nudity, had spent days lounging on nude European beaches, had posed as strippers and prostitutes on assignments. But suddenly, the idea of Creed listening to—or watching—her masturbate left her off balance.

And sent a forbidden thrill through her body.

"How much of a show did you get?"

She could picture him stroking his dick as he stood outside the door, listening to her moans, her cries that escaped no matter how hard she bit her lip. If he only knew that the man she'd been fantasizing about had been him, that she'd imagined him on his knees in front of her, his pierced tongue working her deep, hard, wet.

"Let's just say I know you're a true blonde."

Oh, God. He'd seen her. He'd seen everything. Lust throbbed through her, so pure and rich that she shook with it.

"Well, I hope you have a great memory, because that's the most of me you'll ever see."

No matter what, nothing could happen between them. She might not be able to shock him intentionally, but what would happen if, in her excitement, she sent out a supercharged bolt of electricity? What if his own desire lowered his resistance or something?

Dev would be pissed if she killed a guy he'd practically grown up with.

"That's probably for the best," Creed said, "but it's not what either of us wants."

Arrogant ass. "You have no idea what I want. Now get away from me."

Creed didn't move, simply watched her with a heated gaze that made her swallow repeatedly.

"I said, get away from me," she ground out, pleased at how her breathlessness made her sound even angrier.

She punctuated her order with a hard shove against his chest, and then she slipped out of the chair. When his hand closed around her wrist, she snapped.

The look on Creed's face when he found himself slammed against the wall was priceless. Of course, she'd bet that the look on her face when he grabbed a fistful of her hair and brought his mouth down on hers was just as amusing.

CHAPTER
twelve

Haley stared at the blank screens and listened to the dead silence. Dead, and in need of an autopsy.

At some point during the night, her battery backup, which should have been good for forty-eight hours, had gone belly-up.

Thank God she'd archived all data after she and Remy had rinsed in the cool shower and before they'd fallen together into an exhausted heap on the bed.

The thump of feet hitting the floor made her heart kick against her ribs. She wasn't ready to face him yet. Would he regret letting her in on his secret? Would he be willing to let her perform some tests? And what would she tell him when he started asking questions?

Because he would. The storms had diverted his attention last night, but today, with clear skies and a few hours' sleep, he'd want details regarding her work, her employer and her equipment.

Lying would be easy enough, but with Remy's secret out in the open, every hour she delayed starting the recruitment process could potentially bring the enemy that much closer to learning his secret. Telling Remy the truth before he asked would be best, but she needed to get the timing just right, needed to read the atmosphere that had nothing to do with weather.

And that was the most worrisome part of this whole deal, trying to read a human instead of the weather. She could time the approach of a cold front by the way insects grouped on tree bark, but predicting Remy's reaction when she told him why she was really here? Impossible.

And fascinating. The man was like a hurricane, predictable only in that damage was a given. Except Remy's damage was to himself, and as far as she could tell, no one had been around for the post-storm cleanup.

God, to be so alone in what he went through...it made her chest hurt. She understood *alone* far too well, but his secret put him into a category of isolated she couldn't even comprehend.

The bedroom door tore open, and she jumped, banged her hip on the table. Wincing, she drew back the waistband of her shorts and nearly gasped at the sight of her tattoo, its black lines raised and reddened, as though it were new and not eight years old. How had she missed that when she got dressed this morning? Well, she had been pretty occupied with the rest of her aches and pains, the scrapes and cuts from her tumble down the ravine, the bruises from the wild sex....

The bathroom door closed as she gingerly traced her fingers over the tattoo's pattern, the Strategic Air Command patch from her military days. Maybe she'd been bitten or stung by some kind of insect. Whatever had happened, she probably should see a doctor when she got back to ACRO. Have the damned thing finally removed, something she'd tried to have done six months ago, only to have the doctor's laser break when he started.

Thumping footsteps startled her again, and jeez, it sounded like someone woke up cranky.

But when Remy walked into the living room, he appeared calm, cool ... and gloriously naked.

Honed muscles cut sharply across his upper body, the early-afternoon light emphasizing details she hadn't noticed last night. The thick length between his legs drew her admiring gaze, and she bit her cheek, forced herself to look elsewhere. Like at his butt, when he angled himself away.

"Good morning," she said, sounding a little more breathless than she'd have liked. Breathless *and* stupid, seeing how morning had passed two hours ago.

"Hey." He grabbed his bag and dug through it.

"There are donuts—"

"We don't have time." He threw on a pair of jungle-patterned cargo pants. "We need to get gas for the generator before it gets dark. We can pick up some food while we're out." Pulling a black T-shirt out of the bag, he glanced at her feet. "Good, you've got boots on. Let's go."

She couldn't argue, because with her battery backup dead, she needed power to run her equipment. "Okay, but can we talk first?"

"We'll talk on the pirogue," he said, moving toward the door.

She stopped dead in her tracks. "The what?"

"It's a boat."

"A boat? As in, it floats? On water?"

He halted at the doorway and frowned at her. "What's wrong?"

"Nothing."

"Don't lie to me, Haley." He moved toward her, and she saw that he'd grabbed the knife he'd worn last night. "I hate being lied to."

"And I hate being given orders."

He arched an eyebrow, but the firm set of his mouth softened, and she wondered if maybe going out on the pirogue was more about him wanting to get to know her than it was about being in charge.

For some reason, she hoped for the former, when the latter would have been infuriating but better for the security of her career and personal goals, none of which made room for a man.

"I don't like water. There's a reason I joined the Air Force instead of the Navy. No swimming requirement," she said finally, and if he thought he'd get another word out of her, he'd been through one too many electrical storms.

She'd hated water since she was six, when she'd fallen off a pier because her parents were so busy making out that they hadn't been paying attention. Fortunately, her dad had heard her screams and pulled her out before she drowned, but the memory had stuck with her, and she'd never gone more than knee deep again.

Something in her expression must have betrayed her, because he reached out, cupped her cheek. An instant, sizzling spark arced between them, and she knew he felt it too, because his eyes flashed with confusion and annoyance.

"I'll take care of you."

He swallowed her protest with a kiss, like he thought she'd swoon and follow him anywhere just because he could do things with his mouth that were probably illegal in this godforsaken state.

Of course, when he slipped his tongue inside her mouth, tasting of toothpaste, she did sort of melt against him. Her body went all pliant and hot, and her mind went all blank and dizzy.

She swooned, dammit.

His tongue swiped her mouth, tickling her gums, her palate. He caught her bottom lip between his teeth, drawing a long, loud moan from her. The sound signaled her doom, and Remy pressed his advantage by turning the kiss into something hard and deep and hungry.

When he finally pulled back, they were both panting, and his eyes gleamed with satisfaction.

"C'mon, *bebe*," he said, taking her hand. "We have a lot to accomplish."

"I need my cell."

She grabbed her backpack containing her phone and firearm on the way out, ignoring him when he told her a cell phone wouldn't work in the bayou. She followed him to the garage, where he gathered a gas can and a flashlight, and then he led her down the muddy driveway to a dock that looked about as sturdy as a Popsicle-stick fence.

She hoped he didn't notice how her legs trembled as she climbed into the flat-bottom boat to take a seat on one of the two benches. Remy remained standing and pushed off the dock, using something he called a paddie to steer them through chocolate water clogged with weeds and rotting trees.

"So," he said, ten minutes later and in the middle of God-knew-where, "you said you wanted to talk. About what?"

Placing the paddie on the floor, next to her backpack, he sat across from her and braced his forearms on his thighs, resting his palms on her knees. She tried not to look at the water, or grip the sides of the boat too hard.

"Last night."

"Is there something you want to tell me?"

Shit. In her head, she'd rehearsed what she'd say, but now, under his intense, curious gaze, she drew a blank. All her careful planning had taken a dive right into that alligator-infested, insect-ridden water.

Her concentration scattered even more as his hands drifted upward in a slow, squeezing, massaging action. "Haley?"

"Right." She cleared her throat, at a complete loss, which was something that never happened. "Awkward morning-after thing, I guess."

"Does that happen to you often? You know, awkward morning-afters."

Well, that pretty much made her throat close up. Before she could choke out an indignant "No!" his fingers dug into her thighs, not hard, but firmly enough to let her know he wanted her undivided attention.

"You aren't married or anything, are you?"

"At this point, does it really matter?"

"Last night it didn't," he said, in a bitter voice that told her how much he hated that fact. "Today, with my head clear, yeah. I don't poach, and if some irate husband is going to come after me, I'd like a heads-up."

Hurt and anger churned up like a dirt devil in her belly. Did he think she was the type to cheat? Then again, he didn't know her at all, and she grudgingly admitted that she might have wondered the same thing if the situation had been reversed.

"I'm not married. And to answer your next question, I'm on the pill, and my last full physical two months ago came up clear." ACRO made all its employees run the gamut of tests every six months—tests most doctors had never even heard of.

A sharp nod was his only response. What had happened to the Remy of last night? The one who might have been half-crazed, but who also burned with life and passion. She could talk to that Remy. This one was too cool, too emotionally distant, and she couldn't read him at all.

One thing she couldn't deny: Today's Remy retained all the sensual skill of last night's version. The pads of his fingers tortured her with a measured amount of pressure, no doubt designed to draw out the required response, to make her seek his touch the way she needed it. Firmer. Faster. Higher.

Instead, she sought composure in a gulp of musty bayou air and forced her hands to release the sides of the boat. She planted them tamely on the bench. "Last night you seemed to think my environmental study was bullshit."

"I don't think." He traced a figure eight on her inner thigh. "I *know.*"

Subject displays arrogant tendencies.

ACRO's profiler deserved a high five for that one. Remy couldn't "know" anything. The agency had set her up too well, and her acting abilities didn't suck that bad.

Sitting up a little straighter, she squeezed her legs together, but Remy only smiled, pushed them apart and continued drawing little geometric designs, his gaze fixed where he played.

She huffed. "Why don't you enlighten me on how you *know?*"

"Why don't you come clean about why you're here?"

"For my job."

"Ah." The patterns he made on her skin now seemed random. Like her heartbeat. "So we're back to the environmental study? Are you still trying to pass that bullshit off on me?"

Something flitted around in her stomach, too large and vigorous to be butterflies. "My job was to study you."

He nodded like he'd expected the answer. "Who do you work for?"

"This sounds suspiciously like an interrogation."

His gaze snapped up, caught hers and held it prisoner. "If it were, you'd be in the water instead of on it." A brief smile curved his mouth, as though to soothe her. "Now, who did you say you work for?"

Oh, yeah, this was an interrogation, no matter what he claimed. He'd simply tailored his skills to extract information from a female who was sexually attracted to him.

Smart son of a bitch. Too bad for him she had planned to spill all anyway.

"I work for a secret agency that employs people with extraordinary abilities."

"Like what?"

"Levitation. Pyrokinesis. Channeling the dead." She paused, searched his face for disbelief, but he remained expressionless. "Some can read minds. We've got a guy who can absorb the entire contents of a book or file just by touching it. Another who has webbed feet and poisonous spurs—"

"What about you? What do you do?"

His fingers traced light, straight lines. Curves. Something familiar...Ah, yes. He was drawing her tattoo.

"I study weather at the agency's meteorology lab. I don't have any special abilities."

He raked her with a dark, appreciative gaze. "Don't sell yourself short, *bebe*. You showed me all kinds of special abilities last night." The air whooshed from her lungs at his words. "So tell me, was fucking me part of your job?"

A breeze stirred the trees, and okay, now she got it. The calm wasn't calm at all. This was Remy containing his anger. He lunged forward and slapped his hands on either side of her bench, caging her with his body and thick arms. If he thought he could intimidate her, however, he was very, very wrong.

She might be terrified of water, but Remy Begnaud didn't scare her one bit. Or so she told herself as she looked him in the eye.

"You didn't seem to mind."

Grasping her entire thigh in one hand, he pulled her against him so her butt hung off the edge of the seat. "Does this feel like I minded?" His erection rocked into her center, and while her mind knew he was messing with her, her body spun up with desire. "Was it part of your job? Tell me."

"Or what? You'll pleasure the information out of me?"

She wrapped her legs around his waist and pulled him

close, enjoying the brief startled look that softened his chiseled features before he shuttered himself off again.

"Maybe it won't be all that pleasurable."

Arching into him, she rubbed, taunted, gave him a taste of his own medicine. "Don't try to scare me, Remy. You don't have it in you to hurt a woman."

"How the hell do you know? I've got you alone out here, where no one could hear you scream . . . what makes you think you know me well enough to be sure?"

"Because," she said, "I know you better than anyone on this planet."

He snorted and pushed away from her. "After a night of sex and a couple days in my house? You don't know shit."

Cocking an eyebrow, she leaned forward. "I know that your longest relationship took place while you were stationed in San Diego. She was a Hooters girl named Kimberly Boone, and you dated for twenty-seven days, though you only saw her for fourteen of it. She dumped you the day after a particularly nasty thunderstorm."

He rocked back onto his bench like he'd been slapped, and she rode the momentum.

"I know that when you were being held prisoner in that hellhole in Guatemala, you drew comic strips on the cell walls. I know it hurt every time your teammates looked at you with distrust when equipment failed. Worst of all was when your GPS broke and it wasn't your fault, but they accused you with their eyes anyway. That was the first time you thought about leaving."

It was her turn to lean forward, to maintain control of this tug-of-war for power in which they were engaged. "Now, you want to tell me I don't know anything about you?"

A muscle in his jaw twitched as he stared at her, his expression one of fury and disbelief. "How?" he growled. "How the fuck do you know this shit?"

"I told you, I work with people who have abilities you can't even comprehend." The wind stirred the bayou again, and she frowned. "Well, maybe you can."

"Bottom line, Haley. What do you and your agency of misfits want with me?"

"We want *you*. My job was to make sure you were the real deal. You are. We can help you learn to fully control your gift—"

"Gift? Is that what they told you to say to me? To make me think this is something I should be thankful for?"

"You don't need to be thankful for it, but you can choose to make it work for you. And for the good of the world."

Thunder cracked. Haley jumped.

"The good of the world," Remy mused, looking out over the swamp. "And how were you supposed to convince me to join your special agency?"

Lightning flashed over the top of the trees and in Remy's eyes. "Sex?" He reached for the fly of his cargos, let his long, sexy fingers linger. "Is that your preferred method?"

Her mouth went dry, and she struggled for an answer. Maybe the storm was messing with his libido, would give her a chance to delay the conversation a bit, maybe use sex the way he said, the way the Seducers had taught her.

He stood, rocking the boat enough to make her grasp the sides. His fingers worked the buttons, and each time one slipped through the buttonhole, her body reacted. Her breasts flushed with heat. Her pulse ricocheted through her veins. On the last button, a rush of moisture drenched her panties.

"Was it sex, Haley? Or something way more fucked up?"

With a jerk, he tore open the left side of his pants to reveal a patch of skin at his hip. An angry, reddened patch of skin.

Marked with an exact replica of her tattoo.

CHAPTER *Thirteen*

Dev would probably kill him, but Creed couldn't help himself. With Annika's hand still firmly at his throat, his at the back of her neck and his libido still on high speed from watching her in the shower, his mouth plundered hers.

She was half responding, half struggling, and there was no way he was going to let her go so easily. If she wanted to, really wanted to, she could break his grip. He made it just hard enough for her to talk herself into being held captive by his kiss.

He loved this part, the kissing, because the sensations were always there, everything just starting to heighten, and he couldn't pretend anymore that he didn't think about Annika most of the time he was with other women...since the first time he'd seen her in Dev's office.

Trying to bed the boss's girlfriend wasn't the best way to keep a job, but there was no way he was stopping. Not when Annika's hips swayed against his or her breasts pressed into his chest when he ran the ball piercing in his tongue along the roof of her mouth, and it took every ounce of self-control not to reach up and brush her nipple. Because that would make her run.

He'd never known Annika to be afraid of anything, so for her to have such a fight-or-flight response to his kiss intrigued him. Especially after her forceful orgasm.

He was going to have to bring her in gently.

As gently as he could with her hand tight against his throat. She could kill him with her pinky, and somehow that only added to the thrill.

He reluctantly pulled his mouth off hers, noted her rapid breathing with more than a little satisfaction.

He probably shouldn't have smiled, as that only made her increase her grip on his trachea. "Afraid I'll make you scream?" he asked.

"You're pretty sure of yourself, aren't you?"

"Aren't you?" He let his hand caress the back of her neck for a second, right before he pulled her back in for another kiss. And this time, she didn't fight him. Much.

He didn't bother to mention that he knew she'd yelled his name in the shower. And he wasn't going to be the first to let go. She still held his throat with one hand and braced herself against the wall with the other. With his right hand still firm on the back of her neck, the left was free to roam, along her lower back and then up her side to cup the swell of her breast.

She jerked back slightly as his fingers brushed a taut nipple through her shirt, and he swore she moaned into his mouth.

So much for hating him. Her grip on his throat slowly eased, until her hands clutched his shoulders and she pushed her breast against his hand.

He eased his hand up her shirt, teased her nipples without barriers, and she moaned again, a soft, keening sound that vibrated through him as his fingers neared the promised land.

He slid a finger over the taut peak through the lace of her bra, and she pulled her mouth off his but stayed close, pressed her forehead to his and whispered, "God, that's good."

"It's going to get even better," he murmured as he unhooked the front clasp on the bra so he could worry one bare nipple between his finger and thumb, the way she'd done it herself. She clutched his shoulders hard, as if she was still fighting to stay in control and losing the battle fast, and then she let her hands wander down toward his waist. She yanked his T-shirt up, out of his pants, her cool palms like heaven against his overheated skin, and she kissed him again.

The right side of his body throbbed—sweet, aching agony as she sucked his bottom lip between her teeth and raked her nails lightly down both sides of his chest, pausing to play with the ring on his left nipple.

When he moved his hands down to the waist of her pants, her mouth moved off his, her lips lingering on his cheek and then his neck, and he got it—she was going to follow the tat down as far as it went. He wondered if she'd stop at the waist, catch her breath and get herself together, or if she'd follow the trail all the way down.

She eased away from his hand, which had nearly worked the zipper of her pants down, and reluctantly he let her. He was shivering, splitting nearly in two as she ran her tongue along his chest to trace the intricate tribal patterns that were coming alive under her caress.

When he'd come downstairs, his plan had been to tell her that they were pretty much screwed in this house, that Kat mentioned that the spirit didn't plan on letting them out, and that when he'd tried the doors and windows, they wouldn't open. He also had no cell service and the main phone lines were down.

He was going to have to force the spirit to talk to him more, the way it had earlier. Him, and not Annika. It was the only way to keep both her and Dev safe.

Whether they escaped now or later, the danger in the house was still the same. The closer Annika stayed to him, the safer she'd be.

Shit, he couldn't have made up a better excuse if he'd tried. He hadn't planned on getting screwed *this* way—although, hey, a man could dream. And Annika dropping to her knees in front of him was a definite sight worth seeing.

She traced the pattern under the waist of his pants with one finger while she used her other hand to unbutton and unzip the soft leather. She was going to be in for a few surprises, the first of which she seemed delighted with. He'd always found underwear to be overrated anyway.

She yanked the pants down to his ankles. He watched as she tried to take it all in at once, the way the tat wound around his right thigh and buttock, down his calf and across his foot.

But she hadn't gotten that far, because she was busy staring, openmouthed, at his dick.

"Oh, my God," she breathed. "How . . . Didn't this hurt?"

He shook his head slowly. "I was born with this."

Her hand caressed the right side of his shaft, decorated with the same types of patterns, and the rest of his explanation caught in his throat. He pulled in a harsh breath as she explored his balls, her hand pausing to cup the tattooed one.

"What are the symbols?"

"Native American in origin. And I don't have the patience to explain each and every one to you right now."

Her hand circled his cock, stroked it even as he leaned his head back against the wall and groaned. "That's nice, baby. You going to do some screaming for me?"

"I figured I'd even the score first," she said.

Evening a score had never felt so damned good, especially when she rolled her tongue around the head of his cock and his eyes rolled to the back of his skull.

"Yeah. Oh, yeah," he murmured, just as she shoved his thighs apart impatiently so she could gain easier access to his balls. Her tongue ran down the right side of his shaft, like she knew how much more sensitive it was, and she continued the path down to his right ball. She suckled it gently, took it inside her mouth, and his thighs began to shake.

A long, low moan escaped his throat. She laughed softly and did it again. Fuck, she wanted to hear him howl. And if she kept up this slow, sweet torture, that wasn't going to be a problem.

He brushed one hand over the silken bob of her hair, then let his fingers twine through the soft strands as if that could keep him from sinking to the ground as she took him deep into her mouth.

The warm, wet heat of her mouth and lips and tongue, combined with the way she alternately stroked his balls and suckled him, was rapidly causing him to lose control. As always in sexual situations beyond simple masturbation, his senses started to overload, and he began to straddle the line between pleasure and pain.

He was never sure which one would win out, but he knew that it was rarely pleasure. Sex was always a little bit like a game of Russian roulette. Sometimes, it would hurt less than others, but the hope for that perfect pleasure kept him in constant search-mode, made him resent Kat more and more, since she was at the root of it all.

Her way of reminding him not to get too close with any other women but her.

First, the roar began in his ears, shutting out any other sound, and then his sight began to dim. He closed his eyes to block that out, and lost his sense of smell.

You're shutting down, man.

His fingers went numb and he couldn't tell if his hands were still in her hair.

Sensation would be the last to go and he prayed that the feel of her mouth milking him would not fade away. Not this time.

And suddenly, he was aware of the light zing her fingers created as they dug into his right hip. His cock throbbed and he opened his eyes, and the roar in his ears stopped as he came, a shivering, screaming orgasm that pulsed pleasure to every single part of his body, until he was sure he'd pass out. And he might've too, for just a few seconds, but he caught himself before he slid down the wall completely.

Annika was already on her feet, and he reached out to her, to pull her close. Because he was more than prepared to finish this job.

"We're not done, Annika," he said, his voice rough and heavy.

She brushed her hair back from her face. "Uh, yeah, we're done. I figured if I took the edge off for you, you'd leave me alone."

She looked so serious, even though her cheeks were still flushed and her nipples taunted him through the thin fabric of her T-shirt. She wanted him, that much he knew. What was holding her back was an entirely different story.

"This is about Dev, isn't it?" he asked as he yanked his pants up.

ANNIKA SPUN BACK AROUND, her unspent lust sparking frustrated anger, but shit, she couldn't have sex with him, and she couldn't tell him the truth. Going down on him had been a bad idea. She'd hoped to disperse some of the raging sexual tension between them, but it seemed to have made things worse.

"Yeah," she said, looking him in the eye, because she was one hell of a great liar, "it is. I don't screw around on him."

"You've gotta be kidding me." He gaped at her like she was a fucking idiot. "You can't possibly think he's faithful to you."

"What I think is none of your business."

She pushed past him, but he seized her arm and brought her back around, his expression a conflicting mix of emotions. He respected Dev, but probably thought she was getting a raw deal. How stand-up of him.

"He's not, you know." His fingers tightened around her forearm, and she cursed her inability to shock him. Then again, if she could shock him, she'd never have allowed things between them to go as far as they just had. "He's in love with someone else. And he's got women. Shit, the other day I had to cool my heels for twenty minutes because Marlena was blowing him in his office."

"I don't care what he does with his secretary." Hell, she didn't care what Dev did with any of the women—and, occasionally, men—he slept with, because he always left them in bed to be with her when she showed up in the middle of the night. And yeah, she knew all about his long-lost love, more than even Dev probably realized she knew.

This wasn't really about Dev, though. This was about not sleeping with Creed, something she wanted badly enough to make the situation dangerous.

"You love him, don't you?"

She jerked out of his grip, looked him in the eye, and this time didn't have to lie. "Yes."

She loved him like a too-old brother or a too-young father. He was family, the only one she had. She'd slept with him more times than she could count, both of them fully clothed and tangled together on his couch, where they'd fallen asleep after she'd cried on his shoulder.

No one but Dev had seen her cry since she was a toddler. He alone knew her history, and he alone had managed to reach her when she'd been little more than a wild animal for months after ACRO rescued her. A danger to everyone, she'd been kept in isolation, and had done some serious damage to anyone who came within reach. Even Dev had suffered sprains, dislocations and electrical burns.

He could have had her put down. Instead, he'd saved her. First from the CIA, and then from herself.

"You're going to get hurt."

She laughed at that. "Why do you give a rat's ass? And don't tell me you care if my little heart gets broken."

"I care, because if Dev has you, no one else has a shot."

She didn't have time to be stunned by his admission, because he raked his gaze over her as he angled a little closer, close enough that she could smell leather and sweat and sex, making her wetter than she already was.

"Look," he said, his voice low and rough, "I don't know what's going on between you two, but he's not here. We are. And there's definitely something going on between us."

"Yeah, a few overheated hormones." She rolled her eyes with as much nonchalance as she could muster, when what she wanted to do was melt into a pool of nerves and lust. "I think we can handle it. We'll be home in a couple of days, you can find some biker chick in a local bar and get laid, I'll screw Dev and everything will be back to normal."

Except now nothing would ever be normal. She'd always wonder if Creed might be *the one*. The one who wouldn't end up in an ICU after messing around with her. Dev had spent days covering up that particular incident. But she wasn't seventeen anymore, and maybe...

She shook her head, because this line of thinking could only end in frustration. Her own. Creed's. Dev's when he had to contain the damage she caused or listen to her cry over something else.

Maybe she should call Haley. Annika had no friends, and while she couldn't call Haley one, the parameteorologist was one of the few people at ACRO who wasn't nervous around her, and she was a woman. Surely she'd had man trouble. Then again, she probably treated men like everything else, like they were mysteries to be solved. Weather to be predicted. She probably had charts and graphs that mapped out the male brain. That poor SEAL she'd been set upon was no doubt wondering from what planet Haley hailed. And that SEAL was also the reason Annika couldn't call Haley. They were both on missions, and personal problems needed to be put aside.

She looked at Creed, who watched her with a dark hunger in his eyes, and she nearly groaned, because putting him aside wasn't going to be easy.

And she wasn't sure she even wanted to.

CHAPTER
Fourteen

Now they were going to get down to it. Remy watched Haley's face carefully, because he'd finally started to get some answers, some real answers. Not just the I-like-ball-lightning-and-come-work-for-my-secret-superpower-bullshit-agency explanations she'd been feeding him over the past fifteen hours while she stroked him and Mother Nature simultaneously fucked him.

He'd like nothing better than to show her what exactly that entailed, but more than ever, he needed to remain calm. In control. He'd been trained to do so by the Navy, and he did not plan on giving up any more without shaking Haley Holmes down for some intel. Because whatever the agency she worked for was all about, he wanted to know.

This parameteorologist might be able to handle him in bed, but he was sure she wouldn't be prepared for his methods of interrogation.

And she didn't look prepared, at least not for the unveiling of his tattoo. She just sat there, stared at his hip and then his face and then back down to the ink again. And then she stood and took a small step to close the distance between them, not seeming to notice the way the slip of a boat rocked.

She touched the slightly raised brand, tentatively at first, and then she traced a finger around the reddened edge, just like he'd been doing to hers. Remy forced his breathing to remain even as last night's events came roaring back into his consciousness.

First he'd tried to control the storm, and then it had grabbed him by the throat and rolled him worse than a hungry gator. He'd lost that battle and obviously his fucking mind as well, since he'd showed off his weather shit like he was a circus sideshow freak. And now he knew the partial truth about what Haley wanted from him.

"Where did that come from?" she whispered, as if anyone but the gators could hear them this far out into the swamps.

"I'm waiting for you to tell me that."

"I don't...I mean...Holy shit." She looked up at him, seemed to realize that she was standing in the middle of the boat—on very shaky ground in many senses of the word. She reached out and grabbed him hard, her fingers digging into the skin on his bare biceps, and he steadied her by placing his hands on her hips.

"If you keep rocking like that, we're both going into the water," he said, and although it wasn't a bad master plan as plans went, he'd end up having to rescue her eventually.

"Remy, you have to believe me when I tell you, I had nothing to do with that tattoo. Nothing."

"I don't have to do anything you tell me, *bebe*. And for the record, I don't believe you either."

She pushed back from him, and the pirogue rocked again. He was used to a sway much larger than this, and even though Haley wasn't, she stood her ground. She started unbuttoning her shorts and he went hard at the sight of her exposed hip.

"They look the same," she was saying.

"Yeah, I noticed," he started, but stopped abruptly. It was his turn to stare at Haley's once-smooth tattoo, which was now raw and scabbed. Just like his. "Jesus, what happened? Did I do that?"

"No, you didn't. You didn't hurt me. Not once." She looked at him earnestly, and he remembered the way she'd looked last night, illuminated by the lightning, coming over and over in his arms. He remembered losing control and not worrying that this time there was no one there to catch him.

"There's got to be more you're not telling me, dammit." His voice came out louder than he'd intended. He wanted to grab her and shake her by the shoulders to get her to spill, but a bigger part of him wondered if maybe it was better that he didn't know everything.

"Lie down," she said suddenly.

"I don't think this is the best place to—"

"Lie. Down," she repeated, and there was a fire in her eyes that told him he shouldn't bother to argue.

He shoved the pole deep into the murky water and tied the anchoring line around it to keep them from floating off too far. Then he removed the seat from one end of the boat in order to make room for his body, and eased himself to the deck.

She'd been sitting again while he maneuvered himself, was gripping the sides of the boat hard until he was flat on his back. Then she got onto her knees and half crawled to him. She began to spread herself out over him, placing her palms down right above his shoulders, and leveraged herself above him until his arousal was pressed right between her legs.

For a long moment, they just stared at each other, and Remy wasn't sure if he was ever going to be able to trust anything that came out of her mouth again. Not that it would make her much different from anyone else in his life, but he'd wanted her to be different, although he hadn't realized it until this moment.

"Look at this," she was saying. She'd eased off him slightly, putting more of her weight onto her right side. He propped up on one elbow and looked down. She pointed toward her tattoo and then at his. "Watch," she said softly, lowering herself down.

Remy watched as the two tattoos headed toward each other, a perfectly matched pair when they were in this very familiar position. He waited until she lowered herself onto him all the way and neither of them could see the tattoos anymore.

"I have no idea how this happened. You have to believe me about that. There's no way I could've done this to you while you were sleeping," she said.

"Maybe your supersecret agency did it while I slept," he said, and she furrowed her brow and shook her head, although it didn't look like she was all that convinced it couldn't have happened. And if it had, what the hell kind of place was he being asked to work for anyway?

"I'll ask one more time, Haley, and I want an answer," he said. "Tell me what's really going on here."

"I told you what I know. I work for an agency—"

"Of freaks. Yeah, I got that. Where is it? Who runs it? What's its purpose?"

"They're not freaks. You're not a freak."

"Christ, you're not going to try to turn this into a therapy session, are you? Because I don't usually fuck people who try to mind-fuck me. It's too complicated, and I don't need any more complications in my life than I already have." He tried to move her off of him, but she didn't budge easily. "I'll roll you right into the water if I have to."

"Go ahead. But if I drown, you'll never get the answers you want," she said.

"Oh, I'll make sure you don't drown, *bebe*. You'll just get waterlogged, and then you'll beg me—"

"The way you begged me last night, Remy?" she asked. He noticed her breathing had become quicker, as had his. He was pushing his arousal up into her as she continued. "Last night, out in the rain, you didn't even realize what you were saying. Begging me to hold you and make you come."

"And you did that."

"I did. And now I'm telling you what you need to know. I can't tell you the name and location of the agency until you agree to give it a chance. Then you'll be taken to a secure location to meet with the agency's head, where you can ask all the questions you want."

"How many freaks are there?"

"We currently employ about five hundred *people*. Not all of them are Special Operatives. And so far, none of them can do what you do."

"So, what, I'm a freak among freaks?" he asked, and then held up a hand. "You know what? Don't answer that."

He put his head back, closed his eyes and let the gentle rock of the pirogue soothe him.

When he was younger, eight or so, he used to sneak into the swamp at night, take this old pirogue and push her through the muddy waters until his arms ached and sweat ran down his back and he was far enough from shore that anything seemed possible.

Most times, he wished he'd just get picked up by a group of pirates or bandits and taken away to places that could give him the action and adventure he craved, away from people who knew him.

He hadn't found it until he entered the SEALs, and even that hadn't lasted nearly as long as he'd hoped. This agency Haley talked about was just another team setting, and there was no way in hell it was going to work. Besides, he'd already gotten messages from two firms looking for mercs. Looking for him.

We heard you were one of the best.... We need men who can think on their feet ... function independently.

Of course, if he couldn't function in a team setting, he had no hope for the most intimate kind of team there was. But he'd always known that anyway.

He had nothing left to lose, except he didn't plan on acquiring anything else *to* lose. Ever.

"The agency ... there are people there who can teach you things. I can teach you things," she said.

He shifted slightly under the weight of her body, which made the pirogue rock. She grabbed his shoulders and he pushed up on both elbows, forcing her into a straddling position.

"Like what? What the hell can you do to make anything different?" he asked.

"Did you ever stop to think that maybe there's a way you can keep it from controlling you? A way you can learn to actually use it more effectively?" she asked, and he let out a long, bitter laugh.

"Control it? I don't want it at all, Haley. Don't want to harness it, encourage it, or think about it," he said.

"That's not true. You have harnessed it. I've seen you do it."

"Trick of the trade," he muttered. "Can I get up now? We really do need to get gas before dark hits this place."

"Remy ..."

"I don't want to talk about this. Not now. We got a long way to ride, *bebe,* and somehow I don't think you want to do that in the dark."

She pushed off him reluctantly, zipping up her shorts, and disappointment settled in his stomach. And other places. He followed suit, but not before staring down at the tattoo, much in the same way he had when he'd discovered it. Then he began to push-pole through the water.

Last night, he'd been asleep less than an hour when the soreness woke him, and in the lamplight he'd brought into the bathroom with him, he saw what he'd thought was a bruise.

When he'd realized that he'd been tattooed without his consent, he'd barely contained his fury. But he did, mainly because he didn't want to wake up Haley with a storm caused by his rage. No, he'd had other plans. He'd stalked out to Haley's equipment and tried to gain some much-needed intel. He'd been unsuccessful in breaking into the heavily passcoded and secure machines, mainly because his diverted anger channeled itself into an electric impulse that shorted out the wiring and killed the long-life battery.

First thing you do to the enemy is you cut off comms, then supplies, and finally the escape route. Now that all three had been taken care of and he had some answers, he still wasn't sure what to do.

"You planned this, me coming here?" he asked, not bothering to turn around to her. He eased them through the murky swamp under some low cypress tree branches and just concentrated on forward motion.

"Yes. This was planned. I needed to meet you."

"Where's my old man, then?" he asked.

"I'm not sure where he went."

"But you said he was all right the last time you saw him. Was that true?"

"Yes, he was fine, Remy. He was the reason you were discovered."

He turned to face her. "You gave him money, didn't you?"

"Yes."

"Figures." He paused when he heard the laughter coming from around the bend. Old Joe sold gas and supplies from a small shack sitting right on his family's property. The main house was a big, ramshackle beauty that was home sweet home to Joe's wife, one son and six daughters. A family far enough away from Remy and his own daily drama that they shouldn't recognize him after eight years away.

If he didn't call up a storm, they'd be all right. He'd held it together for this long, he could do it for another half hour.

THE SOUND OF MUSIC and laughter punctuated by the sharp crack of fireworks grew louder as Remy guided them through the swamp. He'd shut down after their conversation, his expression discouraging further talk, so Haley passed the time by studying storm damage; the scattered fallen branches and bent trees didn't compare to the beating the Begnaud house had taken.

Mother Nature seemed to have a bone to pick with Remy.

Through the curtain of tree trunks and moss-draped limbs, Haley spied a boathouse and dock, which Remy angled the bow of the boat toward. As they approached, the aroma of roasting pork and pungent spice replaced the smell of stagnant bayou, making her mouth water.

The pirogue bumped up against the dock, and someone shouted. A lot of someones, actually. From Haley's estimation, there were at least a hundred people, of all ages, mingling, dancing and setting off fireworks in a sprawling backyard. A barbecue pit burned steadily in the side yard, and two huge tents had been set up nearby, one housing tables and chairs, the other providing cover for long tables of food.

Remy waved and secured the boat to the pier. Several people raised their glasses in greeting—surprising, given last night's angry mob scene.

"They seem...welcoming," she said.

"Different parish. I haven't been back here in eight years. Plus, they're mostly three sheets to the wind." He held out his hand, and she took it, stepped carefully onto the creaky boards.

"What are we doing here?"

"You said you were hungry."

"We're going to crash the wedding?"

"Not crash, we're invited." He pointed to where some guys holding beer cans waved wildly.

She arched a brow at him. "Drunk people waving equals an invitation?"

"Around here it does."

"Right. So what's the plan? I distract them with my fascinating meteorological knowledge and you siphon gas out of one of the vehicles?"

He fixed her with a flat stare. Like she'd been serious. "These people own a country store and a one-pump gas station."

They'd barely made it off the dock when a group of men, some in shorts and tees and some in various states of formal dress, approached.

"T-Remy. Been a few years," said a wiry guy with a goatee. His red-stained tuxedo shirt hung loose around his waist and gaped open at the chest—clearly, the party had been going on for a while.

Remy nodded warily and angled closer to her, like he expected trouble. God, had people treated him so badly during the course of his life that he automatically assumed the worst? It made her want to hug him, protect him, which was ridiculous, because she'd never met a man more capable of protecting himself.

"I hope we're not interrupting," Remy said.

The guy's gaze drifted to the can in the boat. "Only if you're here for gas."

Haley sensed more than saw Remy go taut, but before he could reply, goatee guy grinned. "Man, this is a party. I got married!" His buddies whooped and clanked their plastic cups and beer bottles together, spilling liquid onto their clothes and shoes. "So here's the thing: I'll get my dad to open up the shop for you, but only after you join us for some gumbo and bounce."

Remy shook his head and smiled in a way that made her suck in an admiring breath. He hadn't smiled like that for her, and a ridiculous twinge of jealousy pinched at her.

"David, you always were a little touched in the head."

David laughed and gestured to a woman dressed in what could only be described as gypsy garb and a bridal veil. She hurried over, followed by a gaggle of similarly dressed women.

"This is my wife, Amber." David hooked her tenderly around the neck and pulled her close. "We did sort of a gypsy-themed thing to honor her wacky side of the family."

She gave him a playful punch in the gut. "Speaking of wacky, your paw-paw wants help fixing the roof leak." She finally spared Remy and Haley a look. "These your friends?"

David and Remy exchanged uncertain glances. "We went to high school together for a while. Will you take his girlfriend and introduce her around?"

Before Haley could protest either the girlfriend thing or the offer for introductions, Amber grabbed her arm and dragged her toward the house. "What's your name?"

"Haley, but I—"

"C'mon, girl, we'll get you ready to party."

Remy vanished with the guys as though she'd never existed, so Haley allowed Amber and friends to take her inside the house. They led her to a frilly bedroom strewn with suitcases, where they played dress-up and chatted about honeymoons, something Haley never planned to have, even if some small part of her wondered if she'd regret her decision.

The rest of the chatter was drowned out by her own thoughts, ones like how the hell Remy had been branded with a mirror image of her tattoo. She hadn't marked him, and she doubted he'd been responsible, so that left outside influences.

She'd worked at ACRO long enough to know that anything was possible, but could ACRO have arranged something like this from a distance? And if they had, why?

"Close your eyes."

Haley sighed, waited while Amber applied eye shadow and mascara. It felt weird. She hadn't worn makeup since the time her Air Force station chief had forced her to attend a unit award ceremony.

"Voilà!" Amber stepped away, and Haley nearly fell over when she looked in the mirror.

The woman staring back at her wasn't a plain-faced scientist who'd grown up with hippie-granola parents. Haley had never in her life worn blue eye shadow or glittery mascara, let alone a bright yellow blouse and a red, gauzy skirt. Dark, crisp pantsuits had always been her style. If her weather station staff saw her now, they'd laugh themselves into coronaries.

"You're gorgeous," Amber said. "Your boyfriend isn't going to know what hit him."

"He's not—"

She cut herself off. Amber had been excited to do this, and it was her wedding day, so Haley didn't have the heart to disappoint her. Besides, she hadn't had a boyfriend in … well, years. Pretending for a couple of hours wouldn't kill her.

Her mind flashed back to the many ways Remy had held her, kissed her, looked at her so possessively—pretending to be his wouldn't be a hardship.

The problem would be tamping down the tiny voice that wanted it to be true.

CREED HAD THOUGHT ABOUT PUSHING IT, about grabbing Annika and pulling her back toward him, and he almost did. She did want him—he could tell by the way she'd licked her bottom lip when she'd looked at him, by the way her nipples had still been hard beneath the thin cotton of her T-shirt. And he'd never, ever been able to experience his own pleasure unless he brought himself to orgasm. The idea that maybe the one woman he most wanted was the one who could break this spell Kat had him in was enough to make him weak-kneed. Again.

But when the floor beneath his feet had begun to vibrate with an intensity he knew could neither be good nor related to sex, he moved away from the wall and closer to her to let whatever was pushing through know that Annika was off-limits.

He had enough trouble with flesh-and-blood men wanting Annika, he wasn't about to let a ghost take him down. At least not a ghost he didn't know. His own spirit would be the biggest obstacle, but he'd cross that bridge when he got to it.

"What's going on?" she asked, and he noted that she'd instinctively moved closer to him. At her words, the entire house seemed to shudder, and a loud crash emanated from upstairs.

Annika moved on reflex to pull her gun, and then realized what she'd done. She reholstered it quickly. "Maybe we should get out of here."

"Yeah, well, there's one problem with that plan. We're trapped here," he said, and the ghost slammed a picture off the wall in the foyer as if to confirm what he said was true.

Still, she looked at Creed in disbelief and marched over to the front door as if she'd had it—both with this house and with him. And as much as he would've loved to have been wrong and have the door open when she touched it, he knew it wouldn't.

She tugged and then played with the lock before tugging again. Then she threw him a look over her shoulder.

"Why aren't you talking to it?" she asked as she walked over to try a window. Same deal.

"I'm waiting on Quaty to come back—she helps me to

communicate. That's why this ghost is frustrated—it's trying to reveal something to me, but I can't understand much of what it's saying." Kat had hightailed it out of there after his nap, pissed as hell at him for watching Annika in the shower but also spooked from the house's ghost. Which was never a good sign, because Kat was rarely afraid of anything. Even the blow job didn't bring her back. No, he'd need something bigger.

"I thought the Bell Witch's name was Kate Betts," she said, and for a second he wondered why Annika would bother having researched the Bell Witch.

"That's a rumor," he scoffed. "And completely wrong. The spirit's name is Quaty, but everyone who heard it misinterpreted it and thought she said Katie instead."

"But I've heard you call her Kat."

"I do that because it pisses her off."

She snorted, like she understood Kat's stance all too well. "So how do you get your spirit back once you've pissed her off?" she asked.

"There's only one surefire way I know that works."

"Care to share?"

"Sex."

"Sex?" she repeated. "You mean, if you and I get it on, your spirit will magically appear?"

"Yes. Kat's extremely possessive."

"She didn't show up when I was blowing you," Annika pointed out.

"She will, once I'm inside of you," he said.

She pressed her lips together and shook her head slowly. As if she really, really wanted to kill him. "So once you're inside me, we'll have two pissed-off spirits in the house?"

"Got any better ideas?"

She started pacing and then stopped right in front of him. "Okay, first of all, does that line work?"

"What line?"

"The whole sleep-with-me-if-you-want-to-see-my-spirit line? Do you use it on all the women you're with?"

"I don't have to use it on other women—they all want to sleep with me on their own accord," he said, and could've sworn he saw a hint of jealousy in her eyes.

He'd told the truth in this case—Kat would be pissed if he slept with Annika. Because he'd wanted to for a while, dreamed about her, even, and that would certainly cause a ghost snit.

"You know, I could tell Dev that you're being extremely inappropriate."

"You paying me back for the last mission, Annika?" he asked. "Because I think you and I both know I did the right thing. I might want you—badly—but I'd never do anything to compromise a job. Ever."

"And you think I would?"

"You have before," he said quietly—and yeah, this was so not the way to get laid. Or get into Annika's heart.

Her hands fisted and raised, and he merely held up his own hands.

"I don't want to talk about what happened on that mission," she said finally. "I just want to get the hell out of here. The option you mentioned isn't viable, so find another."

"We can wait it out, but this spirit is pretty stubborn," he said. "It's been here a long time—fifty years, at least. It knows a lot of secrets and it wants to share some of them."

"Obviously you can communicate with the damned thing—" she started, and another painting flew off the wall in warning.

"It doesn't like to be cursed at."

"And I don't like being locked in some place without my consent!" she yelled at the ceiling above the window at the top of the stairs, where he'd told her the portal was. And before he could stop her, she'd started to climb the main stairs, which was a really, really bad idea.

"Annika, come down from there," he called.

"I don't have to listen to you. Maybe this thing wants to talk to me. I'll listen. We can bargain."

"You know as well as I do that spirits don't work like that," he said, but she was too far gone.

He wasn't sure if she was more upset by his suggestion of sleeping with him, or the fact that she *wanted* to sleep with him. And if her love for Dev was the reason—well, for some reason that wasn't exactly ringing true to him. Or maybe he wanted her so badly that he'd chosen not to care about how his boss was going to react.

He took two deliberate steps toward the stairs, glancing back and forth between the pictures on the wall in case they decided to fly at him. Of course, the elaborate—and enormous—crystal chandelier that hung directly above him was something he kept an eye on as well.

The matching one—a tiny bit smaller but still just as deadly—hung at the top of the stairs, which Annika was rapidly approaching. He looked up and saw the plaster around the base of the chandelier was cracking.

With lightning speed, he was up the stairs, locking an arm around her waist and rolling with her down the steps, even as the heavy ornament came crashing down at the top of the stairs, shattering as it went and continuing to roll directly at them.

Creed got to his feet and dragged Annika with him into the safety of the hallway between the foyer and the kitchen. She shook slightly, but she was unharmed, except for the bruises they were both going to be feeling from their fall.

"Dammit. Dev's going to kill me," she said, trying to get her legs under her. But he wasn't ready for her to go back to normal just yet.

He took her by the shoulders, which she squared under his touch, and he looked directly into her beautiful blue eyes. "You need to listen more," he said fiercely. "There are people who have your best interests in mind. Who want to help you, if you'll just let them in."

He knew the basics about Annika—the bare bones about how she'd been raised and why she'd been brought to ACRO. That explained a lot about why she didn't trust, but until she did, although she might become a great operative, she wasn't ever going to be whole. And Creed didn't think that was any way for her to live.

"And you're one of those people?" she asked, her voice softer than he'd ever heard it.

"Yes, I am."

She stared at him for a long minute before she spoke again. "Go to hell, Creed," she said, twisting away from him and taking off up the back stairs before he had a chance to stop her.

CHAPTER
Fifteen

Remy Begnaud Sr. didn't need to do his drinking at the ramshackle dive bar he'd frequented for years, not now that the Haley girl had paid him a handsome sum in exchange for T.

He'd tried hanging out in classier places than the Bayou Lantern, had bought the Widow Johnson fancy-shmancy cocktails at all of them, but he'd been so far out of his element he might as well have been on the moon.

Besides, he thought, as he downed a shot of whiskey and followed it with a beer back, when he passed out here, no one called the cops. And today Widow Johnson had made it clear that she didn't want to be called either.

"Eh, Remy, how dat boy o' yous?"

A heavy hand came down on Remy's back, and Leon Breaux, a flabby old geezer who talked like his jaw had been wired shut, swung onto a stool at the bar beside him.

"Ain't seen him," Remy said, even though it wasn't true—he'd gone to see T earlier, but T'd had the meteorologist in the pirogue and the situation didn't look welcoming.

"I hear tell he back. Done brung dat storm wit 'im."

Remy signaled Ross, the bartender and owner, for another round of whiskey and beer. "Ain't my problem, Leon. I told you, I ain't seen him."

But he had, over and over. In the nightmares that had plagued him every night since he'd cashed the meteorologist's check. His boy came to his dreams, accusing, asking why his daddy had sold him out. No matter how hard he tried to tell T it was for his own good, nothing changed. The dreams always ended the same way, with T sending a bolt of lightning into Remy Senior's body, vaporizing him with a sizzle.

Ross came back with the drinks, and Remy swallowed them both, his hand so shaky he spilled down the front of his wifebeater. He loved his kid, dammit, and he wanted what was best for him. Maybe he wouldn't win the Father of the Year award, but he'd given T food and shelter, things he himself hadn't grown up with.

And he'd never, ever treated T like he was nothing but an inconvenience. Truth be told, the boy had probably saved Remy Senior's life, kept him from doing something stupid after he lost Fay Lynne.

And you repaid him by selling his secret.

Remy shook his head, tried to force the words out of his brain, but all they did was rattle around inside his skull. Damn it all to hell. Why should he feel guilty? T owed him for taking him in when no one else would. Remy deserved every cent of the money he got from the woman, what with all the times he'd had to save the kid from being lynched.

He laughed out loud, because wasn't it funny how no matter how many times you told yourself something, you still didn't believe it. He didn't think he could get drunk enough to talk himself into believing he deserved the money. Not when T knew nothing about it.

Tomorrow, first thing in the morning, he was going to go

make things right with his son. Tell him the truth. Tell him he loved him. Hand the money right back to Miss Haley.

Well, he'd play that last part by ear.

"Eh, Remy? You okay?"

He blinked, realized he'd gone someplace he shouldn't have, and now the other man stared at him like he might be a bit worried.

"Leave me alone, Leon."

Leon clapped him on the back again and stood. "You need a ride, you lemme know." He ambled off toward a pool table near the back, where his buddies Billy and Lloyd were arguing over a missed shot.

Remy eyed the entrance, wondering if he'd go through it tonight on his own two feet, because that hadn't happened lately. The door swung open, and he laid bets with himself that Crawfish Matthews would be the one coming in, but he lost that wager by a mile.

It wasn't a crusty old crawdaddy farmer who walked inside, no sir-ee. It was some kind of angel, and all heads turned to watch a little ray of heaven put a shine on the dull character of the seedy tavern.

She looked around as though she'd never been there, and he was sure she hadn't. He'd have remembered a rack like that.

Her gaze fixed on him, and he swallowed hard as she walked purposefully toward him, her hiking boots thumping on the floor, her long, slim legs flexing inside tight-fitting jeans. Her sleeveless, button-down blouse just brushed the waistband of her pants, and when she dragged her fingers through her blond hair, he caught a glimpse of abs ripped like a bodybuilder's.

Day-*yam*.

She parked her pretty ass next to Remy but didn't have a chance to say anything, because Ross tripped all over himself offering her a drink. On him. Somewhere, pigs had sprouted wings.

She shook her head, and Ross's expression fell like a coon shot from a tree. Hell, Remy thought Ross would cry when the angel turned to him.

"Are you Remy Begnaud?"

Yankee accent, so she wasn't from around here. "Mebbe. Who's asking?" he replied, hoping his words hadn't sounded as slurred to her as they had to him.

"My name's Karen Anderson. I work with Haley Holmes."

His gut took a dive to his feet. "She said she was working alone."

The woman nodded. "Change in plans. There's . . . a problem."

"What happened?" Stomach knotting with fear, he clutched Karen's arm. "Where's T?"

"He's at the house. Something's wrong. He's upset and calling for you." She leaned forward and lowered her voice. "We can't get him to turn off the weather."

Remy stood, wobbled, but caught himself on the bar top. "I gotta get to him."

"Wait," she said, looping her arm around his waist. "I'll drive."

He stumbled once or twice on the way to the door, but she was surprisingly strong, held him up like she was a two-hundred-pound linebacker and not a skinny, top-heavy woman who couldn't stand taller than about five-seven.

They stepped out into the humid night air, and she guided him toward the alley. "Parking lot's the other way," he said.

"It was full. I had to park in the back."

"Oh. Okay." Strange. There hadn't been many customers inside, but before he could think too hard on why the lot would be full, the hair on the back of his neck prickled.

Miss Karen had developed an accent, one he couldn't place, but it sounded European. Russian, maybe.

"Wait," he said, slowing. "Who did you say you work for?"

"I will explain on the way."

"I don't think so."

She pulled to a halt and shook her head, not looking at him. "You couldn't simply be a good drunk and follow along."

What came next was a blur of movement and sound and pain. Karen grabbed his arm and yanked it so hard behind his back that he heard a crack, felt a white-hot, searing stab of agony that brought tears to his eyes. A man came from nowhere, clapped a hand over Remy Senior's mouth before he could cry out, and another threw him into the trunk of a car. His arms and legs were useless, bound in some way, though no one had tied him up.

"Hurry," Miss Karen said, "I need a shower after stepping foot in that place." She cursed, a hard, disgusting oath that shouldn't come out of any lady's mouth. "Hakata will pay for sending me on this hick assignment."

From where she stood near the bumper, she peered at Remy with a grin that shriveled his privates until he figured they were hiding up inside his belly. "And you will pay for making me touch you, you insect."

Her fist crunched into his mouth with a sickening, wet thud, and he tasted blood.

"Where's Remy?"

He spit out a tooth and tested a loose canine with his tongue. "Who are you?"

"I ask the questions, asshole."

Her second blow connected with his ribs, and fiery pain engulfed his chest. He coughed, inhaled air in shallow gasps that sucked blood into his windpipe and stung his lungs.

"Let's try this again. Remy's not at the house. Where would he go?"

"Don't know," he wheezed through his split, swollen lips. "Ain't talked to him in years."

A man standing next to the woman reached for the trunk hood. "He's lying, Oksana."

"Really? No shit?" She shot the guy an irritated glare. "I'm so glad Hakata sent a psychic to tell us the obvious." Rolling her eyes, she bent over Remy until her boobs filled his blurry vision. "We can set traps, but if you just tell us where he is, this will go easier on both of you."

"Fuck. You."

She snarled, a nasty, feral sound. Her fist came at his face in slow motion, and then the world went black.

THANKS TO OBSCENELY EXPOSED CLEAVAGE and the sheer, flowing skirt, insecurity followed Haley like a stray dog as she searched the party for Remy. If she lost him now, she'd be in too much trouble to measure on any of her equipment.

She made her way to the huge tent where tables laden with Cajun and Creole cuisine were lined up in rows. No tall former SEAL to be found, but food overflowed from silver serving dishes, and her stomach was growling. She'd eat while she wandered around in search of her charge.

"Tsk-tsk, *chere*." A ruddy-faced man with a thick Cajun accent stopped her as she passed a giant tub full of liquid. "Why don't you have one of Leo's special drinks?"

"I, uh..."

He gave a dramatic shake of the head and filled a plastic cup with ice from the chest at his feet. "You don't want to offend me, now, do you?"

She laughed, charmed by the little man who wore only his tuxedo pants, and suspenders over his barrel chest. No shoes, no shirt, not even a watch. "I certainly do not want to offend you."

"Good girl." He filled the cup with red liquid from the tub.

"This here is cherry bounce. A little bit of this, a little bit of that, a tree full of cherries and a tanker truck of white lightning."

"White lightning? That sounds like my kind of drink."

He winked. "*Laissez les bon temp rouler, chere*. Let the good times roll."

She thanked Leo, and keeping an eye out for Remy, she nibbled on sweet beignets and spicy crawfish while she walked around the party, until she ended up on the grassy slope where people danced. Surely Remy wasn't dancing....

She tossed her empty plate into a nearby trash can, but held on to her drink, which turned out to be pretty tasty.

The earthy sound of the music strummed low in her belly, the slow beat tugging at something deep in her soul. The cherry bounce, full of what Leo had called "white lightning," lived up to its name, streaking through her veins like a live wire, sparking nerve endings all over her body. Sensation wrapped around her until she could feel everything—the sultry air, the vibrations from the French accordion...the very night itself seemed to caress her skin.

Around her, the celebration bloomed like a moonflower, as though the wedding revelers had been waiting for dusk to let loose. People had been dancing when she and Remy arrived, but by now, jackets and shoes had come off, ties were loosened or abandoned and several had changed into casual clothing.

Haley kicked off her own boots, and even now as she moved to the music, she wanted to rid herself of the rest of her clothing. The fabric plastered to her body, a barrier between her and the raw essence of the night, where insects and frogs sang from the surrounding bayou, audible between the band's songs.

Grass tickled her toes as she closed her eyes and let herself sway in the center of the dancers. She had no idea where Remy had gone off to, but she wondered if he'd join her, would fit his body to hers the way so many of the couples next to her were doing.

They could pretend to be a couple, pretend to be more than casual lovers. Squeezing her eyes shut, she drew herself into the fantasy, imagined his breath caressing her cheek, his hands pulling her against him until their bodies met and the friction between them caused smoke.

Sweet mercy, she could float around in that fantasy for forever, and for a few minutes she let everything go—her job, her life—and wished they could stay here in the bayou a little while longer.

Lost in her imaginary world, she didn't feel the tug on her dress at first. Then something stepped on her foot, and she looked down to see a small girl, maybe five or so, smiling up at her.

"Dance?"

"I'd love to."

Haley took the child's hand and whirled her around, had the time of her life for a couple of songs, and then someone grabbed her, and she twirled through the crowd, trading partners and enjoying herself like never before. When a strong hand grasped hers and pulled her close, she grinned.

But it wasn't Remy. She peered up at the teen, lanky and tall, straddling the border between boy and man. She tried to picture Remy at a similar age, enjoying himself and trying to pick up women, but something told her he'd skipped this, had gone from kid—if he'd ever truly been one—to man overnight.

She certainly couldn't picture him grabbing her butt as awkwardly as this boy was doing now. She peeled his fingers from her body but held on to his hand. The kid's cheeks burned red, a cute combination of embarrassment and guilt.

"Let me give you a piece of advice, Randy."

"It's Jacob, ma'am."

"Whatever." She pulled him against her, forcing him to

dance. "See, women hate to be groped like that. You'll never get laid if you run around molesting us."

She turned him toward a threesome of teenage girls near the water's edge. "See that blonde with the braids? She's been staring at you. Go ask her to dance, but don't touch her on any part of her body that would be covered by a conservative bathing suit. Okay? Trust me, you'll get a lot further than if you grab her ass like a caveman."

The kid's cheeks turned the color of her cherry drink. "Yes, ma'am. Thank you, ma'am."

He ambled off, and she grinned as he and the blonde joined the crowd. She looked around for Remy, and was finally rewarded with a glimpse of him near the food pavilion, a plate in hand, talking with David. Remy leaned casually against a support pole, appearing relaxed, not a care in the world, but she knew he had his eye on everything and everyone, and he knew exactly where she was, even though he never once glanced in her direction.

Damn, he was fine. Chiseled, hard features, sleek, powerful muscles and an aura of danger and competence that made women drool and back away at the same time.

She drooled, but she'd never back away. In fact, she should go to him, tell him they needed to get back. But moving to the music felt too good to stop. Too freeing. Too . . . sexy.

The gauzy skirt wrapped around her legs, molding to her shape, brushing her inner thighs in the lightest of caresses. She'd never felt so sexy in her life.

Or so hot.

She held her cup to her forehead, let the cool contents ease her fever. She dragged it down her cheek, to her throat, then her chest. The condensation dripped down the cup and onto her skin, tickling and cooling as it trickled between her breasts.

Throwing her head back, she rolled her hips, let herself feel the night, the music, the sensation of cold drink on fevered flesh. No doubt they'd leave soon, and then it was back to the job.

The job that no longer included screwing Remy for science.

A pang of regret wrenched in her gut. She didn't need science as an excuse to sleep with him; she'd do it anyway. But would he want to, now that Mother Nature wasn't messing with him? Probably not, and the idea that she'd been nothing more than a receptacle hadn't bothered her until now.

Sure, he'd been fiercely aroused as he lay beneath her in the boat, but he was a man. A man with a woman straddling him. If he hadn't gotten an erection she'd have wondered about him.

But could he truly desire her now, especially knowing how she'd lied to him?

And why did she care?

Maybe because although she'd had boyfriends, none had ever wanted her the way Remy had.

Needed, not wanted, you idiot.

She sighed and took a drink of her cherry stuff, her eyes still closed. When she opened them, Remy was staring at her. She couldn't breathe, could hardly swallow.

The twilight shadows concealed the intent in his gaze, but nothing could hide the intensity. Around her, the darkness swallowed the party until she could see only Remy. The laughter and music faded until all she heard was the beat of her own heart pounding in her ears. Her tattoo tingled and burned, and she thought back to all the other times it had done the same, and suddenly, she understood what it meant.

Remy wanted sex.

And there was nary a storm to be seen.

CHAPTER
Sixteen

It had been a long time since Remy had wanted sex, because normally he didn't have a chance to want. To desire. To feel. No, it was always a driving, pulsing need that tore through him like the hurricanes he always seemed to be right in the center of.

But seeing Haley, her body swaying to the zydeco beat, the flowing skirt brushing her calves and damned near see-through, the way the neckline of the peasant blouse accentuated her full breasts . . .

He ached for her when he should be running from her—far away. And he couldn't decide which feeling was going to win out. He wanted her, but the idea, the feeling of being a normal man was almost too overwhelming for him. He shifted, the bulge in his pants becoming more obvious. His tattoo began to draw attention to itself, to tingle and burn, and he saw Haley had her hand pressed against her own tattoo.

The air was different around here. He hadn't actually lied when he'd told her earlier that the bayou was a magical place. He'd always believed it was, now more than ever.

That same magic connected him to another person in a way

he couldn't begin to understand. And he was strangely calm about it.

The physical exertion of fixing the roof had released some of the tension he'd been holding on to since discovering the tattoo, but the work was nowhere near what he should've needed to relax. He'd had one drink, and although the brew was strong, it wasn't nearly enough.

He wondered how they could know about his drawings, his dreams, what he'd wished for so long ago that it almost seemed like it had happened in a different lifetime.

The true love spell one of his father's girlfriends had taught him had come first. A childish whim of a lonely kid playing with something he didn't understand and wishing so hard for a girl who could understand him. The drawing in his sleep had come next—always the symbol that was Haley's tattoo that he'd included in the spell as a way for him to actually tell when that true love arrived, drawn crudely at first, perfected in his waking hours when he spent his time coming up with comic book characters. Superheroes.

But he wasn't paper and pen or that same little boy. No, he was flesh and blood man, mixed with magic. And he didn't need a tattoo to let him know how he was starting to feel about Haley.

When a slow, steady beat began to play and couples started to melt into each other, Haley motioned for him to come closer.

He pushed away from the tree and ambled toward her, his pace deliberate. Predatory.

He stood before her for a second before taking her into his arms, pressing his body to hers, their hips swaying together as one unit.

"The bayou seems to agree with you, *chere*," he murmured.

"I didn't think there was this much fun to be had in a swamp," she said. She held up her wrist to show him the ribbon she'd tied around it. From the end dangled a fake gold wedding band. "I pulled the lucky trinket from the cake."

He chuckled softly. "The women always think that's the lucky trinket. The guys don't always have the same reaction."

She smiled up at him. "Your friends are nice."

"They're not my friends."

"They seem to like you."

He smiled. "I guess they do."

"I like you too, T-Remy," she said. "Even though you're a moody pain in the ass, I like you."

He wanted to answer her, to ask for more, but he couldn't. Instead, he pressed his arousal against her while her hands caressed the back of his neck, moved into his hair and pulled him down for a long, slow kiss.

"Let's go, Haley," he said when they broke apart, his voice timbered low and heavy; he knew he wasn't going to be able to wait much longer for her.

"I have to give these clothes back," she said.

"If anyone's getting you out of those clothes, it's going to be me," he told her. "We can do that right here, if you'd like."

His nostrils flared slightly, seeking her scent, and her cheeks flushed. Wordlessly, she took his hand, grabbed her boots, and followed him down to the dock. She let him pick her up and place her in the boat, and when he pushed off, all he could think about was finding a private spot under the tall cover of cypress to lay her down and take her.

He couldn't remember when, if ever, the last time was he'd really enjoyed sex, when he'd actually shattered under someone's touch.

Yeah, he got off, but it was always like someone else was at the wheel, and fuck, he was tired of that. He wanted to—needed to—feel, and Haley made him shiver in all the right places.

Normally, it was all about release, keeping the woman safe and keeping his sanity. With her, it was different. He could explore. She knew, and she was still here. Wanted more. Part of his brain, the part trained from an early age never to trust, wondered at her motive, because he knew he wanted far more from her than just a release.

The part that wanted to shatter told him to continue thinking with his dick. Because he planned to explore every bit of her with his tongue, his mouth....

Nothing to lose, T-Remy. Nothing to lose ...

HALEY LOOKED STARTLED when he steered the boat into a deserted cove. For a minute, she actually gripped the sides of the boat in fight-or-flight mode, until he peeled off his T-shirt. And then she smiled, rubbed her own hands over her breasts, her face bearing the dreamy look of too much alcohol and pent-up desire.

"I don't get this," he said, his voice rougher than usual. "I should hate you for the way you tricked me, should be telling you to go back to your agency with a big fuck off from me to them. But I can't."

"Then don't," she said, making it sound so simple.

Desire was supposed to be simple. Uncomplicated.

He refused to think about the fact that they might be mindfucking him, that Haley was in on a plan to hypnotize him into joining her agency. Wouldn't allow himself to think about anything but the feel of her body in his arms.

Dusk was threatening, but while they still had light, he had plans. He unbuttoned his pants, enjoying the way she bit her bottom lip when he let them drop.

For the second time that day, he eased himself to the bottom of the boat and propped himself onto his elbows.

"Come here, *chere*," he said. She reached under her skirt and pulled off her pink underwear first. And she got down on her hands and knees and held her skirt out of the way while she crawled over to him. She positioned herself on top of his prone body, her hand circling his erection to guide it inside of her.

She let the skirt drop as she pushed against him, drove him

so deep inside of her, she let out a muffled cry that scattered some magnificent frigate birds from their nesting place in the nearby trees, their cries mingled with hers as they escaped over the water and he escaped into her.

He lowered himself from his elbows, put his head on the deck and let his hands roam up underneath her shirt, loving the softness of her skin. She threw her head back as she rocked against him, and he let his fingers trace her nipples slowly.

"Never been like this," he murmured. Everything felt different, as if he'd been lulled into some sort of trance. Her nipples puckered, hardened as he rolled them in his fingers.

"Take this off, *bebe*," he urged. She pulled the blouse over her head and untied the skirt and they were both naked in the middle of the swamp in a boat that hadn't seen this much action since he'd been in high school, and that paled in comparison to this.

And as she lowered her weight down to his completely, he took one last look at her tattoo moving to meet his.

"Go slow, Haley." He grasped her waist and kept her from moving as frantically as she wanted to. "Just for a minute."

She wouldn't last a minute. Already her inner muscles had begun to contract around him, and fire raced through her nerve endings at every point of contact.

"I need to move," she moaned, but he dug his fingers into her hips and held her still.

"I need this to last."

His words tugged at her heart. Their other encounters hadn't been much more than hot, brutal races to the finish, and she imagined that his entire sexual history wasn't much different.

Crazily enough, her sexual past was the exact opposite. She'd never been afraid to experiment, but mostly she shocked her partners with her longing to test erotic boundaries. As a result, sex rarely ended up as anything other than a pleasant diversion from work.

Sex with Remy was so much more. Everything with Remy was so much more. Mind-blowing. Addictive. Pure adrenaline.

Desire rippled through her veins as she watched him watching her, his expression a heady mix of need and want. Lowering her mouth to his, she brushed the tip of her tongue across the seam of his lips, tasting cherries and white lightning.

"Kiss me, Remy," she murmured. "Make love to my mouth, if you won't do it any other way." She wriggled her hips for emphasis, and he gripped her harder.

His eyes darkened dangerously, and then he took her mouth with a hunger she hadn't anticipated. Shock gave way to pleasure as his tongue thrust deep, stroking against hers in a fierce, wet mating. One of his hands came up to tangle in her hair, and she whimpered when he pulled her head back, just far enough away that his breath fanned over her lips, but they didn't touch.

"Remy—"

"Shh." He held her, her neck wrenched askew so she couldn't move, but she wasn't in pain. Then, so slowly she thought she'd die, he flicked his tongue over her lips, teasing, forcing little gasps from her every time she opened her mouth to let him in.

But he never came in. He just teased her mouth with tiny kisses, licks, and the occasional flirty suck.

And all the while, he held her captive, making her head swim with arousal and her sex release a stream of silken liquid down the length of his shaft. It took every ounce of self-restraint to keep from grinding her mound against him.

"Please," she whispered, not sure what she was asking for.

"This was what you wanted, *bebe*." He took her bottom lip between his teeth and let his hot tongue rasp slowly over it before releasing her. "You wanted me to make love to your mouth. Imagine me doing this between your legs."

A sob escaped her and she struggled to move her head, her hips, but his grip tightened, rendering her completely immobile and helpless.

"Open for me."

She shuddered and obeyed, moaned when his tongue rimmed the O of her lips and then pushed inside to taunt her tongue with long velvet strokes and then quick, firm stabs that made her weak.

"This is what I want to do to your pussy, Haley." He circled her lips again, like he had done to the entrance of her sex last night, and this time she cried out, so desperate for release she was shaking with it.

Still, he tormented her, lapping at her, tracing her lips, sucking delicately on her tongue, all the while dominating her even though she was on top. She strained against the prison of his grip, to no avail. It was frustrating. Maddening.

Erotic as hell.

Finally, with a butterfly brush of his lips against hers, he pulled back, pierced her with his dark gaze. "Ride me," he commanded. "Now."

Releasing her, he arched with such force her knees came off the deck. Fire consumed her as she pushed herself up to brace her palms against the muscular wall of his chest. She pumped her hips, driving short, hard strokes up and down the length of his cock. Oh, it was good, so good that when the boat started rocking, she didn't care. She surrendered to it, letting the rhythm enhance her thrusts.

A low, rumbling sound arose from his chest, the vibrations shooting all the way up her arms. Beneath her palms, his heartbeat pounded. Inside her, his shaft swelled and pulsed as her orgasm hovered at that terrible place between torture and ecstasy.

She reached behind her, planted her hands on his thighs and arched her back, spreading her legs wide. The position exposed her to the night air and Remy's gaze, which she felt like a hot brand.

"Touch me."

His thumb slipped between their bodies, and for a moment he held it there, where they were joined, so that every thrust brought the caress of his touch to both of them. Then, slowly, he swiped the callused pad up through her slick folds, stopping just before he touched her where she needed it most.

She hissed in frustration. "Damn you, Remy..."

Something like a panting chuckle came from him, and she growled, reached between his legs and cupped his balls. He sucked air between his teeth, and it was her turn to smile. She raked her fingernails gently over the tightly drawn-up sac and then pressed firmly against the smooth, delicate patch of skin behind them.

"Ah, fuck," he rasped, and the breeze rattled the trees, surrounded them a split second before he pounded into her with violent, jackhammering thrusts.

His thumb slid up, pushed her button so skillfully she plummeted over the edge of release and took him with her. He came in hot jets that seemed to go on forever and splashed against the entrance to her womb in bursts of sensation, wrenching sobbing cries from deep inside.

"Remy, oh, Remy..." She fell forward, collapsed on his heaving chest.

He quivered beneath her, and when he brought his hand up her back, she could have sworn it trembled. His fingers splayed over the curve of her spine as they both tried to catch their breath.

By the time she could breathe without huffing, darkness had fully engulfed the bayou, but the moon left plenty of silver light. Haley pushed into a sit with Remy still inside her. He winced, and she realized she'd pushed against his sore ribs.

"I'm sorry," she whispered, and bent to kiss the dark bruise.

He sucked air between his teeth. "It's okay."

"How did it happen?"

One finger trailed idly along her calf as he tucked his other arm behind his head. "Some assholes jumped me in my apartment parking lot."

"Did they rob you?"

"Nah. I don't think they were after money." His expression grew troubled. "Didn't realize that until now."

Warning alarms clanged in her head. "What makes you say that?"

"They were too organized."

He shook his head as though trying to forget it, but she couldn't do the same. If his attackers were more than petty muggers, they could belong to Itor. Which meant they'd moved faster than anyone at ACRO had foreseen. And they could very well know where Remy was right now.

She needed to contact Dev. Immediately.

"We should probably go. I need to get my equipment working." She eased off him, ignoring the emptiness as he slipped out of her body, and reached for her underwear.

"Wait." He grasped her wrist. "What now?"

"What do you mean?" But she knew. And her heart seized, because she had no idea what to say.

"Where do we stand, Haley? And where does your agency come in? Because I still have a lot of questions."

Agency questions she could answer, even if the answer was nothing more than "I can't say right now." But the personal questions . . . those were more complicated.

"Are you willing to listen to what I have to say without getting mad?"

"I can't promise that."

She nodded, expecting as much. "Let's talk when we get back to the house, then."

As gracefully as she could in the rocking boat, she pulled on her clothes, and he did the same. Then, as she shrugged into the peasant blouse, he went deathly still.

"Do you hear that?"

Her pulse rate tripled. "Hear what? I don't hear anything." If he said alligators, she'd die.

"Exactly." His sharp gaze took in the area, his profile hard in the light from the moon. "It's too quiet. Something's wrong."

Oh, God. She could stand in the path of a tornado, could be buffeted by hailstorms, but being in the middle of a dark swamp scared the bejeezus out of her. "What do we do?"

"We need to get back to the house." He reached for the paddle, and started moving them silently through the water, his biceps flexing in a way that would have made her mouth water if it hadn't gone all dry and sandy with nerves.

"What—" she swallowed hard "—what could it be?"

"I don't know. Poachers, maybe." But his expression spoke of something worse. The wind that whistled through the trees confirmed it.

"Or?"

He closed his eyes, the savage concentration in his expression so severe that a muscle twitched in his jaw, and then the wind died. When he opened his eyes again, they glittered with a fierce light.

"All I know is that I've been in too many shit situations to ignore my gut instinct."

She hadn't been in a lot of shit situations, but she did have a gut instinct.

And her gut told her that they were, indeed, facing poachers.

Only the prey these poachers were after was human.

CHAPTER
Seventeen

"Annika! Dammit, open the door!"

After God-knew-how-long of pleading, reasoning and, finally, shouting, the tone of Creed's voice changed. Annika backed away from the door and hit the backs of her knees against the bed. Her world had spun off its axis, and for the first time in her life, she didn't trust herself. Not with him. If he so much as looked at her—

The door crashed in. The frame splintered. Wooden shards flew across the room, and for a second she thought the not-so-friendly house ghost had gotten pissed again.

But Casper was the least of her worries.

Creed filled the doorway, fists clenched, gaze possessive and hotter than the hell she'd cursed him to. Powerless to move, she stood there as he stalked inside. Every heavy step vibrated the floorboards and sent tiny shock waves up her legs to the place between them that ached.

When he stopped in front of her, she saw only the broad wall of his chest as it rose and fell with deep, frequent breaths. Her own breath came in painful fits and starts, and she became acutely aware of the hardening of her nipples against the edges of her bra, which she hadn't bothered to fix after he'd loosened the clasp earlier.

Creed hooked a finger beneath her chin, and she shuddered as he lifted her face until their gazes locked. The raw desire swirling in his eyes tangled with hers, and that fast, it was over. She'd lost the battle.

Male triumph lit his expression. He didn't bother to hide it as he stepped back and waited while she lifted her T-shirt over her head. Before she could drop it to the floor, he was on her and she was on the bed, his mouth crushed to hers. An electric tingle spread across her skin, a reminder that she shouldn't do this. But then her bra was gone, and her shoes and jeans next, and Creed's fingers were stroking her inner thighs and nothing mattered but his touch.

The velvet strokes of his tongue against hers drove her mad, and the slide of the piercing there made her wonder how his tongue would feel in other places.

"You aren't running this time," he said softly, so sure, so arrogant, but the fight had gone out of her.

"No." Despite her actions over the last few hours, running wasn't in her nature, and it was time to face some of her demons.

She helped strip him of his shirt, but then he pressed her back onto the bed and grazed his lips across her collarbone as he worked off his boots and pants. The sight of his naked body brought a rush of hunger, an animal need for skin-on-skin contact. If she had all night, she'd lick every one of the tattoos that marked the right side of his body, but she had a few minutes at most.

The more worked up she got, the more danger Creed might be in.

Right now, though, the danger was to her, because he'd taken her breast in his mouth, and before she could catch her breath, he cupped her sex, pressed inward with the heel of his palm until the pressure made her whimper.

"That's it," he murmured against her skin. "I want to hear you."

She didn't want him to hear her, to know how weak she was, how she couldn't control her own body when he was in the same room, let alone doing erotic things to her. All she had to do was tell him to stop. . . .

Not a chance. Not when his tongue rasped over her nipple, sending flame-hot sensation licking deep into places his tongue hadn't yet been.

She moaned, threaded her hands through his silky hair and held him there. She could feel moisture pool between her folds, and she twisted, trying to find relief in his touch.

"So demanding." His voice was deep, rough, edged with wicked intent.

He pulled off her underwear in a flash. This could end in disaster, but right now she didn't care. She wanted his mouth trailing down her belly like that, his tongue swirling in her navel as his fingers stroked her swollen pussy.

His hungry gaze lifted and held hers as though asking permission, and she answered by spreading her legs wide. Heart pounding, she watched as he kneeled between them and lowered his head.

Panic flared at the first puff of hot air against her sex. No one had done this to her, and she squirmed with both impatience and nerves.

"Easy," he whispered, and held her thighs with gentle pressure as he used his thumbs to spread her slick flesh. "I've wanted to do this for so long. . . ."

She shivered at his words even as her skin burned.

The first, tentative swipe of his tongue through her valley brought her off the bed with a cry. A low, humming sound welled up from deep in his chest, and he drove his tongue inside her, eating her in earnest. Sensation shot through her, electric pinpricks that started at the place where Creed's ball piercing flicked over her clit and ended in her fingertips.

"Creed," she gasped, and his tongue moved faster, dancing in her hot honey and then thrusting inside her.

Too much, it was too much. Her skin tightened until she thought it would crack, and her womb began to clench, and oh, God, lightning crackled through her veins.

"Stop!" She pushed him away, scrambled back on the bed, her entire body shaking and her sex quivering with the need to climax. "I'll shock you. I can't control it. Not when I come." She was babbling, but her body and mind were a mix of sensations she couldn't contain, which obviously affected her mouth as well. "You seem to be immune, but..."

Creed crawled up her body, his eyes nearly black with lust, and gripped her hip as though ensuring she wouldn't run. "You've been trying to shock me?"

Swallowing dryly, she stared at his hard cock, the bulging, purplish head and the veins she wanted to trace with her lips. She knew how he tasted, salty and metallic, and her mouth watered, relieving the dryness.

"Annika?"

"Right. Yeah. I've tried to light you up a few times. You piss me off a lot."

"Well, if I'm immune..." He grinned, a sinister, sinful grin, and slid his hand between her legs before she could protest. "Let's see what happens."

"But..." But the last time a man had touched her intimately, with nothing but his fingers, she'd nearly killed him.

"Shh. I'll take my chances." He pushed a finger inside her and covered her mouth with his, and she was already so primed, so ready, that when his thumb circled her clit, she exploded.

Her body jerked off the bed as every cell seemed to

vaporize, ignited by heat and electricity and Creed's talented touch. She heard a scream, and somewhere in the back of her foggy mind she registered Creed's groan, the way he twitched, and, oh, God, she hoped she hadn't electrocuted him.

She trembled, unable to function on any level until her body stopped writhing and her skin stopped sizzling, and then Creed was on top of her, peering into her eyes in amazement.

"Holy shit," he panted. "That was so fucking hot." His hand stroked the length of her side, stopping now and then to cup her breast. "It was like my piercings were connected. Like electrical conduits. Fuck, Annika, I felt your orgasm."

"I'm just glad I didn't fry you."

But damn, she felt free like never before. Her fear was gone, along with the fear of the fear. She hated being afraid, hated worrying about Creed when she'd never worried about anyone in her life.

Best of all, she could have sex.

As though a weight had been lifted, she wrapped her arms around his shoulders and arched her hips into his rock-hard erection.

"Now. I want it all." She had never been one to drag out her wants. Instant gratification was more her style.

"Yes, ma'am," he said, and shoved her thighs apart with one of his. "Dammit. Hold on. Condom."

"I'm on the pill," she said stupidly, her nerves making her mouth run without the benefit of thought. Of course he knew she was on the pill. Like many agencies, ACRO required all female field operatives to take birth control. "And I don't want to feel you through a condom. Not for my first time."

"*Our* first time."

"Well, yeah. But it's my first time ever."

He blinked. "Could you say that again?"

"First time. You deaf? I'm a virgin." And geez, was he ever

going to get on with it? He just kept staring at her. It was enough to make a girl paranoid.

"But...Dev?"

She rolled her eyes. "I'm not sleeping with him. I let guys think I am so they'll leave me alone. I've never had sex because, you know, fifty thousand volts into a dude's tool...I mean, I've gotten guys off, but—"

"Yeah, I could've not known that." He moved over her, swallowing audibly, his gaze taking her in like she'd given him some kind of great gift. A Ferrari or courtside pro basketball tickets instead of a stupid cherry.

A shard of irritation speared her. "Are you just going to stare at me all night?"

His eyes cut up to hers sharply. "Hell, no." He stretched over her and sucked her earlobe between his lips. "God, Annika," he murmured, "to be the only man who's had you..." He shuddered, and she hooked her calves around his legs to bring him in where she needed him.

"Then have me." She reached between them and grasped his cock, squeezed, fascinated at the way the tattooed side burned hotter than the other.

Lifting her knee, she made room for his slim hips between her thighs, and guided him to her entrance. He hesitated, looked down at her fiercely, possessively, and her breath caught.

"I don't know what to do," she admitted, hoping he wouldn't think she was completely inept. She had experience on the giving end—she'd made sure of that—but receiving like this was a new thing, and she despised being an amateur at anything.

"I'll teach you."

He pushed, entered her gently, millimeter by millimeter, then pulling back and starting over again. She'd have complained about the time he took, but his thick length stretched her deliciously, sliding over nerve endings that fired and popped, unaccustomed to the slow, erotic massage.

Creed's groan rumbled in his chest, tickling hers. "You're so tight. So wet. Wrap your legs around me."

She did, and desire pooled and pulsed. She'd waited so long for this, and she wasn't in the mood for slow and easy and sappy. She wanted rough and wild and a big, fat, emotional disconnect.

"Fuck me, Creed. I won't break."

"I don't want to hurt you."

"Jesus!" She rocked up against him, sheathing him fully inside her. A sharp stab of pain made her suck air, and he went completely still as she caught her breath.

He watched her with a cocky I-told-you-so expression, and then he ground against her and she swallowed a cry at the exquisite sense of fullness.

"I want this to be good for you." He pulled nearly all the way out and then drove deep. "So good you never forget."

Pleasure ripped through her, making her squeeze him tight between her thighs and grip him hard in her hands. No way in hell would she forget.

His hard muscles rippled beneath her palms. She dragged them down, grasped his firm ass, felt it clench as he pumped into her. Something sizzled inside, coiled tightly all through her womb at the beginnings of a release she knew would make all others pale.

"Yes . . . Creed, oh, Creed . . ."

Panting, he opened his mouth against her throat, pulled her tight against him. "Come, baby. Come for me."

His voice threw her over the edge, into a well of searing pleasure. Sparks stung her skin, pierced her flesh, dissolved her organs. Blinding flashes of light burst behind her eyelids, burning the erotic image of Creed's expression of ecstasy into her brain.

He grunted, filled her with a hot splash of semen as her spasms squeezed his cock so hard, he seemed to be locked inside her, bonded by white-hot heat and slick passion.

Too weak to move, she lay beneath him. His breath feathered over her shoulder. The fingers of one hand stroked her cheek. The other hand gripped her ass, holding her hard against him.

He was heavy, but it was a good heavy, the kind that probably made women feel all secure and safe, two things Annika didn't need any man for. When she did suffer the occasional moment of insecurity, she had Dev.

"You're squishing me."

"Sorry." Creed rolled off her and pulled her onto her side so he remained inside her, his shaft still throbbing. Each pulse made her pussy spasm with pleasure.

"Is it always like this?" she asked, feeling a little stupid and naïve.

His gaze bored into her with such intensity, such focus that she fell completely still. "It's never been this good."

Oh, God. She had no idea how to respond, but when he leaned in and brushed his lips over hers in the softest, gentlest kiss she'd ever experienced, she responded by breaking away.

Heart pounding ridiculously, she rolled off the bed and grabbed her panties from where they hung on the bedpost.

"What are you doing?"

She didn't look at him as she dressed. He was too sexy, too gorgeous, and she didn't need the distraction. "I want to be ready in case your overprotective shadow comes back in a snit and wants a piece of me."

"Annika," he said, bracing himself on one elbow and watching her, "there's no need to rush off. The house seems to have settled for now. I think the entity that lives here knows it can't have you. The fact that it tried to dump a chandelier on you was a big clue."

"What do you mean it knows it can't have me?"

"I won't let it." His voice was a low, resonant drawl, and suddenly she realized that Creed was more than just another nerdy psychic. He was a warrior, and far more lethal than she'd guessed. "There's only room for one possession here."

Whoa. Okay, apparently she wasn't finished being in virgin territory, because having a conversation like this was the first. "I really have to go."

"We should talk."

Avoiding his gaze, she tugged her jeans over her hips. "Look, I don't need some girly post-fuck cuddle. Thanks for popping my cherry, but I'm cool, okay? And it wasn't like I was saving myself for someone special, so you don't have to worry about me clinging like a moon-eyed twit."

She pulled on her shirt and didn't bother with her shoes because she had to get out of there. The room was closing in and it had nothing to do with the damned ghosts.

"I'm going to grab some food. Ciao."

The sound of Creed's feet hitting the floor chased her out the door. Not that she was running. She was just hungry.

And she wished Dev would call with her next assignment, one that would let her kick some ass, because she was ready to kill something. Too bad most of the people in this house were already dead.

CREED COULDN'T LIE TO HIMSELF—his pride swelled at the thought of being Annika's first, and a sudden, fierce urge to call her *his* tore through his heart.

No wonder she was running.

Before he could untangle himself from the sheets to go after her—again—the familiar chill began at the base of Creed's spine, working its way slowly up the back of his neck and moving finally into his scalp, which felt pulled tight against the force of Kat's machinations.

"Welcome back, babe. Thanks for all the help," he muttered. Kat's response was a light breeze and a squeeze to his right biceps, which meant she was going to check out the spirit for herself. Annika had left the door open, and Kat closed it lightly on her way out.

His phone's distant buzz distracted him—set to vibrate, the sound was muffled, the cell buried on the floor among the pile of his discarded clothing. Cursing, he sifted through the pants and shirt until he uncovered the phone and checked the caller ID.

Dev.

Well, at least the phones were working.

"Yes, Dev," he answered, as he struggled to pull his pants on and the door opened. Kat was back, a little too fast.

"What happened?" Dev's voice crackled in interference probably caused by the house.

So many ways to answer that one and none of them appropriate enough to be appreciated by the man who was ultimately his boss.

"Whatever lives here isn't all that happy, Dev. It wants out." That was, at least, the truth. But Kat knew better and he shivered visibly as she made direct contact with him again.

"Is the spirit loose?" Dev asked.

"Not fully. Is that what you want?"

Dev ignored his question. "How is Annika?"

"She's all right," Creed said.

"You know she's going to take a while to warm back up to you, but once she does she'll be fiercely loyal. Protective."

"Dev..."

"Listen to me, don't be too hard on her. She comes across as all tough, but really..."

She's mine. "She's a cream puff?"

Dev snorted. "I wouldn't go that far."

No, you wouldn't. But I did.

Kat jabbed him in the ribs for that thought.

"Are you going to be able to get more of a read?" Dev asked.

"Kat's back—she should be able to help," he said. "But things are getting dangerous. This thing locked us in the house, cut off comms."

"Do you want to pull out?"

No, he hadn't wanted to pull out at all. "Fuck!" he yelled when Kate pinched him.

"Creed?"

"Shit. Yeah. Sorry, that wasn't directed at you." He sighed, pulled a hand through his hair and tapped his tongue piercing lightly against his front teeth before he spoke again. "I think we'll be all right. I'll know more in about an hour."

"Take care of Annika," Dev said.

"Will do, Devlin." He clicked the phone off and stuffed it in his pocket. "Don't start with me, Kat. I need your help," he said as he yanked his shirt over his head, grabbed his boots and stomped off barefoot to find Annika, still muttering.

"Who are you talking to?" Annika was standing in the kitchen, drinking a Diet Coke and eating from a bag of chips.

"Kat's back."

"About time. Maybe now we can get to work," she said.

She was going to try to pretend they didn't just have mind-blowing sex, that her first time wasn't off-the-charts amazing. And Creed wasn't going to let that happen.

Neither was Kat, because the bag of chips was ripped out of Annika's hands and thrown across the room.

"Hey!"

"Kat, cut that out," he said.

Annika folded her arms across her chest and glared at him, and he would've probably, at that moment, reached out to grab and kiss her, but that familiar chill gripped his shoulders, telling him that Kat was about to make contact with whatever in the hell ruled this house.

His personal life would have to wait. "Let's go," he said. "This thing's ready to talk again. And it's finally agreed to leave you the hell alone."

CHAPTER
Eighteen

A few minutes earlier, Haley was riding him. Now Remy wondered if she'd really been taking him for a ride the past couple of days. But the way her lips pressed together and her hands fisted told him that she was just as concerned by the invisible visitors as he was.

"Are they yours?" he asked, his voice so soft as to not even be a whisper. "Your agency?"

She shook her head and pulled a Glock from the backpack she'd brought with her into the pirogue earlier. He yanked his own gun out of the other side of the boat—a Sig Sauer—and for a second they just stared at each other.

This was his team now. And at least he knew she knew how to shoot. Shoot first, ask questions later—and he was going to have an awful lot of questions for Haley.

Stay down, he motioned, and she followed him off the boat and into the soggy marsh that bordered the back of the house, still hidden by the heavy drape of the cypress trees.

At first glance, there was nothing out of order—nothing

obvious. No footprints. No signs of forced entry. Nothing that would show others had been here, or had gone inside.

But that wasn't true at all. Because any sign of the two gators who lived along this back path was gone, and he smelled the tinny, heady scent of fresh blood.

Haley tried to walk ahead of him into the house, but he put an arm out to stop her, shook his head.

My equipment, she mouthed.

He shook his head again, more than prepared to haul her out of here if she didn't start cooperating. But he caught a sudden flash along the west side of the property out of the corner of his eye and realized that they were being tracked by someone with a scope.

Without warning, he turned and fired.

Suddenly he found himself slammed against a tree, his feet dangling, fighting for a breath as though an invisible set of hands was wrapped around his neck. He heard gunfire; Haley shooting. To his right, he saw a man, his arm outstretched and a look of intense concentration on his face. He couldn't warn Haley, not with his neck in a choke hold, and he couldn't lift his gun, not with how his arm had somehow been pinned to his leg. This was crazy. Impossible. And not going to happen.

He didn't need to concentrate, not with the fury that shot through him. A tingle swept his skin as he glared at the man, and then a gust of wind roared through the bayou, knocked that fucker off his feet, and then Remy was on the ground, sucking in gulps of air.

He grabbed Haley by the arm and hauled ass to the cypress trees by the marsh, which would provide at least limited coverage.

"We go on foot," he said. "I won't be able to lose them fast enough in the boat."

She nodded, grabbed her pack from the pirogue. He did the same and they took off. She'd gathered the skirt up as much as she could, and her legs were going to be cut soon by the brambles they were forced to run through, but he was impressed by the way she moved.

He'd have to take them deeper into the bayou—in the dark, it wasn't going to be the prime place to be, but he had plenty of experience to keep them both safe from the elements.

"Here." He grabbed her, pulled her back against the trunk of a cypress, with its heavy branches enveloping them in enough cover. He wasn't winded, and Haley's breathing was only a little fast, which meant she was in good shape.

"We won't lose them for long," she said.

"Something's coming," he said, and she looked at him sharply. "Storm—it's not mine. And it's going to be bad."

The tattoo began to tingle, and as he brought his hand down to rub his hip, he noticed Haley had begun to do the same. A mirror image.

"Do you think you can bring the storm in faster? Make it more severe?" she asked, and he eyed her to make sure he understood what she was actually asking.

"You want me to help the storm along?"

"Yes. I'm just not sure what's coming is going to be enough to stop this particular group of people," she said.

"You want to elaborate more on 'this particular group of people'?"

"I will, but later. Let's concentrate on the weather for right now," she whispered, her warm breath tickling his ear. His cock stirred, his entire body on high alert in several different and conflicting ways. "Do you think you can do this?"

If he couldn't, they didn't stand a chance, because whatever these people wanted from them, they weren't stopping.

"I've got to stay still, concentrate," he said.

"Can I help?"

"You already have," he said, his eyes lingering on her breasts, and she smiled. It was tough enough trying to control the weather and his sex drive, but Haley was encouraging him to make weather, and the situation necessitated it. But doing that came with a price and she didn't seem to mind paying. She was fucking turned on by his little weather show. And her being turned on was making him want to take her, right here. Again.

That would have to happen later.

He tore his gaze away, watched the sky from the shadows of the trees and let loose every bit of excess energy, which he would've normally shoved down deep so it wouldn't translate into some kind of major weather. But at the moment he had Mother Nature's complete cooperation, and she was going to have his.

He thought about the way his life had been turned upside down, worse in the past twenty-four hours than he'd believed possible, thought about the way his dad sold him out for money and thought about those people rummaging through his house. The thunder boomed, loud enough to make Haley jump at its suddenness. And then the fog began to roll in, thicker than he'd ever seen it, and if Haley hadn't been holding him, he wouldn't have been sure she was there anymore.

He took a few steps backward, until they were clear and he could see the fog like a wall in front of him, cutting them off from their pursuers.

"That should work for now. Come on," he said, tugged her wrist and led her away from the rain and fog that hid them . . . and hopefully knocked out the enemy's comms. At least now the fuckers would have trouble mobilizing if they'd come by boat or air.

From what Haley had told him about the operatives from her agency, he wasn't sure what these people were capable of. Then again, he wasn't sure what he was capable of—but he was going to find out soon.

"Where are we going?"

"Someplace I haven't been in years," he said. He wasn't sure the deer blind was still there, hidden in the moss and high above the marsh on four-foot stilts, or if it would even be viable, but it was better than nothing. Although they weren't getting the worst part of the storm—the part he'd created—Mother Nature was still giving them a deluge.

Another mile in the driving rain and they ended up by the stilts that kept the structure from getting flooded. He'd spent a lot of time here as a kid—his own private place, where he could think and dream and draw his comic strips, where he was the superhero and invincible. And now, as he ducked to walk underneath and press the planks with his palm to check their stability, he noticed the initials he'd carved over fifteen years ago.

He'd done that the first time he'd found the place—after a particularly bad day at school when he'd been singled out more than usual, accused of casting weather spells and breaking the front windows of Jean Marie's daddy's store. He'd stayed up there for two days, until Remy Senior had come to get him. His old man had brought him food, had climbed up and sat next to his son, had waited for T to finish the food and tell him what had happened. His father had told him that running away from problems usually only made them worse and had urged Remy back to the house again.

It made perfect sense that his refuge from the past would provide shelter now, although Remy knew well enough from experience that the trouble following him wasn't going to stay away for long.

"This should hold without a problem," he said. "Let's get in out of this rain."

He hoisted her up, holding her fast because she was soaked and he could barely see through the driving rain, and finally she dragged herself in. Then she actually reached out a hand to help him up. He smiled, shook his head and yanked his body unceremoniously into the old structure.

It creaked, but it held. Haley had already moved toward one corner so she could see out both the small windows—one facing north and the other east—her gun drawn. Covering him.

"We're safe for now," he said. "Unless you think they could get through that storm."

"I think it's bad enough to hold them off for a while. Besides, they don't know these swamps the way you do. I have a feeling this is off the maps."

"Yeah, it is. But these people must have other ways of tracking us."

She nodded. "I just hope they don't have Trackers."

"This marsh doesn't hold tracks," he said.

"No, not like that. Trackers are people who can see psychic footprints. They see auras instead of actual tracks. Doesn't work in water, though, so we may be okay."

"What kind of people do you deal with?" he asked, and the look of concern on his face must have been obvious, because she reached up, touched his cheek.

"Don't worry about me, Remy. I can take care of myself. And you." Her clothes clung to her, and God, it was obscene for him to be this turned on now, but the tie between lust and danger was impossible to ignore.

"I need to know more about this enemy we're up against," he said.

"And I need to make sure you keep up the weather," she murmured, her fingers already untucking his shirt from his waistband. She yanked it up, then ran her hands along the flat of his abs. His nostrils flared and his breath seared his throat while he concentrated on her and the weather.

"What more do you need?" he asked.

"Tornados," she said. "Or a microburst. Something that will screw with their communications and their ability to move. Something big."

He nodded, watched as she knelt down before him, unzipped the straining fly and freed him.

"You can do this, Remy. I need you to do this."

His fingers twined in the softness of her hair as her mouth enveloped him. He shuddered at the warmth of her mouth against his rain-chilled body and forced himself to just let it go, to be Haley's hero for this moment.

He'd never had to do this before—force a storm to grow more powerful than the atmospheric conditions would naturally allow. But for what seemed like hours after she'd stopped him twice from coming, Haley pressed her naked body against his and they kissed and fondled like teenagers making out in their parents' living room, seizing the moment and not caring if they got caught.

Finally, the frenzy built beneath his skin until the electricity shot off his body and he felt the earth shifting beneath their feet. A howl like an oncoming train echoed in the distance as he concentrated on the coordinate points where he'd last seen the enemy, and when she let him sink into her warm heat, he prayed he'd done enough.

OKSANA MINSKY CURLED HER FINGERS into her palm until blood began to drip down her nails. "Imbeciles." She ground her teeth but succeeded only in grinding her temper even hotter.

"You imbeciles! We had him. How could you let him get away?"

Niles, the pasty-faced Brit whose extraordinary telekinetic powers made killing him a waste, turned to her, muddy and sopping wet after the downpour and tornado that nearly killed them all. "We had no way of knowing Remy had such control. Perhaps if you and Apollo had tortured more information from his father, we wouldn't be standing here like bloody fools."

Her fist plowed into his face, producing a satisfying crunch, and he fell backward, clutching his nose. "Only one of us is a *bloody* fool."

She'd needed no reminder regarding her failure. The formidable empathic abilities that had helped her lure Remy Senior out of the bar had allowed her to steer their interrogation in directions most likely to gain the responses she required. Unfortunately, the feelings of guilt that rolled off him in unbearable waves had probably enabled him to resist all her forms of torture. The man hadn't spoken a single word about his son. Not even when they took his pinky finger.

Oksana didn't doubt that they could've broken him, but they hadn't had time. Setting the trap for the younger Remy had been their priority.

"We have the ACRO agent's equipment." She supposed the speaker, an excedosapien with remarkable strength, thought he was being helpful, but like most excedos, the trade-off for his enhanced physical abilities was a serious lack of brainpower.

"Her computer will have safeguards. The moment we attempt to retrieve the files, the data will be destroyed. It's useless."

Cursing, she slapped a mosquito feasting on her arm and hoped her next deployment would be someplace more civilized. She hated capture missions, by far preferring the undercover spy trade that allowed her to work alone like she had with the KGB. Itor offered better pay and more interesting assignments, suited for her empathic talents, but sometimes, like now, she wished she'd never left the other agency.

Because although failure in the KGB meant punishment, failure for Itor meant far, far worse. She wasn't looking forward to telling Apollo, the team's leader, about their fuckup here.

"Niles, if you're done bleeding, call Apollo and tell him to proceed with plan B. And tell him to make it extra-painful." She stared into the tornado-twisted copse of trees where Haley and Remy had disappeared. "If I have to pay for this, so will that ACRO bitch."

HALEY PEERED THROUGH THE HAZY DARKNESS at Remy's muscular outline as he prepared for battle. He'd strapped his knife to his arm and another to his ankle. Practiced hands fastened a chest harness into place, and then, after checking the ammo, he slid his pistol into the holster.

"You always go on vacation prepared for World War Three?"

She expected a smile at her teasing, but instead he shot her a look devoid of any and all emotional traces of the hot sex they'd just had. Apparently, he could dismiss their physical connection much more easily than she could, given that her body still hummed with post-orgasm afterglow.

"This wasn't a vacation. It was an ambush." Closing his eyes, he concentrated, and the rain and wind pounding through the bayou increased in intensity. The tornado had ripped a path south of them, but had fizzled after his climax. "One you set for me when you paid my dad to lure me here."

"I know it's too late for an apology, but for what it's worth, I'm sorry." Guilt tore through her as she checked the ammo in her own weapon. "The bad guys weren't part of the plan."

"Then what was?" He crouched next to an opening that looked out over the trees. "Were your people going to lock me in an invisible choke hold instead of whoever the hell is out there? And how did they do that anyway?"

Sinking down near him, she placed her gun next to her and

tried not to cringe when her shredded skirt stuck to the cuts on her shins. "Telekinesis. One of their agents must have a lot of power."

"That's great. What else do I have to watch out for?" When she didn't answer, because she wasn't sure how, he turned to her. "Haley? I need to know what we're up against."

"I don't know. Itor is pretty secretive, and I'm not an operative, so I'm not privy to all the intel." A breeze sliced through her wet clothing, and she shivered, rubbed her arms. "But based on what I've seen at my agency, we could be dealing with powerful psychics, people with natural night vision, people who can communicate with animals or plants, superhumans with radar or superior hearing, speed—"

"Speedsters, Brawlers, Mentalists," he murmured. "Are you asking me to believe in the existence of multiple agencies full of comic book superheroes and supervillains?"

"Yeah, well, hello, Mr. I Control the Weather. What's that called in your comic book world?"

"An Elementalist." He jammed his fingers through his wet hair, leaving unruly tufts. "It's just . . . Shit."

"What, Remy? You can tell me."

His dubious snort told her exactly how much he thought he could tell her. He peered out into the darkness, his mouth a grim slash, and the wind that had started to die down picked up again.

"It's been difficult enough for me to accept what *I* do," he said finally. "So the idea that there's a whole world of people out there who are like me, who I've been reading about and drawing since I was a kid . . ."

She stood because sitting was making her crazy, but there was no room to pace in the creaky little shack. "There are a lot more than you think."

"So who are these Itor guys? Where are they located? What government do they work for?"

"They work for whomever hires them. We think they have a central command, but they also have several small cells scattered around the world."

"What about your agency?"

"We work out of one location, but there's talk of expanding." She threw back her head and looked up at the ceiling, and immediately wished she hadn't. Even in the darkness, she could see misty spiderwebs the size of her head hanging from the boards. "We've got to get to a phone. My boss needs to know about this. They can get us out of here."

"I can get us out of here."

"Haven't you been listening? We're not dealing with a handful of gun-toting terrorists."

"I can—"

"No, Remy. You can't. I know you aren't a team player, but for once, you need to trust someone else."

"And you're that someone? You, who has been lying to me from the second I met you?"

"Not everything has been a lie."

"Name one thing that hasn't."

Her heart shifted in her chest as though warning her not to admit anything personal. But Haley had never been one to follow orders, not even ones that came from her own mind and body.

"I wasn't lying when I said I liked you."

His body went rigid, and then he swung around. "That was probably the biggest lie."

Why she should care whether or not he believed her was a mystery to her, but the fact that he didn't, that he blatantly rejected her admission, made her burn with humiliation.

"Think what you want," she snapped. "And keep being an asshole, because that way maybe I can stop liking you."

A long pause broken by the sound of rain on the roof settled into the tiny shack.

"Ah, hell," he muttered. "I want to believe you. Don't know why. But I do."

It was crazy, the way she'd wanted to slap him one minute, and now she wanted nothing more than to climb into his lap and let him hold her. Especially because they might not have much time left. Either Itor would capture them or ACRO would rescue them, but either way, their moments alone were numbered.

"I hope you can," she said quietly. It had been a long time since she'd asked anyone to have faith in her. After all, if her own parents couldn't believe in her, how could anyone else?

Knowing she shouldn't, because every touch chipped away at the emotional barrier between them, she reached for him, but a stabbing pain in her temple stopped her short. Cringing, she pressed her palm to her forehead. Now was not the time for a migraine. Not that this felt like a migraine, but...

A bolt of agony tore her skull apart. She cried out, dimly heard Remy repeating her name over and over. She grasped his wrist, tried to look at him, but images floated into her vision.

Remy's father. Battered, bloody and nearly unrecognizable. A man was beating him, kicking him. Then he turned, his thin, angular face filling her vision.

"You, Ms. Holmes, have caused us a lot of trouble. The way you caused your parents a lot of trouble by being born despite your mother's attempts to terminate her pregnancy with herbal remedies."

Dear God, how did the man know that?

"Bring Remy to us, and we'll forget the time and effort you've cost us. Agree now, and we'll make you rich beyond your wildest dreams."

"Never," she shouted, and she felt Remy's hands come down on her shoulders, his concerned voice asking what he could do.

The man smiled sickly and pain stabbed her brain like punctures from a nail gun. "Tell Remy we have his father, and if he wants to see him alive, he'll come to Lafayette. South Red Rover Road. Three o'clock tomorrow." The man slammed his boot into Remy Senior's face. "And Haley, don't speak a word of this to ACRO, or I swear to you, I'll skin this man alive and send you the remains while he's still twitching."

The image fizzled, but Haley still couldn't see, could feel only the warm trickle of blood running from her nose and the dull knock of a pounding headache. She felt Remy's hands on her body, but she couldn't hear him. Dizziness and nausea gripped her, and the world spun, just before she toppled over and everything went dark.

CHAPTER
Nineteen

Remy had had plenty of medic training, had done his fair share of plugging gaping bullet holes in his teammates—and himself—with his bare hands. He'd carried unconscious men across a field of raging gunfire, and held their hands while they lay dying. And still, he'd never had the tear of absolute fear cutting through his heart like it was right now, with Haley draped unconscious in his arms.

"Haley...*chere*," he whispered, cradling her head in his hands. She wasn't waking up and her pulse was rapid, but she was breathing.

He'd caught her before she'd fallen to the floor and now he let them both sink down gently to the wooden planks. He rested his back against the side of the structure, facing the window, and pulled her closer between his legs so her upper body rested against his, her head on his shoulder. And he rocked her, whispering in her ear to *please wake up* because Christ, he couldn't lose her. Not now, not when he'd just found her.

"Please, Haley...come back to me."

She moaned a little, clutched the front of his shirt with her fists. "Remy..."

"I'm here. I'm here and you're safe."

"Hurts so much..."

"Don't talk, just rest."

"Can't. There's trouble. I have to call—"

"We've no way to communicate with your agency, unless in that bag you've got a phone that actually works," he reminded her.

"But they've got him...hurting him. Badly. Threatening to torture him. Already started..." She closed her eyes again and he fought the panic that rose in his throat.

She's just resting. And as much as he hated to wake her again, he needed to know what the hell was happening. "Haley, you need to tell me what's going on," he said quietly.

Her eyes opened, her pupils slowly returning to their normal size. She hesitated for a second before she finally spoke. "Itor Corp—the enemy—they have your father," she said.

Threatening to torture him...Already started...

Shit. His mouth went dry, because his father didn't deserve that kind of treatment. Not when Remy himself was their main target. "They're using him to lure me in," he said.

"I'm so sorry. It wasn't supposed to happen like this. If we'd known Itor was this close, we would've just taken you."

He wanted to answer her, but he was wrung out. This wasn't going to be just any mission. This was the mission of his life, and he had no choice but to accept it.

"Shoot first, ask questions later, right?" he muttered.

"It would've been for your own protection. The world's protection. In the wrong hands..."

He ran his fingers through his hair and heaved a deep, ragged sigh. Because he got it. Finally, he got it. "I'm a menace. And you're hurt because of me."

"No, Remy. My job's dangerous. With or without you."

"But you said you usually don't get this close to the potential operatives—you're not usually in the line of fire."

"I was trained in case I needed to be. We can get help to your father and have my agency come rescue us."

"I don't ever sit around and wait to be rescued. Just not in my nature."

"It's too dangerous for you to attempt this on your own."

"I don't have a choice," he said.

"Yes, you do. Get us out of here, and then I'll contact my boss. ACRO will help you get your father out of this."

"What, with no strings attached?"

"Everything comes with strings, Remy. But they're not going to force you into ACRO against your will. I won't lie to you, though, if you don't join, they'll do whatever it takes to ensure you aren't a risk to yourself or others."

He ran his fingers through his hair again, the enormity of the entire situation suddenly feeling too heavy for his own shoulders.

"I'm a risk right now, to you especially. Dammit, Haley, let me go alone."

"No. You're still vulnerable. You need me," she said, her brown eyes trained on him. Seeing him, not the man who could control the weather. "And I need you."

And as much as he wanted to refuse, to argue, he knew there was no way he could leave her here alone. She was still weak and far too vulnerable, and his sense of chivalry wouldn't let him desert her now.

The tattoo on his hip began to tingle, and she was looking at him with that now familiar lust in her eyes. Desire had never been this right, and he'd never been this calm or this content, even with the immediate threat bearing down on him.

Somehow, some way, he was gaining more control over himself, and he suspected that Haley had something to do with that, whether or not it was something she was conscious of.

"Do you really think you can help me manage my so-called powers?"

"There are trainers at ACRO who can help you as well. It'll just take time."

"Right now we don't have the time. We're going to have to improvise if we want to get out of here safely." He eased away from her slowly, stood, and then helped her to her feet. She was slightly unsteady at first, but after she stretched and massaged her neck, he saw that she was suffering no lasting effects from whatever those monsters had done to her.

"We'll be able to get out—Itor wants us to get out. They want us to come to them," she said.

"Why didn't they break into my mind?" he asked. "Wouldn't that have made more sense?"

She stared at him and he could tell she was deciding whether or not to hold back. She chose not to, and for a minute he wasn't sure if that was a good or bad thing. "Planting images, which is what Itor did to me—basically forcing a psychic image into my mind—can cause permanent damage. They'd never do it to you, you're too valuable. To Itor, I'm disposable."

"Not to me, Haley," he said, his voice holding more emotion than he would normally let show. "Come on, let's go find a way to contact your agency."

THEY'VE BROKEN INTO HER MIND, *Devlin. Planted horrible images. I can't get much more of a read on her right now . . . I keep seeing Remy's father.*

Two of the three psychics assigned to Haley, sitting in different rooms on either side of the main house, came rushing in to report the news an hour after he'd asked Marlena to put out a trace on Haley.

He'd left them still trying to see what Haley was planning

next. In the meantime, he needed to get some help into the Bayou, and fast. Fortunately for him, two of his best operatives were free to help him on this case.

Free, and in the process of trying to kill each other. Never mind that they'd made a complete shambles of the newly redecorated rec room, which Dev noted the second he used his CRV to see what the problem was.

"What the hell is going on here?" he demanded of Ender, an excedosapien with superspeed and a magic way with weapons, who was also known as Tom Knight to a select few at the agency. Ender was six feet, three inches of lean, lanky muscle, and Wyatt Kennedy, who was putting his special gift of telekinesis to good, solid work by throwing anything that wasn't nailed down at Ender's head, matched him in height but was the polar opposite in coloring, with his dark hair and eyes.

Both were stubborn as hell, although Wyatt tended to get along with people better than Ender did. Hell, anyone got along with people better than Ender, who prided himself on being as much of a loner as being part of this agency would allow.

"Someone's been putting up wanted posters of Ender again," Wyatt said. He was pinned half under Ender, but he managed to make a heavy piece of metal artwork fly across the room at Ender's head.

Ender, of course, was too quick for that, and in seconds the melee threatened to begin anew. The men were pretty evenly matched, although Ender would never admit that.

"I know it was you, you asshole," Ender told Wyatt, holding the dark-haired man down by the throat.

"Enough!" Dev bellowed. "One of these days, you're going to kill each other."

"One of these days, I'm going to kill him," Ender corrected.

"Today, you're going to need him to help rescue a new recruit," Dev said. "Follow me."

He walked toward his office, his CRV slightly dimming since he'd been up all night. Again. He heard the soft footfalls behind him, the carpet purposely thick and lush to keep the main house a place of calm and tranquillity.

"Marlena, don't interrupt me until there's word on Haley," he said, feeling her constant presence at the large desk outside his office.

"Yes, of course, Dev." Her voice was soft, but there was worry there. Whenever a potential operative as big as Remy was up for grabs, everyone was on edge. They'd had one or two get away in recent months, and while they hadn't seen the effects of that just yet, Dev knew the fallout wouldn't be good. He already had a man planted deep inside Itor in order to try to extract those particular operatives before Itor broke their minds for good.

But that paled in comparison to the job that lay in front of him now.

Once he entered the familiar space of his private office and heard the door shut behind them, he let himself fall back into his leather chair and turned his CRV sight off again.

Immediately, his other senses kicked in at high speed, and he felt the tension in Wyatt's shoulders and in Ender's lanky frame—like any men preparing to go on a mission, their adrenaline, already on the rise from their fight, was palpable.

"We haven't heard from Haley in over seventeen hours." Dev drummed his fingers on the heavy oak desk. "Something's gone very wrong." He told them what the psychics had told him, because he'd never ask men to go into a mission without having all the facts.

"Itor's been moving in faster than ever," Wyatt said quietly, and Dev caught the note of speculation, and suspicion, in his tone.

Itor had begun to know things about ACRO and her inner workings that they never should have been able to figure out. Not without actually being here, and being privy to classified information.

"Yes, Itor's been particularly up on things as of late," Dev said.

"Which means it could all be one giant trap," Wyatt said.

"As always," Dev agreed. "I figure that once I get closer, I'll be able to tell if that's true."

"You're not going in," Ender said.

"Don't tell me what I can and can't do. Last time I looked, you weren't in charge."

Ender snorted. "I have no interest in being in charge of this asylum."

"I've asked you not to call it that, especially not in front of the new recruits," Dev said.

"I was just trying to make Wyatt feel more at home," Ender said, and Dev put his hand out before Wyatt could make a move. Still, the already broken glass ashtray rumbled from the garbage can next to his desk, proving Wyatt wasn't fond of jokes about his mental stability.

"Bottom line, Dev," Ender continued easily. "You stay. I'll go in and rescue the SEAL. I'm used to rescuing them, since they can't save their own asses." Ender was former Delta Force, and never failed to let others who had served in other military branches know exactly how he felt about them.

This time, Dev felt part of the ashtray whiz by his face and heard it crash into the wall, leaving Ender to mutter and curse.

"You deserved that," Dev told him, then pressed a few buttons on the computer in front of him to make sure the helo was waiting to take the men to their next location. Dev sighed.

As much as he hated to admit it, Ender was right—if Dev himself went, he'd be risking too much.

Taking over as head of ACRO meant spending less and less time out in the field. It worked the same way in the military, and Dev missed the rush of the fight, the tense way the men in front of him waited for action, like animals waiting to strike at a moment's notice.

"Both you and Wyatt are going in on this one. More if we need them," Dev said.

Wyatt was a former SEAL—he could relate to Remy the way only another member of the teams could. Ender, of course, could relate to no one, but he was a damned fine operative. And Dev thought about calling in Annika as well—her special brand of electricity might well help rein in Remy's powers somewhat.

"Do you want us to take care of Itor or just bring Remy in?" Wyatt asked.

That was the million-dollar question. Because as badly as Dev wanted Remy safe and sound, within the confines of this compound, until he had learned enough about his own powers to protect himself and the world around him sufficiently, Dev also knew that Remy needed to prove himself to the most important person of all—himself.

A man's got to come in on his own terms, his father used to say, and Dev understood that. The military men especially needed to walk in, pride intact and ready to rock hard into this new phase of their life.

The ones who hadn't been given the choice, who'd been shunned and stripped of responsibilities because of their powers, had the harder transition. Rather than just sinking into the warmth of a place where they could finally be accepted—and not be all that different—they grew suspicious. Ill-tempered. Hard to control.

They'd have to approach Remy the way they'd approach a wounded animal, especially now that Remy Senior was in danger.

"Let's show Remy that he can function in a team setting," Dev said finally. "If he can't be involved, he'll bolt and try to do it on his own. Right now, that's suicide."

In his mind's eye, he saw Wyatt and Ender glance at each other in silent understanding, right before he heard the soft thwack as his operatives shook hands.

FOR THE ZILLIONTH TIME, Annika wondered what the hell Dev had been thinking when he'd sent her to this Disney haunted mansion filled with moody ghosts and one annoying ghost hunter.

At least the spirits weren't touching her anymore. She'd never been able to feel ghosts, not the way people with a natural ability could, but she'd felt Casper trying to pull her and Creed apart before her nap, and then an hour ago, Casper wrapped its icy fingers around her throat. On instinct, she'd charged herself with enough juice to power the space shuttle, and whatever had been touching her had fled.

And then told on her. She knew because Creed had pegged her with an exasperated look before explaining how shocking spirits was not a good idea.

Tattletales. No wonder Creed got along with them so well.

Now she crouched on her heels and watched Creed do his thing as he communicated with the dead who, in her opinion, weren't dead enough.

How he could tolerate lying shirtless on the cold marble for hours was beyond her. He didn't appear to be uncomfortable, at least. In fact, though his arms would flex now and then, and sometimes his abs would tighten, revealing one fine six-pack, he seemed perfectly relaxed.

Damn, she wanted to reach out and smooth her hands over all those hard muscles. She wanted to kiss the look of fierce concentration right off his handsome face, to make him open his eyes and worship her with them like he had in the bedroom.

Right now, though, he belonged to the netherworld, a place where she was a stranger, and she was happy to keep it that way.

Energy sizzled along her nerve endings, and the lights flickered. Creed's body went stiff, and his eyes shot open, stared with haunting emptiness at the ceiling.

"Creed?" Tentatively, she reached out. A chill sank deep into her bones at the feel of his clammy skin.

Shit. Was this normal? She grasped his wrist to check his pulse, and cool whips of air wrapped around her.

"Get away from me," she growled at the entity, letting her body flood with energy. "Get away, or I'll light you the fuck up."

A shrill, angry cry vibrated the house, but the spirit snapped back. Creed's pulse beat weakly beneath her fingertips, too thready for comfort. Unsure what to do, she looked up at the flickering lights.

"You'd better not hurt him, whoever the hell you are."

"Aww, you really do care."

The gasp that escaped her pissed her off, but at least Creed was okay. More than okay, if the glint of humor in the depths of his eyes was any indication.

"I don't give a shit what happens to you." She twitched a shoulder in a nonchalant shrug. "But Dev does. That's why I care."

"I don't believe you," he said, tucking one arm behind his head.

"And why's that?"

He gave her the cocky grin that infuriated her every time. "Because you're still holding my hand."

She jerked away like she'd been burned. A lot of less-than-complimentary names for him came to mind, but the distinct ring tone of her cell saved him from the humiliation. She drew the phone from her pocket. *Dev. Thank God*.

"Please tell me you have a new assignment for me."

A sigh crackled over the airwaves. "You aren't playing nice with Creed, are you?"

Oh, she'd played, but it definitely hadn't been *nice*. It had been naughty and wrong and yet she wanted to do it again. Which was even more wrong, since she still couldn't stand the guy.

"Just get me out of here."

"I'll have a helo there in half an hour."

She arched a brow. "Seriously?"

"You're going to join Wyatt and Ender in Louisiana. They're already on their way to help out Haley. I'll have all essential materials to bring you up to speed in the chopper."

"Will I get to beat up bad guys?"

"Most likely."

Grinning, she thanked Dev and hung up. Creed was sitting on one hip, braced by one arm, the other resting atop his knee. The way his legs spread drew her gaze straight to his crotch, to the impressive bulge behind the leather fly.

Heat flushed her body, and she tore her eyes away because as much as she'd love to go another round with him, she couldn't. Not now. She'd gone twenty-one years believing she couldn't have sex, and the idea that now it was possible but probably only with Creed had rocked her hard. She'd never needed anyone for anything, and she wanted to make sure that if she slept with him again, it would be because she wanted sex, not because she needed it. Or needed him.

"I'm outta here." She pushed to her feet and headed to her bedroom to grab her shit.

"Annika..."

She stopped, but didn't look at him. "Don't." For a moment she stood there, waiting to see if he would say anything else, and when he didn't she took the stairs two at a time.

She couldn't put her fists in enemy faces fast enough.

CHAPTER
Twenty

Haley didn't have time to think too hard on what Remy had said about her being disposable.

Not to me, Haley.

Even now, as they kept to the shadowy back streets of the town Remy had led them to, she shoved aside what he'd said. There'd be time later to panic, to fully comprehend how close she'd let him get to her.

And how close she felt herself getting to him. No question about it, she was in way over her head and rapidly losing the strength to tread water.

Grunting when what she wanted to do was curse, she adjusted the pack on her back and concentrated on how much her feet hurt. Her boots had become soaked when they'd run through the swamp, and the wet leather had rubbed her skin raw. Her feet hadn't suffered like this since basic training, when her new combat boots had been implements of torture.

"Haley? Are you all right?" Remy asked, coming to a halt near a row of hedges between two houses.

"Yeah." She hadn't realized the pain had caused her to fall behind. "Sorry. I'm a little distracted."

He eyed her warily, like he sensed her lie, but she was careful to not limp or wince or in any way reveal her pain. If he knew, he'd do something manly and stupid, like carry her.

"Give me your pack."

"I already told you I can handle it."

"We've been over this. Remember what happened last time you tried to do something by yourself?"

Her tattoo tingled, and she nearly smiled, recalling the lesson he'd given her on the dining room table. Then she realized that though he'd changed his tactics, he was still trying to order her around.

"Giving me an orgasm isn't much of a threat. I'm keeping the backpack. And I need to try to contact ACRO now that we're out of the swamp. Maybe I have a signal."

She shifted the pack, and he must have thought she was going for her phone, because he stayed her movements by grasping her arm. "Don't bother. I shorted out your cell."

"You what?"

He shifted his weight and had the decency to look sheepish. "Yeah, well, I was pissed about the tattoo last night."

"You really should work on your temper."

"Later. Right now we need to grab my dad's truck and find a pay phone."

A dog howled nearby, a mournful cry at the moon, and she hoped Linda, the lead psychic of the Triad to whom she'd been assigned, was right about the power of the full moon to enhance psychic conduits.

"No. Itor knew things they shouldn't have known, so I don't want to use a nonsecure landline, in case they're listening. I'll do the backup thing."

"Backup?"

She nodded, wishing it hadn't come to this. She'd never

communicated psychically before, except in controlled tests, and despite Dev's assurances that it would work, she had enough skeptic in her to make her nervous. What she hated most was that psychic comms were one-sided, so she'd have no way of knowing if her message had been received.

Still, it was all they had.

"I need a quiet place." She'd attempted to make the connection earlier, in the bayou, but her head had hurt too badly to make it work.

Though the streets were mostly empty, it was Saturday night, and even in a small town—or maybe especially in a small town—people liked to party, and headlights flashed ahead.

Remy took her hand and led her down a side street to a parklike grassy area with stone benches. "Will this work? What are we doing, anyway?"

She looked at him standing before her, his clothes wet and muddy like hers, and thought about how they'd been in a similar state last night, when they'd had sex outside the house during the storm. When he'd looked at her like no one ever had, like she was a lifeline.

Her parents had looked at each other like that.

Heart pounding, she once again fought down the panic that gripped her, and cleared her throat, eager to get back to the job.

"Before I was sent here, I was bonded to a team of three psychics. It's supposed to allow me to send messages." Bonding with a Triad was an option offered to all agents before a potentially dangerous mission, but because she wasn't a fully trained field operative, her participation had been mandatory.

"Uh-huh." He folded his arms across his broad chest. "So you're calling the cavalry with your mind?"

"I'd think you, of all people, would be open to the possibility."

"I'll believe it when I see it."

Yeah, she would too.

She sat and pulled him down next to her. "Just keep an eye out for psychotic-looking bad guys."

Closing her eyes, she relaxed like she'd been taught, and then visualized a blue stone in her mind. A brilliant oval-cut topaz, spinning like a top. When the stone began to hum and then glow, warmth infused her body, signaling a connection with one of the psychics assigned to her.

As though aggravated by the link, her head throbbed, bruised by the earlier psychic assault. She wondered if ACRO knew about the attack. Linda had mentioned that even without a deliberate connection, Triads would instantly become aware of trauma to an assigned operative.

The mind cries out when the body is injured.

Quickly, because the pain intensified with each passing second, she fed the stone images of what had happened so far—Itor attacking, she and Remy escaping into the dark bayou and then slipping into town.

She felt herself starting to tremble as the agony of the connection deepened, drilling white-hot nails into her brain. Linda said that images were more effective for communication than words, but Haley could no longer think, and instead screamed inside her mind, *Itor has Remy's father. They want us to go to Lafayette. We'll make contact when we arrive at a hotel.*

"Haley? Haley!"

Remy's voice ripped into her, severing the link. She snapped open her eyes, and immediately plunged into a bone-deep chill. Shivering, she rubbed her arms, and Remy pulled her into his warm body.

"You were shouting. Shaking so hard I thought you were seizing. Are you okay?"

Okay might be an exaggeration, but at least she no longer

thought her skull would shatter. "Better now. But I could use some aspirin."

His hands ran up and down her arms in long, soothing strokes, and she burrowed as close as she could get, let herself relax into his strength and heat. He smelled like bayou and ozone and man, and she didn't think she'd ever been so comforted by any scent.

"What just happened?"

"I told ACRO about our night," she said against his chest. "We need to get on the road and to a hotel."

She just hoped Remy Senior's truck would be at the bar where Remy said his dad went every night, because she didn't want to have to steal a car. The last thing they needed now was to be arrested.

"We don't have time for a hotel."

"It's where my agency will meet us."

"No offense, Haley, but I'm not going to trust my dad's life to your psychic airwaves."

She pulled back and looked up at him. "I know I haven't given you a lot of reason to trust me, but I'm asking you to have faith in this."

"You're asking too much."

Pain sliced through her. "I thought you said you wanted to trust me."

"Wanting to and being able to are different things." He wrapped a lock of her hair around his finger, and then drew it across her cheek in a long, tender stroke. She instantly softened at the contrasting sensation of his callused pad and her silky curl on her skin, and her body melted against him, her heart thawing like the polar ice caps.

"I trust my gun and my gut," he said after a short pause. "So far, neither has let me down."

Like you have. His unspoken words hung above them like

black clouds in the cool air. She scooted away and stood. "We need to go."

He came to his feet and pulled her into his arms again. "Haley, ask me to do anything else." He tipped her chin up so she had to look into his eyes. "Just not that. I can't gamble with my dad's life. He wasn't the best parent in the world, but he's all I have."

"You'll have so much more if you just give ACRO a chance."

Give me a chance.

The stray thought rattled her, and she broke free once more, as though she'd spoken out loud. The distance didn't help. She kept thinking crazy things, like, *Trust me. Give me a chance. Make love to me until nothing exists but us.*

Yeah, treading water had just become impossible, and Haley was sinking fast.

THE MOTEL WAS OLD, off the map, and the bed creaked to high heaven every time Remy or Haley moved. And they were going to be moving a lot, now that they had a room to themselves and nothing else to do but wait.

After Remy had hotwired Remy Senior's truck and they'd hightailed it out of the bar's parking lot and out of the bayou, he'd noticed Haley seemed quiet.

At first, he'd attributed it to what had happened to her. Every time he thought about someone breaking into her mind, hurting her that way, his anger would rise. Which wasn't good, not for a mission like this. Anger wasn't the healthiest emotion to carry into battle with you; it could throw off your game if you weren't careful.

But she'd insisted she was all right, and the closer they got to Lafayette, the more time she spent reassuring him that everything was going to be all right.

Now, in the motel room, she was still trying to take his

mind off things—and although it wasn't completely working, she was doing a damned fine job.

"Mmmmm, that's nice, Remy," she murmured, from where she sat straddling him on the bed.

She'd showered while he did a perimeter check outside their room—it was on the second floor, overlooking the street, which was exactly what he'd wanted—and when he'd come back inside, he'd stripped her towel off as soon as he'd gotten a chance.

First, he'd insisted on using the antibiotic cream and bandages on her ankles and feet, guilt tugging at him that he hadn't forced her to let him carry her pack—or her—through the marshes.

Damned stubborn woman.

Then he'd gotten distracted by her naked body, and had kissed his way up her calves even as he massaged her feet.

Now he sat up against the headboard and took his time to just play with her perfect breasts, sucking one nipple and then the other, until they turned a deep rose color and the peaks stiffened and she was begging him for more. He tortured her for a little longer, licked and blew softly on each taut peak.

She shivered and grabbed at him and he really wished they could stay here in this piece-of-shit motel room forever.

Plans were going to be made later—for right now, it was all about Haley.

"Better than nice," he murmured, trailed his tongue between her breasts and let his hands trail down her bare buttocks.

She pressed her sex against his groin. "You've got too many clothes on," she said. "Let me help you with that."

"I could use a shower," he said.

"No, not yet." She nipped along his neck. "I like the way you smell—like the bayou and fresh rain."

She helped him out of his shirt and moved off him so she

could slide his pants down. And then she licked her way over his chest and stomach before he could get ahold of her again.

She crawled between his legs, and he smiled, because he'd never met a woman who enjoyed giving oral sex as much as Haley did. And right after he thanked his lucky stars, he leaned on an elbow, before he lost control of his senses and urged her backside toward him.

She looked at him over her shoulder teasingly. "Why, *chere*, are you asking what I think you're asking?"

"You bet your ass," he said, gave hers a playful slap and let her straddle his chest with her legs.

She was already so wet for him, and he buried his face against her as she licked the length of his cock and both their bodies jerked in unison from the pleasure.

He moaned against her, then tongued the hard nub of her clit. She tasted so sweet, like he could settle in and live here between her legs for a good, long time, and he caressed her thighs with his hands while he sucked and licked for her pleasure.

He was more than aware of how his own body was responding, the way his muscles tensed with need, and Jesus, her tongue was everywhere, licking his balls and that hypersensitive area right behind them that made him practically jump off the bed.

His toes curled as she held his thighs apart, balancing her body weight on them, and in turn he spread her wider and used his tongue to plunge as deeply inside her as he could get. She bucked up, but he held her in place with his hips as the patter of a soft but persistent rain began to tap the window.

She wiggled against his face, her own moans vibrating around his cock, and she was so ready, her fingers digging into his thighs as she worked his shaft up and down. Just one long suckle on her clit and she was coming against his mouth and he was coming in hers and the thunder boomed right outside their room in appreciation, the rain a steady drum of applause.

Yeah, Mother Nature was certainly showing her sense of humor. His skin tingled with the electrical currents from the storm he'd just drawn in toward them, and Haley turned her body around to nestle against his chest. She ran her fingertips up and down his biceps and he felt her body relax into his.

"Mmm, you still smell like rain. What were you doing outside earlier?" she asked, her voice husky. Her eyes were heavy-lidded, and he was prepared to let her drift off while he protected them until dawn came.

According to Haley, the magic men were supposed to show up at some point soon, and he needed to be equally prepared for when they did and if they didn't.

"I was just shoring up this place," he said. "It lacks an adequate security system and I don't trust those Itor people as far as I can throw them. Especially because they seem to be able to throw *me* with no problem." He frowned at the memory and she kissed him lightly on the forehead.

"We'll get them, Remy. I know how worried you are about your father."

He shrugged. "He's the only family I have. He never showed it the way I wanted, but I know he cares about me on some level. Was the only one who did."

"Not the only one now," she said, and twined her legs through his, and God, he really wanted to believe her.

"Don't you think we should talk about all of this?" he asked finally. "I know you need sleep, that you've been hurt, but we've got something going on between us."

She pushed herself off his chest onto her elbow so she could look at him. "You know I had nothing to do with this," she said, touched his tattoo that already looked more healed since that morning. Hers was healing at an equal rate.

"There's something between us," he repeated. "You know all about me. You told me that, back on the bayou," he reminded her. "You know my past history with women."

"Enough to know that you've never wanted a history."

"Enough to know that I *couldn't* have one, Haley. There's a big difference."

"And now you want a history? With me?" she asked, and he wasn't sure if she actually wanted him to say yes or not.

"I don't know if it's the tattoos or the weather or the spell I threw when I was ten . . ."

"What spell?"

He paused, wondering if he was really going to admit this to her. "When I was younger, when I knew I was different . . . Shit, this is embarrassing."

"Tell me, Remy."

He took a deep breath and continued, told the story quickly before he chickened out. "I wanted someone who loved me, loved me for me. In spite of my weather shit. Someone who understood it, and me. And so I threw a spell and asked for all of that. And that night, for the first time, I had the dream." He swallowed hard and Haley stroked his arm. "I dreamed about the symbol. This symbol." He pointed to her tattoo.

"You've been dreaming about this since you were ten?" she asked. "No wonder you freaked when you first saw it."

"Yeah. That was something I never expected to see. I'd forgotten about the spell. Given up on finding someone. But I'd never stopped drawing this symbol." His finger traced the tattoo, the one he could—and did—easily draw in his sleep. "Never stopped dreaming about it."

Haley sat up completely, drew the sheet around her as if

she'd suddenly gotten a chill. "What are you telling me? That you summoned me? That this is all some kind of voodoo curse?"

HALEY STARED AT HIM, unsure how to handle this. It wasn't that she didn't believe him. She just didn't like the idea that a damned curse may have put her life on a course she hadn't set for herself. Not when her entire adult life had been about doing what would give her the most control—over her career, over her personal relationships.

"Tell me, Haley, why is it that you call my ability to control the weather a gift, but what we have together is a curse? What kind of criteria are you basing this on? And who the hell gets to make that determination? You?"

Okaaaaay. "What got up your ass?"

"Your finger, once or twice."

"That's very funny."

"Glad you're amused, because I'm still wondering why some things you can't explain are gifts and others are curses."

She rubbed her temples, unsure of her own answer and thinking that the fact that it was two in the morning didn't help her state of mind. "I don't like to think my life has been predestined like that."

"And you think I do? You aren't the only one with a tattoo, *bebe*. And you sure as hell don't spend your days worrying about whether or not you're going to hurt someone or compromise a mission because of a fucking strong wind."

He was right. She was being unfair. Very unfair, especially considering that his life had been one big storm track influenced by forces he couldn't control.

"I'm sorry," she said softly. "I just...I've never wanted to fall in love. I've avoided it all my life. So to think that some spell might influence my feelings against my will..."

"Why wouldn't you want to fall in love?"

Shrugging, she swung her legs off the bed. "Didn't you say you wanted to get something to eat?"

Remy grabbed her wrist. "Haley?"

He didn't say it, but she owed him. Owed him for lying to him, for having him brought to Bayou Blonde... which had led to his father being taken by some of the most evil villains on the planet.

"Love makes you give up things," she murmured. "It makes you selfish. And blind."

His gaze bored into her with such intensity that she had to look away. "Where is this coming from? Did some guy hurt you?"

"No, nothing like that." She pulled loose from his grip. "Look, I don't want to talk about it, okay? My parents are dead and buried—"

"Ah."

He said it like he'd figured it all out. Psychoanalyst Remy Begnaud had discovered what made her tick. Good for him, because she had yet to figure it out.

"Did they have a bad marriage?" he pressed, and she cursed his training as an interrogator. The tone of his voice, so level, measured, was meant to lull her into thinking she could share and that he would understand. "Did one of them cheat?"

"Cheat?" She barked out a bitter laugh. "My parents had a very loving relationship. Unfortunately, that love didn't extend to me."

"They didn't love you?" He sat up, grasped her arms and pulled her back against his chest.

"They did." She wiggled to escape the intimate hold, but when his fingers began to knead the tightness out of her shoulder muscles, she softened up like cookie dough. He had a way of doing that to her, and she was starting to like it, damn him.

"But?"

"But their love for each other was so absorbing and extreme that everything else—jobs, house, friends, me—came after, far after. It was all very Ron and Nancy Reagan."

Her parents believed their relationship couldn't be stronger or healthier, and they were probably right, but Haley had always felt left out, and as a result had always viewed love as a weakness. Love meant forsaking all else for the affections of one person. No way would she fall into that trap. Her career, her self-esteem, were too important to watch it go down the drain because of a man. Her mother had never seen anything wrong with giving up her own career, but in Haley's eyes, her mother had given up everything.

"So what happened to them? You said they were dead."

His thumbs worked on a particularly stubborn knot, and she groaned, willing to tell him anything now. The man was good. Too good. He'd have her confessing all her sins and even making some up if he kept up this blissful torture.

"Mom died of cancer a year after I joined the Air Force." Haley had attended the funeral, but her dad had refused to speak to her. Heck, she hadn't spoken with either of them since she'd sworn in. Before she and her father could resolve their differences, he had died, too. "My dad was gone six months later. Doctors couldn't find a cause, but everyone who knew him said he'd died of a broken heart." She swallowed the sudden lump in her throat. "See what love does? It makes you weak. Kills you."

Warm breath feathered over her scalp as Remy pressed a gentle kiss to the top of her head. "It also gives people something to live for," he whispered.

Tears stung her eyes. Dammit, she wasn't going to cry. She refused to let her parents hurt her more than they already had.

"Can we be done with the mushy stuff now?" She playfully kissed his hand and shot for breezy. "I really am starving. Maybe we can get a to-go order from the Denny's across the street."

He wrapped his arms around her and pulled her even tighter against his chest. She was completely unprepared for the depth of emotion his embrace coaxed out of her. Never had she felt so safe. Years of loneliness vanished in an instant.

Loneliness she hadn't even known existed.

"You stay here," he said softly. "I'll feed you."

He climbed out of bed and pulled on his pants and shirt, which were still wet and caked with dirt after their escape from the bayou. He checked his weapon with skilled, easy grace, and an inappropriate shiver wracked her body. Military men had never been her thing, had always chafed at her inner feminist, but her deepest, basest female instincts couldn't help but appreciate a man who could handle himself and keep her safe.

Then her heart, which had felt all comforted and safe, jumped to her throat as the door flew open.

Twenty-one

"What the hell...?"

Remy had rolled himself and Haley off the bed to the floor, kept her down while he drew his gun and pointed it toward the doorway, but it was too late. If the man standing in the middle of the room, who'd materialized out of nowhere, had wanted him gone, Remy would be gone.

"It's okay, Remy. He's one of ours," Haley said. She'd shifted and pulled the sheet down to cover herself. Remy noticed that the man at least kept his eyes respectfully averted from Haley, but the sneer he had especially for Remy wasn't hidden at all.

"If I'd been the enemy, you'd have been dead, SEAL," the man growled. The guy was his height, a little lankier, but Remy bet he'd have put up a hell of a fight if it had come to that.

Former military, if Remy had to guess. He wondered what the man's special skill was, beyond appearing out of thin air.

"Christ, Ender, you've got to stop doing that." Another tall man appeared in the open doorway. His dark hair was long, nearly to his shoulders, and he closed the door behind him. "Are you all right, Haley?"

"I'm fine. But I'd like to get dressed," she said. "If you could all give me some privacy for a second so I could get to the bathroom, that would be great."

Remy watched the two men turn away and then shifted his attention over to Haley. Who looked back at him. "You didn't say I couldn't look," he said in a low voice, and the man named Ender snorted.

Haley mouthed, *Be nice . . . they're two of ACRO's best*, and then shut herself in the bathroom. When Remy brought his attention back to the men Haley thought so highly of, they were already facing him. "You must be Remy," the dark-haired man said. "I'm Wyatt Kennedy, and this is Ender."

"Ender?" Remy asked.

"Yes, Little Remy," Ender said, and it was Remy's turn to growl.

"Come on, guys—this isn't the time for a cock-block contest," Wyatt said. "We've got work to do, and not a hell of a lot of time."

Remy checked his watch and nodded. "What's your plan?"

"You mean you didn't come up with anything while you were waiting?" Ender asked. "Oh, right, you were too busy—"

"Ender, come on," Wyatt stopped him. "His old man's in trouble."

Ender sighed, loudly. Then he turned and started rifling through the bag he'd brought in, unpacking a laptop and assorted weapons.

"Aren't you better off doing that in your own room?" Remy asked.

"This is our room," Ender stated.

"No way. You two aren't staying here," Remy said.

Ender growled. "You don't tell me where to stay, SEAL."

"Remy, man, we can't risk leaving you two alone," Wyatt explained, stepping in between Remy and Ender.

"I've done all right so far." Remy fought the urge to bare his teeth at Ender.

"Yeah, you have," Wyatt said, putting a hand on his shoulder, as if to calm Remy down. It worked, momentarily. "But that's not good enough now."

"You have no idea what you're up against," Ender added.

"And you're going to explain it to me?"

"Those are my orders." Ender frowned as if he disliked both the orders themselves and being ordered. Remy got that all too well.

"What now?" he asked.

"Now we work. Unless you need sleep." Ender said it as if sleep were for the weak. On that, Remy couldn't help but agree. Without another word, Ender pulled his weapon and walked out of the room.

"Where's he going?"

"He'll reset the perimeter alarms. They work on normal enemies," Wyatt explained. "Not on people like us."

"Is he always like that?" Remy asked.

"Pretty much."

"How the hell do you stand it?"

"He's not that much different than you and me, truth be told, Remy. Besides, I owe the guy. He's the one who rescued me and brought me into ACRO five years ago."

"What were you doing before that?"

"I was with the teams," Wyatt said, and Remy suddenly knew that his old man was going to be all right, after all.

HALEY STOOD IN THE BATHROOM, cheeks burning at having been caught naked in bed. Worse, she had nothing but towels to wear.

After she and Remy had checked into the hotel, she'd tried

to contact the Triad again, but her head had nearly exploded, so she'd broken down and called Dev while Remy did whatever SEALs do outside. Then she'd showered, used the opportunity to wash her clothes, and now her garments dripped from where they hung draped over the rusted shower rod.

"Haley?" Remy tapped softly on the door. "Your buddies brought us some clothes."

"My heroes."

She took the khaki BDU pants and black T-shirt from Remy, grateful for ACRO's foresight. Or second sight. Didn't matter. Important body parts would be covered.

Once dressed, she dragged her fingers through her hair and stepped out of the bathroom, to find the three men overpowering the small room with their presence. Ender had turned his chair so he could prop his long legs up on the window ledge, the laptop balanced at his knees. He looked relaxed, like he was surfing the web for pleasure, but she wasn't fooled. She didn't know him well, but Ender's reputation more than preceded him, and she knew he had deadly aim.

All three men were deadly, with or without their special abilities. Even with Wyatt's riotous personality, she didn't mistake for a second the danger that lay beneath that demeanor.

Remy sat next to Wyatt at the table, maps of the area scattered between them. Remy looked up first, smiled, although his eyes held a more serious glint than they had earlier.

He was in mission-mode. A shiver of pure, female appreciation skittered through her, and once again, she wondered when her preferences in men had gone from suits and ties to cammies and combat boots. One thing was certain: after this, there would be no going back to corporate casual.

Wyatt turned to her, his lean, lanky body screaming with excess energy and a surplus of sensuality. Rumor had it that in addition to telekinesis, he had the power to seduce anyone, female *or* male, without even trying. Haley believed it, had in the past fallen victim to the same sexual yearning other women claimed to feel in his presence, but now, thankfully, she felt nothing.

"Haley, did those bastards show you anything besides Red Rover Road? Anything that can help us pinpoint a likely location for Itor to set up shop?"

Her head throbbed at the reminder of the heinous violation. "I saw a countryside. Marshy fields and barbed-wire fencing." She plopped down on the bed and grabbed the med kit Remy had left out after bandaging her feet. "And a three-way intersection...I think the crossroad is called something like Washington." A red haze of pain obscured the memory, and she sighed. "I'm sorry. I can't be sure."

"It's okay. We'll find it." Remy ran his finger over the map. "Could it be Washout? I've got a Washout Road bisecting Red Rover about twenty miles outside the city limits."

"Good call," Wyatt said, tracing the map point with a pencil.

She rolled up her pants legs and dabbed antiseptic on her shin cuts while Wyatt dug through a pile of maps and charts and pulled out a satellite photo. "There're a shitload of isolated farmhouses and crap in the area."

Cursing, Ender dug his cell out of his jeans' pocket. "I'll call Resources. I can't get anything on my computer."

"What are you talking about?" Haley asked, feeling a little useless.

"We need property and rental records. If we can get a list of houses that have been rented recently, it could help us locate Itor's local base of operations."

Remy shook his head. "It's hard to believe they could be so easy to lose in the bayou but that well set up here."

"Believe it, SEAL." Ender stood, paced while he spoke to someone on the phone.

Wyatt leaned back in his chair and kicked his booted feet up on the air-conditioning unit beneath the window. "Don't underestimate them," he said to Remy. "Even if they fucked up in the bayou. Haley, what kind of operatives are we looking at? Did you see anything?"

"I only saw two men. One of them was telekinetic."

"Telekinetic how?"

Remy rubbed the back of his head as though he could still feel the blow when he hit the tree. "Asshole picked me up and tossed me about twenty feet."

Wyatt scowled, and Remy glanced between him and Haley. "Why? What's up? Are there different kinds of telekinesis?"

"Most telekinetics are like you and me. We can affect *things*. You rearrange the weather. I can toss inanimate objects around." To prove his point, Wyatt sent one of Haley's boots sailing over Ender's head and into the door, which earned him a dirty look and a return trip of the boot thrown with a deft arm.

"That could come in handy," Remy said.

"Yeah, it does. But I can't directly affect living things."

"Why not?"

"Humans and animals are protected by auras that naturally shield telekinetic energy. It takes a special talent to bypass the aura. Those who can, can either affect a body on the outside, like what happened to you, or they can affect the inside. Stop a heart from beating or cause a stroke." His expression grew grim. "You don't want to meet up with one of the latter."

The map in Remy's hand crumpled in his fist. "Was it someone like that who hurt Haley?"

Concern softened Wyatt's dark eyes when they flickered over her. "No. That fucker is a special brand of psychic. There's only a handful of them in the world. Thing is, they can't just mind-rape anyone at the drop of a hat. They have to possess deep, intimate details about the person."

She hadn't known about that limitation to the mind-rape power. Hadn't wanted to think on any of it too much—had let Remy and his magical methods of persuasion in bed distract her from the fact that someone had used her mind—and her past—against her.

Dev had always promised the utmost privacy for his operatives. Something was going wrong at ACRO, and that thought made her head ache residually.

"Whoever it was knew things he shouldn't have known—about ACRO, about me," she admitted, and Remy moved toward her. He sat next to her on the bed, reached out to massage her neck with a strong hand while Wyatt looked at her with concern.

"Dev will want to talk with you when you get back, to figure out how Itor could have gotten the type of info they needed," Wyatt said quietly.

She nodded, because Dev had already told her as much. For now, though, her eyelids had grown heavy, and it was all she could do to listen to the guys' plan. She put aside the med kit and stretched out on the bed, just to rest her eyes.

It seemed like five minutes later when Remy shook her shoulder gently, but a glance at the cheap bedside clock showed that she'd been asleep for three hours.

"We have food, *chere*."

The smell of bacon, eggs, and pancakes brought her out of her fuzzy, groggy state, and she gratefully sat up and took a Styrofoam plate of food.

"Did you guys figure out where Itor might be hiding?"

Remy nodded and sat next to her, close enough that his heat wrapped around her like a comforting blanket. "There's a trailer near that intersection we discussed. It's well hidden and was rented out just three days ago."

He'd showered and wore clothing identical to hers, though

his BDU pants were camouflage-patterned. Worry lines creased his forehead, and she reached for him, took his hand.

"We'll get your dad."

"I know. I just keep thinking about how I want to rip those bastards apart for what they did to you. Once we disperse from the vehicle, all I'll care about is getting my hands on them."

Ender made a gun with his forefinger and thumb. "All I care about is shot geometry, wind and distance."

"Snipers." Wyatt rolled his eyes. "But speaking of wind, we could use a weather briefing if you're up for it. We're going to hit them an hour earlier than they said. Two o'clock."

She nodded, glad to have something to do. Part of the ACRO weather station's duties included weather briefs for every mission and flight, and giving the reports had always been one of her favorite aspects of the job.

She ate while she used Ender's laptop to download current model analyses, radar images and observations.

"Well, boys, it looks like prime bad-guy hunting weather. Partly cloudy, eighty degrees, seventy percent humidity. Ender, winds will be from the southwest at around seven knots. There's also a narrow band of light showers to the west, but it shouldn't pose a problem. Remy might be able to draw on it for a little extra power."

Ender took a break from shoveling bacon and sausage into his mouth to crumple his coffee cup and toss it into the trash. She'd never seen anyone eat so much meat. His cholesterol must be through the roof. "What, exactly, can you do, SEAL?"

Remy froze with his fork halfway to his mouth and shot Haley a look of uncertainty.

"It's okay, man," Wyatt said. "You don't have to hide it anymore."

The way Remy shifted, just slightly, on the bed told her he

wasn't ready to open up to complete strangers about something he'd kept buried for his entire life.

She cleared her throat. "He can rapidly alter the local atmospheric conditions to create fog, wind, rain, hail . . . and he even spun up a tornado in the bayou."

Wyatt grinned. "Cool."

Ender snorted. "What's the catch? There's always a catch."

"Strong emotions can spawn weather I can't command," Remy muttered.

"That's a control issue. ACRO can train that out of you." Ender's hawklike gaze lit on Remy with predatory intensity. "I'm talking about the kryptonite. What is it?"

Remy bared his teeth. "Do you tell everyone what yours is? You want people to know about your kill switch?"

The testosterone in the room built like a summer storm, but before it reached critical mass, Wyatt tossed a pen at Ender. "He's right. Unless we need to know . . ." He glanced at Haley. "Do we need to know? Will he compromise the mission if he snags kryptonite?"

"I never have before," Remy said tightly, and Haley shook her head.

"He'll be okay." There was no severe weather on the way to mess with his libido, and besides, if worse came to worst, she'd be there with him. "So when do we go in?"

"Not we," Remy said. "Us. You're staying here."

"The hell I am."

Wyatt swallowed whatever he'd been chewing. "Annika is on the way, and if Remy can do what you said, we should be more than fine."

Ender merely pointed his plastic fork at her. "You're a liability. You stay."

She huffed. "I realize I'm not a field operative. But I'm possibly your only communication connection with Itor."

None of them appeared to be convinced, so she played the danger card. "What if they decide to mind-fuck me again while you're gone?"

"She's got a point," Wyatt said, and Remy shook his head. "I don't like it."

"That's because you're thinking with your dick," Ender drawled.

Remy turned to her. "Do I still have to be nice?"

Ender tossed his empty plate into the trash. "I hate to agree with Wyatt on anything, but he's right, Haley has a point. If they invade her mind again, they might cause some serious damage before we could get her help. She can go, but she stays back."

For some reason, she felt like she'd been accepted by the popular kids for the first time in her life. And for the first time she'd be on the front lines, in the action instead of supporting the mission with weather reports from behind the scenes.

"You stay way back." Remy's eyes were fierce, his voice deep and low. "I don't want them coming near you."

Before she could bristle at his order, Wyatt cleared his throat. "Remy, man, speaking of coming near..."

Bracing one lean hip against the table, Ender sent Remy a look of warning that shot chills down her spine. "Don't let them take you." When Remy opened his mouth to argue, Ender held up his hand. "I know you think you're such a bad motherfucker that they can't force you to work for them, but they have ways. And in their hands, you're a walking WMD."

"Yeah? And what about in ACRO's hands?"

Wyatt shook his head. "We don't work like that. Itor sells services to the highest bidder. Everything we do is for the good of the United States and its allies. Which means we won't force you to work for us. But you've seen how they operate. We want you to join us of your own free will."

Haley held her breath, hoping Remy wouldn't ask what would happen if he refused, and fortunately, he didn't.

"We'll see what happens after this is over." He pierced her with a heated stare. "There are a lot of things that need to be settled."

CHAPTER
Twenty-two

Dev's family mansion was still full of company, but much lonelier since Annika took off. Creed stood in the kitchen, staring at the abandoned bag of chips on the floor and her soda, while he took a gulp of his own.

She'd looked a little worried when she'd left him, which was cool. She'd never seen him when he went into one of his so-called ghost-talk trances, probably freaked a little when he seemed to lose consciousness.

Which meant she cared.

And although he wished she were still here, for many different reasons, helping to bring in a new operative safely was something good for Annika to be a part of. Dangerous, but good.

He wondered if the psychics who followed most of the members of the ACRO team—three psychics per operative, all on duty for eight-hour shifts so each operative had emergency coverage twenty-four seven—might sense the way he felt about Annika. He thought he had enough self-control to keep it under wraps.

But this being Annika's first time, her mind would be more vulnerable. Confused. He hoped that the psychics' code of honor and silence held true, because he didn't want such delicate information getting back to Dev. Not that way.

He checked his watch, saw that it had been nine hours since he'd been alone here. Hours of Kat arguing with the spirit, of physically and emotionally draining work, and they hadn't gotten any further than discovering that whoever was locked inside this house wanted access to Dev.

Which Creed had figured out from the second he'd stepped over the threshold, so he hoped it wouldn't take nine more hours to extract additional information.

He massaged the back of his neck, before Kat took over that job for him, easing some of the tension that had started his temples throbbing. Of course, part of the tension was her fault in the first place.

"Are you ever going to let me have my own life?" he asked her. He got no response beyond a light touch to his forehead and a slight throb along his right side.

No, neither Kat nor Annika seemed the type to share him with anyone else. Then again, Annika hadn't promised him shit.

A loud slam brought him firmly back into the job, as his attention was being demanded.

The doors on the second floor opened and shut, and he slugged the rest of his soda, tossed the can and stripped off his shirt again.

He lay down on the bare marble floor at the bottom of the staircase. The spirit wanted him closer to the portal, but there was no way that was going to happen.

He closed his eyes, concentrated on drawing in the spirit's power and finally got a vision.

A young boy, maybe fourteen. Brown hair. Lanky, like he hadn't yet grown into himself.

Dev. Walking through this house, down the main staircase.

"You know Dev," he said, and Kat said yes, the spirit knew Dev very, very well.

"I have questions—from Dev," he said.

"I want to talk to Devlin directly," it said, and Creed's eyes opened. It was rare that a spirit spoke directly to him, instead of going through Kat. A strong spirit.

"You can't talk to Dev," he said out loud. "You're going to have to deal with me first."

"Devlin sent you."

"Yes."

"He wants to know about the kidnapping," the spirit said. "And something more. Something about an infiltration."

"Yes." Dev had mentioned kidnapping, but Creed had no idea what the spirit meant by the infiltration. Still, he'd run with it. "Dev wants to know about both."

"You'll have to let me out to get that information," it said.

"You'll have to take that up with whatever put you here. I don't have that power," he said, and the house roared with anger, with pain, and the emotion pierced through him. He turned on his side, curled up to protect himself as the shrill sounds continued to batter their way through him.

He wasn't sure how long it went on, and then he became aware of a touch against the back of his neck, urging him to lie flat again. A touch that wasn't Kat's, but still, he uncurled his body, kept his eyes closed and did what was being asked of him.

Another touch, this time on his chest—soft at first, and then more insistent. Again, not Kat's. Then the caress moved down toward his abs, and he froze.

No, this ghost was giving off vibes for a direction he didn't swing.

Kat knew that, and he knew her overprotectiveness would

kick in shortly, but she was going to let the spirit push it a little, because they both needed answers.

"Who are you?" he asked, even as what felt like fingers tickled his sides.

"Dev knows," it said, and Creed felt his shoulders and hips press to the floor.

It was going to try to hold him down. Kat caressed his shoulders, her way of telling him not to worry, to just listen.

Yeah, easy for her to say. Because this spirit couldn't be trusted. Not that any spirit could, really. They were all tricky.

A thin sheen of sweat covered his chest, his right side pulsed with excess energy and he could smell the electricity floating in the air that always accompanied a true haunting.

People liked to think that hauntings were nothing more than urban legends, scary stories to tell around the campfire and laugh about later.

Oz always used to say that ghost stories were not for little kids, and nothing at all to joke about—ever.

"Tell Devlin I'll be waiting for him, that I want him back," the spirit said, and with one final touch to Creed's cheek, it was gone.

Creed was well aware of his own breathing, ragged and harsh, and when Kat attempted to help him, he jerked away.

"I'd never let anything hurt you," Kat told him.

He turned his back on her, and she let him walk away, into the kitchen, didn't follow him. He sank into one of the chairs around the old table and rested his head in his shaking hands, feeling the reassuring rub along his shoulders.

It was one of the few times he willingly allowed Kat to comfort him.

THEY'RE IN TROUBLE BUT GOOD, Dev's father always used to say whenever he'd get that look in his eye, and the terrible headache followed, so even from the time Dev was very little, he knew that the gift of second sight was something not to be envied.

Trouble from the mission involving Remy was inevitable. Expected. Even though Dev sensed it, there was nothing he could do now but wait. Wait, have backup ready to go at a moment's notice and try to rid himself of the searing pain he always got when one of his operatives was hurt or in trouble.

But there was no rule that said he had to wait all by himself.

"So good," he murmured after he'd tongued a taut nipple, an act that elicited a primal moan and a thrust upward from the hard body trapped beneath his. His balls tightened, the familiar thrill clenching his abs, and the ache in his head began to lessen in response to his body's shift in pressure. But not before the voice of memory started playing inside his head.

You love it when I suck your nipples, don't you, baby?

He shook his head softly, continued to suck on the hard, pebbled nipple. His cock throbbed as his fingers traced the sensitive underside of the arms bound to the headboard. He paused at the inside of the elbows and continued up the forearms, past the tick of the pulse point beneath the leather straps that bound the man with the dark hair helpless against Dev's caresses.

Let me tie you down, Dev. I love it when you fight....

"I can fuck the worry right out of you," the man named Rich, one of ACRO's newest Seducers, trained in the art of sex and the art of keeping his mouth shut tight, had told him when he'd walked into the house less than fifteen minutes earlier. His voice was husky, the tone cocky, which was just the way Dev liked his lovers.

He had used his second sight briefly to study Rich, the way his black hair was shorter than Dev normally liked, but still long enough for him to twist in his fingers, the way his eyes were more light brown than chocolate...the way he was never going to compare to Dev's memories.

Nothing ever would.

Rich had moved forward boldly, had jerked Dev's robe open and off his shoulders, and Dev had steadied himself and let the hot mouth nip and suck down his chest, toward his abs. He let the talented tongue tease his belly button for a few minutes with tight, probing circles that made his cock ache before he'd pushed hard against Rich's shoulders and pulled the man from his knees.

I'm going to fuck you until you pass out....

"You're the one who's going to get fucked tonight," Dev had murmured, his hand holding firm to Rich's biceps in a grip that showed there was no room for arguments. Or memories.

Three in a bed was too crowded.

Rich hadn't argued, had let Dev lead him up the stairs. Dev had him stripped and bound within minutes, and Rich seemed to find it fascinating that a blind man could be in such command of everything, had told him so as Dev had strung the man's arms over his head, pausing to suck hard at the tender skin of his neck before sliding down the younger man's body.

And now Rich was begging to be fucked, moving his body against Dev's in that demanding way that only someone tied down could understand, his groans driving Dev to that place he needed to be.

Dev grabbed what he needed from the bedside table, rolled the condom on his cock and squirted a generous amount of lube onto his fingers. He worked Rich's tight hole as the man drew a sharp hiss in through his teeth, and then he began to relax under Dev's machinations.

Dev worked two fingers inside Rich, preparing him, even as he bent his head between Rich's legs to nuzzle the man's cock, taking it into his mouth with a long, slow slide.

Rich's body jerked upward, his wrists pulling against the restraints.

"Oh, yeah...don't stop." Rich pushed back against Dev's fingers, even as he added another one, and Dev played his tongue along the tip of Rich's cock, teasing, tormenting with mouth and fingers, instructing Rich not to come, until the man's body shone with sweat and his pleas were incoherent groans.

He crawled back up Rich's body, flipped the man's legs over his shoulders and entered him, pushing the head of his cock inside hard enough to gain entrance. Rich's back arched and he moaned.

Pain with pleasure, baby...

Dev waited until he felt Rich's body adjust to the intrusion and then he slid farther inside, reveling in the tight fit until his balls slapped Rich's ass.

"Jesus, fuck me now, Devlin. Hard," Rich panted, totally out of control and loving every minute of it.

Dev leaned in and kissed Rich with a ferocity that had built up over the past weeks, when he'd tried to make do with Marlena, with other women, with his own hand and cold showers.

It never worked. No matter how hard Dev tried to push the memories—the needs—down, when they roared to life, his inability to drive Oz out of his mind and his bed always shocked him. It was always when he finally hit the end of his rope, when he couldn't suppress the feelings anymore, that he would break down and bring a man to his bed to try to exorcize the demons Oz had left behind.

And even though Rich didn't look or smell or taste like Oz, if Dev turned off his second sight, he could use the rest of his senses to conjure up the right smells, the right tastes, and instead of fucking Rich he was fucking Oz, hearing Oz's moans and other sounds from the only man he could totally let himself lose control with.

Rich's ass tightened around Dev's cock until his balls were

hot and full and he slammed into Rich with a frenzied need, hitting his prostate over and over, until they were both slippery with sweat and Dev had to hang on to the bed with both hands just to stay in place.

I want in deeper, Dev. Want to be all the way inside....

He released Rich's hands because he needed to feel arms around his back—strong ones, ones that could hold him down if they needed to, and he moaned the name, *Oz*, against Rich's mouth until he came, his body shuddering with the release he'd waited for, his heart ripping out of his chest all over again.

Remy walked outside the motel room to breathe in some fresh air, clear his head and prepare for the mission ahead of him. Because staying in that close proximity to Haley without being able to touch her, or talk to her about their future, was killing him.

Of course, Ender was outside too, leaning against one of the black Humvees, drinking a coffee. He handed one to Remy without saying a word.

"Thanks," Remy said. "Is there one for Haley? I'll bring it in to her."

"It's a job, man," Ender said, pointing to the extra coffee, which was obviously for Haley. "Don't get too attached to her. ACRO's got policies against shit like that."

"She didn't worry about that when she came to get me," Remy said, grabbing the coffee off the car roof.

Ender snorted. "Sex is fine with ACRO. That's how she got you to cooperate in the first place, because all female operatives know that men think with their dicks. But the relationship shit? Out of the question."

"I never said anything about a relationship—" Remy started, but Ender held up his hand.

"I've seen you mooning after her. Forget about it."

"Are we ready yet?" Wyatt asked.

Remy turned and saw him lying on the hood of the car, wondered how long he'd been there and how much he'd heard. But Wyatt merely slid off the car when Ender said, "Now," and got into the backseat of the car Remy would ride in with Haley.

According to the plan, they would take the Itor house from four locations. Wyatt would take the east on his own, with Remy and Haley driving him as far as necessary and then letting him out to hoof it to the right location, in case the cars were spotted. Remy and Haley would continue along to take the north, and Remy was given permission to stay with Haley, after much arguing and a final, put-his-foot-down, I'm-the-right-one-to-protect-her command. To which Ender just snorted and Wyatt smiled.

Ender and the operative they called Annika would take the south and west, respectively—all of them would abandon the cars when they were a quarter mile from the location. They should have the element of surprise on their side, especially since they'd be there an hour earlier than the time Remy himself was supposed to meet Itor.

"I'm ready," Haley said from the door of the room. She had her bag slung over her shoulder and she closed the door and walked down the stairs and toward Remy. He handed her the coffee, ignored Ender's smirk and watched as the woman he assumed was Annika pulled into the parking lot.

"I just want to talk to Annika for a second," Haley said, but Wyatt shook his head, spoke through the opened backseat window.

"We don't have time. We need to move," he said, and Remy saw that Annika was already pulling out, with Ender right behind her.

He and Haley climbed into the car and within minutes they were driving along the back roads toward their destination, headsets in place but not talking. Remy could actually feel Wyatt's pent-up energy as though it were creating its own electric field.

He shifted in his seat and realized he'd been lucky that the weather had held out this long. Although, just being around Haley made things easier on him. Ever since the tattoos...

He glanced over and saw that, even though Haley was looking out the window, she was rubbing her hip, the one with the tattoo.

Man, this was one strange deal.

"Pull over here, Remy," Wyatt said.

"I thought you wanted us to get farther?" Remy said, although he did what Wyatt asked.

"Ender wanted it that way. I don't answer to Ender." Wyatt checked his equipment and then gave Remy a slap on the shoulder. "See you on the inside."

Remy watched Wyatt take off into the trees, and within moments, he'd lost sight of the man.

He recalled the private meeting he'd had with Wyatt and Ender last night too, long after Haley had gone to sleep. One that discussed backup plans. Last resorts.

The last resort plan wasn't much different from the one he and his SEAL teammates used to discuss, but there was so much more on the line if Remy got captured by Itor than there ever was with the U.S. Navy.

He pulled onto the road and started driving again. Haley was still rubbing her hip thoughtfully. And Remy started to feel the familiar tingle along his skin, even though the skies were mostly clear. He chalked it up to wanting Haley and tried to ignore the feeling.

"Are you all right?" he asked her finally, when the silence

grew too thick between them. The humming had started in his ears as well, and he needed to take his mind off that.

"I will be," she said. "What about you?"

"I will be," he repeated, and she smiled. "I do have one question for you," he said, unsure whether it was the intensity of the upcoming mission that made his heart beat so fast, or what he was about to ask.

"Okay," she said, biting her bottom lip nervously.

"Did you fuck me as part of your job?"

She drew in a sharp breath, but she didn't answer.

Fuck.

You know Ender's a prick, so you can't trust him fully.

But still, he knew he could trust Ender with his life. He figured he could trust Haley too, but he wanted more than that from her. So much more, it physically hurt while he sat there and waited for her to find her voice.

"Why would you ask me something like that?"

"I know why you came to the bayou. You knew all the rumors about me. And the only way you could test your theories..."

"Was to get you into bed," she finished. "ACRO wanted me to get the job done by any means possible."

"And you're good at your job, aren't you?" he asked, aware that his voice sounded raw, and more aware of how stupid he was to have this conversation minutes before he was going to head out, risking his life.

"Remy, no..."

"It's all right. I understand. I do. I'm all about doing anything it takes to get the job done," he said, his life as a SEAL flashing before his eyes.

"I am too, but caring about you was never part of the job. It wasn't supposed to be. I can't believe that it happened." Her voice caught and he wished he could pull over to the side and take her in his arms. As it was, all he could do was grab her hand and squeeze it hard.

"I know how scared you are. I'm scared too," he admitted. "I've never been in love before."

He allowed himself to take his eyes off the road for a second, because he needed to look into hers after his admission.

"You love me?" she asked, stared at him and crossed her arms in front of her. Not exactly the moment he'd hoped for, but then again, what the hell was? And for the first time, he didn't care about going out on this particular ledge.

"Yeah, I love you. And I'm going to do whatever it takes today to keep you safe," he said, and then felt a jolt of electricity down his spine and clutched the wheel hard. "Haley, something's wrong."

"WHAT DO YOU MEAN, SOMETHING'S WRONG?" Haley asked, shaken out of the I-love-you moment she hadn't been sure how to handle.

Then she sucked in a breath like she'd been burned, because, oh, shit, she'd rather deal with the love stuff. Ahead of them, black clouds rolled in like a series of inverted tidal waves. A white wall of hail obscured the road only yards ahead.

"Tell me you're doing that. Are you doing that?"

"Hell, no." Remy slowed, but they plowed into the weather so hard, she flinched, certain the windshield would break from the force of the ice balls beating down on them.

The noise, deafening and painful, made her shout into her headset at the other team members. "If you guys are outside already, take cover. We're in for some rough weather."

Rough and...wrong. Not one forecast model had indicated even a possibility of weather like this. And the striations in the cloud formations, the shape of the hail...she'd never seen anything like it.

Ice crunched beneath the Humvee's tires as Remy steered through the obscuring veil of precipitation. Visibility fluctuated, but she could make out a shape ahead. She squinted, gasped at the same time Remy bit out a guttural, "Fuck!"

He slammed on the brakes, and she grasped the Oh Shit bar as the vehicle skidded and spun back-end-first into a gully, just missing the four black sedans blocking the road.

"Not good," Remy muttered, slamming the Humvee into first gear and gunning it out of the ditch. Three more vehicles moved into position in the road, coming from the direction they'd just traveled, trapping them.

"Uh, Remy..."

"Yeah, I see. We're going right through them. Hold on."

He stepped on the gas. The engine cut out. Men in cammie jumpsuits swarmed out of the cars. Some carried weapons. Others, she suspected, *were* weapons.

Remy grabbed her arm and yanked. "On the floor." Then he smiled. The nut actually smiled. "Time for some twisters."

Nothing happened. If anything, conditions improved. The hail had turned to rain, though wind still whipped through the narrow valley.

"What the fuck?" The concentration on his face turned it red. Veins bulged in his temple. "Something's wrong. I can't do shit!"

Haley peeked over the dash. A tall, lean man moved toward them, his hands empty, his gaze trained on Remy. He made a brusque motion with his hand, and a shot rang out; the driver-side window shattered.

"Get out of the vehicle," he shouted, and Remy bared his teeth, shook glass out of his hair.

"Fuck you."

The man shrugged. "Do you want your father alive or in pieces?"

Remy swore under his breath. "Let Haley go. Release her, and I'll cooperate."

"Remy, no," she whispered harshly, but he didn't acknowledge her.

"Itor does not negotiate."

Remy opened his mouth to say something, but only a strangled grunt came out as his body was pinned against the seat. "I hate these fucks!" he spat.

Men closed in on the truck, and panic sent Haley's heart into overdrive. She scrambled toward Remy, but the passenger door flew open, and hands seized her feet. She screamed, kicked viciously, relishing the thud of her heels connecting with flesh.

Remy bellowed in rage. "Get your goddamned hands off her!"

She grabbed the seat, dug in with her fingers, but another set of hands joined the first, and a rough yank broke her grip. The sharp bite of a needle stung her thigh, and then she was on the freezing wet pavement, a woman bent over her, leering. The woman yanked Haley's headset off and crunched it beneath her boot.

"You're a serious pain in the ass, Ms. Holmes," she said in a tinny Russian accent. "If my orders weren't to bring you in alive, I'd gut you and leave you to bleed to death in the road like a car-struck deer."

Remy's curses and threats buzzed around her head, and she wondered if the Itor people were as impressed with his creativity as she was. She was pretty sure some of the things he proposed doing to them were anatomically impossible, but then, she didn't think it was possible for her to be carried away by evil scumbags and not care.

Whatever had been in the syringe had been good stuff. It

wasn't until she'd been placed in the backseat of one of the sedans that she began to care.

Because she could no longer hear Remy's shouts. She could, however, hear his roar of pain.

"SHIT!" ANNIKA RAN AS FAST AS SHE COULD, her feet crunching through hail, her wet clothing sticking to her like she'd climbed out of a pool. She arrived at Remy's Humvee where it had been left in the ditch. Ender was already there, testing the engine, which wouldn't turn over. Wyatt skidded to a halt next to her.

"Son of a bitch," she panted. "It was a fucking trap."

Ender rarely passed up an opportunity to bluster, but he remained tight-lipped, his expression as grim as Wyatt's. By mutual silent consent, they ran back to Ender's Humvee, climbed inside, Wyatt in the rear seat, Annika in the front passenger, and then Ender let loose the tirade he'd been holding back.

"How the fuck could we have gotten it wrong? That trailer is the only logical place for them to hole up, and there's no way they could have seen us coming."

Wyatt snared the maps out of the back of the vehicle. Ender took a handful, and glared at Annika. "You afraid you'll get a paper cut, princess?"

"Shut up." She peered out the window, looking for a visual on whatever was making the hair on her arms stand up with a static sensation. "I think . . . I think I can find Remy. Or at least get us in the general vicinity."

Wyatt peered at her from over the top of a satellite photo. "How?"

"Something's radiating a shitload of energy. Like a nuclear power plant. But different. Bizarre. Almost feels artificial. It's got to be Remy working his weather mojo or something." She pointed to the roiling black clouds overhead. "Did you notice how fast those suckers came in?"

Ender and Wyatt exchanged glances, and Wyatt shrugged. "We ain't got dick. Can't hurt to see where her spidey sense leads us."

Ender started the vehicle, and Annika closed her eyes, let the tingle behind her lids be her guide. "Head northwest."

The truck spun out in the gravel and then hit the road with a burn of rubber. Adrenaline careened through her veins, heightening her senses and enhancing the electric sizzle just under the surface of her skin. She loved this part of her job, the hunt, the chase, and then the climax of battle.

Hopefully there'd be a battle. First, they needed to find Remy and Haley. If those fuckers hurt Haley, Annika would shock every one of them until they looked like burnt bacon. Haley might be an uptight prig, but she was the closest thing Annika had to a girlfriend. And really, maybe she didn't know Haley as well as she thought she did, because the woman at the hotel had more closely resembled an untamed jungle woman than a parameteorologist with a stick up her ass.

Maybe she'd taken to heart Annika's suggestion to make Remy horny. Good. Haley had needed to get laid in a serious way.

Like Annika had.

The thought made a burst of heat explode in her gut, and she damn near groaned. God, it had been good with Creed. Feminine instinct told her it could get even better. She had no experience, and he'd been trying to be gentle, but if they ever let loose on each other...oh, man. Images popped into her head like an old reel movie—hot, wild, swing-from-the-chandeliers sex-fests, starring the two of them.

She shifted in her seat, aching already, inappropriately. An ACRO operative and a potential operative had been taken.

Sex had no business being on the brain. Creed had no business being in her thoughts at all.

"Annika? Still northwest?"

"Yes." She opened her eyes and studied the cloud-choked sky. The electrical tug was growing stronger...just as she knew the tug toward Creed would. Years of sexual frustration had built up, and now that she had an outlet, she planned to use it.

She just hoped Creed didn't want more from her, because she had nothing but her body to give.

CHAPTER
Twenty-four

Remy grunted as his wrists were bound separately, arms spread and strapped to a metal bar above his head. He was forced to kneel on the soft dirt of the barn floor, his ankles bound together as well. He felt the second prick of a hypodermic in his biceps and the medicine burned through his veins. Not a sedative this time. No, for what was coming now, these assholes wanted him wide-awake and ready.

They hadn't simply relied on the sedative the first time either—they'd knocked him over the head, and he was still seeing double.

He looked up at his captors, a man and a woman, waited for the inevitable questions about his abilities, but none came. Instead, the man walked behind him and Remy heard the whir of something wooden and unforgiving whiz through the air seconds before the slam to his kidneys jolted him forward.

The woman crossed her arms and smiled.

Remy didn't make a sound. At first. And then he forced out a long moan, right before they hit him again. And again, and the cry that he let out was more anger and frustration than hurt, but they wouldn't know that.

He hated showing any weakness at all, but he'd learned long ago that giving people what they wanted made things go easier on him. They wanted to think they were hurting him so badly, he was going to let them.

What they were doing was no walk in the park, but he'd had worse.

His head ached and he wondered if they'd done something to him beyond pumping him full of drugs, because he still wasn't able to conjure up as much as a raindrop, no matter how hard he concentrated.

"Again," the woman commanded, and Remy steeled himself for the next blow, forced himself to take stock of the situation.

The woman was pretty—tall, blond, icy. She leaned close to him, whispered in his ear, "Pain and pleasure, T-Remy. I can give you both." And yeah, he'd be willing to bet she could.

But when he didn't answer, she responded by running her hand down his T-shirted chest, not stopping until her hand covered his crotch. "Why don't you give me a chance? I know what you need."

"You have no idea what I need, lady. And it's certainly not what you've got between your legs," he said.

She pulled away and the man delivered another quick slam to his shoulders.

"Manny, put that down and get away from him. You as well, Oksana." The sharp voice snapped him to attention, and the guy who'd been getting his jollies trying to break Remy down did an immediate cease and desist. Oksana smirked one more time and then blew Remy a kiss.

"See you later, T-Remy. I'll make sure of that. You'll be a much better playmate than your father."

Remy dipped his head and retched. The cold sweat he'd broken out in was helping to loosen the bonds on his wrists, but it was going to be a painful way to escape.

"I'm sorry, Remy. Sometimes my associates take too many liberties. It's hard to get good help these days." A British accent. Cultured. Smooth.

Remy lifted his head, pissed that he'd started seeing double again.

The man was shorter than he was, stocky, and he made no effort to hide the .44 Magnum he wore in a shoulder holster over a pin-striped, button-down shirt, complete with a tie, like he was going out to dinner instead of conducting an interrogation.

"My name is Charles," the man continued. "Welcome to the party."

"Where's my father?"

"In due time, T-Remy. In due time."

"You've got me now, so you don't need him for anything. Just let him go."

"Such loyalty." Charles lit a cigarette and blew smoke rings, which hung in the humid air.

"I held up my end of the bargain."

"Ah, but that's just it, Remy. You didn't follow the rules. You were supposed to come here alone—and you have to understand, we can't take chances. Not with ACRO breathing down our necks, even though the three ACRO agents who followed you have been properly disposed of. But I'll bet you understand what it's like to have ACRO trying to back you into a corner."

He wasn't giving Charles the satisfaction of answering anything, but Charles didn't seem particularly upset by that.

"You've got a lot of training under your belt," Charles continued. "But none of it's going to be able to save you in the end. Not when you've been the victim of a very powerful curse. A curse that no one has been able to get to the bottom of, no matter how hard they try."

It's a gift, not a curse, he heard Haley's voice echo in his ear. But as much as he wanted to believe, there was an entire lifetime of pain and humiliation to back up the fact that gifts weren't supposed to bring this much heartache.

Haley. At the thought of her name, which he'd been trying his best to keep out of his mind in case they were somehow able to read it, the tattoo began to tingle.

He thought about thunder, tornados, anything. And still, he couldn't bring anything on.

He coughed, then groaned at the pain that effort caused along his rib cage. Charles was by his side in a second, a water bottle in his hands.

"Have some water, Remy."

He looked up at the man. "Where's Haley?"

"What if I told you Miss Holmes is being very well taken care of?"

"What if I told you that I don't believe a fucking word you say?" he asked. Charles nodded as if in agreement, switched on a video monitor mounted near the door, and Remy got an eyeful of Haley, sleeping peacefully.

She's all right. Relief surged through him, and he wondered how long that feeling was going to last. "What about my father?"

"He's not as comfortable. But, then again, you really don't want him to be, do you? Not after what he did to you. Because if it wasn't for him, you wouldn't be in this situation."

"I want to see my father," he repeated, hating the validity of Charles's words.

"Fine." Charles flipped the monitor view to a room where Remy Senior was being held. His father had been beaten, looked scared, hurt, lost. "Is that what you wanted to see?"

"What do you want from me?"

"We want you to come work for Itor."

"Thanks, but I already have a job."

"With ACRO? What, you think they're going to save you, Remy? They've got you right where they want you."

Remy didn't answer, but that didn't matter.

"You're nothing but a weapon to them. They're lying to you if they tell you anything different."

"And how do I know you're not?" he spat before he could stop himself.

Charles smiled, as if he'd been waiting for Remy to ask that question. "They're planning on making you their caged pet, to keep you locked away like the family skeleton in the closet until they need you for something. Just like your own father tried to do. Poor, loyal Remy falls for it every time."

The words stung him to the core, but he forced his body, his facial muscles to stay relaxed. I-don't-give-a-fuck mode. He was about to tell the guy to screw off, to kick Charles's legs out from under him, to break out hard. Then Charles started speaking again, his voice low and relaxed.

"Haley fucked you, didn't she? Fucked you until you couldn't see straight, until you couldn't tell up from down. Until you thought you were in love with her. And now you think you should follow her anywhere. Even into ACRO."

Remy clenched his teeth and tried not to listen, but Charles was dredging up fears that played inside his own head and refused to go away, especially after he'd professed his love to Haley.

"That's how ACRO does it, Remy. They use sex to get what they want. And they want you—badly."

"And what you're offering is so much better, right?" he asked, flexing his arms so the bindings around his wrists clanged against the metal pole. "Is this how you treat your operatives?"

"I was just trying to give you a taste of what ACRO will do

to you. They were planning to put you in a cage, Remy. Lock you up like a dog to keep you safe from yourself. They weren't going to train you and let you live the way you want to—with freedom and power. They were going to try to save the world from you."

Remy's gut clenched, because he didn't want to believe anything this guy said. But fuck, his weather shit was dangerous—and so was Remy himself in the wrong, and maybe even the right, hands.

Charles moved in closer. "Everyone you love and trust betrays you. It's the way your life was meant to be, starting with your own momma."

Remy began to hyperventilate, air pulling painfully through his lungs. He heard screams before he passed out completely, and realized that they were his own.

Dammit, his mental game had gone to shit since he'd met Haley.

When he came to seconds later, it wasn't because his breathing was under control. Rather, the tingle that made his skin feel too tight was back in full force.

"Storm's coming, T-Remy," Charles whispered in his ear.

"SHE'S COMING AROUND."

Haley's eyes fluttered open. The backs of her eyelids felt like they were coated with sandpaper, and she groaned as they scratched her corneas. Bright light above made her wince, and, disoriented, she turned her head away.

Lying down. She was on a bed.

Two strange men wearing jeans and sweaters stood next to her. One, a tall blond, held a glass of water. The other, bald and stocky, helped her sit up. Thunder cracked, and her head nearly split open.

"Have a drink," Baldy said, his German accent deep and guttural. "You'll feel better."

The temptation to knock the glass out of Waterboy's hand was intense enough to make her shake, but her mouth was so parched she couldn't refuse. She gulped the entire contents as Baldy held her. She wanted to ask about Remy, but if Itor believed she cared, they'd exploit both her and Remy's feelings.

Baldy released her, stepped back. He watched her for a moment, then frowned. "I'm not getting much," he said to the other man. "Her parents are protecting her."

Caught off guard, her mouth dropped open. Quickly, she snapped it shut. She'd been through too much military and ACRO POW training to let them rattle her.

"Protecting her? How?"

"They're not talking, and they're keeping others who might talk from coming around."

Waterboy huffed. "Ms. Holmes? Do you possess any kind of special ability?"

His nasally American accent annoyed her. Especially since he was playing for the wrong side. She smiled and shoved the glass at him. "Thank you for the water."

"Let's go," he said to Baldy, and then he turned back to her. "Mr. Mikos will see you shortly."

They started out of the tiny, sparsely decorated bedroom, but at the doorway, Baldy turned to her. "Your father said he loves you." His brow furrowed over troubled eyes, and she wondered if Itor was, perhaps, not his first choice of employer. "Your mother...she said she's happy to see you've finally fallen in love. She's showing me some sort of drawing. A fist holding lightning. Something about soul mates."

Baldy shut the door, and she tried not to tremble. No doubt he was messing with her head, but the mere idea that her parents were actually protecting her and trying to talk to her... well, it rattled her, just like he'd intended.

"T..."

The faint voice jolted her out of her emotional mire, and

she stood, her feet thumping on the hardwood floor. Three steps took her to the window, where she peered out from the second-story room into the gray daylight. Fields, trees and a gently sloped hill surrounded the house, isolating it from civilization. A ramshackle barn rose out of the pasture behind the house like an ugly wart, and as she watched, the front door opened, spilling weak light into the gloomy day. A man slipped out, but before the door closed, she caught a glimpse of the interior.

Chills ran up her spine at the sight of a metal table, the kind used for autopsies. A cage. Tools. Medical equipment. They were keeping Remy there. She didn't see him, but she knew.

Unsure of her plan, she tugged on the window, but naturally, it had been nailed shut. She had to get out. Had to get to Remy somehow.

"T."

The voice again. A man's. Louder. It hadn't come from outside. She moved to the wall near the bed. "Hello? Is someone there?"

"Where's my boy? Where's T?"

Oh, God. Remy Senior. "Mr. Begnaud? It's Haley. Haley Holmes. Are you okay?"

The distinct sound of a fist striking the wall made her jump. "Where is he? What did you do to my son, you bitch?"

"Mr. . . . Remy, I'm a prisoner too. We're being held by a foreign agency that wants your son."

"Your fault," he shouted, and she resisted the urge to tell him he was the reason both agencies had been after Remy in the first place. The guy was probably half out of his mind by now anyway.

"He'll get us out of this," she said, hoping he'd believe it, because she wasn't sure she did.

She moved around the room, listening to Remy Senior throw curses at her as she looked for a way out or anything she could use as a weapon. She tried the door. Locked. The heat ducts were too small to allow a cat comfortable passage.

Nothing. The only furniture consisted of the bed, a nightstand and an old dresser. She couldn't even reach the caged lightbulb on the ceiling when she dragged the nightstand beneath it. Breaking the bulb would have at least given her a shard of glass for a weapon.

Frustrated, she sank down on the bed. Her skin itched, probably a reaction to whatever they'd injected her with, and her tattoo had begun to tingle. Maybe another side effect...

Lightning flashed, and her tattoo began to burn. Definitely not a side effect. The storm was affecting Remy, and shit, what was going to happen if they couldn't be together when his storm fervor hit full force? If he was restrained, which, no doubt, he was, he wouldn't be able to relieve himself.

What if there's a storm and you don't get sex?
I have to. She makes me.

Fear knotted her stomach. Would he go crazy, maybe even die if the pressure couldn't be relieved?

She raced to the window, looked out into the growing darkness. The lights inside the barn had been turned off, dousing the sinister effect. She could easily have been gazing out the window of a bed-and-breakfast onto the quaint, sprawling farm surroundings.

It wasn't right. Evil should look evil. It should reek like rotten flesh, not smell like the pine cleaner and fabric softener that wafted around her room.

Helplessness gnawed at her, making her muscles quiver, her bones soften. A suffocating sensation tightened in her chest, and she wanted to drop into a ball of despair, wrap her arms around her middle in defeat, spread her legs and imagine Remy there, his fingers, his tongue....

She blinked. Where had that come from? Looking down, she saw that she had pushed down the waistband of her cargos and was rubbing her tattoo. It pulsed and sizzled, and the sharp ink outlines had risen up so her fingertips could read them like Braille.

Weak, shaken and confused, she shuffled toward the bed in almost a dreamlike state, sinking down on it as though her body had gone boneless. Closing her eyes, she took deep, slow breaths, wondering if the drugs had messed with her system.

A sudden, searing firestorm spun through her like a tornado of flames. She gasped. Her eyes flew open. The scent of musk, ozone ... *Remy* ... washed over her, until she could detect him on her skin, in her clothes, her hair. His essence permeated her every cell. It was as though he were there, inside her, possessing her completely.

She could feel the hunger rushing through his veins. His heart pounding in his chest.

His very soul merging with hers.

Slowly, as if moving quickly might break the connection, she eased back on the bed and absorbed him until his life force intoxicated her. Her senses reeled, even as her mind tried to stay focused, tried to figure this out. But in the end, it didn't matter how all this had happened, because she was with Remy, and somehow he was making love to her.

Twenty-five

Something strange was happening. One minute, Remy was practically hanging by his arms, numb, muscles screaming in pain, his senses assaulted by manure and grass and ozone.

The next, he was lying between Haley's legs—and God, it was soft and warm. He inhaled the scent of woman, brushed his lips against her neck and figured he must've been hit by lightning. Must be unconscious or dead to be able to see this, feel this so clearly.

"Haley," he whispered against her skin, scared to look up and see her face, because this mirage could disappear that quickly.

But when he heard her whisper his name back, he knew something had gone right. The tattoo, which had continued its slow burn, now throbbed as if it had a pulse of its own, as if his heart and soul were connected to the ink embedded in his skin.

If the marking connected him to Haley, then it most definitely did contain the best part of him.

Focus, Remy. She's helping you through this storm. Concentrate—don't break the connection.

The connection had the power to shed their clothes—which was good, since he didn't exactly have a free hand.

"Bebe," he murmured, slid inside her without any further talk. Her hips moved to meet his and she thrust against him, while lightning tore at the sky.

They'd somehow been transported to each other and to the center of the storm, open to one another as well as the outside elements. His mouth skimmed her breast, her nipple, even as rain mixed with hail tore at him, sliced at his bare back, as he moved his body to cover hers completely and shield her from the elements.

Focus on me, Remy. Only me.

He pressed his head against her, her sweet, hot sex holding him inside, helping him ride out what could've been a painful experience thanks to his bound hands, which left him no way to give himself relief during this storm. Instead, waves of pleasure stroked him, Haley's nimble hands swept his body—and he shuddered over and over into her.

Thunder boomed overhead, pulled his senses outward. His breathing was audible, sharp, his chest tight, and he flickered between where he was, arms straining against the restraints, and where he wanted to be, back inside Haley, where it was safe.

She's not safe, though. Never will be, as long as you're around.

He'd always known that, but the tattoo connecting them confirmed it. He had a strong suspicion that just removing the ink wouldn't break their bond—one put in place long before he'd ever met or fallen in love with Haley Marie Holmes.

It was time to do the right thing. The hero's choice. He had to be ready for the last resort plan, because if Ender, Wyatt and Annika were really gone, he was in pretty big trouble. And from the way Charles had been talking, so was the world if Remy got into the wrong hands.

While he strained against the bonds, one of them loosened.

In a minute, he'd be hands free, and there were more than a thousand means of destruction around this old barn to fashion a weapon.

But Haley was tugging at him, pulling him back down to her, like she was going to fight his plan till the last.

REMY. PLEASE . . .

Haley's emotions swirled and tangled with Remy's, so fast and furious that every time she reached out to capture and hold one, it slipped between her fingers. Love, sadness, joy . . . it was all there, but she couldn't get close enough to any one to absorb the significance behind it.

Around them, the storm roared, though some distant part of her knew she was warm and dry on a soft bed. They floated in the heart of the tempest, hail and wind and lightning spinning beneath them, above them, all around, but she cared about nothing except how Remy felt inside her.

She wrapped herself around him, using more than her arms and legs—her entire being surrounded him and kept him with her, because something else tugged, trying to draw him away. Pain and sadness . . . and worse, resignation.

Shh . . . love me, Haley.

She didn't hear the words, but she felt them, just as she felt him move inside her, felt her heartbeat and panting breaths synchronize with his.

His hands were everywhere at once, caressing her breasts, drawing seductive patterns on the skin of her back, framing her face to hold her for a kiss that transmitted the rapture of loving so deeply, so wholly that the world around them ceased to exist.

They rolled together so neither was on top for more than a moment, but never once did they come apart. His cock filled her to overflowing, and God it was good, the way he drove into her, every powerful stroke taking her to the very edge.

The textures, the sensations, they were more intense here. Sweet, sharp pleasure built with each clever tug of his fingers on her nipples. Pure flame streamed through her sex, as though a fuse had been lit.

Her mind spun with lust—sexual, mental, emotional. *This is love,* she thought. *This is how it should be. No pain. No fear. Just trust.*

It was a high she'd never experienced, and as Remy thrust inside her, kissed her savagely yet tenderly, she shattered. Her orgasm ripped through every organ, her brain, took her apart at the molecular level. Remy went with her, and it was as though lightning had struck, seared them together in a possession of ecstasy that went on and on.

I love you.

I love you too.

Now there were no secrets, and she knew his heart. And he knew the truth of hers, as well. She loved him beyond anything she'd ever believed possible.

You'll be safe now, he told her. *I'll make sure of it.*

The connection began to weaken, like they were on two ends of a rubber string that had started to stretch and crack.

I'll make sure of it? What was he talking about?

The string broke, throwing her violently back into the farmhouse bedroom, but not before she caught Remy's last secret. The one that ripped through her like a bullet.

Rolling over, she lost her lunch on the floor.

Remy was going to make sure no one used him as a weapon or hurt those he loved.

He was going to take his own life.

HALEY STAGGERED TO HER FEET, her body shaking as she stumbled to the window. She'd break out, jump to the ground, stop him somehow.

The door opened, and she whirled, the sudden motion making her dizzy.

A man stood there, a scrawny, short guy wearing glasses. "Come with me, Haley," he said in a deep, calm voice she didn't expect from such a small man.

This was her chance. She could get away from him, make a run for the barn. Before the thought could go further, he grasped her wrist. Instinctively, she jerked away, but her arm snapped back to his hand.

Strings of white goo stretched between his palm and her wrist.

"No escaping, said the spider to the fly," he murmured, and she shuddered. ACRO agents unnerved her at times, but this guy's creep-factor shot right through the troposphere.

He pushed her ahead of him, and the goo lengthened so she was forced to lead as they moved through the old farmhouse that had been transformed, on the inside at least, into a crazy den of technology and Itor agents. Clearly, they'd been operating covertly here for at least a few days, probably to ensure plenty of backup.

She had no idea which of the half dozen or so agents on the main floor below possessed special powers of any kind, but it didn't matter. Were they completely normal humans, she couldn't overpower them and escape.

Especially not with the scary little nerdman attached to her and right on her heels.

"Keep going," Nerdman said, in his mild-mannered voice that made him all the more frightening. He prodded her with a finger, and she started up the staircase in front of her.

At the top of the stairs, he pointed to a door at the end of the hall.

"Go inside."

"What's in there?"

Nerdman pushed his BC glasses up on his face. "The man who decides if you live or die."

Chills ran up her spine, and her gut knotted. "I think I'll pass. Take me to the barn."

Laughing, Nerdman snapped the sticky stuff off her wrist and opened the door, which creaked ominously. Tables laden with beeping equipment and flashing screens filled the room. A dark-haired man sat at a desk, his brown eyes focused like lasers on her.

"Please come in, Miss Holmes," he said, in a pleasant, Greek-tipped voice.

"Do I have a choice?"

He twirled a pen between his slim fingers. "There's always a choice. You may go back downstairs, but I warn you, my operatives are bored and looking for sport, so doing so will be like tossing a cat into a kennel."

"Well, then," she said, entering and slamming the door in Nerdman's face, "I suppose there's not really a choice, after all."

"Smart girl." He gestured to a chair across from his desk. "But then, I'd expect as much from a parameteorologist whose parents were attorneys."

Rubbing her wrist, she sat, when all she really wanted to do was beat the snot out of the man. "Am I supposed to be impressed by the fact that you know all this? Any lame phone psychic could snag that out of my head."

Suddenly, her head snapped back as though an invisible fist had slammed into it. Blood exploded from her nose.

"Let's get one thing clear, Ms. Holmes, I'm not psychic."

Pain throbbed, undulated through her sinuses until her brain ached. Blood flowed in a slow stream from her nose, over her lips and off her chin, but she made no move to stop it, even when he pushed a box of tissues toward her.

"No, but you sure are a bastard."

He smiled, stood and looked out the small window behind him. Lightning forked in the distance, and thunder rumbled through the room. She wondered again about Remy, and tried to tamp down the panic that held her in a tight grip.

Play it smart, Haley. See what this guy wants, and then use it to save Remy.

Smart, that was fine and dandy, but she cursed her lack of special powers, which might have made her useful in this situation. As it was, she was helpless, nothing but a liability, like Ender had said. Remy had told her he loved her, that he'd die keeping her safe, and oh, God, she couldn't let that happen.

When her mother died, her father had wasted away, and while she'd like to think she wasn't as weak as that, she now understood the power of love. Her career had always come first, because she'd believed love would dilute her passion for weather, for her work. But Remy only strengthened it. Without him, her job as a meteorologist would never be the same.

"I don't suppose I can meet the man who broke into my mind?"

"Sadly, he's now out of the country." The acid dripping from his voice told her he wasn't as sad as he pretended to be.

"Why am I here, Mr. . . . ?"

"Mikos. Apollo Mikos." He turned to face her. "You're here because Itor doesn't have a parameteorologist."

"Maybe that's because people in my field have ethics."

The unseen fist slammed into her gut, and she doubled over, coughing and wheezing.

"I have great control over the air, Ms. Holmes, so you might think about how you answer my questions." He emphasized his point by wrapping an invisible rope around her throat and tightening until her breath cut off and she fell to the floor. The noose loosened, and she lay gasping, every breath like sucking hot embers into her lungs.

"I-I'm just—" She gasped, and swallowed blood that had drained from her sinuses into her throat "—just thinking that torture might not be the way t-to recruit people."

His laughter rang in her ears, which already buzzed from lack of oxygen, as she used her wobbly arms to push up on onto her knees.

"We don't torture everyone. I wasn't tortured, for example."

That's because you were already evil, you asshole.

Yeah, she kept that thought to herself and thanked God he wasn't a mind reader. His hand appeared at her side, but she shunned it and stood by herself. Waves of dizziness forced her to brace herself against his desk.

"We have enticements." His long stride took him to a metal box roughly the size of large microwave oven. "Do you know what this is?" He gestured when she shook her head. "Come look."

She staggered a few steps, and he opened the top of the box. Lights flashed, needles on gauges flickered . . . and her step faltered, her coordination a victim of her utter shock.

"My God," she gasped. "That isn't . . . it couldn't be . . ."

Apollo grinned, and in any other situation, she'd have thought he was handsome. Vile, but handsome. "It is. Itor's pride and joy. The IWX-1 Meteorological Generator. It almost makes your boyfriend obsolete."

She sucked in a harsh breath. "He's not my boyfriend. I barely know him." It was stupid to lie, she knew, since psychics had probably already sifted through her brain, but dammit, she had to try.

"Perhaps not, but he cares about you. Which, of course, works for us."

"Bastard," she growled, and winced, waiting for the blow to come, but it never did.

"I do believe we already covered that." He turned a dial on

the machine, and the reading on the wind gauge increased. "How do you like our little toy?"

It was unbelievable. Really cool, if ACRO had it and not the insane monsters at Itor. She'd give any one of her five senses to be able to study the thing.

"Why are you interested in Remy if you have a machine that can do the same things he can?"

"Our machines create effects that are widespread instead of precise. For example, we can create conditions favorable for tornado formation, but we can't aim the funnel where we want it to go. The machines are also limited by the fact that they can only create weather if the necessary environmental factors are already in place. Our intelligence indicates that Remy can create intense conditions at any time, and aim them exactly where he wants them."

Most of what he said went straight into an ask-later file in her brain, except for the most pressing question, one that chilled the blood in her veins. "You said 'machines.' You have more than one?"

"This was our prototype. It's compact, portable, but can produce only very small, weak storm systems, like what you see going on around us. Our IWX-2 is one hundred times more powerful, has produced category five hurricanes that have devastated hundreds of miles of U.S. coastlines." He leaned in, spoke softly as if telling her a secret. "We've boosted its power, and we think we can wipe entire states off the map next hurricane season."

Nausea bubbled up in her throat. Devlin had been right when he put in the order for her lab to find evidence regarding the existence of said machine.

"Why did you bring this smaller one here?" The moment the question was out of her mouth, she knew. "To counter Remy's abilities. If you control the atmosphere, then he can't."

"Your brilliance will be an asset to Itor," he remarked dryly.

She ignored him. "How did you know it would work?"

"Join us, and we'll share our secrets," he replied, and she nearly laughed because his vague answer told her enough.

"Ah. You guessed."

Apollo looked at her with a new appreciation. "I misjudged you."

Apollo turned away, took a step toward the desk, and before she could think things through, she lunged, shoved him between the shoulder blades while hooking her foot around one of his, like her ACRO martial-arts trainer had taught her.

"Misjudge this," she snarled as he went down, and before he fully hit the floor, she pounced, brought her bare foot down on his head as hard as she could.

He grunted, blinked, and then his eyes closed. Quickly, before he regained consciousness, she ripped the phone from the wall and ran back to the weather machine. She brought the phone down hard into the electronic face of the device. Again. Again. Switches broke, and the glass faceplates on the gauges cracked. But it wasn't enough.

Behind her, Apollo groaned. She spared a moment to whack him in the head with the phone, and felt no remorse when blood ran down his face from a deep cut in his scalp.

"Now you know what it feels like, bastard."

Panting, she scurried back to the machine. It whirred, and inside, something sparked, but the damned thing kept running. Figured. She'd seen equipment at the weather station break at a harsh glance, but this thing must be powered by the Energizer freaking Bunny.

Bracing her palms against the cool metal, she pushed as hard as she could. The machine probably weighed as much as Remy, and it scraped with agonizing slowness across the table on which it sat.

The sound of fabric on wood flooring whispered behind her. Shit. She didn't have much time.

Spurred on by adrenaline and the realization that she was going to die no matter what, she shoved as hard as she could. The machine teetered on the edge of the table.

Apollo cursed, his voice mushy, like his mouth was full of marshmallows.

She shoved. Something crunched into her ribs. She cried out, pushed one last time.

The machine fell to the floor with a crash and splintered apart.

Outside, the thunder died away. Inside, it was just beginning.

It had taken nearly every bit of mental strength Remy had to break the connection he'd felt with Haley.

One more hard tug on the restraints and one wrist was freed. He flexed his hand to rush some of the blood back to his fingers even as he maneuvered his other wrist out of the leather restraint.

He had to be ready. Problem was, he was used to doing things to *save* his own ass. Figuring out how to get himself killed was something entirely new.

You've only got to do it once. If it came to having to take his own life...

If he rushed Charles or Manny, they'd just shoot to bring him down—he was worth too much to them alive.

Weather-wise, he was still impotent.

Something about the way that last storm had hit him didn't make sense. It had seemed unnatural. For the first time, it hadn't felt like he was in a tug-of-war with Mother Nature.

Stop thinking and just do what you need to do. There were

plenty of weapons lying around the barn, things that could take his life quickly.

He grabbed a scythe from a hook on the barn wall and weighed the tool in his hand. It was heavy, uncompromising; it would do the job. But shit, he'd have given anything for a bullet right about now.

As he walked to the center of the barn, something imperceptible shifted—pressure changed, and the air around him buzzed with static energy. Like the atmosphere had been freed from something horrible. He drew in a deep breath through his nostrils.

Maybe one last try . . .

He started with something easy—rain. When he heard the light sprinkle on the roof, his heart soared, and he quickly threw in thunder, lightning, hailstones the size of golf balls. Then baseballs. Then—

"Are you trying to fucking kill me?"

He whirled around, scythe held out in front of him, to find Wyatt standing at the door of the barn, his arm over his head to shield him from flying hail until he entered.

"I couldn't do that before, I was blocked," he told Wyatt.

"Yeah, I know. But you can now." Wyatt paused. "So you planning on working the farm, or are we going to do a little take-down?" Wyatt eyed the scythe and then looked directly into Remy's eyes, because he knew what Remy had been thinking. He shook his head. "We've all been there. Some of us more than once. It's not your time."

Remy realized he'd been gripping the metal so hard, his hand shook.

"Put it down, man. It's not your time."

"How the fuck will I know when it is?" he asked Wyatt quietly.

Wyatt just shrugged, pulled a Sig Sauer out of his pants. "Want this?"

Remy stared at the gun and at Wyatt for a long moment. Then he dropped the scythe and walked toward the former SEAL. He took the cool metal in his palm, the heavy weight comfortable and familiar in his hand.

"I'm going to the farmhouse to get Haley," Wyatt said. "So far, she's still alive, but she's not going to be for much longer. I can't keep watching her or I'll burn out my other powers. And I really don't have time for a therapy session." As Remy watched, gun in hand, Wyatt walked out of the barn and then raced up the hill toward the farmhouse.

He turned the gun over in his hands and swallowed hard. Because there was always going to be someone with some kind of machine to fuck with him, someone whose powers were always going to be greater than his. There was always going to be danger surrounding him.

That's why you learn to rely on a team. Those words rushed back at him. His first instructor from boot camp had said them. And his BUD/s instructor. His team was still alive and well, and they needed his help.

Son of a bitch. He took off after Wyatt, the need to save Haley, to see her, surpassing everything.

THE PERIMETERS OF BOTH the barn and the main house were strangely quiet and free from the activity Remy would've expected to see. Itor had to know he'd escaped, and surely they'd be sending someone—probably more than one someone—after him. But how many? Before they'd knocked him out in the car, he'd noted at least ten guys.

He pressed his back against the outer wall of the house, in between a window and the partially opened front door. Wyatt had already disappeared inside, and now Remy heard shouts and a strangled groan.

He slammed in, gun drawn, to see Annika throw her hand out and electrocute an Itor agent.

"About time you showed," Annika said. "I've got this. Perimeter's stable. Your father's safe. Back up Wyatt and go get Haley."

Remy followed the trail of bodies, most of them looking more knocked out than dead, up to the third floor.

He burst in behind Wyatt, saw Haley and a guy standing in the center of the room, and Remy raised his weapon. But Wyatt shoved him back.

"I'm in fucking charge here," the former SEAL said in a low, controlled voice that brought Remy instantly back to the team mind-set. No more time for lone rangers here. "If you kill him now, he'll still have her. She'll go down with him."

Remy stayed back and let Wyatt do what he needed to do, even though watching Haley struggle for every breath was fucking killing him.

"Let her go, Apollo, and you won't be harmed." Wyatt's voice rang out through the empty space, but Apollo didn't appear to be listening at all. "One last chance, and then I can't be responsible for what's left of you."

Apollo snorted in response, tightened whatever psychic grip he had on Haley's body, because she gasped and grabbed for her throat.

Wyatt's body stiffened, almost imperceptibly, and then things began flying around the room. At first, they merely hovered by Apollo's head, but they were enough to distract him, because Remy saw Haley's breathing come a little easier.

"Guy needs all his concentration to kill someone like that," Wyatt told Remy. "I specialize in being that one annoyance you can't ever get rid of. No matter how hard you try."

A puff of air grazed Remy's cheek, and then Wyatt flew

backwards, crunched against the door frame. The objects in the air froze like they'd been suspended in Jell-O.

Haley's distress had lessened, but she still struggled for breath, her eyes wild and rolling. Remy gripped the gun hard, wanting to do something, anything, to help her, but as hard as the wind blew outside, it didn't do jack inside.

"Shit!" Wyatt peeled himself off the wood, and the objects in the air started moving slowly again. "Partition. This guy's good."

Wyatt sent a printer spinning toward Apollo, but at the last second, Wyatt's head flew back and the printer merely struck the other man a glancing blow off the shoulder.

"Partition?"

Wyatt growled, beaned Apollo in the face with a stapler. "He tied off his connection with Haley so he can divert some of his power to use against me." He impaled Apollo in the leg with a pencil, and Wyatt's head flew back again, his lip split. "He can't make Haley better or worse while his power to her is anchored."

The room exploded with flying objects; Wyatt kept jerking as some invisible force struck him. The window shattered. A lamp crashed against the wall. A desk chair came across the room and finally nailed that bastard in the back of the head. Apollo released Haley from the mental grip as he slammed to the ground, out cold.

Wyatt pulled out his gun and shot the man, execution-style in the back of the head, and nodded in satisfaction.

"Evil like that isn't allowed to share my planet. Get her out of here," Wyatt told Remy, who'd rushed to Haley's side.

Remy tried to rouse her, checked her pulse, but Wyatt was yelling at him again.

"Get. Out. And stand down if anyone gets in your way,"

Wyatt said, starting a storm of his own with equipment flying around them when another agent crashed into the room, gun drawn and ready to fire.

"He's mine," Remy growled, drew the Sig Sauer fast, with no hesitation, and shot the man dead. Without waiting, he grabbed Haley and ran with her out of the house, not sure where the hell he should take her.

Go to the road. Find the main road.

The ground beneath his feet began to shake with that familiar vibration Remy was usually grateful to hear. This time, it became immediately obvious that whoever was in the fast-approaching, low-flying helo was not friendly. And then the Itor agents who'd been running in the opposite direction minutes earlier were suddenly headed straight for him, and he had his hands full of Haley.

Annika cut in front of him, Wyatt by her side. "I'll take the men, you take the helo!" Annika shouted to Wyatt, and Remy waited in a holding position behind their human shield, clutching Haley, prepared to use his own body to protect her if necessary.

But one by one, the men stopped running, actually dropped to the ground, their faces twisted in pain and bearing the shock and awe that could only have been put there courtesy of the man Haley had said possessed extraordinary sniping skills.

"Dammit, Ender," Annika grumbled loudly over the roar of the impending helo.

"The fucking helo's still mine!" Wyatt yelled.

"Go, Remy. Straight into the woods," Annika said. "Don't leave Haley alone—that's your assignment now."

Remy didn't argue, sprinting against the force of the wind brought on by the blades of the chopper, trying as hard as he could not to jostle Haley, and ran until he could barely breathe, until he saw the black concrete trail that cut a swath into the mountainside.

The explosion that happened seconds later rocked the ground so hard, Remy nearly lost his balance. But he kept running, across the road and into the wooded area on the other side.

He ran for at least ten minutes, until his head began to spin. Camouflaged by the fall foliage, he stopped and turned back to see if anyone was behind him. When he saw he was alone, he knelt down on the ground, still not letting go of Haley, talking to her softly in Cajun French, asking her to *please wake up, chere.*

She didn't. For a second he closed his eyes and put his forehead to hers, until Wyatt's voice came quietly over his shoulder.

"Remy, the helo's waiting." Wyatt knelt down beside him and felt for Haley's pulse, the way Remy had done seconds before.

"She's not waking up. And my father—"

"She'll get medical attention once we're off the ground. Let's go—we need to get you out of here. Your father's safe; Ender already put him on the helo."

Remy nodded, his training kicking in. The danger wasn't over. Never would be really, he realized about ten minutes after boarding the helo and laying Haley down on a stretcher next to his father, who was also unconscious.

The helo, which was supposed to be gaining altitude, suddenly shuddered and shifted.

"What the fuck?" Ender called out.

"We're losing altitude!" the pilot responded.

"Shit." Wyatt pressed his face to the window. "Itor. They had a second helo and they're following. They have a Mech on board."

"What the hell is a Mech?" Remy asked.

"The guy can manipulate engines. I can't do shit about it, because we're not on the ground—I can't throw anything at it, except this helo."

Ender cursed under his breath, muttering about preparing to bail, and Remy stared out the window and then back at Haley.

"I can take down their helo," he said with a quiet calm he actually felt.

"Can you do it without taking us down too?" Ender demanded, and Annika and Wyatt turned their stares to Remy. He glanced over at Haley, who was being made as comfortable as possible, then looked out the window.

"I don't plan on dying today," Remy said. He moved away from the group a bit, closer to one of the windows, as the helo jerked again. He steadied himself with a palm pressed against the glass, the anger at Itor and what they tried to do to Haley, to his father, to him, rising in his chest.

Eyes closed, he concentrated on exactly what he needed—something that wouldn't make him too out of control, since all his normal options regarding release were severely limited.

He opened his eyes, stared at the other helo—his skin tightened and tingled, their helo slammed to one side and a bolt of lightning came down in a perfect angle to slice through Itor's helo and take it down.

"We're back on track!" the pilot yelled.

"Get us out of here now!" Remy roared.

Behind them, the helo had virtually disappeared from the sky in a fiery burst that rocked their own helo. Thunder boomed and a heavy rain tailed behind for a few seconds, but Remy closed his eyes and took some deep breaths, and dammit, he did it.

"Excellent," Wyatt said, clapping Remy on the shoulder. "We'll make the connection with the jet within fifteen, and then we'll blast back to ACRO."

Remy nodded, moved to sit next to Haley for the entire flight and just prayed.

CHAPTER
Twenty-seven

When the jet set down at the ACRO compound, Remy was more wrung out than he'd ever been in his life. He still had no idea what the hell he was going to do next, and the woman who'd guided him through the last difficult days was out cold.

He was scared to death that she'd never wake up.

Touching her hand as they wheeled Haley off first, he watched them spirit her away to receive further medical care. And then he buried his head in his hands, tried to block out all the white noise hammering his skull. His body ached for so many different reasons, and his mind felt twisted and unsteady.

When he finally stepped out into the predawn light, he saw that Ender and Annika were long gone, but Wyatt was waiting for him out on the landing strip. The man was lying on his back on the frosty tarmac, staring at the sun as it peeked over the distant line of pines. He was wearing sunglasses, but still....

"Hey." Wyatt stood when he saw Remy approach. "I was trying to move the clouds around, but Mother Nature isn't that cooperative."

"Tell me about it," Remy muttered. Thunder rumbled in the distance in response, and he just shook his head. "Can you take me to see Haley?"

"Not right now. But she'll be all right—we've got the best medical care here."

"So where do I go now?"

"You've got places to be," Wyatt said, turning Remy in the direction of another tall, well-built guy, who looked to be in his mid-thirties. He wore black BDUs as well, and he reached out a hand for Remy to shake.

"Remy, it's good to finally meet you in person. I'm Devlin O'Malley."

Head of ACRO. Wyatt nodded to both men and took off toward one of the large houses.

"Good to meet you too, sir," Remy said automatically to Dev.

"Come with me," Dev said, and even though the tone was pleasant, Remy knew it was nothing less than a command, and he followed him away from the landing strip and toward the road.

Two large ACRO guards appeared from around the other side of the jet, to flank either side of them, and they walked in silence until Dev stopped him outside a large black van.

One of the guards knocked on the back door and then swung it open. Remy Senior sat inside, his head bandaged, looking guilty. And old.

"T, you're all right. Itor told me—"

"They said a lot of things to get what they wanted," Remy interrupted. "I'm fine."

"I'm all right too," Remy Senior said. "These people, they said they're gonna send me someplace. Give me a new identity."

Remy wondered how the hell ACRO was going to accomplish Remy Senior not revealing anything, especially when the guy'd been drinking, and decided that he didn't want to know.

"T—"

"I forgive you," Remy said, his voice raw, his body suddenly weak with emotion. He didn't mean it—yet—but he knew he would at some point.

"You'll be able to see him, once we get him settled," Dev said from behind Remy. "Right now, it's safer for him this way. And I know you don't want anything to happen to him."

"No, I don't," Remy said. "I don't want anything bad to happen to anyone because of me."

"You can't control everything, Remy. You can only do the best you can," Dev said, and moved back.

"I'll see you soon, Dad," Remy said, leaning down to give his old man a hug. Remy Senior hugged him back.

"I love you, boy," Remy Senior said. Remy nodded, and the guards shut the door on the man who'd been Remy's father all his life. His only father.

In seconds, Remy and Dev were ushered into the back of a large black Humvee, complete with tinted windows and bulletproof glass.

"We'll go to my office—a mile up the road. Can you grab a bottle of water for me? I've turned off my second sight for a while," Dev said, and Remy hadn't realized that Devlin was blind until just then. Devlin's eyes were clear, bright, and Remy had assumed that his nonblinking stance had more to do with military training than anything else.

"I do blink, but it's habit." Dev smiled.

"You can read my mind too?" he asked.

"Everyone always asks me the same question about the blinking. Sometimes the best part of being psychic is screwing with people's minds."

The car stopped and both men got out, walked into a beautiful old Victorian house that was made with reinforced steel and bulletproof glass, although the average person walking through wouldn't have noticed those safeguards. Remy followed Dev up the winding staircase and into a large office, where a woman sat behind a desk.

"We'll go into my office," Dev said. "No calls, unless it's an emergency, Marlena."

Devlin's office was large, lined with bookshelves and computers and, Remy noticed, no windows.

"I'm safer without anyone being able to see in," Dev said. "But you don't care about that. You want to ask me something."

"I want to know about the tattoo."

Dev stared at him with that unblinking look. "For this, I'll turn the sight back on. Show me," he said finally, and Remy unbuttoned his pants and pulled them down to expose the tattoo on his hip. Dev reached out to touch it and he said, "It's Haley's."

"Yes."

"And you've been able to gain more control since it appeared."

"Yes. And I want to know how and why it connects me to her. Why she put it there."

"She didn't put it there, Remy. You two obviously have some kind of connection—one that we had no idea of when we sent her to find you."

Remy refastened his pants and then sat heavily on the leather couch, and Dev took the chair across from him.

"I don't know if I want that connection anymore," he said roughly, ran his hands through his hair and blew out a frustrated sigh. "I don't want to be responsible for putting her in danger. Not again."

"She seems to be the only one who can ease your needs during the storms. You're calmer when you're close to her. And when you're not with her, the tattoo can connect you."

What Devlin said seemed so freakin' logical. But Remy already knew that love and desire were anything but. "There's got to be a better way than having us connected for life with the tattoos."

"If there is, we don't know what it is yet. And we don't know if it will hurt either one of you if we try to remove the tattoos. Right now, doing nothing is the safest bet for all concerned."

"Who's the 'all concerned'?"

"Just the entire free world," Dev said, and calmly told Remy the many ways in which his weather power could be used, and abused, ways Remy had never even given thought to.

His hands shook, his mouth dried and he sank back in his seat. "It's just like the Itor guy said. I'm a fucking menace," he mumbled.

"In the wrong hands, yes."

"In any hands."

"That's not true. If you decide to sign on, we can help you over the hard part, the part where you feel you won't ever be allowed to live a normal life." Devlin leaned forward, elbows on his thighs, and looked right into Remy's eyes. "You don't have to do this alone anymore."

"I've never lived a normal life," Remy admitted. "Except with the SEALs, but even then, they never saw me as normal."

Dev fished a piece of paper out of his pocket and handed it to Remy. "That's over. And I see you as very normal, if that helps. So sign this, and you'll be part of our team."

Remy took the paper out of Dev's hands, scanned it quickly. "What, for the next six months, I'll be living, eating, breathing ACRO? One day off every six weeks? Getting my outside time doled to me by the warden in charge? And this is supposed to make me happy?"

"It's supposed to make you the best operative you can be. You're responsible for finding your own happiness," Dev said. "But I can do something to help with that. I'll send you happiness every night, if you want. Blond, brunette, redhead—all three if you think you can handle it."

"I don't get how this happened," Remy mumbled.

"There are so many things we can't explain, Remy. I can't explain your powers, or why they were given to you, or why I have the powers I do. The best we can hope for is to learn to control them and use them for good, as hokey as that sounds."

Remy rolled his neck from side to side to try to ease the sudden ache he felt in his head, and then he looked Devlin in the eye. Because he knew Devlin would know he was doing that, would expect it. Deserved that respect for all he'd done for Remy.

"I can't sign this. Not right now. Not until I see Haley and get some things straightened out."

"You won't be able to see her until she wakes up. I can put you up here on the compound until that happens, keep you safe until you decide."

"Thank you. I appreciate that."

"I know what it's like to have the life you once knew taken from you," Dev said, his voice quiet. "But don't wait too long to make up your mind, Remy. I want you trained, better than you've ever thought you could be trained."

Remy nodded, stood and shook Dev's hand. Dev pressed a button on his desk. "Marlena, will you send someone in here who can take Remy to the guest house for the night, please?"

HALEY HATED DOCTORS almost as much as she hated pounding headaches and creepy little men who produced sticky web stuff like Spider-Man gone bad.

"Your CT scans are clean, Ms. Holmes," the cute, way-too-young doctor said. "Your ribs are bruised, and you're working on a couple of black eyes, but we'll give you some pain meds and ice packs. If it still hurts to swallow and your voice hasn't returned to normal by Tuesday, come back in. I don't suppose I can talk you into staying overnight?"

"We already discussed this."

He started to say something, but when she glared, he snapped his mouth shut, jotted something on a chart and then said, "Most of the trauma, including your loss of consciousness, was caused by psychic bruising. I do think after a few days' rest, you'll be fine."

Great. She might be physically fine, but mentally? There was a reason she hadn't signed on as a superspy operative. Other than the utter lack of special ability, of course. She was a wuss. And she really disliked being beaten and strangled.

Fortunately, she didn't remember much after Apollo crushed her in some sort of invisible vise, but she did recall waking as medics wheeled her from the ACRO jet, and being confused because Remy hadn't been there.

No one could—or would—say where he was now, or why he hadn't come to visit her during the fourteen hours she'd been stuck in the tiny ACRO clinic. Dev had sent word that Remy was fine, but that was all she knew.

Wincing, she eased out of her bed. Her clothes had disappeared, but she found combat boots and a folded stack of black BDUs in the corner chair. She reached for them, but the curtain swept open and she grabbed the gaping back of her hospital gown instead.

"Do you think I could have a little privacy?" she asked, her voice hoarse and raspy from Apollo's air-choke.

"I've seen it all, darlin'."

Haley whirled, found herself face-to-face not with the cute doctor, but with a fifty-something woman whose white badge identified her as a medium from the Paranormal Division, but who was currently working in the Medical Division's Psychiatric department.

"Who are you?"

"Dr. Helen McIntyre. Call me Helen. I'm a counselor. All operatives are required to attend at least one session with me following a mission, but the Special Ops director figured that since you're injured, it would be best for me to come to you."

"It wasn't a mission," Haley grumbled. "More of a kidnapping. And Jason isn't my boss."

"Not now that you're back, but Devlin is, and he agreed."

"It still wasn't a mission."

Helen rolled her eyes. "You're as stubborn as your father says you are."

Haley managed to sit on the bed before she fell over. "You can see them? My parents? That Itor guy wasn't lying?"

"I can see them. And they love you. Very much."

It was Haley's turn to roll her eyes. "Lady, they have you *so* fooled."

Helen pulled the chair out of the corner and took a seat. "You don't believe they loved you at all?"

"Does it matter?"

"It matters because they don't want you to be afraid to have children."

"Wow," Haley said. "That came out of left field. I haven't even thought about kids." Which was only partly true. She hadn't thought about them before Remy, but now...maybe children could be a possibility.

And though she knew in her heart that she would love her children wholeheartedly, the memories of how her parents had cast her aside in favor of their own love affair gave her pause.

Helen thumped her on the head with one finger.

"Ow! What was that for?"

"From your dad. He said you've learned from their mistakes, and the connection you have with your children's father will only intensify your feelings for the kids, so to stop lying to yourself, and to me."

Haley sucked in a harsh breath that hurt her ribs. "Have you seen him?"

"Who?"

"Remy." When Helen stared at her blankly, Haley huffed. "You know, *the father of my children*."

An impish glint sparkled in Helen's green eyes, and Haley knew she'd been played. Psychics and their weird sense of humor.

"I caught a glimpse of ACRO's newest golden boy earlier, and I have an appointment with him tomorrow."

Relief turned her inside out. She'd trusted Dev, but to hear Remy was okay from someone in person . . .

"Can you tell me what's up with the tattoos?"

Helen tapped her lips and stared over Haley's shoulder for so long, Haley began to wonder if the other woman had gone into a trance.

"Clever," Helen murmured, and then shifted her gaze to Haley.

"What's clever?"

"It's a little complicated, but . . . do you believe in soul mates?"

"You're kidding, right?" Haley crossed her arms over her chest and winced when her elbow smacked her bruised ribs. "The Itor guy brought it up. I threw down the bullshit flag then, and I'm doing it now."

Helen clucked her tongue and puffed up like one of the laying hens that Haley's parents kept in their backyard. "Everyone has a soul mate, but few make contact with each other while living one of their many human lives. Soul mates primarily spend time with each other on the Other Side." Haley's skepticism must have shown on her face, because Helen huffed. "What? Don't look at me like that. I'm trying to explain this."

"I'm listening," Haley muttered.

Helen leaned forward and touched Haley's knee in an oddly comforting gesture. "According to your spirit guide, many lifetimes ago you and Remy worked out a way to know each other in human form. The tattoos. His childhood spell activated them, and if you sit and think about it, you'll realize that you two are meant to be."

"I already have," she said quietly, because although she might still be a little skeptical about the soul mate thing, she did believe that she and Remy belonged together. What she'd felt back at the Itor house had been too powerful to deny. "But I don't suppose you can tell me what's up with Remy's weather ability? Is it related to this *soul mate* thing?"

"I'm sorry, but I can only discuss that with him."

Haley sat there, numb from too much mystic overload anyway. "Are we done now?"

"Yes," Helen said, standing. "I'd like you to make an appointment at my office next week."

"Is it mandatory?"

"Let's call it voluntary, but if you don't show up, I'll put in an order to make it mandatory." She smiled a kindly grandmother smile, which didn't work, not when this woman gave off a tough-old-bird vibe.

"I guess I won't argue, then."

"That's wise. I always win." She patted Haley on the head like she was a troublesome child. "And there's someone else here to see you."

Remy? Haley's heart went ballistic. Dr. McIntyre stepped out of the curtained cubicle. A few moments later, Dev walked in, and Haley had to smother a sigh of disappointment.

"How's the new Meteorology department head?" he asked, as he moved unerringly to the chair next to the bed.

"I guess that answers my question about whether or not I got the promotion." Which was great, but for some reason, she wasn't nearly as excited as she would have been just a few days ago. Too much had happened. Life, for one. Love, for another.

"You did." Dev rolled his shoulders as though he'd stayed too long in one position, like at a desk. "You handled your assignment as well as you could have, given the Itor fuckup."

"What happened, Dev? Before I left for Louisiana, you told me Itor wouldn't make it that close to us."

His jaw tightened and flexed, and she figured he'd need to see a dentist if he kept grinding his teeth like that. "I don't know why or how we got caught with our pants down. I don't know how they got private information about you either. What you tell our counselors stays between them and you—and me if I need to know—but it's possible that someone broke into the office...."

"Or that one of the counselors is responsible for leaking information."

"Speaking of counselors, how'd the session go?"

"I'm sure you know." The blatant attempt to shift away from the subject of a possible traitor inside ACRO annoyed her, and her reply came out sharper than she intended.

"Is there something you'd like to say?"

She turned away, stared at the blue and white stripes on the curtain. "I want to know why Remy hasn't been here to see me."

"Mission's over, Haley. Why do you want to see him?"

Leveling a look at him she knew he could somehow see, she said, "Because he was more than a mission."

"Ah." He lounged back in his chair, hooked his combat

boots at the ankles. "I expected him to sign on today. He refused until he sees you. So go home, get some rest, and I'll have him brought to you tomorrow."

Little butterfly wings fluttered in her belly at the thought that she'd get to see Remy, as if she were some lovesick teen. "And then?"

"I need you to work up a training plan to cover the weather segment of his instruction. When you called me from the hotel you said he still needs work on some aspects of his control?"

"Yes. But now that he's in an environment where he no longer has to hide his gift, where he's encouraged to use it, I think he'll master it in no time."

"And the sexual consequences?"

Her cheeks burned. "I doubt it will ever be easy. Mother Nature influences his sex drive the way it influences sunlight-deprivation depression and the change of seasons. And the tattoos, well, they had an unexpected side effect."

"I know. Your Triad picked up on it. The tattoo connection will be helpful when he's out in the field and the weather goes to hell."

Great. The Triad probably got a mind's-eye full. "I want to sever the Triad link before I go home."

He nodded. "Of course. And I know you're tired, but I'm going to need to know everything you learned about Itor's weather machine. And once you finish Remy's training plan, your first priority will be to determine the location of the thing." He speared her with a look that penetrated despite his sightlessness. "I'm sure I don't need to impress upon you the importance of finding it."

She shook her head. "The more I think about it, the scarier the whole thing is. If their machine is half as powerful as Apollo said, it could generate F5 tornadoes in cities like London or Seattle, cities unprepared for that kind of force. Or it could unleash hurricanes so destructive that scientists would have to revise the Saffir-Simpson Hurricane Scale. Itor could pound the U.S. coasts with category six hurricanes one after another."

The nightmarish possibilities ran through her head in slow motion. Hundreds of thousands could die. The country would be plunged into financial ruin. Anarchy could destabilize the government.

She stood, managed not to wince at the multitude of aches, and Dev came to his feet as well.

"I'll get on it immediately. But can I ask one favor?" Dev inclined his head, and she continued. "I want more training. Lots and lots of operative training. With every kind of self-defense instruction you've got." She clenched her fists at her sides. "No one is going to make me feel helpless again." And no one would ever again make Remy feel like she was so helpless that he needed to kill himself to protect her.

"You got it." Dev stuck his hand in his pocket and looked inward, as though seeking a specific kind of calm. "E-mail your mission report in the morning, and copy Special Operations and RSO. Remy's new supervisors will want to know everything that took place."

No doubt. Jason, the Special Ops director, seemed to have his fingers in all pies. Akbar, the Rare Special Operatives department head, probably did too, though he was much more subtle about it.

Dev didn't wait for her to reply, simply slipped away like a ghost.

The cute doctor entered and handed her an ice pack and a bottle of pills. "Take one every four hours for the pain. They'll help you sleep."

"Great. Thanks." She snatched the pills and escaped as fast as her stiff body would carry her. On her way out, she dumped the bottle into a garbage can. She didn't need painkillers and the deep sleep they brought. Not when she wanted to be clear-headed when Remy came to see her.

She needed to feel him inside her, his strong hands on her, his mouth consuming her until they were both reduced to one soul, like what had happened when Itor had them. And she needed to tell him how much she loved him, because although she hoped he'd felt her love during the mind-sex—assuming the experience had even been real—she hadn't spoken it out loud. He deserved the truth, and hopefully he still felt the same way.

Dev slept restlessly that night—tossed and turned and even took a cold shower at one point to keep the ghosts at bay.

It didn't work. He was calling for his car by four in the morning, was in his office working fifteen minutes later. Poring over lists of ACRO employees, putting his focus on operatives with Special Abilities and wondering how the hell a mole could be working at ACRO and he couldn't sniff out that person.

He ran his hands through his hair and sighed deeply. There was someone he could call to help, but he wasn't ready for that. He might never be ready, not unless the agency was in major danger. And there was still a lot more that Dev himself could—and would—do to stop this from cycling out of control.

He jerked his hands out of his hair as the familiar burst of energy traveled over his skin—it was a light touch because there was a wall between them, but he knew that Creed had come home.

Creed could handle this one with him.

"Devlin, Creed is here to see you." Marlena knew Dev had

been waiting for the ghost translator to return from his old family mansion.

"Send him right in," Dev said, sat back in his chair and waited until he heard the door open and again felt the energy that Creed always sent out, stronger now. It wasn't an unpleasant feeling, more like tiny prickles on the skin.

Creed being Creed, he cut right to the chase. "What's happening, Dev?"

Dev didn't need to use his second sight to see that Creed was shaken—he could hear it in the man's voice.

"Are you all right? You're not hurt, are you?" Dev asked.

"I'm fine, man. But you're not going to be."

Dev nodded. He knew that—now he just needed a way to reassure Creed. "I can take care of myself. You know that. Now, can you tell me what you've learned?"

"There's a traitor here, Dev. At ACRO," Creed said. "But you knew that already."

Dev nodded slowly. "I suspected. I just needed confirmation."

"Well, I would've liked some additional information, but I couldn't risk staying there. That thing wants out, and badly. If I'd stayed..."

"No, you did the right thing. Does Annika know?"

"She left right before the spirit decided to start talking."

"Then let's keep it between us," Dev said, knowing he could count on Creed for that.

"The weather guy's here?" Creed asked, and Dev nodded.

"He's here. Hasn't signed on yet, but I think he will. He seems to have made the mistake of falling in love," Dev said, and wished he didn't sound so cynical. But a night of sex always brought that out in him.

Creed snorted in response, like he understood. And maybe he did, on some level, since the spirit that seemed to live as part of him interfered with the man's love life quite a bit.

"Is Annika back?" Creed asked finally.

"Yes—came and went out on assignment again."

"You don't give her a break, do you?" Creed asked, and Dev got a particularly sharp shock from Creed. He wondered for just a second if Creed knew about the electricity he gave off, or if the man had been taking lessons from Annika. But Annika wanted nothing to do with Creed, so sharing tips didn't seem possible.

Dev laughed. "She asked to go out again. Don't tell me you miss her. I never figured you for the sentimental type. She's not exactly one herself."

"I know more about her than you think," Creed said, and Dev briefly wondered what that was supposed to mean. "What do you want me to do now?"

"I'll let you know. For now, I want you to stick close to home," Dev said. "We're both going to have to stick a little closer to home."

IT WAS WYATT WHO ENDED UP dropping Remy over at Haley's house the next evening.

After a restless night and one full day in a comfortably furnished guest house that was double the size of his place on the bayou, and a few thunder and lightning storms that he was pretty sure he was behind, especially when he woke up after a particularly vivid dream about Haley, Remy got a visit from the former SEAL.

"She woke up last night—she's sore and she's hoarse, but from what Dev says, she's going to be fine," Wyatt told him before Remy got in the car. "She refused to stay overnight for observation."

"Stubborn," Remy muttered.

"Yeah, kind of reminds me of someone." Wyatt still wore the sunglasses from yesterday, had a blue bandanna wrapped around his head and now he blasted AC/DC from the car stereo, so they both had to yell to be heard as he turned a corner that led down a long, curved dirt road. "I never thanked you for saving my ass."

"You saved Haley—consider us even."

"*You* saved Haley. Now you have to decide if it's time to save yourself."

Remy nodded. "You're sure this place doesn't use cages, torture...."

"Only for the bad guys, Remy. Only for the bad guys." Wyatt jerked the car to a stop in front of a house. "I'm guessing I shouldn't bother to wait for you."

"If things don't go well, I'll find my way back," Remy said, climbing out of the vehicle.

Wyatt nodded, and with a wave barreled back down the road, singing "Back in Black" at the top of his lungs.

Remy walked across the wide-planked porch, past the swing-seat and the potted plants, and knocked on the door, wishing he weren't so nervous, that he'd brought flowers or something she might like. He heard thunder rumble overhead and made a point of trying to control his nerves before she opened the door.

He didn't have to wait long, and was greeted by a smiling woman with the hint of black eyes and the sharp breaths of someone whose ribs had been hurt.

He knew the feeling.

"Hey," he said, because all he really wanted to do was grab her and kiss her, open the white button-down shirt she wore and slide off her khakis, but figured that talking first was probably the way to go.

"Hey yourself," she said, holding the screen door open for him. "Come inside."

"You should be lying down. Resting," he said.

"There's no one else to answer the door. Besides, I knew you'd be coming."

Her house was big—open and airy and casual. A place he wouldn't mind spending more time in. She'd led him through the foyer into a sunroom toward the back of the house and now they sat together on the couch, turned in to face one another. And all Remy wanted to do was kiss her, but he reined himself in.

"Nice place," he said. "Did ACRO find it for you?"

"They did. They've been really good to me," she said. "You met Dev, didn't you?"

"I did. He's who he seems, isn't he?"

"Nothing fake about him," she agreed.

"I've been really worried. That's why I stayed here—at ACRO. So I could make sure you were all right."

"I'm glad you did." She paused. "I kind of figured, since there were a few unexplained thunderstorms in the area."

"Yeah, well, you know how that goes."

"You know, ACRO could probably help you get to the bottom of what's going on with you—why your pull with Mother Nature is so strong," she said, but he'd already started shaking his head.

"That's not what I'm after."

"Don't you want to know how you can do what you can do?"

"What's the point of knowing the how, Haley? I know I didn't get this power because of a spider bite or because I faced my fear of bats to fight evil in the world. I'm not a comic book character. I'm real—and I don't care if I got these powers because I was born in a hurricane or because Mother Nature picked me out as special. All I know is that ever since I've met you, everything is better. I'm calmer, more in control, even when I'm not right next to you. That has to mean more than any explanation ACRO could ever come up with."

"I guess I can understand that. For the record, I've never seen you as anything but a man."

"Well, that's good," he said, and she smiled again and the urge to kiss her got stronger.

"Are you going to join ACRO?" she asked.

"I needed to talk to you first. About joining. About us."

"Don't join just for me," she said quickly. "I want you to make that decision for you. I want you to be happy."

"And I want to make sure you stay safe, no matter what happens to me. No matter what decisions I make. First I need to make sure that I wasn't dreaming about the way I can keep you safe and still remain in control," he said. "I mean, when I was captured in that barn, we had sex. Mind-sex. Unless the drugs they gave me were really powerful . . ."

"You felt it too?" she whispered, reaching out to touch his cheek.

"*Felt* being the key word. I was inside you, Haley. You helped me through the storm."

"It was amazing. I was right there with you," she said, and automatically put her hand on the hip where her tattoo was. His own tattoo had begun to tingle the second he'd walked through the door.

"What does this mean? I know in the car you said that you couldn't let this happen. But I could've sworn, in that barn, I heard you say . . ."

"I love you, Remy."

"Yeah, that's what you said."

She laughed, a wonderful sound. "I know that's what I said. And I meant it. I love you."

"You love me," he repeated.

"Yes."

"You look like hell," he said.

"You sure know how to sweet-talk a woman."

He drew her close, his touch gentle but firm. "Damn straight I know how to sweet-talk you, *chere*. I know what you like, know all the spots that make you cry out my name when I touch them," he murmured against her neck.

"Then do it," she whispered.

"No way, *bebe*. Not until you're fully healed."

"I can't wait that long to have you inside me, Remy. I won't break."

"No, I guess you won't." He captured her mouth in a long, deep kiss that told him her words were the real deal. "And now you need to lie down," he said, picking her up carefully and walking her in the direction of the stairs.

"My bedroom's—"

"I can find your bedroom," he said, and got to the top of the stairs and headed instinctively toward the room that would have the best unobstructed view of the night sky. When he nudged the door open with his foot, he was greeted to a picture window overlooking the lake, and a bolt of ground lightning.

"That was you, wasn't it?" she asked.

"All me," he agreed, and laid her gently on the bed. "Now, you just let me do all the work."

She put her arms to the side. "You won't get any arguments from me."

"Good," he said, and then he kissed her. Her mouth was warm, tasted wonderful—like sweet wine and sunshine, and fuck, he was never going to be able to get enough of her. Never.

His tongue played against hers while his hands skimmed along the outside of her shirt, moved along the curve of her breast until he couldn't stand it anymore.

One button at a time, he opened her shirt, kissed his way down the exposed path as he pushed the fabric aside and then unhooked her bra. He paused for a second to growl at the dark purple bruises near her ribs.

"It's not that bad," she said as she guided his head to her breast—letting him know that even when he was in charge, she was really the one running the show.

He didn't mind a bit, loved the way her mouth curved when he bent and scraped his rough cheek across her nipple before he took it in between his teeth.

With a turgid nipple in his mouth, he let his hand drift between her legs, stroked her sex through the fabric until her hips jerked and she was telling him to *take the pants off of her now.*

"Bossy," he murmured as he unbuttoned and unzipped her pants.

"Proud of it," she said, her breath hitching as he worked her other nipple in his mouth.

"Stubborn too," he said as he pulled the pants off her legs, along with her underwear, leaving her exposed to him in the moonlight streaming through the window.

"Yes," she said as his finger found her cleft and stroked it deftly. "Remy, please . . ."

"Yes, *bebe,* I will," he said. And even though he wanted to touch her, taste her, dip his tongue into her heat and spend a long, leisurely night making her come over and over, he was so fucking hard, he wanted—no, needed—to be inside of her right now.

He spread her thighs, groaned at how she managed to be so tight and so wet at the same damned time and rocked his way into her gently, his mouth finding hers again. Palms down on either side of her, his biceps shaking slightly as he took her, keeping his strokes long and even so she stayed comfortable.

"I can't get enough of you," he breathed against her mouth. "I don't think I'll ever get my fill."

"Touch me," she moaned, and he slid one of his hands between their bodies to touch her core. The pad of his thumb stroked her clit, and she cried out, and he was so close to the edge he could see flashes of light behind his eyelids.

He pumped deeply inside her, her slick moisture creating a devastatingly hot friction.

He threw his head back, his teeth clenched, bared. A low, harsh rumble started deep in his chest, and he was aware of the hot tingling electricity that shot between them. Then he drove upward, and her hand rose to pull his mouth down to hers, where his kiss muted her cries of pleasure.

Her orgasm happened seconds before his, a deep rippling that threw him over the edge with her, until he couldn't see and he could barely breathe and he let go inside her, filling her with hot spurts of semen.

Moments later, he caught his breath and realized he'd partially collapsed on her, his cock still pulsing inside her, and he found himself wishing they could stay in this position forever.

But they couldn't, and he eased away gently and rolled next to her on the bed, staring up at the ceiling in the darkness. Instinctively, his hand reached out to touch her hip, began to trace the tattoo like he was drawing it, and he wondered if it was always going to be this good.

"I don't know what to do," he admitted finally. "I've never been really close to anyone."

"You just keep doing what you're doing, and I think we'll be fine," she said, her voice still slightly breathless as she leaned on her good side and traced his tattoo with her finger in a way that mimicked what he was doing to hers. "We'll figure it out together."

Together. That had a really nice ring to it.

Outside, the ground lightning continued to strike, as if Mother Nature agreed with Haley. From now on, he'd be dealing with two women, and he wouldn't have it any other way.

Epilogue

Somewhere in the distance, thunder rolled, and Haley's heart stumbled.

Bundled in a blanket on her front porch swing, she looked out at the building cumulonimbus across the orchards surrounding her old farmhouse. The property, five miles from ACRO headquarters, had been one of the agency's incentives to sign on. Not that she'd needed incentives. The job was more than enough.

A squeaky meow warned her a mere heartbeat before Geordie, the cat she'd rescued from a shelter a few weeks ago, jumped into her lap. She stroked the purring furball as she sipped her mulled cider, noting how flavorless it tasted, just like everything lately. Even her favorite black walnut ice cream had become bland and unexciting. She'd give anything for some jambalaya and cherry bounce right about now.

Lightning played tag between two dark clouds, and a low, menacing rumble of thunder unraveled across the horizon, growing louder. Shivers spread over her skin, reminding her of how it felt to touch Remy, how the very atmosphere between them sparked and sizzled. How touching him was like grabbing a high-voltage fence, but without the pain.

Fat raindrops pelted the ground, and the apple trees bowed to an icy gust of wind from the late-autumn storm, and she gathered the blanket more tightly around her. Geordie'd had enough, and darted through the cat door into the house.

Squeezing her eyes closed tight, Haley felt the breeze envelop her like one of Remy's intimate embraces, and if she thought hard enough, she could almost smell the extraordinary scent that was uniquely his, a combination of musk and man and ozone, something only a meteorologist could appreciate.

Thunder cracked, closer. A sane person would take shelter, but Haley remained where she sat.

She opened her eyes. The branches swayed, reaching for the low deck of storm clouds. Dead leaves tumbled across the yard.

From the wrong direction.

She blinked. The storm had shifted, its base swirling in a rare clockwise rotation. Below the base, a wall of rain had formed, and from out of the precipitation, Remy emerged.

Her heart went crazy. She stood, dropping the blanket. His intense blue eyes captured hers. Her pulse drummed in her ears, drowning out the thunder that now continued nonstop.

Remy stopped five yards from the porch, and suddenly the storm died down, leaving nothing but the soft whisper of light rain. Water ran in rivulets down his black leather jacket, and his jeans were soaked, but he didn't seem to notice. And, oh, he looked fine, bigger than she remembered. Stronger. More confident, which was saying something, given that in the bayou he'd radiated a certain arrogance. Now, after the first phase of his training, all traces of hesitation were gone. He'd grown into his gift. Mastered it. Nothing would take him down.

They stared at each other for a full minute before she swallowed dryly and said, "I see you've learned a few things."

He gave a sharp nod, flinging water droplets to the ground. "A few." Lightning flashed in his eyes, and she realized none had flashed in the sky.

Even so, thunder rumbled overhead.

"I've missed you," she whispered. "Six weeks is a long time."

"Too long, and I've only got twenty-four hours off, so come here."

She ran to him and flung herself into his arms. Her heart kicked against her rib cage, and through their layers of clothing, his heartbeat answered, thumping against her chest in an identical rhythm.

Dipping his head, he traced the shell of her ear with his tongue, and she felt the distinct bulge of his erection against her belly. "You were right, Haley. I needed ACRO. I needed you."

She put a hand to his cheek and brought his gaze to hers. "I was always so afraid of needing someone the way my mom did. I didn't want a man to define who I was. So I substituted a career for a man, and without knowing it, I let my job define me instead. I need you too, Remy. With you, I can be so much more than a meteorologist." Going up on her tiptoes, she brushed her lips over his. "I love you."

"Then show me."

A hot wash of need hummed through her veins, and she dropped her hands to his firm butt and rocked against him, making clear exactly how she'd show him. "Just try to stop me."

His laughter rumbled deep in his chest, making her already hard nipples ache. "Why would I do that?"

"No idea." She moaned as he cupped her breasts and kneaded them between his palms.

She reached up, pulled his head down to her throat. "I want you to promise me one thing," she said, throwing her head back so he could ravage her neck with his mouth.

"Name it."

The rain had stopped. The air had gone still and had somehow gotten warmer. And in the distance, over Remy's shoulder, a sliver of blue slashed the sky. "Don't ever be afraid of hurting me. You know, during storm sex."

He took a half step back, frowned at her. "Haley, it's safer to do it through the tattoos."

"Now that you've gained so much control over your gift, do you think your urges will still be as strong as they were?"

He looked stricken, like he should be ashamed, like he didn't want to divulge, even to himself, that he hadn't mastered every aspect of his talent. "Yes," he admitted, "but like I said, we can be apart now during the worst of it, use the tattoos instead. I can control the urges that way."

"But Remy," she said, in a low, husky voice she barely recognized as her own, "I don't want you to."

His throat worked on a long, hard swallow. "Are you saying—"

She shoved him, knocking him off balance, and while he stood there, stunned, his erection straining against the front of his jeans, she wriggled out of her T-shirt so fast, a seam split.

"Yeah, I'm saying." She sauntered up to him, poked him in the chest hard enough that he took a step back. "Don't you dare hold back. I won't break." She lifted her face to the sky and closed her eyes. "Give me all of you. Everything."

The next thing she knew, she was in Remy's arms, twirling in a sudden warm downpour, and around them, lightning danced in the sky, circling them in a ring above her house.

"It's beautiful," she gasped. "What else can you do?"

"You have no idea, *chere*." He nuzzled her neck, took her down hard to the ground so that he was on top of her, his thigh between her legs, pressing against her center, which needed him like she needed to breathe. And around them, the air electrified a split second before a flash of in-cloud lightning lit the sky—and stayed lit. "But I'm gonna show you. Are you ready?"

Her whole body shuddered with pleasure. She looked into his eyes, intense and filled with passion. She was ready.

Ready to ride the storm.

About the Author

SYDNEY CROFT is the pseudonym for two authors who each write under their own names. This is their first novel together. Visit their website at www.sydneycroft.com.

Dying for more action
with the **ARCO** team?

Look no further!

Read on for the next novel
in this hot new series

UNLEASHING
the
STORM

BY SYDNEY CROFT

Coming soon from Delta

UNLEASHING THE STORM

ON SALE MARCH 2008

CHAPTER *One*

Kira Donovan would be dead by now if Ender needed her to be, another victim of his steady hand and expert marksmanship which were part random gift of nature and part the result of years of training.

He lay in familiar sniper position, on his stomach on the broad, grassy slope overlooking the farm, mentally lining up one perfect shot after another as the woman he'd been sent to persuade walked in and out of the dilapidated barn without a care in the world.

She was going to require a hell of a lot of training to bring her up to spec. And she was going to have to stop wearing those shorts and T-shirts that showed off too much tanned, curvy flesh, too, because that was much too distracting for everyone involved. Mrs. Freakin' Doolittle and her merry band of animals were going to have a rude awakening.

He sighed, put his forehead down against the cool earth and breathed in the scent of nature mingling in his nostrils that always seemed to be a part of him, no matter how hard he'd tried to get away. And even though he *so* didn't want this assignment, he was here, and he had a job to do. And his jobs always got done.

Speaking of done, what hadn't been was the beautiful woman he'd picked up last night, someone who shared his tastes in bed and his penchant for no-strings relationships. That had to be the real reason for his hard-on.

They'd just gotten to the handcuffs portion of the evening when he'd gotten the call from work, something he couldn't ignore. Dev, the head of the Agency for Covert Rare Operatives which employed him, and Ken, his direct supervisor, had laid out the plan for him, which meant taking the redeye from the Catskills, New York, compound to bumble-fuck Idaho. Ender had just shaken his head in a combination of disbelief and no-fucking-way.

"Why me?" he'd asked. Because he'd worked for seven years as one of their top Convincers, the guy who brought home the big catches. He liked being able to go in and pick off the men and women who'd already been briefed to some degree about the agency's dealing in Special Ops of a very different kind, was always prepared for one of these rare ability types to go off the deep end, but never had much more than a casual, passing acquaintance with them. Except for Remy— one of ACRO's newest acquisitions, an operative who could control the weather—mainly because Ender thought the SEAL was too damned cocky for his own good and he enjoyed taking Remy down a peg or two every now and again.

But he did not want to be one of the people who actually had to recruit the talent.

"You've got patience," Ken said.

He snorted. "Patience when I'm waiting for the right shot, yes. My patience where new recruits are concerned is severely limited, and if you mean patience where women are concerned —well, I just went from bad to worse."

"You've got the background for the cover. You grew up on a farm," Ken continued.

"Shit," he'd muttered, because he'd put his shit-kickers away years ago when he left the farm, and the horse, behind and never looked back. He'd hitched around the country for a year doing odd jobs, whatever he could get his hands on—same went for women—and finally, when he hit seventeen he hit the nearest recruiting office. He wanted different—college—something. And the Army had given him that; Delta Force and covert ops even more. His parents had given consent, grateful that he'd finally called to tell them he was still alive.

He'd finally appealed to the head of ACRO. "Come on, Dev. You've got plenty of other guys who could handle this one—guys whose job it is to do this. What the hell do you need my talents for on this one so early in the game?" he'd asked.

Dev had smiled, and with his usual straightforwardness, simply said, "Because if she can't be convinced to join us within forty-eight hours, you're going to have to kill her." Ender had grabbed the file and left the office without another word. Ken hadn't wanted a trail—needed a quick in and out on this one because of the target's highly specialized and unforeseen increasingly urgent needs, and the less people seen on and around the farm, the better. So it was good-bye Ender and hello Tom Knight for the next forty-eight hours.

If he had his way, the job would be done in twenty-four. Whatever it took, no holds barred, he was going to drag Kira the animal whisperer kicking and screaming into ACRO, or he'd carry out his alternate orders. From what information he'd gleaned from her files, she might actually enjoy being tied down, especially during this time of year.

If it could only be that easy, a seduce-and-convince special, normally Wyatt Kennedy's favorite means of persuasion. An ACRO operative who specialized in deep undercover Ops, Wyatt was convinced that ninety-nine percent of women would roll with just the right kind of persuasion, and the other one percent would require a tranquilizer gun.

Ender had both plans covered.

Mixing business with pleasure had never gotten in his way before, and from what the first contact person, a psychic who'd volunteered at the sanctuary, had reported, it might be the only way to get Kira on board. ACRO's psychic had claimed that Kira's spring fever was a major issue and, according to Ken, utilizing Kira's insatiable need for sex during this time was supposed to be part of Ender's master plan. An open invitation.

Now, palms down, he pushed up from the ground, and headed toward the barn, taking the main route that led from the driveway. Bag slung over his shoulder, he looked like a man who'd walked in from the one Greyhound Bus Stop in this one-horse town, without many possessions or cares.

Still, Kira came out of the barn and headed right in his direction like she had a honing device on him. He hadn't spotted any cameras, but he'd been told she was paranoid.

"Can I help you?" she asked, her voice brisk, businesslike and not at all like the soft tones he'd figured on. Immediately his own needs gained quick interest and let him know they'd demand to be heard sooner than later.

God, she was pretty—naturally pretty, all long, light brown hair and full, pouty lips, wide amber eyes and a body to freakin' die for. Yeah, he'd let her work him in more ways than one, if she was game.

"Hey, I'm Tom. Your new man for hire," he said. He hadn't used his real name in years, preferred the anonymity of Ender and the images it conjured up, especially at work. It kept most of the assholes, and everyone else, at bay. Because, at heart, he never was a social kind of guy, and things were not going to change if he could help it.

He approached her, palm out, and she hesitated, the skittish side he'd been expecting showing through. Finally, she extended her hand, her palm rough from work, her shake strong and sure.

"Hello, Tommy," she said.

"It's Tom," he said, then cursed inwardly and shrugged, like, *It's all cool with me.* "But, whatever, it's all good."

Yeah, real fucking slick.

She didn't smile, but the corner of her mouth pulled up slightly. "You're right on time."

"I try and make that a habit," he said, became aware of something sniffing his ass and turned to find a goat staring at him. It didn't look happy, either.

"Do you also make it a habit to spy on people?" she asked, and he turned back from the animal to her.

Son of a "No ma'am," he said.

"So you just decided you wanted to stare me down for an hour and a half then?" She'd crossed her arms across her chest, and he let his eyes skim her breasts before meeting her gaze and smiling.

"I got here a little early and wanted to take a nap. Didn't want to bother you or anything. And then I saw you, walking back and forth from the barn and, well . . ." He shrugged. "Shit, I'm a red-blooded man, Kira."

That part was more than true, and standing this close to her, inhaling the scent of apples and honey and cloves that surrounded her, despite the other, more pungent smells close by, was killing him.

She narrowed her eyes at him, and he held his breath because he couldn't screw this up this soon. Something was wrong—very wrong. He'd never been spotted, not like that. He'd been hidden, camouflaged, and he was good enough at that to know that she'd gotten her information about his watching in some other way than stumbling on it herself.

When the goat poked him in the back again, everything suddenly became clear.

KIRA WATCHED PEEPING Tom for a long moment, allowing Cheech time to sniff him out. The little Nubian goat was a great judge of character, and if he indicated that Tom needed to be watched, then that's what she'd do.

And frankly, she'd watch him anyway. She'd never been one for the rugged, outdoorsy type, but something about Tom grabbed her in places no man had grabbed for a long time.

Not since her last spring fever.

Now that April had come again, the yearning had begun, the fierce, primal burn that permeated every cell and told her she was days, maybe hours from the insanity that would consume her for upwards of four weeks.

She'd been getting antsy, had been unable to concentrate on simple tasks. And simple tasks in the presence of males . . . forget it. It was definitely time to scope out potential partners and give her battery-operated toys a rest. She'd just figured her other hire, a dark-haired, brawny hottie named Derek, would be the first mate she took this season.

But now, as she studied Tom Knight, with his piercing blue eyes and sun-streaked blond hair that was too long for a military cut and too short for a surfer, she began to think he might be more fun until he wore out. High, chiseled cheekbones, firm mouth . . . yeah, he may not have been her type, but during this time of year, all men were her type, and besides, she wasn't looking for happily ever after.

There'd never be one of those. Not for her. Not for someone people thought was psychotic if they didn't believe she could talk to animals, or were terrified of if they did believe. Because she didn't just talk to animals. She understood them, communicated with them through words and body language and scents, but mainly, mental images and sensations that transcended most human understanding.

And the other aspect of her gift, the part that was more of a curse—well, people *really* didn't understand that.

Cheech gave Tom a head butt and then, with a low bleat, told her he'd keep an eye on the man. The goat seemed to think it was strange for a human to lay on the ground the way Tom had, and Cheech wasn't going to trust him anytime soon.

"Ma'am?"

She blinked, realized she'd been so busy in her own world that she hadn't heard anything Tom had said, and the way he was watching her, like he didn't enjoy being ignored, made her a little jittery.

"I'm sorry. What did you say?"

"I asked if maybe I could move in? Get started working?"

His voice, powerful and compelling, rolled through her like a muscle-deep caress, and she wondered if his effect on her was a result of her growing need or if he always talked with a rough, erotic edge, as though urging a woman toward orgasm.

"Right." She started up the drive toward the guest house, and motioned him to follow. "I don't know how familiar you are with Rainbow Ridge Sanctuary..."

He settled into an easy, long stride next to her, and the warm breeze brought his scent to her, a powerful mixture of grass, woods, and sun-warmed man no one else would have smelled unless they'd been on top of him. Which, she thought as she glanced at him, sounded like a nice place to be right about now.

Yeah, spring fever was kicking at the barn door, and it was only a matter of time before it broke out at a dead run.

"I know it sits on roughly forty acres, and that there's a public and private side." He looked over his shoulder, frowned at Cheech. "Is that thing going to follow us everywhere?"

"Just you. He's suspicious of strangers."

"Great," he muttered, and then turned his attention back to their surroundings. "I'm guessing this is the private side."

She nodded. "The people who own the sanctuary live on the front twenty acres with the exotic animals. Fifteen or so volunteers help out over there, and they charge a small admission for people to visit. Down here"——she waved her arm in an expansive gesture——"we take care of the domestic animals."

He slowed to avoid stepping on Peepers, a crippled mallard duck she'd rescued last year from a kid who'd grown tired of his Easter present. "I thought you were in charge of the whole place."

Nodding, she bent to run a finger over Peepers' smooth green head, which put her at crotch level with Tom. Heat billowed from him, heat and seductive male scents, and oh, she needed to be alone with him. Soon.

"I'm the manager," she said hoarsely, and straightened. "So I do the hiring, and I oversee all the animal care and training. I live down here with you and Derek."

"Derek?"

"He's my other hire. You two will share the upstairs part of the guest house. The bottom floor is mine." She thought she saw a flash of irritation in his eyes, but it was gone so quickly she might have imagined it. "Is there a problem?"

He shrugged and ignored Cheech when the goat gave him a head butt for the sheer pleasure of it. "I was under the impression I was the only hire."

They started walking again, his boots crunching gravel, his tread lighter than she'd have expected as they navigated around flocks of farm fowl and three sheep that refused to give way. Tom didn't miss a beat, moved with her to give the animals a wide berth, and she tried not to focus on the way his lean thighs flexed inside well-worn and well-fitting jeans with every step. Or the way the muscles in his bare arms looked strong enough to effortlessly pin her beneath him.

"Two of my guys quit suddenly a couple of weeks ago. One of them went on vacation and never came back, and the other got up one morning, packed, and left before I knew he was gone."

The kind of labor-intensive, low-pay work they did in a

place like this had a tendency to weed out all but the most dedicated animal lovers, but it had still been odd to lose Jack and David like that, and in such a short a span of time. Especially since they'd been there for her last year during her time of need, and they'd seemed happy to stick around for this one.

Maybe she shouldn't have cut them off when she'd no longer required them. Then again, she knew full well the consequences of trying to maintain a relationship outside her fevers.

"I hired Derek to replace one," she said, "and you to replace the other."

They arrived at the sizable guest house she'd partly remodeled with the money she made under the table here at the refuge, and she mounted the rickety steps. "Watch the banister—it's pretty well shot."

"I can probably fix it," he said, bending to pat one of the three dogs lounging on the porch. When Cheech clattered up the steps and demanded attention, Tom scratched the goat's brown back.

"That's okay—Derek already offered. I guess he's a carpenter in his spare time. He's going to paint the house as well, as soon as he gets some time."

"As long as it's under control," Tom said. "It's always good to have someone handy around."

She bit her lip. Tom had no idea how handy *he'd* be to have around. In more ways than one.

"You and Derek will always use the back entrance stairs to the upper floor, but I'm taking you in this way so you can see the place and meet the kids."

"Kids?"

"The house critters. Mostly rescues I can't allow outside without supervision."

She opened the door, and fur exploded as dozens of cats scattered and dozens of dogs came running.

"Fuck. Me."

Tom stood there wearing a shocked expression she doubted people saw much. He quickly recovered and plastered on a neutral mask, but his sharp, focused eyes took everything in. She got the distinct feeling he was cataloging the furniture, the animals, the entire dwelling in his mind.

"Is that a bobcat?" he asked, as they walked inside and shut the door, only to be surrounded by several happy dogs and one extra-large cat.

"That's Rafi," she said, going down on her heels to scratch the bobcat behind the ears as he rubbed against her hand. "He was on a butcher table, about to be killed for his fur when he was rescued." Her stomach churned, as it always did when she thought about how close he'd come to a painful, lingering death. "The people who rescued him from the fur farm only had enough money to buy him and one other cat. The rest..." she trailed off, unable to talk about it.

She straightened, waved the animals away, and they all bounded off like a bunch of kindergartners released for recess. "So this is where I live. Nothing fancy. Thrift store furnishings." She gestured to the left, where the only pieces of furniture, a stained blue love seat and tiny television, made the room seem bigger than it was.

"Living room there, dining room to the right, my bedroom and den in the back. Those stairs ahead lead up to your room, but like I said, you'll use the back entrance." She took a key off the rack on the entryway wall and handed it to him. "The door on the right is yours. Derek is on the left. You'll share a kitchen and a bathroom. Sheets and towels are in the wardrobe next to your bed, which is a twin, so don't expect to have any comfortable nights with guests."

"Comfort isn't usually a concern." He swung his gaze back to her, let it blatantly take in her body from her lips to her thighs as though the mention of a bed had made him picture her in his. She could certainly picture being there, could imagine his lean, hard body against hers. The potent energy surrounding him, the aura of power and eroticism, promised that time shared between the sheets would be something to savor.

"Anything else, Kira?"

"Yes. We start work at five A.M. You can break for lunch anytime between eleven and two. We work until six. You and Derek can each have one weekend day off. Work out between yourselves which day you want, Saturday or Sunday. I work both. If you need to run to town for anything, groceries or whatever, you can take my truck parked out back. Just ask first. Ditto with my computer. You can use it, but ask. And there's no internet connection."

"Why not?"

Because Big Brother can watch your every move. "I like my privacy."

He gave her the usual "you're a nut case" look, and then rubbed the back of his neck. "Is that all?"

The way he said it, flat and emotionless, had sounded innocent. But she suspected that inside, he was bucking her authority as fast as she could throw it at him. This man did not like being told what to do. How odd that he took this kind of job—when he'd called this morning about a position, she'd been pleased with his farm credentials, but now she had to wonder if the largely man's world background made him a little edgy when a woman called the shots.

So it was with great pleasure that she said, "There's one more thing. Under no circumstances will you consume meat on this property or in my presence. I'm a strict vegan, and while I won't begrudge you eggs and dairy products, I will not tolerate the consumption of animal flesh by humans at this refuge. Understood?"

A vein popped out on his forehead and began to pulse. Though there were no other outward signs of his annoyance and unease, she could smell the potent mixture coming off him in waves.

He smiled, hefted his bag high on his shoulder, and said,

"That's cool." And then she watched his fine backside while he took the stairs three at a time, as though he couldn't wait to get away from her.

But she knew better. Because along with the other smells, she'd caught the scent of lust, pure and simple.

Closing her eyes, she allowed the tantalizing smell to invade her senses and trigger systemic responses she should be trying to suppress, for a couple of hours at least, because after that, there would be no suppressing anything.

But Tom . . . there was something different about him, an earthy animal magnetism she'd never encountered. After eleven years of suffering for a few weeks a year, she knew her body, and she'd been sure she had a couple of days to prepare for this, but it seemed as though Tom's presence had brought the fever on early. Fighting it seemed pointless.

Clenching her fists at her sides, she threw her head back, let her heart rate double, let it flush her body with blood that had heated up a couple of degrees. Her nervous system sparked like someone had struck a match to it, and every nerve ending tingled with hypersensitivity until her skin was on fire. Deep, frequent breaths brought crisp scents and life-giving oxygen into her lungs, and she could almost feel each individual cell distribute the fuel to the pleasure centers that had begun to swell and pulse and crave what only a man could give her.

It had begun.